Kristen Callihan is a child of the eighties, which means she's worn neon skirts, black-lace gloves and combat boots (although never all at once) and can quote John Hughes movies with the best of them. A lifelong daydreamer, she finally realized that the characters in her head needed a proper home and thus hit the keyboard. She believes that falling in love is one of the headiest experiences a person can have, so naturally she writes romance. Her love of superheroes, action movies and history led her to write historical paranormals. She lives in the Washington, D.C., area and, when not writing, looks after two children, one husband and a dog – the fish can fend for themselves.

Visit Kristen Callihan online:
www.kristencallihan.com
www.facebook.com/KristenCallihan

Kristen Callihan

Evernight

The Darkest London

piatkus

PIATKUS

First published in the US in 2014 by Forever,
an imprint of Grand Central Publishing,
A division of Hachette Book Group, Inc.
First published in Great Britain in 2014 by Piatkus

A CIP catalogue record for this book
is available from the British Library.

ISBN 978-0-349-40607-7

Printed in Great Britain by Clays Ltd, St Ives, plc

Papers used by Piatkus are from well-managed forests
and other responsible sources.

MIX
Paper from
responsible sources
FSC® C104740

Piatkus
An imprint of
Little, Brown Book Group
100 Victoria Embankment
London EC4Y 0DY

An Hachette UK Company
www.hachette.co.uk

www.piatkus.co.uk

For Juan

*It is because of you that I am able to write
this or any other book.*

Acknowledgments

My deepest and most profound thanks to:

The team at Forever, who work so hard to turn my words into a proper book.

My agent, Kristin Nelson, for always having my back.

My editor, Alex Logan, who, after all this time, still manages to teach me a thing or two. Darkest London would not be the same without you.

The reader. Without you, Darkest London doesn't live.

Special thanks to Brenda Novak Auction winner and now harassed *Evernight* chambermaid Sara Anne Elliot.

EVERNIGHT

EVERNIGHT

Prologue

I never saw so sweet a face
As that I stood before.
My heart has left its dwelling-place
And can return no more.

—John Clare

The dream was always the same. Only it was not a dream but a memory, and his body knew it, reacting to the terror imprinted upon his very bones with the same infirm jerks as if responding to that long-ago torture. Trapped within his mind, he could not escape, but lay helpless as it came for him yet again.

Always the same. Strapped by gold chains to a trolley, he could not free himself as the vacant-eyed thug rolled him along. Overhead, coal-blackened stone arches drifted by, the bed beneath him bumping and rattling on ancient cobbles. His heart pounded, fear churning within his gut. But rage overshadowed everything. It made his fangs drop over the gag that cut into his lips. He held himself still, kept his wits about him. Ignore the fear. Focus.

He had a good idea who had him and why. He'd been careless, and loyal to someone who worked for the wrong side. Jack Talent. His best mate. And now he'd pay for helping him. And it would hurt.

The scent of blood and metal hit him before the doors opened. Then he was in a cavernous room, the stench of suffering rising to a cloying thickness. On the far side, a variety of saws and knives hung against the wall. His insides rolled. He struggled against his bonds, testing them for weaknesses. There were none, and his heart threatened to pound out of his chest.

He could almost tell himself it would be all right. Until the being walked up to him, dark power and insanity humming in the silence. Inky wings rose up from behind muscled shoulders. Fallen angel.

Bugger. Bugger. Bugger.

The fallen smiled down at him, a strange, almost paternal expression. Mad bastard. Cold fingers trailed along his cheek, sending shards of terror through him as they went.

"Mr. Thorne here has been telling tales to those who should not hear them."

Thorne. That was his name. He hadn't realized he'd forgotten it until the fallen had spoken. He'd been drugged. By someone who knew what to use on sanguis demons. He was William Thorne. And he was mired in a world of deep shit.

Will bucked, the gold bands cutting into his torso. Hot blood ran over his ice-cold flesh. He snarled against his gag, the sound ineffectual and small.

The fallen ignored him and walked over to a worktable set off to the side of the room. He picked up a long, ivory-handled bone saw.

And Will's entire world stopped, his ears buzzing and his skin prickling. He could not look away from the saw—the dull, rusty saw. Bile rushed up his throat, burning and pooling in his mouth.

Slowly, and with great relish, the winged mad-fuck let the steel blade catch the light as he turned back towards Will.

A prayer old as Cain, and just as desperate, flew through his mind. His breathing grew rapid and raw. Desperation had him looking away. And then he spotted her.

An angel. Huddled on the floor. Eyes of twilight, raven black hair falling in a wild riot about her pale face, she was the most terribly beautiful creature he'd ever seen. *Help me. Please. I beg of you.* Surely an angel could destroy a fallen.

But she did not move. She merely stared at him without a trace of emotion. Will ought not be surprised. He was a being of Hell, not of Heaven. How could he expect an angel to come to his rescue? Still, he tried. *Please. Please. I am not so very vile.* He was, but surely she would have pity.

"Shall we try our newest creation?" the fallen asked her with soft menace.

Betrayal slammed through Will so hard he cried out.

The angel came to her feet, and he heard clattering.

"Stop." Her voice was cold, mechanical. "We haven't chloroform."

Not an angel, but one of the fallen's pets. Will gagged, his vision going blurry, and he fought once more for his freedom.

"Not to worry," came the voice of the fallen, "it will not affect the procedure."

When the fallen bent over him, the bone saw in his hand, Will lost all control, bucking so hard that the trolley rocked. He strained until his muscles tore with white-hot agony. He did not stop.

"Come now, Mr. Thorne. I am giving you a gift. Blood such as you've never tasted, a bit of my power, the gift of shadow. Should you survive, you will possess a body stronger than you could imagine."

Fuck you.

"Ingrate," snarled the fallen as if he'd read Will's thoughts. Good.

Hard hands came down upon him. A metal tube smashed between his teeth. Blood, thick and delicious, poured over his tongue and down his throat. Will almost laughed. Ironic that he should have such a glorious last meal. Instantly his pain dulled, the muscles along his arms and torso itching as they knitted. Dark magic. Jack's blood.

It did not stop his panic.

The ragged blade tore through his flesh. White colored his vision, and he screamed. And screamed. Agony clawed through him as the saw hacked at his sternum. He became pain.

The fallen's voice sliced through it all. "Come, Miss Evernight, and see your creation be born."

Evernight, Will thought wildly, his mind needing something to latch onto. And then he saw her, standing at his side, a motionless statue, her dark blue eyes watching his pain with detachment.

When they ripped out his heart, and he finally succumbed to blissful oblivion, he held onto one thing: his hate for his tormentor and the one with the angel's face and the devil's mind. Evernight.

Chapter One

~~~~~~~~~~

London, October, 1886

She was being hunted. Of that Holly was sure. Heart beating a hard rhythm against her ribs, she lay still and silent upon her bed and waited. All was quiet, save the wind, which rustled the leaves on the tree near the house. The silver disk of the moon, shining bright against the ink-black sky, peeked past the corner of her window. And somewhere out there, something stalked her. She could feel it coming for her, the certainty of it like a heavy hand pressing upon her heart.

Odd thing to be hunted when one could barely work up the courage to leave one's house. Rather like a rabbit hunkered down in her warren, waiting for the fox. Then again, she wasn't quite so helpless. Her home was built like a fortress. And, up until now, her safeguards had worked.

Last week, the electrified inner fence had fried a demon to a crisp. The foul stench of burnt flesh had hung over

Mayfair like a pall, drifting into the house to permeate the drapes despite the tightly closed windows and thick, reinforced stone walls. Holly wondered absently what her neighbors made of the smell. But, before the body had even a chance to cool, Felix had deftly taken care of it, leaving no one the wiser.

The week before, Nan had found an elemental male—rather rare—decapitated on the south lawn near the kitchen doors, the victim of a tripwire that triggered a swinging blade designed to catch the unwary across the neck. As for Nan? The pragmatic cook-housekeeper-et-al had merely searched for his head and found it by a mound of ice. So he'd had the power to freeze. Hadn't helped him keep his head, however.

Anxiety tightened Holly's gut and robbed her of sleep. Someone wanted her dead. And she did not know who. Or why.

She could contact the SOS. It was the duty of The Society for the Suppression of Supernaturals, or SOS, to hunt down supernaturals who preyed on others. But then regulators would be swarming her grounds in an effort to protect her. And while she admired and missed her colleagues, she did not want them invading her privacy. Worse, she would be forced to explain to Director Lane why she wasn't capable of returning to her work quite yet. Poppy Lane would see through her hedging and misdirection in an instant. And that really was too humiliating to contemplate.

On the floor below, the clock struck midnight—a soft, usually comforting chime that now had her jumping within her skin. And quite suddenly, Holly had had enough. Cursing, she flung her covers aside and scrambled out of bed. Her feet met with the icy floor, and she marched along, headed for her dressing room. Fumbling in the dark, she threw on a serviceable wool house gown and heavy boots before grabbing her utility belt, complete with knives, spare bullets, and other weapons. She secured it low on her hips, then reached for the handheld submachine revolver she was testing. Heavy and unwieldy, due to a rather large cylinder attached to the base that held 50 rounds of ammunition, the gun needed to be secured to an arm brace for Holly to handle it. Her fingers were steady as she clipped the brace on and left her room.

In the hall, she paused, told herself to move, do what she must. Oh, but she felt the fear. The familiar tight pang of it that occurred whenever she stepped more than a foot outside her front door.

"You won't be going more than a foot," she muttered to herself. "Get on with it, old girl."

Outside was bitter cold and so clear, the moon so very bright, that each blade of grass appeared limned in silver-white light. Poised at the threshold of her door, feet braced apart and hand upon the trigger of her gun, Holly surveyed her land, from the stone stairs to where her front lawn stretched to meet the iron spikes of her gate. Nothing stirred. Even the breeze had died, as though holding its breath.

She was not fooled. She could feel him out there. Watching. Waiting.

"Show yourself, you coward." Her voice sounded small and thin in the empty expanse of the front garden. *Thud, thud, thud* went her heart. Her breath rasped in and out of her lungs. Ice traveled along her spine, making her fingers tense upon the handle of the gun. *Easy. Easy.*

Though there was not a cloud in the sky, shadows began to coalesce over the garden. Dense, black, and complete, it swarmed along the grass and crept up the sides of the house. Instinct had Holly spinning left and raising her gun as the dark shadow hurled towards her.

The gun went off in rapid succession, each shot punctuated by a loud clang as the bullets ricocheted off of some kind of metal that sparked on impact. It was all she registered before the thing was upon her, and cruel, icy fingers gripped her throat even as the hard body slammed into her. They crashed into the door, her bones rattling, her breath choked from her lungs. A flash of silver, two long white fangs gleaming, and eyes—terrifying, mindless—locked on her with complete hatred.

She would die now. Even so, she reached out, her hand connecting with something smooth and hard.

Power surged through her in a rush so fast and strong that her head spun. The body pressing into her froze on a gurgled gasp. Everything went painfully still—the night, her heart, her breath. She couldn't move, her fingers stuck against a cold curve. The shadows around her cleared, and she stared into a face of aching beauty and bone-deep terror. Whatever sort of being she held captive by her touch—for he'd yet to move either—was made not of flesh but of metal, shining bright and gleaming in the moonlight.

The sharp angles of his features, the high, sculpted cheeks and knife-blade thin nose, seemed familiar to her. But the thought fled in favor of the strengthening hum coursing through her. Oh, but she knew this power. It was as much a part of her as her bones. Metal. It was hers to command. Her friend.

Holly didn't have to think. The metal responded as if being called home. And on the next draw of power, the male on top of her fell to the side with a clang, lying helpless and unmoving, save for the rapid cadence of breath that hissed between his clenched teeth. Keeping her hand upon his cheek, she scrambled to her knees and peered over him. His eyes, wide and wild, stared back.

"It is unfortunate for you," she said, "that you are made of metal."

A low, animalistic growl rumbled in his throat, and fear danced along her spine. Holly didn't let it show. She studied the creature, trying to think of what to do with him. She wasn't sure how to kill him, nor if she ought to. He held answers. How to get them was another matter.

He was in pain. She could see that now. It vibrated through him, pulling at the clean, sharp lines of his face. That face. She knew him. Spots danced before her eyes as panic and guilt speared her soul. She had created him.

Beholding the transformed face of Will Thorne, the terror Holly had felt during her captivity surged to the fore on a wave of shocking cold. Guilt was a bitter stew in her stomach. She hadn't let herself think of him. Hadn't wanted to. From the day Jack Talent and Mary Chase had freed her and Thorne, she had tried to put him and the whole incident out of her mind. And while she'd been able to successfully relinquish all thoughts of Thorne, her life was lived in an effort to not think about the hellish moments that had played out in the dark cellar they'd shared.

Now here he was, glaring up at her in accusation. And she could only return that gaze by going numb. *Feel nothing. Retreat to that safe, quiet place of logic and facts.*

Holly reached up and hit the small brass button by her front door. A series of hisses and buzzes sounded in the dark night, and then Felix's faint voice crackled through. "Yes?"

"It's me. I need assistance. Presently," she added, before letting the button go.

Thorne was beginning to shake and pant like a horse that had been run to ground. His gaze had yet to leave her. The last time she'd looked into his eyes, rays of black and silver had radiated from his cornea. Now his irises were entirely silver. Platinum, actually. The hard metal that made up his clockwork heart had invaded every inch of his flesh. Even his hair, once a brilliant snow white, fanned out in silken skeins of shining platinum. Quite beautiful, this metal man.

Deadly too, if the promise of retribution in his eyes ever came to fruition. She would see that it did not.

"I shall not hurt you," she said to him. If he understood was another matter. He appeared completely maddened. More animal than logical being.

Another growl gurgled in his throat, and she could feel the hatred vibrating from him.

Felix yanked open the door. Now fully dressed, save for his cravat, he assessed the situation in a glance and pocketed the gun in his hand.

"I need this removed." She held up her arm, encumbered by the brace and useless gun.

Felix knelt next to her, and his nimble fingers quickly unbuckled the leather straps. It was a relief when the heavy weight came off.

"Prepare the West laboratory," she told him.

"As madam wishes."

He was gone in the next breath. Only to be replaced by Nan. The older woman was wearing her orange, India-print housecoat and a frilly nightcap. "Another devil." She nodded, and her pinned grey curls threatened to bounce free. "'Least you caught this one."

The "devil" frozen beneath her fingertips tried to stir. Fighting his imprisonment. Holly was not certain how long she could hold him, nor did she desire to test it. "I'm taking him to the West laboratory. Hold his feet steady when I lift him up."

Nan's mouth fell open, but Holly did not give her time to question. Taking a deep, bracing breath of cold air, she rose to her feet, keeping her fingers curled about his cheek, and Mr. William Thorne's body moved with her as though he were lighter than a feather. Nan balked, but she quickly ran around the hovering body and took hold of his ankles.

The whites of Thorne's eyes flashed, and Holly knew he was desperate to look about, confused as to how she'd been able to levitate him.

"You, Mr. Thorne," she said to him, "appear to be formed entirely of metal. As I can control metal with a thought, so do I have control over you." She gave him what she hoped was a reassuring look. "Try to relax, why don't you? And then you can tell me why you are here to kill me."

Chapter Two

~~~~~

Try to relax? Not bloody likely. Will's mind had cleared enough to take stock of his situation. He had no memory of how he'd arrived at where he presently was, or what had occurred. He'd known only his objective: hunt down Holly Evernight, and destroy her.

Now she was here. At last. Right next to him, walking with determined strides, her profile a pale and perfect silhouette stamped against the darkened halls.

Hell on earth, how did she do it? How did she keep him floating in the air, unable to move or to speak? Her cool hand lay on his cheek, an almost tender hold. Yet he knew it was only there to keep him trapped. Hate and rage bubbled hotly through his limbs. All for naught. He could not bloody move.

But he hurt. Intensely. Constantly. Pain was a keening wail in his mind. It blinded him. It also gave him something to hold on to. Her scent surrounded him. Iron and fire, the unctuous scent of motor oil, and beneath it all...lilacs. Likely her bath soap, for it was not a strong perfume. The strange combination felt familiar to him, and he reasoned that he must have remembered it from their last meeting. Must have tracked her by it.

No, that wasn't right. Someone had told him where to find the reclusive Miss Evernight. Only he could not remember who.

Gods, his head felt brittle, as though it might shatter. His clockwork heart clicked a steady rhythm. Did she hear it? Did she remember the apparatus she'd foisted on him? He needed to get free and rip out the fleshy heart of the beastly woman who'd ripped out his. He tried to move again. A failure.

"You are wasting your energy." Her voice was all cool tones and dark shadows. She did not even look at him. "Calm, and we can have a chat when you are settled."

Have a chat. Perhaps over tea? He'd cut her tongue out first.

They turned down another corridor. Far above him, the ceiling turned from dark, coffered wood to high, graceful arches of white. *Arched ceiling. Lying helpless on his back as they rolled him along.* Panic blackened the edges of his sight. And with it went his hold on the pain. It crested over him, a violent wave that crashed down and made him shudder. *Too much. Too much.*

Inside himself, he thrashed, trying to get away from it. A whimper broke from his unmoving lips.

Midnight blue eyes glanced down at him, and the faintest of furrows wrinkled between the dark wings of her brows. Lovely and heartless. A cold diamond of a woman.

She brought him into a small, wood-paneled room, strangely warm and cozy, when he'd expected an icy cellar like the one she'd inhabited before. A fire crackled in the hearth, and he craved its heat. The world spun as she turned him, and he caught sight of the matronly lady who he'd all but forgotten about at his feet, her plump face drawn in a scowl. Then his captor set him down on some sort of high table. But she did not remove her hand.

He hated her touch. Hated that she could control him in this, when she'd already destroyed his life.

Like a giant insect, she bent over him, inspecting his face in her detached manner.

"You are in pain." She leaned closer, and her loose, inky hair swung down, the strands cool silk against his neck. "Where does it hurt?"

Everywhere. Another strangled sound escaped him. He fought to keep silent.

But as if she'd heard his internal thought, she nodded brusquely. "I am going to attempt an experiment."

Like hell! He strained, tried to thrash, and got nowhere.

"I will stop if I notice any damage."

Hateful woman. I'll kill you.

A flicker of sympathy went through her eyes. *Hate that as well.*

"Leave us," she said to the old woman. The woman drifted off like a ghost, out of his line of sight. Out of the room.

Then Evernight took a deep breath, her pert breasts rising beneath her frumpy grey housecoat. He didn't want to notice her blasted bosom. Any other thoughts he might have had about the matter fled on a tide of liquid warmth that rushed over him. Relief. A soothing balm.

He shuddered as it sank deeper. The horrendous pressure that constantly weighed down his flesh eased, and he breathed deep. God. His vision blurred. God.

"It's all right."

Evernight's voice.

He turned his head towards the sound and realized that he could move. Absolute lethargy weighed him down. Warm all over for the first time in his memory, he could do no more than blink up at this strange woman who still had a hold of his cheek. Touching him. He could not remember the last woman who'd done so. He knew he'd had many women, but the particulars were lost in the dark mire of his thoughts.

"What did you do?" His voice was rust and cobwebs. It'd been so long since he'd used it. With a shaking hand, he touched his jaw. Flesh there. Not cold, hard metal.

Evernight's wide eyes did not blink. "Drew the metal back."

He took another breath, his chest hitching. "I'm going to rise now."

Her lips thinned. "I expect civil behavior, Mr. Thorne."

A rasping laugh made him wheeze. "Do you now? A word of advice. Become accustomed to disappointment when dealing with me."

She pressed her fingertips into his cheek with just enough force to make her point. "Shall I reverse the process?"

Cold, calculating insect. "You have intrigued me sufficiently that I will withhold execution for the moment."

Her perfectly sculpted face stared down at him without any inflection of feeling. "Generous of you, Mr. Thorne. I shall do likewise. For I too am intrigued."

Slowly, she removed her hand. He felt the loss immediately, a spot of cold on his cheek and a slight increase in pressure on his chest. It worried him. More so when fingers of pain started to spread from the cavern surrounding his clacking heart.

She frowned down at her hand, rubbing the tips of her fingers together as if they bothered her.

"What did you do to me?"

"Why do you want to kill me?"

They spoke over each other.

When she simply stood there, her delicate features unmarred by an expression of feeling, he huffed. "Well?"

"This is my home, Mr. Thorne. You answer my questions first, and then I shall answer yours."

Had she not relieved his pain, her neck would be twisted and her blood oozing down his throat this instant. But in truth, he might have wept for joy for the mere fact that he could once again speak in coherent sentences. He needed an answer, and he'd played enough card games to know when an opponent would not fold.

"You do not strike me as obtuse, Miss Evernight," he said. "However, if that is how you want to play this, then fine." He grabbed the front of his woolen tunic and ripped it open, exposing his chest. "Here is your answer."

There was no satisfaction in seeing her flinch as her gaze landed upon the tangle of platinum threads that ran from the top of his sternum to the bottom of his ribs. It only fueled his rage. "Here, where your pretty work began and my happy life ended."

Her slender throat worked on a swallow. "What do you remember?"

Will's clockwork heart whirred audibly within his chest. "Every damn moment. Right up until you and that thing ripped the beating heart out of my chest." Things had gone hazy after that, for which Will was grateful.

The pink bow of her mouth tightened. "His name was Amaros. He was a fallen. Diseased and mad. He thought he would prolong his life with a clockwork heart. Only he was too much of a coward to try one out before the operation was perfected."

After he'd been freed, Will had experienced a few moments of lucidity before the dark, confused state he currently lived in had descended. His friend Jack had explained what happened, and that Will had been given a clockwork heart as if he were a fucking machine. Will knew that much, but no more.

Oh, but he never forgot *her*. Evernight. His true creator. "You were his pet."

"Pet." Her mouth took on a bitter slant. "I suppose you could say that. Bound hand and foot, and his to command." Her dark eyes flashed with pain and anger. "Yes, I was his pet."

"Forced? I saw you standing there. You did not help me! You did not fight. Sell me another story, for this one wears thin."

She held his gaze as she lifted her arms, holding her delicate wrists out before her. "Chained. And soul sick to watch what he did."

Will glanced down. Thick, pale scars marred her skin. He forced himself to meet her gaze again. "Did you or did you not create this heart that beats in me?"

"I did."

"And did you or did you not know what it would do to a demon should that bastard play mad scientist with it?" To put a machine into a demon was an aberration of nature. Everyone knew this.

"It was my intention to create a heart that worked well enough for Amaros to put one within his own body," she said. "That was his ultimate plan. Once he did, it would have made him weaker. Then I could kill him." The little line between her brows returned. "Yes, sacrifices had to be made. But, had I not tried, the death toll would have gone higher. It was an unavoidable consequence of an unfortunate situation."

"You are a cold little thing, aren't you?" He leaned closer, wanting to see her flinch and disappointed when she didn't. "Unfeeling and detached from any trace of humanity."

"What would you like me to say, Mr. Thorne?"

"Show some bloody remorse!"

Her eyes narrowed a fraction. "You came here to kill me, and you speak of remorse?"

On a curse, he stood, needing to get away. But it was as if she'd attached steel hooks into his ribs, and with every step he took to distance himself, the hooks dug in deeper, his pain intensifying. He stopped short and rounded on her. "For the last time, what did you bloody do to me? Why do I feel this way?"

Her head tilted. "I don't understand."

"Here." Will slapped his chest. "It hurts here when I draw away from you. I crave your touch, and not in a pleasant way, but as if I will soon be crippled with pain if I do not feel it." It burned to admit this, but the truth could not be contained. "Why? Why is this so?"

Evernight frowned down at her hand before her expression went completely blank. She stood stone still, oblivious to him, studying her palm.

"Answer me," he snapped, coming up close to her. Hell. Even that was sweet relief. The heaviness around his heart eased a touch. He had to fight the impulse to grab her hand and press it against his chest.

"Hush," she said, not moving. "I'm thinking."

"Oh, well, jolly good. I'll just sit here in silence, shall I?"

She ignored his sarcasm. "Please do."

Will's fangs erupted, the sharp points puncturing his bottom lip. He tasted blood, and his nostrils flared. One long suck at her neck, and she'd be unconscious. Another few deep pulls and she'd be dead. His cock stirred at the thought of breaking her skin, cracking through it like the delicate shell of a Trinity cream. Delicious.

Hands low on his hips, he shifted his weight from one foot to the other, fighting his baser urges. Not that she even noted the danger. She merely stared at her hand with blank dispassion. Then, as if breaking from a trance, she drew in a breath and lifted her head. Before he could say a word, she moved closer and pressed her smooth palm to his scar.

He nearly swooned. Clutching the chair at his side, Will swayed into her space, lured by the luscious heat and pleasure that she gave him with that simple touch. A moan escaped him.

"Interesting," she murmured.

He would kill her. Just for that. "I do believe I hate you, Miss Evernight."

Firelight caressed her skin as she gave him the smallest of smiles. "Your sense of humor is odd."

He hadn't been joking.

"It appears, Mr. Thorne, that your clockwork heart is a constant poison to you."

"Oh, well, brilliant." And not at all a shock. He slapped the back of a nearby chair, sending it teetering.

"Your demon makeup sees it as an unwanted host—"

"Stating the obvious, darling."

"But instead of trying to fight it, your body is attempting to reorganize itself, transmuting on an intracellular level."

"Plain English would be preferable."

"In short—"

"Too late for that, I'm afraid."

"To survive, your body tries to accept your platinum heart by letting the metal take over your flesh. Which only succeeds in driving you to madness and giving you great pain."

"Another obvious statement."

Evernight let out a small huff. "Do you always interrupt people?"

"I cannot remember. If they were as pedantic as you, I'm certain I did."

Her black winged brows snapped together. "Fine. I shall use small words and simple phrases."

"At this point, I shall be thankful if you can manage as few of them as possible."

A small click sounded in the silence, as if she'd snapped her teeth together. He couldn't be sure, for her calm tone did not change when she spoke. "I can control metal. When I touch you, Mr. Thorne, I can tell the metal to retreat. I can ease your pain. When I do not interfere..."

"I am buggered," he finished, feeling ill.

"In a word, yes. Yes you are."

As expected, Thorne reacted as if Holly had struck him. He reared back, his white hair swinging over his shoulders, and snarled, showing the tips of needle-sharp fangs. "Fucking hell." It sounded more like *fook-hen 'ell* to Holly's ears.

It was strange hearing him speak now. In all their time together in the nightmarish imprisonment, he'd never uttered a word. But she knew the sound of his screams quite well. Suppressing a shiver, she pushed that thought aside. His voice was pleasant, smooth as cream, but with the sharpness of a proper, upper-crust London accent. Well-raised, then. But beneath it, there was a thread of something deeper that came out more when he was agitated, such as now. It wasn't Scots, more like what one would hear in Northern England, with the dropped "h"s and breathy endings of words as if he were swallowing them. Exotic and dark. Holly had heard the like before in other demons. Notably the Sanguis who were believed to come from the north.

Sanguis. The blood drinkers. Fiends who thrived on blood and sexual relations. Logically, Holly knew that it was wrong to fault someone for something they have no control over. Sanguis were as their creator made them. And yet, even though she tried to see it that way, a shiver of disgust over their choice in libation came over her just the same. Nor did she particularly trust demons. Far too many of her colleagues had been hurt or deceived by them.

She wondered idly if he spoke demonish. But then swatted that thought away as he stalked about the room, his muscled arms gesticulating wildly. "Am I to be this mad thing? Incapable of a rational thought unless *you*," his lips curled on a bitter face, "are near me?"

Thorne halted and strode back to her, the torn ends of his tunic flapping, displaying a well-defined torso and that scar.

That scar had haunted her deepest dreams. Nearly a foot long and comprised of gnarled platinum threads, like a tight network of tree roots. From that scar spread a small lake of platinum, washing over the expanse of his upper chest. It radiated ever outward as he moved.

"Tell me," he said, his voice still dark and strange, his eyes flashing black and silver, "why shouldn't I kill us both now and take you to hell with me?"

"Can you destroy yourself, Mr. Thorne?"

The taut wall of his abdomen clenched as he glared down at her. "No," he shouted. "No, I can't. Satan knows I've tried. But I simply dissipate. To shadows! Fuck." He pushed off again, a mass of restless energy. She envied that. She was so weary at this moment. Using her power on Thorne to that extent had utterly drained her. Holly braced her hip against the edge of her desk and hoped he would not notice.

"You say you turn to shadows. Have you the ability to leave your body in spirit as the GIM do?"

GIM, or Ghosts in The Machine, were spirits that refused to move on once dead. As lore went, an extremely old and powerful Primus demon named Adam could be called upon to restore the spirit's body and give them immortality. There was a price, however. Adam gave the body a clockwork heart, and the soul was contractually indebted to him for a time of service. Should the soul fail to comply, Adam simply stopped the heart, and the body would die.

With his clockwork heart, Thorne was modeled after the GIM. Only he was a demon, whereas GIM were once human.

"No. I am either lamentably solid or mere ether." He made it sound like a fault, but Holly saw a greater advantage in his ability. For at least his body was never left empty and vulnerable.

"There is something I do not understand," she said, watching him prowl.

He snorted rudely.

"You say you are here to kill me as revenge against what was done to you. Did you send the others?"

Thorne pivoted on his heel. "You mean to say there are

others who yearn to wrap their hands about your pretty neck?" His smile was not nice. "Why am I not surprised?"

Really, the man was most amusing. "Mr. Thorne, did you come here of your own accord or did someone send you?"

He paused and peered at her. "I . . . Hell, I don't know." On a sigh, Thorne tossed himself into a chair and grasped his hair with both hands as he hunkered forward. His voice came out muffled and pained. "I don't even know how I got here. Or what I've been doing since I was freed. How long has it been since that night?" He lifted his head and looked up at her.

Really, his eyes were most beautiful, almost feminine with their long, dark lashes and the slight tilt at the corners. With his smooth, unlined face, he appeared nothing more than a young man, lost and frightened. "You've scars upon your wrists," he said. "Time to heal at least."

She found it an effort to speak. "It is nearing on a year. It is the first of October, in the year eighteen-eighty-six."

"A year." He winced before letting out a chuff of air. "Why did it take me so long to come for you?" He did not speak to her, but scowled down at his large, clenched fist. "You are the only thing I have thought about."

She was sure many women would love to hear such a sentiment, if it weren't for the "so I could kill you" that was left unsaid.

A soft blanket of silence fell over the room. Enough that she noticed the gentle patter of rain coming from outside the windows.

Thorne ran a tired hand over his face then straightened. "Just how many have tried to kill you, Evernight?"

"Including you, four attempts thus far."

"And you truly have no notion as to why?" He appeared highly skeptical.

"You are the only one I've had an opportunity to ask. The others died."

His elegant brows lifted. They were not white as his hair was, but a dark bronze color. Holly forced her attention away from silly things and addressed the matter at hand.

"I have excellent security in place, Mr. Thorne."

"No doubt," he muttered then rose. He was not a great hulking brute like his friend Jack Talent, but lithe and lean, and above average in terms of height. Perhaps an inch over six feet, which made him a foot taller than Holly. His eyes, beautiful though they might be, were also those of a predator. They glinted now, calculating as he came close.

"Yet you could not kill me," he said in that deep Northern voice.

"Not yet."

He stopped before her, and she caught the scent of wool and something sharp like wine. "Has it not occurred to you that in learning your advantage over me, it has become easier for me to get at you?"

He radiated heat like a small oven now. Demon heat. She wanted to recoil, but did not. The corners of his mouth curled, showing a hint of fang. "Tell me, can you fight against a shadow? Keep one out of your little fortress here?"

Coolly, she faced him head on. "What are you waiting for, then, Mr. Thorne?"

His humorless smile grew, but she noted that he was now shaking slightly, and the corners of his eyes were tight. Platinum crept up his throat, edging up to his jaw,

and it snaked down his abdomen, dipping into the tiny
well of his navel. He twitched when it reached there.

"Here is what I propose," he said, as though he were
not in increasing pain. "I shall keep you safe, help you find
out who wants you dead, and stop them. In return, you
agree to cure me and keep me pain free for the duration."

As she watched him, he swayed on his feet, a small
movement, but clear nonetheless. His lids fluttered, the
platinum threads in his irises getting thicker. "Well?" he
rasped.

She ought to let him wait, the cheeky, annoying bastard, but it *was* her heart that chugged away in his chest.
And so she pulled what little reserves of strength she
had and let her palm rest once more on his smooth chest
where the metal had made it so very cold. He shuddered, a
breath of sound leaving his lips, as she pulled at his pain.

"All right," she said, looking at her hand upon him. So
strange to see it there. "But this shall take some thinking."
For if she was correct, she'd have to touch him almost
constantly.

Chapter Three

Relief, Will realized, could work like a drug. It flooded his system, making him weak of knee and frighteningly close to whimpering. However, he fought back the urge to draw her close, to drop his forehead to hers and weep with gratitude. She might not have been the hand swinging the sword that slashed through his life, but as sword maker, she was responsible in her own way.

He shook himself out of his muddled analogies and followed as she turned and headed out of the room. In the hall, a man waited. He was fairly young, likely in his late twenties, and polished in the slick manner of a London toff. Will eyed him with distaste. Had Evernight a man? She hadn't said, but the unfeeling woman would be just the sort to keep her paramour waiting.

"Felix," she said without breaking stride, "have the blue room made up, please."

Servant. Good.

Felix looked Will over with dark eyes full of distrust. "Very well, Miss."

"Is the blue room next to your room?" Will asked her.

She faltered a pace. "Why?"

He crowded her and then, giving in to the urge to touch her, caught up her hand. When she tried to pull away, he held fast. Touching eased his pain, and she had promised. "I don't want to roam far should I have need of you," he said, with a certain dark glee.

The halls were too shadowed to tell, but he swore a blush stole over the high crests of her cheeks. Her butler, or whatever he was, wasn't able to contain a soft gurgle of shock.

"Ignore Mr. Thorne, Felix," she said. "He is merely trying to get a rise out of you."

Clever girl.

"Yes," Will admitted, "but it is also the truth. I fully intend to comply to the terms of our agreement."

Gas lamps flickered on the newel post at the top landing, coloring her skin peach as they climbed the wide center stair. "The blue room," she said coolly, "has a door that joins to mine."

Will's toe caught on a riser. Scowling, he jumped lightly up the next one as if to appear that his bumble was intentional. Not that he fooled the smug Miss Evernight.

"I assumed you'd need to be near for the same reasons," she went on in her smooth way.

"I don't like you," he told her again, and to remind himself.

"Of course not." She and the butler stopped before a door midway down the third floor hallway. "Nor do you need to."

In the odd way of English houses, the blue room was not done in blue, but in shades of grey. Flamed walnut paneled the walls. The only nod to blue was a vivid, deep blue lapis lazuli fireplace mantle. A staggering display of wealth for a simple bedroom.

Evernight managed to detach herself from him, and the heavy weight of pain immediately returned.

"Bathing room." She pointed to one of the paneled doors at the far side of the room. "My room," she said of the other door.

Two maids entered, one holding a coal scuttle, the other bedding.

Evernight ignored them and headed towards the connecting door to her room. "Come."

Will followed, feeling a bit like a dog, and wanting to growl just the same.

He wasn't certain what he expected of Evernight's room, but not this . . . clutter. Four large tables were pushed up against the available wall space. Heaps of mechanical parts in various stages of development lay upon them. At the end of each table rested a toolbox. Before the fireplace stood a massive desk, upon which tottered two towers of leather notebooks.

Her bed was made of cast iron with a canopy. It seemed more a cage, though masses of plump, linen-clad pillows and a down-filled comforter made up for the austerity. Her only other concession of comfort came in the form of a wide, red velvet chaise lounge drawn up before a wall of windows, hung with ivory damask drapery.

Evernight stopped next to her desk and turned up the lamp there. As she gathered up a stack of what looked like small metal disks from the desk, Will walked over to the window. Below them, a wide stone terrace ran the length of the house, stepping down to an unadorned lawn that met the river Thames. Two sets of iron gates surrounded the property. Efficient if one wanted to dissuade human thieves.

"You know you are being hunted," he said, watching rivulets of rain run down the windowpanes, "yet you sit here like a rabbit in her warren."

"The house is well fortified." She placed a disk on the floor in one corner of the room and moved to the door that connected his room to hers. There she set another little disk. "My safety precautions have dispatched three supernaturals."

"Hmm." He roamed over to a table and picked up an apparatus that appeared to be some sort of half-formed pocket watch, only it had a tiny lens on its face.

"Do not," she bustled over and took the thing from him, "touch my work."

"I won't damage it." But he had to smile at her proprietary tone.

"Maybe not, but it might damage you." Carefully, she set the watch down and turned to face him. "How shall we proceed?"

"You can start by telling me everything you can about your activities leading up to—" He stopped short when she uttered a strangled cry and tugged his arm to get him away from the table. "Oh, for God's sake," he groused, "I was only leaning a hip against it."

"I told you to stay clear of my—"

Will bent down and scooped her up.

"Mr. Thorne! Release me at once."

"In a moment." Will held her close and headed for his room. "I cannot think in here, not with you admonishing me like a high-strung governess."

"Then simply tell me that and let me walk on my own volition." Up close, her lashes were thick and long, her eyes indigo. A tiny freckle graced the outer corner of her left eye.

He might have done what she requested, but he found he enjoyed annoying her, and he had his hands on her, which eased him. Regardless, he let her down with an ungracious drop the moment they were back in his room. She wobbled on her feet and uttered a ribald curse beneath her breath. "I was not yet done in there."

"What? Placing those little disks?" Will asked. "What are they anyway?"

"Another safety measure." She appeared far too smug about it.

"I see." He didn't ask what, fearing the explanation of the mechanics would bore him to tears.

The maids had gone. His bed, an ornate affair of ebony wood, was made and turned down for the night, and a cheery fire crackled behind the grate. Will sat upon a small sofa before the hearth—for his room had a normal sitting area—and patted the space next to him.

Evernight, who was shaking out her skirt, gave him a quelling look.

Hell, he would enjoy this as much as demonly possible. "Come, Evernight. Hold my hand and ease me."

Her look of disgust grew. "You do realize that I could put you into a world of agony with just one touch?"

"But you won't." He leaned back and stretched his legs out. Lucidity and comfort were wonderful things. He almost felt like his old self. Almost. The constant weight and annoying whine of his heart was still there. As was the thick push of metal clawing along his chest. But at least he was cognizant. "Now tell me what you have been doing all this time?"

She sat next to him, but before he could grab hold of her, she turned and touched his pinky. Just that. It was effective, however. "I have been here, working on my devices."

"Here," he repeated. "For nearly a year?"

She gazed into the fire, and golden light played over her pale face, highlighting its curves and the deep wells of exhaustion beneath her eyes. "Yes. As I said." Before he could ask her why, she turned and pinned him with a stare. "I ought to tell you now. I cannot provide you with blood."

Will's gaze flickered to the pulse beating at the tender hollow of her neck before meeting her eyes once more. Weariness and caution there. Disgust, too. He bristled. "I do not recall asking for your blood."

"I was not referring to myself, of course," she went on plainly. "I meant that I cannot have blood brought in for you. I realize that makes me a bad hostess, but there it is. I cannot condone it."

A hostess? Is that what she fancied herself to be in this scenario? "And I suppose you do not eat all manner of beasts here? Rare roast beef with your pudding?"

"None that are bipedal, Mr. Thorne."

Touché.

"You should know," he said, "that blood is not the only thing I take for nourishment."

He almost laughed at the way her expression grew closed off, that small nose of hers lifting in a haughty manner. Oh, he knew precisely what she was thinking now.

Not that she let it show in her neutral tone. "I thought that sanguis only imbue blood and—"

"Fuck anything we can get our hands on," he supplied helpfully.

She blinked. Then stared.

Will rolled his eyes skyward. "Aside from all that, I can drink most beverages. Except for lemonade."

"Why not lemonade?"

"Because I hate it." He laughed when her eyes narrowed. "Hot chocolate," he told her, "is my favorite."

He stood. Time to get her out of his room. Talk of tupping and quenching his thirst had him growing hard, and he didn't want a show for it. Had he any hint that Evernight might allow him to crawl into her bed, he'd work his more base pains out that way. A good long tup could do much to restore him. But he rather thought she'd put a knife to his bollocks, not that he wanted to get them anywhere near her. She'd be the type to lie there and think of England.

"Hot chocolate," she repeated, her nose wrinkling as if puzzled. "Truly?"

Will turned to regard her. "Energy, Miss Evernight. You understand the concept, do you not? Life force lives within blood." And other bodily fluids he wouldn't mention now. "It exudes out of a body while tupping. Sanguis thrive off that. As for chocolate?" He shrugged. "It gives me a rush of pleasure to drink it. And that appears to be enough. Other sanguis have their own personal drink of choice that does the same."

"A strange breed," she muttered, drifting off towards the door.

"When you humans can explain why eating the endless list of things you decide to cram into your mouths makes more sense," he responded dryly, "I will agree to that claim."

She stopped. Slowly, she turned to face him. Just as slowly, a smile spread over her lips, and Will forgot to breathe. Hells bells, she was lovely. A glowing light in the darkest night. What a man might do to receive smiles such as that over and over again. No. He would not think of *her* in that way.

"Point to you, Mr. Thorne. Good night."

*   *   *

Holly stared, as she often did, at the familiar outlines of her room. Next door lay a demon, one who had wanted her dead. One who now needed her too much to kill her. She ought to be wary of him. Instead she nearly hummed with anticipation. A good puzzle, a proper challenge, were her favorite things in the world. He was that in spades. But when she thought of his pain and confusion, guilt loomed up and dampened all other emotions.

It continued to rain, leaving the room dank and shadowed as morning came. Janelle crept in on cat feet and stoked the fire, adding coals. She did not tidy—no one but Holly was allowed that task in here—but held the door open for Sara Anne, her newest maid, who brought in Holly's breakfast tray.

The scent of fresh coffee and warm sweet buns filled the air. Holly pushed to sitting as Sara Anne set the tray on a table by her bed.

"Mr. Thorne shall require a large pot of chocolate," she told the girl. "Have cook make it as thick and rich as she can."

"Yes, mum."

Holly sank her teeth into soft, warm bread, and then she heard the crash. A moment later, the connecting wall between hers and Thorne's room shuddered. Instantly sparks crackled and blue bolts of electricity snaked over the wall, followed by a bellow of rage from the other side. The two maids flinched, fear and horror holding them in place.

"Stay here." Holly whipped out of her bed and, turning off the electric field she'd placed between their rooms, hurried to seek out Thorne. Only to find chairs upended and a set of curtains torn from their hangings.

A flicker of movement had her turning even as strong arms came around her and she was hurtled bodily to the floor. Knowing her attacker was Thorne, she instantly wrapped her limbs around him and held on. They skidded across the floor, rumpling the heavy carpet and pulling her nightgown tight on her throat. They came to an inelegant halt halfway beneath the coffee table before the hearth.

Ears buzzing and head throbbing, she clung to the hard body on top of her. Something sharp scraped her neck, and she lost her breath. Fangs. Bloody hell.

Holly sent a bolt of power through Thorne, freezing him. Which only made him heavier. His cold cheek pressed against hers, the long strands of his hair covering her face and threatening to fall into her mouth. She resisted the urge to pummel his back.

"Are you calm?" she snapped.

When he said nothing, she realized that he was under her thrall and not capable of speech. Cursing, she pulled back on her power until he went limp against her. His chest lifted on a breath, and then he rolled away.

The table upended with a crash, and he swore. In an effortless glide, he rose, hauling her up with him. Head spinning, she leaned against the smooth, hot wall of his chest. But when his arm came around her waist, Holly stepped quickly away.

"What in the bloody blazes has come over you?" She barely refrained from shouting the question.

Thorne huffed through his nose and raked his long hair back from his face. Standing in the weak morning light and wearing nothing more than a pair of loose, black linen trousers that hung low on his narrow hips, he fairly gleamed. Over half of his torso, both arms, and the left side of his face were entirely platinum. He shook. Whether it was to keep still or from pain, she did not know. Likely both reasons.

A feather floated past her nose, distracting her. He'd shredded his bed. Seeing the direction of her gaze, he winced.

"I did not know where I was." His voice was rusty and dark.

A maid chose that moment to step in, carrying his breakfast tray. Her pale eyes went wide upon seeing the destruction. Holly strode over to her and took the tray from her unresisting hands. "Cleanup can wait, Sara Anne. Please bring my breakfast in here. Thank you."

Carrying the tray back into the room, she eyed Thorne. He'd wrapped an arm about his abdomen, as if holding his suffering in, but when he saw her, he let his arm fall and stood straight and glowering. Sinewy and lean of form, he was more a blade than a battle-axe. She would not look at the tight stretch of his abdominal obliques as they veered down in a sharp V between his solid hipbones. Nor would she note the dusting of dark gold hair that started below his navel and began to thicken at the line of his trousers.

"Pick up the table, will you?" she asked him in perfect blandness.

He reacted swiftly, the muscles along his side flexing as he bent and righted the table. There was something almost indecent about the way he moved his body, all sinful promise and decadent indulgence.

Holly set the tray down with enough force to rattle the china and then poured him a cup of chocolate. Thorne watched her, his nostrils flaring as the dark liquid filled up the white china cup.

"Here." She offered it to him. "Drink up."

But he hesitated, shifting his weight from one leg to the other, then thankfully hiked his trousers a bit higher on his waist. "What the devil did you do to your room? I could not get into it."

He sounded so put out that Holly's lips twitched, but she rather thought it a bad idea to smile. "Employed an electric field, which is quite good at repelling all things metal."

Thorne scowled deeply and ran a hand along the back of his neck. "Smarts like hell. I don't like it."

"When I trust you not to harm me in my sleep, I'll leave it off."

A sound of annoyance left him. "I wasn't trying to harm you. I was trying to see you." He looked off as if not wanting to continue. His gaze ran over the ruined furniture. "I apologize. For the room."

"Accepted. Now take your drink."

He did not say a word as he took the cup from her and gingerly sat upon the sofa. As it was the only place left to sit, she took the spot next to him.

His hand shook as he lifted his cup and drank deeply, his strong throat working on a swallow. The heavy fall of his silky hair pooled at the tops of his bare shoulders. Extraordinary how differently an unclothed Thorne smelled. Like baking bread, stoked fires, and pure, clean platinum.

A lock of hair hid his eyes from her, and she had to resist the urge to tuck it back behind his ear. Such strange hair. Not coarse or tinged with yellow. It was the pristine white of fresh snow, shiny, smooth, and thick. Up close, one could detect glints of silver and pale gold highlights in the strands. The effect of his hair was even more startling in contrast with his unlined, dusky ivory skin and dark bronze brows.

"How do you get away with this hair in society?" she found herself asking.

His head jerked up. Eyes more silver than black stared at her. "You would be surprised by what one can get away with when one carries themselves with enough aplomb. Most think it some sort of infirmity or defect. Not," he added, with a trace of amusement, "that I keep company around many humans."

"You never thought to cut it short?" At the very least, it would be less showy.

His lip curled in distaste. "So I can look like one of them? A proper sanguis male would rather go to his grave than live with such an affront." He glanced down at where his hair ended just below his collarbones. "It used to be longer, reaching the small of my back. But it..." He winced and touched his forehead. "I...cut it." His elegant fingers, tipped with little claws that had shot out with shocking speed, rubbed a spot on his head. "I think because it was a detriment to fighting."

Confusion and irritation clouded his eyes as he lifted his head. "I don't know." His gaze flicked away. "Thank you for the chocolate. For remembering."

"Thorne." She set her own cup of coffee down. "Have you any memory of attacking me just now?"

The corners of his eyes tightened. "It wasn't an attack. I wanted..." He shrugged. "I knew you'd take away the pain."

Knowing he needed more relief, she set her hand upon his platinum-covered biceps. His arm felt like flesh but was cold and entirely smooth. Holly curled her fingers around the corded muscle there, and a shiver went through his arm. Demon hot skin soon greeted her palm.

He held still as she traced her fingers down his smooth

and taut forearm. Even here, veins stood out against hard muscles. Gently, she turned his arm, exposing the soft, ivory inner flesh. At his wrist was a tattoo of a stylized crimson "N" circled by a crown of thorns. She'd seen this image before. On Amaros and his minions. Only the "N" had been in different colors and circled by different images, depending upon the person. Amaros had a pair of black wings sprouting from his.

Thorne peered down at it dispassionately. "To signify my membership in the Nex."

The Nex, an order dedicated to bringing down the reign of humans and letting supernaturals live in the open. An idea that Holly could find merit in on principle, but in practice, knew that it would upset the world order. Despite their weaknesses, humans were far more plentiful in number, and they would not be able to tolerate the idea of the supernatural. Nor did Holly agree with the Nex's methods, which favored fear, torture, and slaughter.

"And the thorns? For your name?" Absently, she stroked the spot. Thorne broke out into gooseflesh, and she let her touch drift off.

"No. It represents sanguis." His expression gave none of his thoughts away.

She moved on to his other arm where the flesh was still entirely platinum. Cold seeped into her hand as she rubbed along the surface, leaving ivory skin in her wake, and revealing yet another tattoo, this one larger. Thorne gave a small start as the black ink appeared. The design was of a long, wicked dagger, wrapped with more thorns. It traversed the length of his forearm, bisecting it with its darkness.

Holly held his wrist in her hand, feeling the pulse beating there, and watched his expression alter from surprise to confusion to a deep frown. "And this one," she asked in a low voice. "What does this one signify?"

"I..." The soft curve of his bottom lip caught on a fang. "I cannot recall. When I try to think of anything more about that part of me, I simply see another wall of black."

"Has your memory been tampered with, do you suppose?"

His brow quirked. "Tampered with or damaged?"

"Your memory is certainly damaged. But the fact that you cannot recall even a glimmer of what this tattoo means suggests that certain memories may have been wiped clean." There were supernaturals who could do such things. Primus, fae, witches.

"It just becomes better and better." Scowling, he looked up at her. "How long do I have, do you reckon? Before the metal takes over again?"

Holly stared off into the dying embers behind the grate. It occurred to her how cold the room had grown. If not for the heat emanating from Thorne's good side, she would be shivering. "I have not had a chance to study you."

A low growl rumbled in his throat. "Study me," he scoffed. "As if I were a specimen under your scope."

He pulled away and went to search for his tunic, only to swear and toss it down upon finding it torn.

"I cannot give you a precise answer unless I have gathered all the facts. Facts require study." Holly sighed at his steadfast scowl. "All right. When do you think you fell asleep?"

His mouth tightened. He would not look at her. "The last chime I remember was at five in the morning."

"You could not sleep?"

He looked at her sidelong. "Sanguis are creatures of the night, love. Day, with its burning sunlight, is the time for slumber." Thorne set his hands on his narrow hips and frowned at the mantel clock. "I must have passed out closer to six."

"Because your pain had started to increase?"

"Darling," he said with a smile that didn't reach his eyes, "the sad truth is that it started the moment you took your little pinky off me, and it did not ease until you touched me this morning."

Which was most unfortunate.

"So then," she said as if not affected, "we parted ways at around two in the morning. You lost awareness at six, but did not rise until," she glanced at the clock, "seven, which is presumably when the metal fully invaded your brain. Which, all other variables aside, gives you roughly—"

"Four hours of lucidity," he finished. "What do you mean, 'all other variables'?"

"Things that speed up or slow down the process. Last night, I observed that your agitation appeared to make the platinum spread at a more rapid pace. Drinking chocolate seems to calm you down, and thus the process as well."

He made a noise of reluctant agreement and turned away from her, as if he did not fancy her watching him so carefully. Which was ridiculous. How was she to help him if he did not let her study him?

"I have some memories back," he said. "There are places we need to visit after breakfast."

"But you are sanguis. You cannot go out in the day."

"No," he answered with false patience, "sunlight burns my kind. It is raining," he gestured to the window, "and I'll be well covered by my clothing—Hell, I need clothing."

Holly stood. "We'll find you something until you can

get your own. My cousin St. John is about your size. I believe he's left some things in his room." She started for her door, not wanting to face him. "However, I shall stay here. I have things I need to do—"

He caught hold of her arm and spun her round. The scent of chocolate and hot metal rose up from him. "You come with me."

She didn't want to meet his eyes. A wall of resistance rose up within her. She needed to get away from him. "You do not need me to come with you."

"I need you to touch me." His cheeks, so sharply etched and defined, tinted with anger. "To keep me sane."

"We've just established that you have several hours before insanity occurs."

A huff of breath escaped him, and his grip grew almost painful on her arm. "Why are you resisting? Do you plan to bar me from the house as soon as I leave it? Because let me tell you—"

"My reasons for staying here are my own." When he moved to speak, she raised her voice. "I have given my word, Mr. Thorne. If you persist in trying to manage me, I shall withdraw it."

His fangs lowered a touch. "Try it and see what happens."

"I'd rather not." She did not want to fight him. She simply wanted to get away and hide.

They stood, facing off, neither one speaking. Her head pounded, panic sending little dots over her vision. He needed to let this go. She could not leave her house. She could not.

Trying another track, Holly gave him what she hoped was a comforting smile. "I understand that you are afraid—"

"The devil I am!" He looked appalled.

"It isn't anything to be ashamed about," she said soothingly. "It's only natural for you to want your hand held—"

"Bloody hell, woman," Thorne snapped, "conduct whatever mad experiments you want. I'll go without you and be glad of the silence." He moved as though to stalk from the room but came to an abrupt halt. His chin lifted in a surprisingly regal gesture. "This is my room. You get out."

Holly ducked her head demurely. "As you wish, Mr. Thorne." She left with due haste so that he would not see her grin of victory.

Chapter Four

———— ❧❧❧ ————

Will hated being shadow. He lost all sense of himself and felt only a soul-deep terror that he'd stay this way, without mind or body. It was a primal thing. And a state of being he did not want to attempt, but he had to if he wanted to travel without being seen. The risk of going mad was less now that Evernight had pushed her power through him. So he thought of a destination, then turned, hoping that his shadow self would take him there. Today he thought of home. His.

Instantly his body dissipated, ice cold invading him. And then total, absolute blackness.

He was not aware of time or distance. He came back to himself in a heap upon a cold marble floor with the shadow of a man bent over him. Will reared, claws out, fangs extended. The man stepped back, hands up in a peaceable fashion.

"Hold," he said. "It's Jack."

Jack? Will panted, his body shaking and sweating from the effort he'd made to solidify. The man before him was a big bastard, and he knew him. Will relaxed only marginally. "What are you doing here?"

Jack Talent, his one-time best mate and the man who'd indirectly led him down his current path, laughed wryly. "I ought to ask you the same thing, mate. You're in my house."

At that, Will's tension left. He stood up straight. "Your house? What the bleeding hell am I doing here?"

Jack's speaking look made him realize he'd said that last bit aloud. "So you did not intend to come here?"

Will rubbed the edge of his jaw, where it was cold and heavy with metal. "I wanted to go to my home." Clearly he had not perfected this mode of travel. "I'm..." He sighed, feeling tired, old, rudderless. "I think of where I want to go, fall into shadow, and hope that I'll end up there."

With a stillness that would be unnatural on anyone else, Jack watched Will. "What precisely did you think before you turned?"

"To go home." Will paused. "No, that's not it. I thought I should go to where I've been living before..." He broke off and scowled at Jack. "Why then did I end up here?" He knew it was no accident. Just as he knew that look upon Jack's face; it was guilt. Well concealed, but there for anyone who knew the man well enough.

"Because here is where you'd been. Before you escaped."

A snarl tore from Will's lips. "Escaped? As though I were a prisoner?" He took a step in Jack's direction, but the big nephil simply stood unmoving. "Did you keep me as one, Jack?"

"You asked," Jack said quietly. "You begged me to."

Will flinched as if hit in the gut. All his ire fell flat. "Why?" It came out a harsh whisper. "Why would I do that?"

"You were growing more mindless. More feral," Jack said. "I agreed to keep you because I cared for you too much, *owed* you too much, to do the alternative and destroy you."

"As if you could." It was a quip because Will was fairly certain that, if any being had the strength to end him, it would be Jack Talent, half bloody angel.

Jack's mouth quirked but he was polite enough not to contradict Will. "I put your possessions in storage. And your funds have been managed by my accountant." He gave Will a quick and rare smile. "You'll not want for blunt any time soon."

A lump filled Will's throat, and he had to clear it before speaking. "Ta, Jack."

His old friend nodded shortly. "It was the least I could do." He rolled his shoulders, his expression growing set, as if coming to an internal decision. "Would you like to see where you were kept?"

Did Will? Cold fingers gripped his ribs at the thought, but he'd landed here for a reason. "All right."

They were silent, the air between them solemn, as Jack led Will to the back of the house and down the servants' stairs. When they'd reached the kitchen, Jack went to the ice pantry and pulled a hook on the wall. Another door opened, revealing another set of stairs going down.

"So, the dungeons for me?" Will wanted to laugh, but he couldn't.

Jack didn't appear any more pleased. "You screamed too loudly to consider anything else."

Well then.

They reached the bottom and a heavy door studded with gold rivets. A door to keep demons in or out. Jack gave him an apologetic look. "Does the gold still affect you? Mary and I were never sure it did any good. You escaped once before when we put you into a gold-lined room." Gold was poisonous to most demons, sanguis included.

But Will had been so altered by his platinum heart that he did not know. One way to find out. He walked up to the door and pressed his palm against one large rivet. It hurt, but only faintly, more of a stinging sensation than actual pain. Nor did his flesh burn. "Well," he held up his unmarked hand, "I suppose that answers that."

He stepped away, and Jack turned the handle on the massive door, setting off a series of scrapes and clicks as the tumblers slid open. Inside smelled of a tomb, and something scuttled out of the light.

It ought not to bother Will at all. His lairs had always been below ground. A safeguard against the sun. But they'd been warm places of unexpected grandeur.

He'd had a life before. It hadn't been perfect, but it had been enjoyable. He'd had women, parties, adventures. Now he'd become a thing to be hidden away. A monster that only one woman could control. For one dark moment, he hated Holly Evernight for the power she wielded. But he couldn't seem to hold on to that hate. Which brassed him off too.

Thin-lipped, Jack flipped a switch, and electric lights hummed as they snapped to life. Will squinted under the harsh electric glow. Rough-hewn bricks lined the space, which was empty save for a raised platform in the center and, in the far corner, a large wooden box from which several thick wires ran up into the ceiling.

Jack's boot heels clicked against the stone as he went to the platform. "Here is where you lay." He seemed pained by the idea. "It was quite an effective prison."

"I simply laid down and stayed?" Will laughed without humor. "I can't believe that."

"No, not until you understand the beauty of it." Jack placed his large palm upon the black, smooth platform. "It's a magnet, Will." He eyed him, solemn and sad. "The power source is in the box over there. One flip of the switch and your metal body was trapped."

Will flinched, the words going through him like the recoil of a gun set off. Sourness filled his mouth. "This magnet, it's an invention. Was it hers?"

It was not surprising that Jack knew precisely to whom Will was referring. "You haven't told me where you've been, Will. Please tell me you aren't planning to go after Holly Evernight."

"I won't tell you that."

Jack glared. "Have you tried?"

Damn, but his friend knew his evasion tactics too well. "Yes."

"Shit and piss, Will, if you've harmed a hair—"

"I have not," Will cut in, "nor shall I."

Jack did not appear convinced. Will wasn't about to try to plead his case.

"You never answered my question," Will said. "Is this thing one of her creations?"

Jack stared at him for a moment longer, as if he was attempting to come up with a better answer. Then he sighed. "Holly created it."

A growl, feral and pained, rumbled through the room. Will realized he was the one making it. Betrayal cut deep. "She knew?" She of the innocent eyes and pleas.

"No," Jack said flatly. "It was an older invention, designed to lift her dirigible off the workshop floor. I thought it might work on you." He shrugged, then his gaze turned hard. "We kept you from her because, to be quite frank, we didn't think she deserved the guilt."

"She made me into this!"

"Is that why you went after her?"

"Of course it is, you muggins! What other reason would I have to seek her out?"

Jack's brows lifted. "You obviously failed at whatever attempt you made on her the first go round. Else I'd have heard of it."

"We are working together on a solution to heal me," Will said through his teeth. He had to give Jack something, otherwise the persistent bugger wouldn't let up.

Jack's expression was grim. "What are you playing at with Holly, Will? For I'll tell you right now, she is my friend, and I'll not have her hurt."

For a moment, Will imagined telling Jack where he could stuff his questions, but he leaned against the brick wall and ran a hand over his face instead, trying to calm himself. Pain made that hard. Metal forced its way up his neck, towards his brain. Already, when she'd promised him more time. Hells bells, would he be able to return to Evernight before he lost sense of himself? Perhaps. She was quickly becoming his true magnet.

"There is a contract out on her life," he said at last.

A sound came from the other side of the room. Jack gasping, and choking it back. "We've heard nothing of this."

"I figured as much. Otherwise Evernight would be better guarded." He glanced at his old friend.

Jack tilted his head and frowned. "Rest assured we'll be tailing her now."

"You cannot. If you are noticed, and believe me, your lot is often noticed, it might scare off a potential assassin. If I am to catch one, that is the last thing I need to happen."

Jack's frown grew. "You ask for a great deal of trust in this. If Holly were to be hurt—"

"She asked me to keep her safe, and I will. She also has refrained from requesting assistance from you and yours. Now ask yourself why?"

"I can guess. Bloody, stubborn, independent woman." There was a wry humor beneath Jack's annoyed tone.

Will empathized. "Regardless of my feelings, I *will* protect her with my life." Will held Jack's assessing stare for a long moment before sighing and running his fingers through his hair. "No more arguing. How did I get free? Do you have any idea?"

"Someone helped you escape here."

"Tell me."

"Not much I can tell." Jack shrugged. "The magnet works off electric power, which was always running. Then one night, it all went dark. I heard you roar." The corners of Jack's mouth lifted. "And I do mean roar. By the time I got down here, you were gone, and the doors were all wide open. There was no sign of forced entry, which isn't a surprise. And nothing else was touched."

"But I'd escaped before, you say?"

"Yes. About a month before your final escape. Mary and I tore through London looking for you, only to return home to find you standing in the front hall. You were covered in blood and babbling about something finally being 'done.'" Jack studied Will as if waiting for an excuse. But Will didn't have any.

Blood. So much blood. He'd been swimming in it, so hot and viscous, licking it off his fingertips. When? Whose?

"Messy of you, Thorne. Draining her dry." A flash of fangs, male hands touching the edges of a female's throat

torn-open. "Not to mention costly. Restitutions will have to be made. She was a favored donor."

He knew that man's voice. Who was he? A glimpse of speaking to someone who wore darkness like a cloak, of demanding something from the man. Or did the man demand something of him?

Then the meaning of those distant words sunk in. Satan's balls, Will had killed a woman. An innocent. Killing was one thing. But to attack and destroy a willing blood provider was the act of an animal. It made him no better than the fiends who writhed about in Hell. His fingers dug into his thighs as he fought the urge to double over and vomit.

"After the first escape, we employed the magnet to keep you secure," Jack said, oblivious to his inner torment. "You were oddly content with the idea, actually."

Taking a deep breath, Will walked over to the platform. He didn't want to touch it. Associations of pain and endless hours of nothingness washed over him when he looked at it. But he laid his palms upon the cool surface. A shudder wracked through him. And then glimmers of a memory flashed through his mind in rapid bright succession like a zoetrope. Of the magnet's constant hum, and the pressure it caused, as if an invisible hand crushed down upon him. Of facing the ceiling, the familiar crosshatch pattern of the bricks, of tracking a spider as it crawled across one of them, and then a hooded figure leaning over him.

"Evernight," the figure hissed in his ear.

Yes, Evernight. The name written upon his very soul. The source of all his pain.

"Holly Evernight. She is the one you want." A cloth pressed to his nose, the scent of a woman heavy upon

it. He knew that scent. He'd craved that scent for what seemed like an eternity. It was she. The one who had made him into this thing of pain and madness.

"She is alive and well in London, Thorne. Follow the scent."

His name was William Thorne. And he would kill Holly Evernight.

"By the blade, be swift and true," the figure whispered. And then the great force that held him down was gone, and he fled, going straight to her.

The memory ended in a rush, and Will sucked in a sharp breath, his head spinning and his heart clicking at top speed. He sagged against the magnetic platform. Will cleared his throat and concentrated on what he knew. "Someone let me go and sent me to her."

Jack's voice, calm and smooth, seemed to come at him from a great distance. "Did you recognize the one who set you free?"

By the blade, be swift and true. Never hesitate, never doubt. He knew those words as if they were etched upon his soul. But had no notion of *how* he knew them.

"No," he said, as another memory solidified, "but I do know this. She was female, and she had purple eyes."

Thorne had been in her house for precisely nine hours and ten minutes. Hardly a significant amount of time spent in his company, especially given that she'd been asleep for six of those hours. And yet, now that he'd gone, she felt oddly altered. Which was ridiculous. He'd only been gone for . . .

Holly glanced at the clock hanging from the wall. One hour and fourteen minutes. Sighing, she tossed her repelling pencil down and leaned back against her chair. In the hallowed silence of the West laboratory, the clock ticked on in an endless echo throughout the room.

A moment later, Felix's scratchy, disembodied voice drifted from the panel on the wall. "Mrs. Talent is here. Shall I put her in the small library, mum?"

Even though he could not see her, Holly nodded. "Very good."

Holly smoothed her sweaty hands down the sides of her worsted wool housedress. It was a plain serviceable affair of dark blue. Certainly nothing that suggested any hint of a woman plagued by agoraphobia. Nevertheless, she felt as though she were about to be slipped under the microscope and be found out.

"Do not be ridiculous," she murmured. "She isn't your enemy. Though let us not fool ourselves. She isn't here for a social call."

And now she was talking to herself. Bloody brilliant.

On that cheery thought, Holly calmly walked towards the library, cool shadows gliding over her and thick carpet muffling her steps. A pulse beat hard at the base of her throat as she came upon the library door and a waiting Felix opened it for her.

Upon entering, her guest rose with a starchy rustle of crinolines. Like Holly, Mary Talent wore blue, but that was where the similarity in their dress ended. Mary's blue wool gown had a gold and red paisley pattern and fit her frame like a second skin. The underskirt was pale gold worsted. The overskirt, in the same paisley blue wool as the bodice, draped with luxuriant folds then swept up to a massive bustle at the back before falling in an elegant train to the floor. Mary always did love her fashions.

Her melodious voice broke the silence. "Holly, it is

good to see you." She smiled softly, but her golden eyes were shrewd, taking inventory of Holly's every move.

"Mary." Holly gave her a quick, but heartfelt embrace. Her friend smelled of rain and fog and spice. A lump rose to sit at the back of Holly's throat. Quickly, she stood back. "It is good to see you too."

They both sat, Mary arranging her voluminous skirts and bustle to the side as Holly plunked down in the nearest chair. As pretty of a picture as her dear friend made, Holly could never abide such a restrictive costume. "Are you well, then?" she asked, before Mary could do the same.

Mary's lips curled as if she knew very well what Holly had done. "Yes. Exceedingly."

"And Jack?"

Mary's husband, Jack Talent, was both a friend and an SOS regulator. A shard of guilt lanced through Holly's chest. She ought to have had them over for dinner months ago.

"Jack is well." Mary's smile grew cheeky. "He's been made a director."

An extremely coveted position in the SOS, as there were very few seats, and the directors ran the entire organization. Life was passing Holly by.

They went silent as Nan entered with a tea tray. She set it down on the table and then left, but not before Holly caught the pleased smile on her face. Holly supposed it was on account of having a visitor for once. She dragged her gaze away from the housekeeper's retreating form and back to Mary.

"Director James stepped down," Mary explained. "Jack accepted on the condition that he still be permitted to work his own cases."

Amusement lit through Holly. "Field work always was his favorite part of the job."

A fond light came into Mary's eyes. "Yes." She cleared her throat and set her glowing gaze on Holly. "I too have been made a director. Director Wilde stepped down as well, you see." She grinned then. "Actually Director Wilde and Director James eloped to Italy three months ago. They are taking the Grand Tour and then settling down in the Tuscan hills."

Holly couldn't help but smile at that. "How very lovely. I did not realize they were so close."

"I saw a hint of it once." Mary's light brown curls trembled as she shook her head slightly. "And if it pleases them, I shall be pleased."

Holly poured and handed Mary her cup. "Cheers on your promotion, dear."

"Thank you." Mary took a small sip before setting her cup down. Her expression was neutral. Carefully so. "I gather you realize that this is not entirely a social visit."

Perhaps Holly ought to be hurt by that, but she was not. Mary respected her too much to pry unless it was under the auspices of official SOS business.

"I did." Holly set her own cup down. "Out with it, old girl."

"We need you back." Mary leaned in with a rustle of skirts. "Quite honestly, I do believe you need it too."

A strangled heat clogged Holly's throat and grew thick in her chest. She willed herself not to fidget. "The SOS granted me a year's sabbatical. The year is not yet up."

Dark gold eyes held hers. "Have you left this house in all that time?"

"I fail to see why that matters." She would not look

away. She would not run out of this room. "My laboratory here is quite functional."

"And you can work just as well at headquarters. Surrounded by like-minded individuals, as opposed to being shut up in an empty house."

Holly hated the pity hiding behind Mary's words. "The house isn't empty. I have my staff."

"And do they challenge you?" Mary volleyed back. "Converse with you as equals?"

Holly turned her head and studied the red marble mantle, featuring a stylized carving of Seshat, Egyptian goddess of wisdom, knowledge, and writing.

"If it were anyone else but you, I might not argue," Mary said gently, "but I consider you one of my dearest friends, thus I feel compelled to say that this isolation does you no good. You need to interact with people."

"I had a visitor. Last night, in fact."

Across from her Mary leaned forward, intruding into view. "Who?"

She ought not have said anything, Holly thought crossly. For this would not go over well. "William Thorne."

Silence was a detonated bomb.

"When was this?" Mary's eyes began to glow in the way of the GIM.

"Last night at approximately ten past twelve in the morning."

"What did he want?"

Holly took a bracing sip of tea before continuing. "Revenge."

"What?" Mary launched to her feet, nearly upsetting the tea tray. Thunderclouds of anger marred her smooth brow.

"It's all right," Holly said. "He was under the misconception that I intentionally tore his heart out to replace it with one of my clockwork hearts." The cup only rattled a bit as she set it down on the saucer. "I managed to disabuse him of that notion."

"Dear God," Mary murmured, looking pale. "Jack and I have been searching for him. He'd been staying with us"—something close to guilt flitted over Mary's features—"but he disappeared recently. We've been most concerned."

Holly could certainly understand why. They ought to have brought him to Holly from the start, she thought with a twinge of irritation. After all, she had created him in a roundabout way. She ought to have been given the opportunity to study him. Then again, she hadn't been very communicative back then. She recalled staying hidden under her covers for a good month after being freed.

"He was quite agitated," Holly said sedately, "but we reached a truce." To say anything more felt like a betrayal of Thorne's trust. Nor was she keen to explain how Thorne found her. There was absolutely no doubt in her mind that, should the SOS learn someone wanted her dead, they would insist on bringing her under their protection. And quite truthfully, she would rather die than admit why she could not leave her home, much less leave it to live in some strange SOS safe house. No, thank you. She'd take her chances with Thorne now.

As she poured herself more tea—mainly to avoid looking up at her friend—she was aware of Mary's hard glare.

"Just how did you 'disabuse him' of his belief?" Mary asked. "When last I saw Thorne, he was violent and not capable of rational thought."

"A lady has to have some trade secrets, dearest," Holly

hedged. With a sigh, she lifted her head. As expected, Mary appeared both doubtful and annoyed. "He is lucid," *now,* "and he shall do me no harm. In this you can trust." Holly hoped she did not have to eat her words.

"Where is he?" Mary glanced towards the door as if Thorne might come charging in, fangs extended, at any moment.

"I do not know."

Mary glared at her. "That is all you will tell me?"

"For the moment."

Silence swelled and stretched between them, one in which Holly met Mary's unforgiving glare, and then Mary sighed. "Very well, have your secrets with Thorne. Only, should you see him again—" and her tone stated emphatically that she knew perfectly well Holly would—"do tell him that Jack and I are eager to contact him, if only to know that he is happy and well."

Guilt pricked at Holly's spine. "I do not know about happy, but I can tell you that he is grateful to have regained his wits." Whether he maintained them was another matter. Oh, but she was mad, mad, mad. She stifled a cackle. Holly Evernight, The Mad Scientist. To think her cousin Sin used to call her Doctor Frankenstein to get a rise out of her.

"Unfortunately," Mary reached for the leather satchel she carried with her, "I have an objective today that does not involve pestering you." Her expression gentled then, which put Holly on alert.

Mary pulled a small framed photograph out and handed it to her. "Do you know this woman?"

Holly studied the portrait of a young, pretty woman with golden curls, doe eyes, and a pert nose. Recognition punched her lower belly, as did a heavy sorrow. "This is Eliza May."

Tight-lipped, Mary nodded. "Yes."

Eliza's eyes seemed to bore into Holly as she fingered the edge of the tooled leather frame. "She is a distant cousin. From America." Holly's great uncle Aidan had immigrated to Boston many years ago and, while there had been a murmur among family members that it was a miracle that he'd married at all, marry he did, and his one child had been Eliza's mother.

"She was to come live with us last year but something happened." Holly shook her head slowly, feeling yet another facet of guilt that she hadn't allowed herself to address for months. "Eliza never arrived in England, though the ship's manifest listed her as a passenger. My father tried to discover what he could, but everything became a bit waylaid when my parents had to care for me."

Holly winced. Poor Eliza May hadn't been forgotten, necessarily, but Holly couldn't help but think that, if she hadn't been in such a state of nerves, her father might have been able to put more effort into discovering what had happened to Eliza. "Father did ask the SOS to help." It sounded like a poor excuse to Holly's ears even as she spoke.

"Yes," Mary put in, her pretty face drawn into a frown. "Unfortunately, he went to Poppy, who assigned an agent on the case, but never told me or Daisy about it. Not that she was to have known to do so," Mary went on in a mutter, "but it would have made a great deal of difference."

Holly edged forward on her seat, her pulse picking up. "You have information then?"

One glance at Mary's expression told Holly it was not happy news.

"I am sorry, dearest." Mary sighed and settled down in a cloud of blue next to Holly. "Last year, shortly after you were abducted, Daisy and I happened upon a woman being attacked. Your cousin, I'm afraid. We tried to help but we were too late to save her."

"Poor Eliza." Holly did not want to hear the details, but she rather feared she knew all too well.

Mary took her hand. "All isn't lost. When we arrived, Eliza's spirit was still there. She did not want to die."

"You made her a GIM?"

As a GIM, Mary could call upon Adam to perform the change, should she find a good candidate.

"That was the idea," Mary said. "However, when Adam arrived, he took Eliza May with him instead of making her a GIM."

"What? Why?" Holly rose and took up pacing. "Where did he take her?"

"I do not know. He was not forthcoming, nor do I know where he goes when he isn't called here." Mary frowned again. "I am sorry. I wish I could tell you more, but I thought I'd give you some hope. And I can say that he did not harm her, nor do I believe he intends to."

"I suppose that is some comfort." Holly's insides grew leaden at the thought of her young cousin trapped with the primus. She glanced at Mary. "Why didn't you tell me before?"

"I did not know. In my new role as director, I was handed a great deal of unsolved cases. I only just came across this picture, recognized Eliza May." Mary picked up Eliza's portrait and held it carefully. "I came directly to you once I put it all together."

"Can you grant me an audience with Adam?"

"I've tried to call him forth. He will not come." Mary's lips pursed. "I suspect he knows what I wish to ask and has no desire to answer."

"Bloody, bothersome demons." Holly had a word or two she'd like to convey to this Adam.

Mary fought a smile. "As you say."

"Well," Holly sighed, "thank you. And if you hear anything further—"

"You shall be the first to know," Mary finished for her.

When Mary had gone, Holly sat in the silence of the library, listening to the sounds of the house settling around her. Quiet as a tomb. It wasn't the first time she'd thought as much. But it was the first she'd considered it her tomb. She'd done this to herself. Yet she could not find the strength to dig herself out.

Chapter Five

―――⚬※⚬―――

Rain pattered on the brim of his hat as St. John Evernight stared up at the house that did not belong to him but was the only home he'd known in London. Evernight House shone bright against the leaden sky, the white limestone along the Greek revival edifice somehow defying the coal-laden fug that coated all other buildings in London. In his younger years, Sin fancied that the house had been enchanted to remain so impervious to grime. Now he knew it had. And perhaps he was the *only* one who did know this.

No, there was at least one soul dwelling in the grand, old town house who knew the truth. He'd be having a hell of a discussion with that one soon. But for now, Sin leaned against a lamppost and clamped a thin cheroot between his teeth.

Tempted by the acrid taste and the faint smell of the fine Turkish tobacco, the urge to light the thing and draw in a lungful of burning smoke was strong, but he fought it. Disgusting habit, as far as he was concerned. And just one

of the things he'd apparently inherited from his father—or
the man who'd spawned him, as Sin thought of him. Considering that his father had been an evil Primus demon
who had tried to claim the souls of Sin's brother-in-law
and nephew, Sin cringed at the idea of being anything like
the bastard.

Inside the library, figures moved about, walking past
the lit up windows. Holly had a visitor. He thought of his
cousin Holly, tucked up within the house where she'd been
hiding out there for going on a year, thinking she fooled
her family with her claims that she was merely working
on new inventions. A rather stunning display of willful
ignorance for someone so bloody clever. Though Holly
was only his blood kin by a distant thread, he'd been
raised alongside her, and she was more a sister to him
than his actual sisters. He worried over her. The worry
grew when he thought of what he would ask of her soon.

From his vantage point across the street, Sin watched
as the house door opened and a slight female figure
emerged. Her step was light as she descended the front
stair. Gliding through swirling billows of fog, she made
her way down the walk of the house, boldly moving past
several traps designed to kill unwanted visitors. She was a
pretty thing, this courageous miss, and he recognized her
as Mary Talent. A Ghost in the Machine, the very type of
being who could lead him directly to where he needed to
go. But a GIM would never betray her maker. And while
Sin knew he could eventually force the GIM to tell him
what he needed to know, he did not harm innocents or
women.

Besides, Mrs. Talent was a friend to Holly and his sisters, which meant she had his loyalty. So he remained
where he was, hidden by fog and shadows. Turning to go,

Sin gave one last glance at the house he'd called home. He should be inside as well, living in comfort. But he couldn't. Not anymore. He would not hurt Holly, nor taint her with his darkness.

When Mary left, Holly decided to do some research. She sent Felix to the SOS library for books containing facts on sanguis, and shadow crawlers, and their earliest lore. He returned soon enough, leaden with heavy tomes, which told her precisely nothing about why Thorne still lived with metal invading his system, or how to reverse the process. Short of pulling out his mechanical heart, she could think of no other solution. As that would also kill him, it was hardly a viable plan. But one thing was certain: he was far better off than early crawlers, who slowly rotted away and needed mechanical limbs to replace the ones they'd lost. Those poor creatures were merely walking dead.

What made Thorne different? Was it that he'd been alive when the procedure had been done, as opposed to early crawlers, who purportedly were already dead when the demon Adam tried to create his first GIM? Could the difference save Thorne?

A blaring sound pulled her from her reverie. Holly headed for the outer hall. An alarm beeped from the brass panel by the front door, and as it did, one of the little light bulbs within the panel blinked. An intruder. In the basement.

A series of loud booms reverberated through the house, the iron doors that led to the basement slamming shut. Felix and Nan entered the hall a moment later. Felix already had one of Holly's multi-fire guns in hand, and Nan's eyes had begun to glow with witchy light.

"I do not think the main floor has been breached," Holly began when the entire alarm panel lit up like The Strand at night. "Hell. Felix, man the West hall, and Nan, you take the East." They hurried off. Though they were hardly weak, her heart began to pound and her insides tightened with worry for them.

Punching a hidden wall panel with the side of her fist so it would open, Holly reached inside the weapons closet, intent upon arming herself, when the entire house went dark.

Complete and utter blackness. Unnatural darkness. She could hear the gas lamp sconces hissing away yet could not see her hand in front of her face. Bloody, bloody hell.

Breath sharp with fear, she pressed her back against the wall and fumbled inside the closet to grab the nearest weapon. Her hand closed over the smooth handle of a whip the second an icy cold wind rushed at her with the power and sound of a freighter.

She heard her own scream of rage and fear from a distance, as she lashed out with the bullwhip. Lashing against air. Cruel masculine laughter echoed in the dark. Something tugged her hair. Holly wielded the whip again, not knowing where to aim. It connected, hitting something large. Not enough. Another pull of her hair, then laughter.

The bastard was toying with her. Gods, and he was *shadow*. Was it Thorne? The very idea sent a surge of bitterness into her dry mouth.

Another hit to her temple had her reeling. She set aside her fear and gathered her wits. Using a push of power, the knives, swords, and throwing stars lined within the weapons closet flew outward, whirling in a tempest around her. She could not see them, but heard the clicks of metal when they struck objects. The laughter increased, but was a bit farther away. Holly pushed her weapons outward, driving the intruder back.

The air grew colder, burning Holly's lungs and thickening the blood within her veins. She shivered, fighting for strength. Her attacker was trying to freeze her.

Then she heard a howl of sheer outrage and the shattering of glass. Grunts rang out, snarls, and thuds of flesh connecting to flesh. The blackness fled as if someone had wrenched open closed drapes. Holly squinted at the sudden return of light. A movement to her right had her focusing on two looming figures. A flash of white, the gleam of platinum. Thorne. He fought a man, tall and fair. The man swung out, his hand pure gold, and razor sharp claws gleamed bright. The claws scraped against Thorne's metal face, sending up sparks.

Holly sucked in a breath. He was entirely metal, just like Thorne. Which meant she could end him. She must have made a sound, for the man's eyes met hers. His burned deep gold. She raised her hand, seconds away from paralyzing him, when he grinned and, with a swirl of black shadows, disappeared just as Thorne made a vicious swipe where his head would be.

Thwarted, Thorne roared, his fangs so long they looked like blades. He stalked forward, his body twitching, his gaze wildly darting about as though searching for his prey.

"He's gone, Thorne."

At the sound of her voice, he spun in her direction, crouched down as if to attack. Dear God, but he was covered in blood. It stained his lips, chin, and jaw. Covered his crisp white shirt and torn waistcoat. His gaze, molten platinum, clashed with hers. He advanced on a growl, stalking her.

"Thorne." Holly tensed against the wall, ready to stop him but not wanting to hurt him. Nor did she have the strength to hold him long; she was more drained than she realized. But he kept advancing, the ends of his frock coat snapping about his thighs with every step he took.

Though part of her was inordinately relieved that he'd returned, the look in his eyes alarmed her for its intensity, as if she'd become the entirety of his awareness. And he was coming for her.

She was prepared to counterattack when he stopped before her and clasped her shoulders with a gentle but firm hold. His lips curled in another snarl. "Mine." He gripped her harder, pulling her towards him. "My Evernight."

As if she were a toy he'd fought over and won.

"Er...yes." Holly put a hand to his chest, holding him at bay and sending what relief she could into him. "I'm here to help you. Now kindly let me go."

He did not relent, but bent closer, his gaze fixed upon her throat with unnerving focus. A sound rumbled in his throat. It was far too hungry, that sound. He smelled of blood. Up close, she could see flecks of it in the snow-white of his hair. Had he wounded her attacker before the man fled? Or was it his own blood?

Whatever the case, she did not intend to provide him with any more of it. "Mr. Thorne," Holly warned.

He seemed past hearing, his voice going rough, faint. "Mine." And then, before she could take another breath, his eyes rolled up into his head and he collapsed in a graceless heap at her feet.

Chapter Six

❧~~~~❧

For nearly seven hundred years, the demon the underworld thought of simply as Adam had lived a lie. That did not bother him greatly. The world was full of lies. What was one more in the scheme of things? But his time was running out, for there was a vast difference between "nearly" seven hundred years and the actual seven hundred years. At least for him.

It ought to be over, the endless lying, waiting, and anxiety. He had what he wanted. What he needed. Hell, the object of his desire was currently attached to him by means of a soundless golden chain, drawn from his wrist to hers. Yet it wasn't enough. He had not yet won. And it was *her* fault. Dour, stubborn, all around pain in his arse, Miss Eliza May.

She made not a sound as he walked along the thin spine of a London rooftop, dragging her with him. She never did. She sought to drive him to madness with her endless silence. And she was succeeding.

He suppressed a growl low in his throat. The urge to

yank the chain and bring her hurtling into his body was high, but he ignored it. He could be silent as well. He *could*.

The whole of London spread before his feet—the glimmering lights, the broken teeth of chimneys and roof lattices, the domes and spires of churches. Eerie drifts of smoke rose up to join the heavy pall of thick, black fog that blocked the light of the moon to those below. Never before had the city been so vast, so capable of both miracles and violence. The world was on the cusp of a great change, and London was at the heart of it.

In the blink of an immortal's eye, everything would be different. He could feel it in his bones. Innocence lost. He'd lived through such times before. But this change would be greater, and irrevocable.

Technology, that grand science which sought to ease man's burdens, would be the catalyst that brought forth horrors they would scarcely understand now. Adam had seen it—the visions, the world torn apart by weapons. Weapons made by intelligent beings such as Miss Holly Evernight.

Oh, but he had a bone to pick with her. She'd created her own brand of mayhem when she'd copied his lovely clockwork hearts. Hearts that had no business going into the bodies of already powerful immortals. It set the balance off. It angered beings far more frightening than he. She didn't even know the half of it. And now one of her abominations, Will Thorne, was with her.

Logic said to destroy the both of them. Thorne for being what he was, and Evernight for her impressive, creative brain. She and her future offspring would be capable of destroying the world as she knew it.

The Nex knew this. They wanted her. Quite badly. The

SOS, in their focus to contain rather than innovate, didn't see her true potential. Not yet.

Adam surveyed the London sprawl, the sounds of coach clatter and men, shouts drifting up to him. Soon it would be worse—louder, more sprawl, more of everything. But wasn't that the point? Because the truth was, he could not wait to see it all. Technology was just as much his passion as it was Evernight's. And then there was the inconvenient but unavoidable fact that she was related to Eliza. So he'd watch over Holly Evernight in his own way and protect her from what wanted to destroy her.

But he'd have to be careful about interfering. Oh, the bitter irony, that he should be highly feared throughout the supernatural world. When, in truth, he was as harmless as a babe. It was a closely guarded secret, known only to another ancient, that Adam was not a primus at all, but a man, twisted by fate and magic into a false god. One governed by rules.

How very much he hated them; they'd bound him hand and foot for hundreds of years. He could not kill, much less harm, supernaturals or humans. Not without forfeiting his very soul. And though he had the power to create an entirely new species of supernaturals and held their very lives in the palm of his hand, he could not command his children to kill in his name. Were it not for the fact that he was impossible to destroy, or to catch, he'd be a sitting duck to any ornery supernatural out there.

Even so, he had powers that were useful to him now. That in mind, he bent his head and concentrated on letting his power flow.

The being he'd summoned appeared before him. The man the world had known as Jonathan Deermont, tenth

Earl of Darby, glared at him with eyes of pure gold. "You rang?" Disdain dripped from his clipped English tones.

Adam smiled, not a pleasant one. "For someone whose pathetic arse has been saved by me, you certainly show little appreciation."

The shifter had been at death's door after he'd been given a golden clockwork heart by the mad fallen Amaros. Adam had used his power to heal him. Thanks to him, Darby kept his sanity and still had the ability to turn to shadow or metal without damage.

Darby's mouth curled. "I find little to appreciate these days. Had I known the true extent of my devil's bargain, I'd have answered differently." Though he did not in any way acknowledge Eliza May, the reply seemed directed at her, as though he empathized with her "plight."

Adam fought for control. Fought not to lash out at Darby and paint himself the irrational beast that *she* seemed to believe he was. "Don't be coy. You knew."

Darby's resentful gaze slid away. "What is it you require?"

"It has come to my attention that your little group has targeted Holly Evernight for extermination."

The heated glare Darby shot him did not escape Adam's notice.

"Yes," Darby said.

"You attempted to destroy her this night."

Darby didn't bother to reply. Nor did Adam need it. He knew she'd survived. Which was good.

"How did you find Miss Evernight's company, Darby?"

Darby's patrician features tightened. "She's hardly the weak and frightened creature I was led to believe."

Pink lines of newly healing wounds criss-crossed the man's face. Had Miss Evernight done that to him? No,

those were demon claw marks. So Thorne was champion-
ing Evernight just as Adam thought he would. Even so, he
could not help but needle Darby.

"Excellent," Adam said. "I was hoping she'd regain her
fighting spirit."

Behind him, though not a sound was made, he knew
she rolled her eyes. Adam ground his back teeth and
forced a pleasant tone. "And the other one? The unnatural
shadow crawler?"

Darby twitched, his expression twisting as though
caught between rage and confusion. "Unexpected."

So Darby and his ilk hadn't sent Thorne. Which was
troubling. Adam had a good idea who had sent him. It
took all his resolve not to glance at Miss Eliza May.

Though he hadn't been bidden, Darby spoke. "Thorne
does not fare as well as I." Golden eyes studied Adam. "I
suppose he was not worthy of the same offer I received?"

How little the young ones understood anything.

"He wasn't a viable option."

At the time of their creation, Darby had pleaded to the
heavens for life, while William Thorne had begged for
death. As Adam could only help those that desired to live,
and Darby had powerful ties that could be exploited, their
fates were sealed.

"Shall I go now?" Darby asked, goading him.

Adam let the question drift off before answering.
"Holly Evernight shall not die. Capture Thorne and hold
him." The newly turned crawler had no idea the threat
he was to Adam. If only Adam could destroy Thorne.
But he could not. He could only keep Thorne contained.
Permanently. "Demand payment for your services for the
contract. But do not kill either of them."

Though he did an admirable job of hiding his reaction,

Adam saw the urge to refuse glinting in Darby's eyes. "Why?"

Why? Adam wanted to laugh, only that old, frustrated rage made it impossible.

"Because I bid it," he said. "Hells bells, does any slave do things without question these days?"

"I'm afraid I'm going to have to understand it a bit more," Darby said without fear. "I may answer to you, but my men deserve more than to follow the whims of one bored primus."

Annoyance ran hot through Adam's gut. While he could not harm humans and other supernaturals, fortunately, he could do whatever he wanted to those who'd given up their souls to his care. Thus he let it out in a pulse of power. Darby flinched, his body going stiff as ice as his clockwork heart stopped. Sweat broke out over Darby's skin as he struggled.

Adam cocked his head. "I ought to stop it forever. But I am not yet done with you, Lord Darby. So let me be blunt, as you are most likely in great pain." Yes, he was; the man swayed on his feet, the color leaching from his face. "You will hold them for me, and you will let this contract go. Or you will answer to me. Am I clear?"

Darby's skin resembled whey now, but he managed a nod. With that, Adam released him. His clockwork heart whooshed into action with an audible sound. Darby fell to his knees with a gasp. He stayed there for a moment, sucking in deep draughts of air.

Adam looked away in distaste. He'd decided long ago that sympathy was a waste of time. He refused to feel any now or ever again. Slowly Darby rose. Hate burned bright in him. So bright his soul glowed with it.

"May I go?" he asked with grudging impatience.

Weary of his presence, Adam waved a hand in permission. With a swirl of shadow, Darby fled. And Adam was alone. Well, not quite. The heavy weight of judgment pressed upon his back. Oh, but he wondered what Eliza thought of this little scene. Neither he nor Darby had acknowledged her, but she'd been watching. Adam knew that well.

As if to taunt him, the wind shifted, bringing forth the subtle scent of autumn pears and Rhenish wine. *Her.* He stiffened, as did his cock. Hell and damnation. He would not turn around and acknowledge Miss Eliza May, she of the hateful glares and endless silence. But he had to at some point. He had to find a way to get through to her. Fuck it, he was nigh irresistible to most beings, alive or dead. A wake of spirits trailed him even now, moaning and wailing for attention. Females and males wanted to bed him. Every bloody one but her. Wasn't it just divine providence that she would be the one to find him repulsive?

Will felt like hell. Or as if he'd been dragged through it, at any rate. Tentatively, he stretched his aching body, and bit back a groan when his muscles protested.

"You're up, then."

He nearly jumped out of his skin. The older woman Nan bent over him, her careworn face taut, as if examining a particularly interesting insect. It reminded him of her employer. His senses had deteriorated so greatly that he hadn't noticed another being in the room with him. Perfect. Bloody perfect.

"Where is Evernight?" From his prone position in his bed, he glanced about and found the room otherwise empty. Had he hurt her too? A memory rose within him, of holding her close, his focus upon the sweet curve of her pale neck, and he nearly gagged at the thought of his fangs ripping through her fragile skin.

Cold flooded his being. If Holly Evernight was no more, he was doomed. That was as good a reason as any for him to feel this…this fear. But no, he was fairly certain that, had he harmed Evernight, he wouldn't be lying in comfort now.

"In her room. And that's 'Miss Evernight' to you, boyo." The woman certainly knew her place, didn't she?

Nan watched him as he sat up. He'd been bathed and was wearing an old-fashioned nightshirt of thick, red-and-green plaid flannel with a bit of ruff along the collar. Of all the indignities he'd suffered, this topped it. He glared down at the offending garment, wanting to take it off but refraining from giving the old bird a show. Not that she'd mind, he suspected. "You aren't an ordinary housekeeper, are you?"

Nan cackled. "What was your first clue?"

His lip curled. "What are you?" Now that he'd paid the woman a bit of attention, he felt her otherness. A low, constant thrum that spoke of ancient forests and unbreakable stone.

She settled into an armchair by the fire. "Forward of you, but I'll answer." She crossed her arms over her chest and gave him an arch look. "I'm a witch. Been with the Evernight family since 1809."

Nan looked a bit worse for wear. Most witches of his acquaintance kept a youthful appearance. As she was a witch of undetermined power, and female, he did not say this, however. Unfortunately, his thoughts must have shown, for her glare grew in strength. "I'm cursed, if ye must know."

"Aren't we all?" Will's chest fairly ached now. Pain was returning. He needed Evernight.

Nan snorted. "I've lost almost all my powers and am bound to stay an old woman when living Here. As I'm no longer welcome There, I haven't seen my true self for quite some time."

Here and There. Here being earth. There being another plane of existence, the place where the more ancient of the supernaturals dwelled or could travel to. Most demons, Will included, no longer had the power to travel back There. They were too far removed from their creator's origins to have a strong enough connection. And then there was Nowhere, the place humans referred to as Hell.

Will liked to think of it as Hell too. And as much as part of him, the dark, pure-demon part of him, felt a certain kinship with Hell, it was not a place anyone in their right mind actually wanted to visit.

Mindful of the witch's watchful gaze, Will left the bed. His head spun for a moment then he steadied. Already the pain of the metal taking over his flesh began to grow. It would never stop. The realization hit him in a wave of despondency.

Will limped over to the fire. He was cold. Bone deep cold. He ran his fingers through his hair before clutching a handful of it. *Focus.* The fleeting thought that Evernight could help him focus had him frowning. He glanced at the connecting door to her room, and the shooting pains in his flesh intensified. "The being I fought. He was a shadow crawler."

"Aye. An advanced one."

Will quirked a brow.

"The older ones that Adam created were beings of rotting flesh and mechanical parts. You and this other, you're different." She squinted at him, as though peering into his soul. "A more efficient model."

"Oh, yes." He gave a laugh. "Quite." His dark amusement died as a thought occurred. "If Evernight made me..."

"You're thinking she might have made that being too?"

"Didn't she?" Will did not know how many experiments Evernight had conducted on Amaros's behalf before getting around to him. His lower gut burned with ineffectual anger. Bloody science. Bloody mucking about with things it ought not touch.

"She only knows of one created. You." Nan stood, her movements graceful and lithe, betraying her supernatural self despite her elderly appearance. When she faced him, her power fairly hummed, and it pricked at his skin, not at all a nice feeling. "That girl has suffered. You'll not make her suffer more."

"And I haven't?" He was this altered...thing. Unnatural. The very nerve of this witch, ordering him about as if he were her puppy. He stared at her, daring her to make him do anything further this evening.

She held his gaze with interest. "You *will* protect her with your life."

Will's fangs began to itch. "She is in one piece, is she not?"

Nan's thin nostrils flared. "So flippant, you are. When you've no idea with what you meddle." The fire in the hearth gave a loud, sharp snap as she tilted her head. "The Evernights are nothing to be trifled with, not if you want to come out of the thing intact."

He snorted. "Spare me the theatrics. Power relies on controlling through fear, of which I have none." None in regard to his life, that was. He'd been far too afraid of losing Evernight's for his comfort.

"I am not speaking of mere power," Nan said. "But ruthless cruelty. Which gives not a fig about fear."

"Ruthless and cruel?" He shook his head. "I hardly see Miss Evernight and her kin as ruthless. Cold and clinical, perhaps."

Nan's stony expression did not crack. "It is not this particular branch of the Evernight family. It is from whence they came." She smiled then, cold and dark. "Tell me, sanguis, what sort of ancient would send witches and elves to guard a family?"

There were bloody elves in this house? Felix. He must be. The bastard was too graceful and handsome to be a mere human servant. Bloody damn it all. This eve was growing worse and worse.

"Have you any notion of what spawned the elementals?" Nan asked. "Not many do anymore. Not many *want* to remember, for fear of calling up that dark power."

To give voice to something was to give it power. Every good little demon knew as much. Will swallowed hard. He had a good guess now but, as Nan suggested, he really didn't want to say.

Unfortunately, she said it for him. "Fae."

Unease settled over Will like an icy counterpane. An old dread that spoke to his soul. Will refused to glance about, no matter how much it felt as though a fae might pop up at the word. Despite the sweet, pretty beings that humans loved to depict as fae, they were anything but kind. As old as primus demons, and just as rare, a true faire could rip a soul to shreds. They were said to be tricksters, and, yes, cruel and ruthless beyond compare.

"Aye, you understand. And the ancient whose blood runs through the Evernight family will not be pleased should one be harmed."

Will shook himself out of his childlike fright. Ghost stories for supernaturals. That was all this was. "If they are so powerful, then why are assassins on Miss Evernight's tail? Why hasn't this great and powerful ancient stopped them all?"

"Good question. Why do you suppose?" Not an answer then. So the old witch was hiding something. Or lying through her teeth.

He merely stared at her, annoyed now. And she gave him a cheeky grin. "Did it ever occur to you that perhaps they want the two of you together?" The words were barely out of her mouth before she went pale and seemed to choke, as if something struck her in the throat. Will was of a mind to fetch her water, but she took a deep breath and appeared unharmed.

"I cannot begin to fathom why her kin would want me around," Will said truthfully. But if they did, it was in his best interest to keep his distance from Evernight. Which would be easier said than done. As if reading his thoughts, Nan nodded.

"Best to start thinking on that, boy." She was still pale, but it was clear that she was done with him. She moved to go, dismissing him with a simple turn of her back. "And stay out of the mistress's room!"

Chapter Seven

Holly had finished the last stroke of her nightly hair brushing when Nan entered the dressing room.

"How fares our guest?" Holly had last seen him being hauled off by footmen after she'd pulled the metal back from invading his lean frame. Nan had promised to look after him.

"Sleeping." Nan picked up an errant stocking that Holly had discarded upon changing. "I checked on him so don't you go checking on him," she added with an emphatic look of warning. "You've warn yourself out."

"I am perfectly fine." Her cheeks heated. "Nor had I intended to seek out Mr. Thorne." Blasted Nan knew her too well by half.

The woman *harrumph*ed before her expression turned serious. "We found something." She held out her palm, in which rested a black dagger. "The wee devil that broke in left this behind."

Holly eyed the thing as though it were a bomb. She knew that dagger. "Leave it with me."

Nan frowned. "I've noticed your experiment has a similar one tattooed on his arm. Best you be asking him why."

"He is not my 'experiment.'" But Nan was correct; she needed to ask. What did the dagger mean?

Time for a change of subject. "Why," Holly asked as she set down the silver-backed brush, "is it so cold in the house?"

Nan's thin mouth went thinner. "The boiler was rattling like an untended kettle. Felix ordered it turned down. I was coming to tell you when you rang."

A sly hint of censure there. Holly's lips curled in a small smile. "My intention was not to question your management skills, Nanny. I'm simply cold and irritable."

Nan made a noise of amusement. "If you weren't questioning everything, I do believe I'd die of shock." She bustled about the room, picking up Holly's discarded boots. "Would you like to see to the boiler now, lass?"

Holly smothered a yawn. "Honestly, no. I'm knackered." She'd likely do more harm than good if her mind wasn't completely on task. The boiler had an intricate design that required one's full attention. Worse, it was housed outside the main building for safety purposes. Holly had no intention of venturing to any outbuildings this night.

"I'll put more coal on the fire," Nan said. And did just that before leaving her.

Coal fires were inefficient and smoky. Something that became fairly obvious when one's efficient radiator heating system decided to die.

Alone in her bed, she hugged a pillow to her chest and moved her feet about to increase the friction, thus bringing forth a bit more heat. She really ought to go out to fix the boiler before the pipes froze. But she could not summon the energy. Rest. She needed rest. So why was she wide awake?

"Bother," she muttered against her pillow.

Her internal debate was still raging when the covers lifted on the far side of the bed, sending a blast of cold air over her.

"What the bleeding hell." Holly whipped around as Thorne slid between the sheets, a mulish expression on his face.

"I have need."

The declaration sent a hot bolt of shock through her center. When she merely gaped, he glared at her. "In pain here, love, if you don't mind."

He slid closer, gathering her up. Holly pressed a quelling hand against his chest. "Your pain is no excuse for invading my privacy. Or getting into my bed!" she added with heat, for he merely snorted and did not let go.

"It is the only reason I'd be here," he said with feeling. "And you cannot find me too distasteful, as you left off your little electric wall tonight."

"An oversight that I am now lamenting," she said darkly.

His eyes flashed silver in the waning firelight. "Your mistake. Now, if you do not mind." He gestured between him and her with his chin. "Get on with it, sweets."

She wanted to throttle him. And would have, if their legs hadn't become entangled, his hot and rough with crisp hair. She tried to ignore that. And ignore the sensation of being pressed bodily against his lean strength. Opening her fingers wide upon the center of his chest, she sent a bolt of power through him even as she pushed him away. "There," she nearly snarled. "Now, kindly leave." Had she been wanting to see him? She must have been momentarily afflicted by a bout of insanity.

Thorne rose up on one elbow, light gleaming over his altered flesh and glowing softly on his natural skin. Good lord above, was he naked? Holly gripped the covers so that she would not lift them and take a peek.

"I'm not going anywhere," he said, as if she'd suggested something utterly ridiculous. "I'm sleeping here."

"You most certainly are not." She'd go mad. He was too much for her, lying as he was in her space, crowding her with his heat and seductive scent. His vitality alone had her body humming with unwanted excitement.

Thorne raked a hand through his unruly hair, pushing the mass of it back, and peered down at her as if she were addlepated. "What do you suggest I do? Lie in my bed, writhing in agony and slowly losing my wits? Until I attack someone, perhaps your pretty maid? Or ought I stay with you and feel a measure of calm? Get some much needed rest so that I might track down this bounty on your head?"

Well, when put that way…Holly shook her head. "Must you lie so close? You're crowding me."

A slow smile pulled at his lips. "Bothers you, does it?" Dark eyes slid along her length, making her feel stark naked as opposed to being covered from toe to chin in layers of eiderdown. "You do seem rather *stirred* up."

"Annoyed is the word to use." Holly burrowed farther under the covers and moved away from him. Unfortunately the edge of the bed was at her back.

He grinned as if he realized the fact, and as if he did not believe her. "I'll behave." His solemn, almost innocent tone belied the evil twinkle in his eyes.

Beneath her hand, his heart pumped a steady rhythm. Holly hadn't realized that she was still touching him. She moved to take her hand away when he growled and slapped his bigger hand over hers. Trapping her there.

"If," he amended, "you keep touching me."

"That is impossible. Once I fall asleep," which was appearing to be less and less likely, "I cannot control where I place my hands."

"I thought of that," he said, far too happily for comfort. Before she could blink, he grabbed her wrist and snapped something over it. "So I thought we'd use these." Another snap rang out, and he lifted his arm to display a cuff upon his wrist and the chain that ran from his to hers.

The cuff on Holly's seemed to burn down to her bones. Rage and unmitigated shock choked her for an endless moment as she stared up at his smug face. She fairly shook with fury.

"You . . ." She gritted her teeth and found her voice. "You put a bloody shackle on me? You sodding chained me," she screeched at his rapidly fading smile. "After *he* did!"

Thorne thrust his chin forward. *Pugnacious little shite.* "Come now. It's silk-lined. Hardly the same thing at all. And it isn't as if I am not suffering the same indignity."

Holly saw stars of red. "Get it off! Get it the bloody hell off of me." Heedless, she punched at his hard, solid chest, each blow of her left hand restricted by the pull of the cuff. "Get it off now, or I swear to God, I will push a sea of hurt straight into your rusty, metal heart." She was screaming now, her throat raw.

The cuff seemed to grow tighter, threatening to break her bones.

"Get. It. Off!"

A solid weight bore her further down into the feather bed. Arms bracketed her, holding her close, preventing her from flailing. "All right, love." A deep voice at her ear. "All right. Just let me."

She wiggled, aiming a knee towards the softer bits she knew were there. A grunt, and she was held more firmly. "Christ's thorns. I'm taking it off, yes?"

The sound of metal clicking shot through her panic, and the cuff on her wrist fell away. A moment later, the hard body on top of her rolled away. Holly sucked in a great gulp of air, the cool rush of it clearing her head, then she bolted upright.

Thorne, bare-chested and hair disheveled, stared at her. Regret and something much like pity lined his expression. In silence they faced each other, both of them panting lightly. Then Holly slapped him. Hard enough to send fiery pain through her hand. Hard enough that his head canted to the side and a sheet of white hair slid over his cheek.

"Don't you ever do that to me again." Holly held her scarred wrist close against her chest.

Thorne stayed utterly still, his head bent, his face averted and hidden beneath his hair. Then slowly he straightened. His eyes, a brilliant striation of black and silver lines, bore into hers. "No. Never again."

Heat prickled behind her lids and at the base of her nose. She drew in another breath. *Calm. Center.* Crisply, she nodded. The silence between them was close and thick. Awkward.

Next to her, Thorne stirred, his throat working on a hard swallow. His torso, that glorious example of sinewy musculature, tightened as the ever-present evil lake of platinum spread in a rapid wave outward from his scar. But he didn't make a sound of pain.

Slowly, she reached out and placed her palm on his chest. Thorne sucked in a soft breath, but held still for her. As she concentrated on easing his pain, she spoke. "I've no desire to freeze my feet, so you'll have to get it, but in the top drawer of my bureau in the dressing room, I keep a collection of hair ribbons."

She could feel his gaze upon her and see his surprise in the clenching of his rippled abdominal wall. She let her hand drop and lifted her eyes to his. Some strange emotion passed over his expression before he nodded and went to do as she asked.

She did not watch him go, other than to note that Thorne wore a pair of flannel smalls that reached his knees and hung far too low on his hips, exposing the crack of a rather taut and very fine arse. Flushed, she studied the starburst pattern on her cover as the sounds of Thorne retrieving the ribbon drifted out from the other room.

Soon the bed creaked under his weight as he slid back into it. The intimacy of it, as if he already belonged there, had her insides tightening. She ought to have chased him out. Why was it that she'd allowed him to stay?

"Here." His voice was soft as he held a long length of red satin ribbon out to her. Wordlessly, Holly took the ribbon and began to wrap it about her right wrist. She favored sleeping on her left side, so this would have to do. Just as silent, Thorne held out his strong wrist for her.

She bound them together with a figure eight wrap, but when she tried to tie the final knot, her fingers fumbled, awkward with the use of only one hand.

"Here," Thorne said quietly, "let me."

Leaning in close, until their foreheads nearly touched and his hair curtained over their bound wrists, he held the blunt tip of one finger to the knot as she pulled the other end tight. Done, Holly slowly raised her head.

Their gazes locked. Holly's mouth went dry, the urge to lean in just a little further making her belly clench.

It clenched tighter when Thorne threaded his fingers through hers and clasped her hand.

"Why," Thorne whispered, "is the ribbon acceptable?"

She answered just as low, though she couldn't say what prompted her to whisper. "It just is."

It wasn't a chain. It didn't clank, or weigh her down. But to voice that would give rise to an old panic. Perhaps he read that in her eyes, for he simply nodded as if it made perfect sense. Then he sighed, his chest lifting and falling with the sound. "Lie down. Sleep. I promise, I won't hurt you. And I'm only here because I have to be."

Was that supposed to comfort her? Instead, it sent a pang of something through her breast. Something uncomfortable.

But Holly did as bided, curling up on her side and letting her arm fall behind her so her link with Thorne wouldn't pull tight. Not that it mattered. Thorne slid in close, spooning his body to hers and bringing their linked arms together before her. Nothing, not even the heaviest cover, felt as secure, as instantly warming as his hold. From the man who'd come here to kill her. Who nearly killed another this day.

"Thorne—"

"Do not waste your breath fussing," he cut in blandly. "It's the only way to lie comfortably." He snuggled in further, bringing parts of him she'd rather not focus on into contact. "And I will keep you warm."

All true. Yet she lay in absolute stiffness. How could she not? She'd never in her life been held by a man in this manner. Never shared her bed with another. Every part of her that touched him narrowed down to an acute focus—of his chin resting just above her head; his soft, warm exhales that buffeted her hair; the movement of his chest against the blades of her shoulders; the hollow of his hips that so neatly cupped her bottom.

Perversely, she fairly twitched with the urge to arch her back and seek out the bulge of his cock with the curve of her bottom. Her cheeks flamed. How perfectly horrid of her. And what would that accomplish? Other than make her look a fool, or give the impression that she was seeking something she didn't truly want. Holly ground her teeth. "I'll never sleep like this."

He made a noise that could either be construed as agreement or annoyance. Perhaps both. "You think I relish sleeping with a spitting cat of a woman?" His hand spread wide over her fist, closing over it. "But I'll try my best." And with that, he was silent.

Oh, but it did not stop, the hot, itchy feeling that coursed through her. His forearm was an iron band about her waist, drawing her attention down to his hand, where the tips of his fingers just touched her belly. He did not move them, but with every breath she took, they dragged along her nightgown, tickling, making her lower belly ache sweetly.

Holly forced herself not to yield to temptation and focused on other things. "Thorne?"

"What now?" he rumbled.

Ye gods, but his rough, sleepy voice did strange things to her insides. Holly swallowed. "The crawler that broke in. I believe I recognized him." She hadn't at first, but lying next to Thorne, a memory had broken free.

She felt him tense and lift his head. "Who was it?" He was alert now. Sharply so.

"I think it was a shifter Amaros brought in." Holly frowned. "Darby, I believe he was called. They experimented on him." She winced when Thorne shuddered as though he could not control it. "It was before I became involved. They put a gold heart in him, but Amaros had said he died."

"You're sure it was Darby?"

"Not one hundred percent," Holly admitted. "He certainly wasn't covered in gold at the time, but his eyes..." A fine tremor worked through her. "I remember his eyes." Those eyes had been so very full of fear and outrage. Just as Thorne's had been. She would never forget any of the victims. She would never forget a second she'd spent in that hellish prison.

Thorne was silent for a moment. "How many others did that bastard experiment on?"

"I don't know. Even one is too many."

They grew silent once more, but the thought haunted her. As did the notion that there could be, at this moment, more than one maddened and murderous shadow crawler roaming London. Would they all come after her?

"Darby left behind a dagger," she blurted out. "An exact replica of the one tattooed upon your arm."

Thorne's body grew so tight that it felt like steel against her back.

"What does it mean?" she whispered.

His voice was a dark night, surrounding her with its strength. "I do not know. But I mean to find out."

Chapter Eight

〜〜※〜〜

I understand you are in need of me?" Thorne entered Holly's laboratory the next morning as if put out for having to be there. His hair hung shining and clean about his face. Though Jack had sent round Thorne's clothes, he was still in a state of dishevel, wearing only shirtsleeves, braces, and a pair of trousers. He took her in on a glance then noticed Felix standing next to her.

"What is he doing here?" Thorne's tone was peremptory.

"Assisting."

The corner of Thorne's mouth pulled down. "With what, pray tell?"

Holly braced a hand upon her desk. "I thought it best that I begin to truly uphold my end of the bargain."

He did not appear to be eased by this information but prowled further into the room, his gaze roaming about as if seeking any hidden menaces. "How do you plan to do this?"

A crisis of nerves threatened to make her voice weak.

Holly stayed firmly in place and took a breath. "Though I am nowhere near being an expert on biology, or the anatomy of demons for that matter, I shall try my best. I'll need samples of your blood, skin, and hair."

Thorne stood stock still. "I am not going to be tied down."

"I am not asking you to do that." She tried to give him a look of reassurance. "You may sit here on this stool. I'll take the samples, and Felix shall label them. Does that sound reasonable?"

With a sour face, Thorne sat. "Let's get on with it, then."

He was silent and unmoving as Holly snipped his hair, but when she attempted to draw blood, she hesitated. He snorted at the action and simply punctured his inner elbow with his claw. Holly's hand was steady as she pushed the tip of a lancet against the wound to draw the dark crimson rivulets of blood down into a small vial.

"I sent a description of the dagger to SOS headquarters," Holly told Thorne.

His gaze lifted from the blood pooling at the bottom of the vial. "How? You did not leave the house."

"Through the use of my photophone transmitter." Holly gestured towards the apparatus that faced the south window of her laboratory. Composed of a polished length of wood, with a speaking tube on one side and a series of mirrors on the other, it worked as an excellent means of communication on clear days.

"It's a complex process," Holly explained. "But, to put it simply, both light and sound travel in waves. When you speak into the cone, the sound waves are directed to the mirror there at the end and then travel in the form of a light wave pattern. That pattern is caught on a receiver comprising a bigger, convex mirror, which vibrates upon being hit by the waves and reformes into sound—"

Looking glazed, Thorne lifted a hand to halt her explanation. "Are you trying to tell me that you can communicate by means of controlling light waves?"

"Well, yes."

A slow, almost wry smile curled over his lips. "Bloody hell, Evernight, but you do humble those of us with plebeian minds."

"It isn't my invention," she admitted, unaccountably flushed from the praise. "True, I've worked on perfecting the processes for farther distances, but the idea is American in origin.

"Mr. Alexander Graham Bell claims to have invented it, though really it was created through a collaborative effort with Mr. Charles Sumner Tainter. In all honesty," she said, "a great inventor needs a healthy amount of conceit. Mr. Bell and, fellow inventor, Mr. Edison would declare they'd created the moon and the tides between them if they could get away with the claim."

Thorne chuckled. "Have you met them? Seems you could teach those men a thing or two."

She bit back a smile. "Perhaps I could. But it is my business not to be noticed by Edison and his ilk." The SOS lived in shadows, and she was content with that.

"The world does not know what it is missing," Thorne said softly, and more warmth flooded her.

It was ridiculous the way his praise flustered her. Holly set down her lancet. "What I was trying to tell you was that I've heard back from the SOS research division. They cannot find any rendering of the dagger or record of assassins who might use it."

"They won't." Thorne's mouth snapped shut, and he

frowned. "Those who take up the dagger don't leave behind a record." He said it slowly, as if feeling his way around the answer.

Holly glanced at Felix, who hovered at the periphery, and Thorne did as well. His lean body went stiff as stone. Holly gave Felix a small, almost imperceptible nod, and the man quietly quit the room.

"Did that just come to you?" she asked when Felix was gone.

Thorne's long lashes swept upward as he looked at her. "Yes. Yet nothing more." Frustration marred his smooth forehead.

"Don't force it. We'll find the answers." Holly wished she believed with the same conviction in which she spoke.

"Meanwhile, I shall feel bloody useless, shall I?" Thorne groused.

"I shall endeavor to appreciate you for your brawn then."

He made a noise of amusement, and they fell silent as Holly returned to her task.

The flesh sample was the worst of it. Holly scraped along his skin to gather tiny particles, but the metal parts at his chest had to be gouged out. He claimed it did not pain him, but the sound of it, and the pressure she had to apply to the blade, had her breaking out into a sweat.

When it was done, she ran her forearm along her brow. "There. I've brought down every reference book on the biological sciences our library holds, as well as a tome on demonology. There ought to be some answers in them."

"Is that it then, for me?" His gaze, when it met hers, was closed off. "Or do you intend to poke and prod me some more?"

Rude arse. It made what she had to say all the more

difficult. But as her health relied on keeping his as well, then she needed to do what was necessary. Holly took a deep breath. "As to what I can do for your health, I have a plan."

" 'Plan,' " Will repeated dubiously.

He was in a foul mood. He'd been out of sorts since waking. Wrapped around Miss Evernight. Ordinarily, sanguis took great enjoyment in sharing a bed with others. After all, they craved physical contact and pleasure.

None of which would describe last night's fiasco. He'd come to Evernight's bed because touching her eased him. And, if he were completely honest with himself, he simply wanted to be there. But he'd mucked it up by chaining her. Will had expected her ire; a part of him had looked forward to it. He'd not been prepared for the blind terror that took hold of her. And he'd felt . . . remorse. The rest of the night ought to have been spent in misery, tied as he was to an unwilling Miss Evernight.

Hell, but he was downright rejuvenated after a night in Evernight's bed. And he'd merely held her.

Which was precisely the problem. Finding peace and contentment with Evernight—two emotions he was certain he'd never found in bed with a woman before—was entirely unacceptable. When awake, the woman was prickly as a hedgehog and about as lovable as a block of ice. Save she'd been warm and languid in sleep, leaning into his embrace as if she needed touch as much as he did. And her surprisingly plump and rounded arse had felt exquisitely perfect pushed up against his cock all night long.

Thank the devil the woman was a sound sleeper or she'd surely have felt his reaction to her lovely bum.

Will had quit the room before she'd had a chance to wake. Now, however, there was something about the tightness along Miss Evernight's mouth that had his hackles rising.

She was reluctant to voice this plan; that was clear. Although not as reluctant as she had been about touching him this past quarter hour. She'd all but quivered with disgust at that, looking at him as though he were a fiend fresh out of the pages of some shabby Gothic novel that humans loved to pen. Given his appearance when he'd returned to her home last night, he supposed he deserved as much. It still rankled.

Instinct prompted him to capture her slim, cool hand. Instant relief. Every bloody time.

She let him hold it for one breath, then delicately pulled away.

"Our agreement was that you'd keep me well," he reminded with a pointed look at her hand.

Evernight smiled her slight, Mona Lisa smile. "Yes, as to that—"

"Do not even try to back out—"

"Calm yourself." She lifted one cool brow at him. "What I was attempting to say is that I had an idea as to how we can make things more effective."

He eyed her warily. "Go on."

She moved across the room, her drab gown making a whisper of sound. While the color was an uninspired charcoal grey, Will was enough of a connoisseur to see that it was made of the finest cashmere and fit her like a second skin. He ran a hand along the plush velvet settee that sat before the fireplace. Miss Evernight, he concluded, was a closet sensualist. Not in the visual sense but in the tactile. She surrounded herself with comfort.

She cleared off a worktable with brisk efficiency. When she placed a thick eiderdown quilt upon the table, he could no longer hold his tongue. "More experiments, Miss Evernight?" He made his way to her, as if the very idea of experimentation did not turn his stomach.

Her cool eyes held his. "Nothing invasive, I assure you, Mr. Thorne."

"Hmmm," was all he could manage. He did not want to get on that table. If she tried to strap him down, he'd make the fuss she'd kicked up last night look like child's play.

"I'll need you to disrobe."

Will halted, his ears ringing. " 'Disrobe.' " The word fell like a weight between them. Surely he'd misheard.

"Yes."

Well, I'll be a devil's get. He reached for the strings of his trousers and tugged them as his heart began to chug away.

Pink washed over her pale cheeks, and she studied the table instead of him. "I'll step in the other room." She took one step then stopped. "Down to your undergarments, please. Cover yourself with the rug there." After pointing to the thick velvet throw folded at the end of the couch, she scurried off without another look.

Will had no idea what she had planned but her discomfort was priceless, and he wanted more of it. He did as instructed, but took off his smalls as well. If she wanted him unclothed, she was getting the full treatment. His grin was wide as he stretched out on the sturdy table and covered his lower half with the throw—though it was tempting to leave that off too. He was far too warm to need it. But he'd behave. Up to a point.

"Ready, Miss Evernight," he called out with evil glee.

Unfortunately, he might as well have been a piece of

furniture for all the attention she gave him. No, she simply glided up to the table and looked down at him with her usual detachment. "Yesterday, after you'd fainted—"

"Collapsed," he corrected. "Men do not swoon or faint. They might collapse, however. After protecting their woman against any and all threats. Although, in my case, it was really more of having a rest, if we want to be precise."

Her lips pursed and twitched at the corners. "While you took your rest, I had to use a significant punch of power to help you." She stared down at him, solemn, thoughtful. "It was tiring for me, which is ineffective in the long run."

He hated the twinge of guilt that pinched his gut. "Is there a point?"

"Yes." She drew up a stool and sat at his side. Suddenly, the vantage point made him uneasy. He wanted to stand and loom over her so that she could not look down her nose at him. But he would be damned if he showed his displeasure. So he lay as if at perfect ease.

"You see," she went on, oblivious, "I believe that it would be better for both parties if I were to take my time about repairing your altered flesh."

"Take your time?" He sounded like a bloody parrot, but he didn't understand.

"Think of it as a treatment, as opposed to a quick dose of medicine." She lifted her hand, but hesitated, as if she didn't want to let it fall. But then she took a breath and rested her hand upon his arm. He felt the touch down to his bones.

"I'm going to..." She cleared her throat. "I shall rub you down, thoroughly concentrating on each area. Hopefully, it will slow the progress of the metal more effectively than simply putting my hand upon your chest."

A slow, wide grin pulled at his lips. "Let me see if I have this correctly," he said, struggling not to crow, "you are going to rub your hands all over my body..."—she narrowed her eyes in distaste, which only made his grin reach epic proportions—"slowly and thoroughly—"

"Really, Mr. Thorne."

"While my part in it is to lie here and take it?" His cheeks ached from smiling. "Is that the plan?"

"If you are going to act like a juvenile, then I shall be forced to leave." Scowling, she moved to stand, but he had his hand clamped around her forearm before her bum could lift from her seat.

He tried his best to be serious. "It's a good plan, Evernight." An excellent plan. One he could not wait to implement.

Her frown of annoyance remained for a moment, then she set her hands upon his arm and closed her eyes. Warmth swept over him. Her lips parted, and her brow furrowed as she breathed in and out, her breasts rising and falling with each exhalation. The whole effect was so similar to one of a woman being slowly and thoroughly tupped that Will nearly groaned.

Sweet mother of mercy, but he hadn't thought this out; his cock reacted as if stroked, rising swiftly and going iron hard. And he'd have to lie here, pretending that her soft, cool hands slowly running along his flesh weren't the very best thing he'd felt in his life. Pretend that he didn't want her to reach under the cover and clasp his aching erection and give it a nice squeeze.

A strangled noise gurgled in his throat. She stilled, her eyes opening a bit. "Does it hurt?"

"No," he managed.

"Do you feel it working?"

Something worked just fine. "A bit."

Nodding, she closed her eyes again and slid her hands over his shoulder and along his chest. Her fingertip grazed his nipple. He felt it in his cods. Bloody hell. He would die before this torture was over.

"If this works as I believe it will," she said, cutting through his haze, "we shall do this daily."

"Very well." It came out as a strangled breath.

Her keen eyes cut to his, and it took all he had to return her bland stare. Almost immediately, her lids lowered, and her attention returned to his body. Relief and torture all at once. Will took a breath and focused on the coffered ceiling above, counting the squares there.

One. Her hands skimmed along his collarbones. *Two*. The stool beneath her groaned as she stood and circled the table, dragging her hands down his opposite arm. *Three*. The warmth of her palms mapped the line of his hip, moving down to his thigh.

Satan's. Balls. He sucked a breath through his clenched teeth. His cock twitched, his stones drawn so tight they ached. Her profile, serene, set with concentration, filled his view. The tip of her thumb skimmed the sensitive skin of his inner thigh, and he broke out into a hot sweat.

Ceiling. Just count the squares on the ceiling.

Then she clasped his knee. He nearly shot off the table.

Evernight's dark brow raised a fraction. "Ticklish?"

It was a knee. A sodding joint. It shouldn't be so sensitive. Her holding it, her lithe fingers stroking the back of it, ought not to make his abdomen clench and his thighs tense. But it did. Will gripped the cover, wadding it over his erection, with fingers that had grown claws.

"Yes," he lied. It was either that or toss the cover aside and pull her down to him. But she wasn't even flushed.

No, Miss Ever-bloody-night simply stared down at the limb she'd uncovered as if it held all the interest of a piece of machinery. Less than, he thought bitterly. Her damned inventions were her pride and joy. He was more like a side of beef.

She moved on, which was no better for him. He'd never known how sensitive his calves, his feet, his damned *toes* were until she'd touched them. Even though he was in sensual agony, his pain left him. His tormented flesh grew lethargic, warm, and liquid as she worked him over.

Until only his cock remained hard as steel. By the time she'd finished with him, with a little encouraging pat and a request that he rest quiet like a good lad, there was no point in denying it: Holly Evernight would be the death of him.

Chapter Nine

Holly knew the moment Thorne left the house. She felt it in her bones, in the leaden weight that seemed to settle within her breast whenever he strayed. It disturbed her that she missed him, that some part of her reveled in his presence. Why? He was a pain in her arse, a rude clod, smarmy, obnoxious. And he'd wanted to kill her.

Despondent and having had little sleep, she retired early. Which she hadn't done since she was six years old. Where had he gone? Would he return? He had to. If only because he needed her to heal him.

Holly wanted to punch her pillow. "Bollocks."

"If mam and da heard you say that, they'd have your hide."

The unexpected voice in her room sent a bolt of terror through her, and she flew upright, the knife at her bedside hurtling through the air at her silent command.

Sin, sitting in a chair by the flickering fire, ducked, avoiding it, only just. "Jaysus, Hol," he said, as the knife imbedded in the wall behind his head and he righted. "What sort of welcome is that to give a fellow?"

Heart still racing, Holly pressed a hand to her chest and struggled for a breath. "The sort that bleedin' eedjits receive when sneaking into my room without invitation." Sin could get her Irish up like no other. "Have you no notion for your own safety, boy?"

He snorted, then rose, his tall frame uncoiling with uncommon grace. "As if you could bring me down." He grinned then, his green eyes twinkling. "It's good to see you, even if it means ducking one of your wee blades."

It was her turn to snort as he promptly plopped onto her bed and leaned in to ruffle her hair. She swatted his hand away then kissed his cheek.

Holly and Sin had been raised as brother and sister. In truth, neither of them had known who his real family was until his sister, Lady Miranda Archer, had arrived at Evernight Hall three years ago. Oh, they'd known he'd been adopted into her family, but they hadn't imagined that he was the lost brother of the Ellis sisters—one of whom was Holly's director, Mrs. Poppy Lane. Their parents knew, of course, but they'd kept that particular secret quite well.

The revelation hadn't changed things between him and Holly, however. They were close. He would always be her baby brother. A pest and her closest friend. With Sin, she felt young and carefree.

"It's good to see you too," she told him. "And mind your boots. I don't want London muck on my bedding."

Grumbling, Sin took off his boots then laid back next to her on the bed, just as he'd done countless times throughout their childhood. Holly sighed and settled against his shoulder. His familiar scent and shape was a sorely needed comfort. "Did you just get in?"

"Close to it." Sin never answered a question directly, which annoyed her to no end. But she let it go.

"How long are you staying?" Holly asked.

He was silent for too long. "I'm staying with Miranda and Archer."

The lump grew. "Oh." So he preferred his blood sister now.

Sin knew her too damned well. "It isn't like that, Hol." He turned to face her, and a lock of his dark, red-tipped hair fell over his brow. "I..." He huffed out a breath. "I still can't control myself properly. Miranda, Poppy, and Daisy are helping."

Sin had a great many powers. None of which he had been able to handle when he was younger. It had been a source of constant worry for their parents.

"And," he added with a cheeky grin, "Archer is teaching me how to fence."

"Oh, well, I can see how sword fighting tops learning your maths," Holly groused. Sin was wretched at his maths, and the task to teach him fell to Holly. When he didn't slip away from the lessons, that was.

His handsome face wrinkled with a great scowl. "I'd rather be skewered, if truth be told." He laughed when Holly shoved at him with her elbow. But his humor soon fled, leaving behind a look that was almost a reprimand. "And you've a guest, haven't you?"

Holly refused to squirm. "Was it Nan or Felix who tattled?" She caught his guilty expression. "Or have you been playing spy?"

Sin flushed then scowled. "He's a sanguis, Holly. Which is bad enough, but there's something off about the demon."

So then, he'd been spying. Sin always did. He'd cling to quiet corners and watch the world move by.

"He's none of your concern."

The bed squeaked as Sin sat up. "Bollocks to that. You're my concern, and so is he if he's staying here. I'll not have some blood-drinking, unnatural, hell-bred—"

"That is quite enough, St. John." She'd thought of sanguis in much the same manner. Before. It upset her now to hear Thorne being described as such.

"It isn't the half of it, Hol. What possible reason could you have to invite such a creature here?"

Holly sat as well. "He's my lover. Are you satisfied now?"

Oh, but it was worth the fib to see Sin burn bright red and start to sputter. "You," he said through his teeth, "are not playing it fair." Cursing under his breath, he reached for his boots. "Putting those sorts of images in my head and *lying* too!" He glared at her over his shoulder. "Oh, I know ye are, ye little harridan."

"So certain, are you?"

"Aye." He stood, his arms crossed over his chest, looking for all the world like a harridan himself. "For if it were true, you'd never willingly admit to it."

No, she wasn't Thorne's lover, but the thought was intriguing. A blush heated her cheeks, and Sin cursed roundly before calming himself with a deep breath.

"Will you not tell me the truth of your situation?" he asked quietly. So quietly that Holly half-feared he already knew. But that couldn't be, because he'd be shouting and making all sorts of demands for her return to Ireland.

"I already have." It sounded exactly like the evasion that it was.

They stared each other down until Holly's eyes burned with the need to blink. She wouldn't. She couldn't.

Finally, Sin broke with a long, put-out sigh. "I didn't come here to fight, aye?" Because he was so tall, Holly sometimes forgot that he was so young.

"All right, all right." Holly held up her hands in surrender. "Let's call pax then."

Some of the starch left his shoulders. "Pax then."

They smiled at each other, but then his faded. He hesitated for a breath. "Just let me say one thing, or I'll never forgive myself. Don't trust the sanguis. Don't … Don't get close to him."

"Why on earth not? And you had better come up with something bloody better than he's a bloody sanguis!"

"He is Nex, Hol." Sin appeared outraged that he should even have to say as much.

"Was," she corrected, feeling the fool for defending Thorne when she knew practically nothing about him. "They tossed him on his ear. And, anyway, how did you know that?"

"I know who he is. Did you think I wouldn't check on what happened to you in that cellar? Try to learn all that I could so that I might help you heal? But you won't let me in. You won't let any of your family in." Hurt tinged his voice. "Why trust him, Hol? Is it guilt that has you keeping him here? Or fear?"

"You go too far, Sin." But Holly wanted to curl in on herself. Was she merely doing this out of guilt? Would she have helped Thorne if he hadn't offered to help her in return?

"Once Nex, always Nex," Sin said. "You ought to know that as well." The quiet reminder was worse than shouting.

He left her, with the quick, inhuman speed he usually sought to hide. Holly ran to her window to catch sight of him, but he wasn't there. Sighing, she moved to the window at the opposite wall, where it overlooked the Thames. There on the water, bathed in moonlight, an odd sight caught her eye, and her heart stilled within her breast.

Rushing to her worktable, Holly grabbed the small metallic cylinder that she'd been testing last month and ran back to the window. With shaking hands, she lifted the device and put it to her ear.

Safely away from Miss Evernight and her tempting hands, Will sat on the back terrace of Evernight House smoking a cigarette and gazing up at the silver-bright disk of the moon, visible for once, on this rare, clear night. Stars lay like glittering sand across the ink-blue sky. A perfect night. When was the last time he'd taken note of the sky?

Years. Long before he'd become Nex.

Absently, Will rubbed the scar on his chest. A breeze kicked up, bringing the briny scent of the Thames over the lawn. He watched the moonlight glinting on the river's dark waters and drew in another deep breath. Candle wax and sulfur, just a tinge of them in the air. Tensing, he leaned in, bracing his forearms upon his knees as he peered at the river. A halo of golden light bobbed along, hovering a few feet above the dark water line.

A growl rumbled low in Will's chest, and he rose, his body at the ready to defend the house. A second later, a small pontoon drifted into sight, guided by two sturdy-looking rowers. Will cocked his head in mild shock. Upon the flat, wooden raft sat a man, proper as you please, before a small dinner table covered with white linen and laid with fine crystal. Light from the brace of candles pooled over the table and danced over the man's face, giving it the macabre image of a skull.

Not bothering to acknowledge Will in the least, the man simply carved into what appeared to be a slab of beefsteak as the pontoon eased to a slow halt before Evernight House. The man reached for his goblet of wine, and Will saw his face in full. Memories, swift and strong, slapped into him. Of his life, his duties. Of this *man*. Nex.

Will leapt high. His body arched through the air, the wind whistling in his ears. He landed lightly upon the pontoon, the craft barely registering his presence.

Aldous Nex finished his sip of wine before gently placing the glass down. "You always loved a showy entrance, Thorne."

"Says the man having his dinner on a pontoon."

Cold, soulless eyes bore into Will. "Take a seat." Not a request.

Will complied. He wanted to know what Aldous, the supreme Nex elder, wanted. Folding his length into the rather dainty dining chair, Will withdrew a case of cigarettes from his pocket. "Smoke?" he offered Aldous.

"Please."

When they'd lit their cigarettes and wisps of fragrant smoke drifted up into the night, Will slouched back in his seat, adopting an indolent pose he knew would irk Aldous, and waited.

The man's thin lips twitched, but he simply enjoyed his smoke before speaking. "Why have you not yet killed the Evernight girl?"

"Was I supposed to?" Will asked idly. Had the Nex sent him to kill Evernight? Why, when they'd cast him out? Vanity aside, there were far more levelheaded agents at their disposal for such a task.

Either his questions were clear on his face, or Aldous

had expected him to wonder as much. "Rumor has it," Aldous said, "that some fortunate soul shall be highly rewarded should he be the one to destroy Miss Evernight. As you always were an opportunist, and have a personal stake in her demise, why wouldn't you try to kill her? Yet here you sit on her terrace, playing guard dog." He stared at Will through a plume of smoke. "Not quite your style, sanguis."

"And here I thought I would never be so prosaic as to acquire a set style." Will shrugged lightly, but the look he gave Aldous was not. "I have a personal stake in your demise too, Aldous Nex."

The man laughed. "You gave away the identity of key agents to an SOS regulator so that he might slaughter them, and yet you have the temerity to resent us being rid of you? Oh, that is rich."

"Agents who abused a fellow onus," Will ground out through his teeth. Though "abuse" was far too weak a word for what they'd done to Jack. Will was only sorry that he hadn't helped Jack tear those demons apart. "We are supposed to protect our kind, not torture them."

Twin flames flickered in Aldous's eyes, reminding Will that this was no mere man. "Loyalty to the Nex, Mr. Thorne, takes precedence above all things."

Which is why, Will supposed, he did not belong anywhere. His loyalties were never blind. "Good thing what I do and why is no longer your business," he said.

"What if I chose to make it my business?" Aldous's tone was mild, almost encouraging. "What if you were Nex once again?"

Will's entire body tensed. And though he'd not moved or even blinked, Aldous noted the effect his offer had upon him. Slowly, the older man inclined his head.

"Acceptance once more. A place with your comrades. A renewed sense of purpose."

"All for killing Evernight?" The words tasted ugly and bitter upon his tongue. But he could not ignore them. Kill Evernight. And life as he knew it would return. But it wouldn't. He'd go mad and die without her. Without his permission, his hand drifted to his chest.

Aldous's gaze followed the movement. "You think of that contraption within you. You believe she can help you."

Will flinched. How pathetic that he was so easily read. "You think you can do better?" His voice was a rasp.

"No." Aldous puffed upon his cigarette. "I think you're doomed without her. Already she has restored your sanity. Very impressive, given the state you were in before."

Will glanced at him sharply. He leaned forward, planting his feet upon the boards of the pontoon. "You knew."

Aldous tapped a line of ash into his discarded beefsteak, where blood had begun to congeal. "You were not my problem then."

Grinding his teeth, Will struggled not to swipe that bland, superior look off his face. Affecting calm, he crossed one leg over the other and took a leisurely drag of his smoke. "Why should I be your problem now? As much as I enjoy flattery, the Nex have more than enough resources to do the deed without me."

Aldous chuckled. "My dear boy, your ignorance astounds me." When Will growled, the elder's laughter ebbed. "What you have become is a perfect killing machine. If only you knew how to control your power." Aldous Nex gave him a look that was almost fond. "Now that your sanity is restored, it would be my great pleasure to personally train you."

Lucky me, Will thought dryly. "There is still the small matter of my being, as you say, 'doomed' without Evernight."

"It was your presumption that I want you to kill her." Aldous's gaze locked onto Will. "I'm asking you to bring her into the Nex."

Will could not have been more shocked if Aldous had thrown him into the Thames. He couldn't even form words.

"Have you any notion how valuable the SOS's head inventor is to us?" The elder's expression went smooth as still waters. "Whoever put a price upon her head was an utter fool to overlook her talents."

A sick sensation rocked through Will. "She wouldn't work for you."

"We can be very persuasive, as you well know." Aldous shrugged one shoulder. "We won't break her. Not entirely. It would be counterproductive. When she is not working, you can keep her as yours." Thin lips lifted. "All and all a good arrangement, I should think."

Save for the woman who would be a slave and an unwilling concubine.

"Well," Aldous reached for his wine, "think it over." He took a sip before regarding Will. "Keep in mind that if you refuse, you will not only be out of the Nex, you will be our enemy." He leaned in, and again his eyes flared flame bright. "Either way, we will have the girl."

Will's fangs throbbed. "With an offer like that, how can I refuse?"

Aldous gave him a pleasant smile before lifting his hand and making a swiping motion. In an instant, Will hurtled through the air, the punch of power cracking his ribs. He landed upon the lawn hard enough to kick up turf and scatter a wave of soil in his wake. The pain in his ribs was but a twinge to the crushing weight of metal as it began to race through his body, robbing his breath and pulling him down into dark terror.

"Mr. Thorne." A soft touch on his shoulder. *Go away.* Something heavy sought to pulverize his bones within his flesh. "Thorne." Another touch, harder now, shaking. "William Thorne."

He tried to swat the hand away. He couldn't move.

"Bloody bollocking hell."

Had he said that? No, the voice had been feminine and prim, despite the crude words. He rather liked that. His body rocked slightly as hands ripped apart his shirt. Fresh air buffeted his icy skin. Perhaps he ought to fight? But he felt . . . safe. Odd, that.

Soft, slim hands smoothed over his chest, making him grunt and his cock rise. He wanted to purr like a jungle cat, stretch himself out for the female, coax her closer and closer, until he struck and made a meal of her. Abdomen clenching, Will canted his hips and a wrist brushed against the tip of his erection. He groaned loud, and the touch fled.

"No." Blindly he reached out, trying to stay those lovely hands.

"Calm yourself, Thorne," said a crisp voice. That voice. *Focus.*

He forced his eyes open. The grey night wavered and shimmered then pulled into focus. Holly Evernight's pale face hovered over him, her lips pinched and her brows drawn. "Be still," she said, "and let me work here."

"Never wanted you to stop," he mumbled through stiff lips. Hell, his head pounded.

Her cool gaze studied his chest as though it were a puzzle to be solved. Then she resumed her cruel work upon him, concentrating her efforts on the thick, twisted coil that made up his scar. He nearly sobbed in relief, and in despair.

Hells bells, but he enjoyed having her hands on his skin. Exquisite torture. Will soaked it up. It felt so good. So bloody good. Like joy and life and pleasure. He wanted her to touch him endlessly. If she never stopped, he'd be perfectly happy. His fangs itched to drop and impale themselves in the plump little swell of her breast. Right above her nipple. He could drink her and suckle her all at once.

A whimper caught and died at the back of his throat, and he lurched upright. "Enough." His voice cracked, and he cleared his throat. "I'm well enough now."

Evernight sat back on her heels, and he truly took in their surroundings. He was on the lawn, sitting in a depression of overturned earth. Right; Aldous had been here, making offers and promises. Will glanced at Evernight. She stared back, placid as always.

"Why are you out here?" she asked.

"Why are *you* out here?" he hedged.

Her shoulders drew inward, diminishing her size. "Believe me, I do not want to be here. But the terrace is safe enough for the moment." With that odd statement, she glanced about before returning her focus to him. "I came to help you." Her eyes narrowed. "What happened?"

Hell, but he couldn't tell her the Nex's grand elder had been here, or that he wanted to keep Holly as his slave. Will kept his gaze on the river and tapped the side of his bent knee as he thought of what to say, but the silence was stretching thin and he panicked. "Bad fall."

" 'Bad fall.' " She repeated his lame excuse with the sarcasm it deserved.

Feeling foolish, Will nodded as though it made complete sense. Then decided to change the subject. "Tomorrow, we shall be going out."

"Oh?" She didn't sound very surprised.

The idle rhythm he tapped grew faster. "We accomplish nothing staying here, waiting for someone to come for you. We must become the hunters, not the hunted."

From the corner of his eye, he saw her arm tense. And then he caught the deadly scent of Christ's thorn wood. His breath stilled. *She wouldn't. She couldn't.* Time slowed as he turned his head, and their gazes clashed. Understanding flared between them, of her cool rage and quiet determination, and what she planned to do. The knowledge punched through him, swift and shocking.

He reacted without thought, grabbing her wrist and hauling her close. Her chest fell against his with a thud and a sharp exhalation of breath. He wrenched her arm upward until the sharp point of her wooden stake pressed into the tender underside of his jaw.

Will kept a tight grip upon her wrist, holding the deadly weapon where it was as she trembled. But defiance lit her eyes, and he did not know if what he felt was admiration or deep hurt. Perhaps both.

"It's a simple thing," he murmured in the ringing silence, "just thrust hard and deep."

Her wide, clear eyes bore into his. "I know."

Oh, he bet she did. The sharp tip of the stake burned his skin, and his sense of self-preservation screamed for him to thrust it away. He ignored it. "Do you wonder if I am so altered that Christ's thorn will not harm me? Is that why you hesitate?"

She appeared unrepentant. "Will it?"

"Do you not smell my flesh burning?" It was a subtle

scent now. Like a stuck match in a stuffy parlor. It hurt. But if the wood went up into his brain, he'd be dead. Just like any other sanguis.

The bones in her wrist shifted as she tightened her grip. Bloody hell. Will pushed the point in deeper, ignoring the pain, refusing to flinch as he watched her. She pulled against his grip, as if fearful that he'd do the job for her. He did not let her go. "Why?" His question came out far too rough and pained. "Why bother healing me at all?"

"I had to be certain." Her eyes narrowed in accusation. "I gave you the chance to answer me truthfully. You failed." The delicate muscles of her throat moved on a swallow. "I heard your little chat, Mr. Thorne."

"And you believe I will hand you over to the Nex? Make you a slave once more?" He wanted to laugh, and to snarl.

Her black brows rose a touch. "You said you couldn't refuse his offer."

"It never ceases to amaze me how utterly sarcasm eludes you."

She let out a huff. "He offered you everything you have lost."

Will was silent, his clockwork heart pumping hard, and then his grip loosened. Slowly his fingers slid along the silky skin of her wrist before his hand dropped to his lap. She kept the stake where it was, her shoulders vibrating with tension.

"Perhaps," he whispered, "I don't want what I've lost. Perhaps I want something new."

She frowned, her expression making clear as day that thoughts whirred within her massive, logical brain. "What do you want, Mr. Thorne?"

If he answered "you" would she run? Likely. The truth was, that answer made him want to run too. So he told her another truth. "To be wanted for who I am, not what I can do for others."

That cool, analytical frown grew.

"Go on then," he said against the puncture wound. "Do it, if that is your wish. For I'm dead without you anyway."

Her entire frame stiffened, intent and determination lighting her eyes. He found himself holding his breath, willing himself not to react. But then the tension drained from her, and she lowered the stake. And heavy silence fell over them. Will gave her time to collect herself.

"You should know," she said after a moment, "I did not want to use this." But she would. And he respected that. Her chin lifted. "The Nex want me."

"Yes."

"They aren't trying to kill me."

"No. Which means whoever is has no loyalties other than to himself." Much like Will, he realized with a rather ugly start.

She looked away, her profile clean and pale against the indigo sky. "I'll never be truly safe."

Gently, he rested his hand atop hers, when what he really wanted was to haul her into his lap and hold on tight. "None of us are. It is a sacrifice of the life we chose," he said. "That doesn't mean we must live it in fear."

Dully she nodded. Will suspected she lived far too much in fear now. It kept her here in this house, an odd little sitting duck. He gave her thin hand a squeeze. "Come, love, we are in this together, are we not?" True, he'd tried to kill her, and she'd tried to kill him. But that meant they were even now.

Her wan, reluctant smile was like moonbeams breaking through a cloudy night. "We are."

A strange sense of elation and purpose filled him, and he stood, holding his hand out to her. "Right then. Tomorrow we go out." And they'd be official partners. Then she had to go and ruin it all.

"No." Her prim face had returned, the starch back in her knickers. "I shall stay here. It is up to you to go."

Chapter Ten

~~~~~~~~~~~

Holly's refusal to go out was not well received by Mr. Thorne. It incensed the man, as if she had personally insulted him by wanting to stay at home. Which was the furthest thing from the truth. Not that she would confide her fears to him. Lord above, but the demon was like a dog with a bone. He would not let the thing go and hounded her to the point of madness.

Why, he asked her, wouldn't she go out? Did she truly think he was trying to trick her? That he wanted to give her up to the Nex? No, she did not. Then what? What was more important than ending the contract out on her life, that she couldn't spare the time to leave her house?

What indeed. That she'd be a crippled wreck the moment she hit the streets, perhaps? Holly calmly maintained that he did not need her to accompany him on his outings.

When his badgering had no effect, Thorne hung about the laboratory like a specter. He settled in a chair across from her desk, his ankle propped on one knee and a leather-bound book in his hands. He made a pretense of studying whatever it was in the book and had even brought a pencil, presumably to make notes. Holly didn't believe it for one moment. Perhaps he thought that if he kept in sight it would wear down her defenses. Well, he was sorely mistaken.

Keeping that in mind, she went to work on the schematics for a submersible ship. The concept was hardly new. Submersibles had been around, in some form or other, since the 1600s. But the Americans had made significant strides with submarines, using them to some success during the Civil War in the 1860s. She'd been corresponding with Mr. John Philip Holland, an Irish engineer who had quite interesting theories on propulsion methods. But she knew they could be improved.

Scribbling away, she soon lost herself in her work, and a measure of warm calm stole over her. That is, until Thorne's voice snapped like a whip.

"Just look at yourself." Thorne tossed his hand up in her general direction.

And here we go.

"I'm rather busy at the moment." She made a correction in her calculations and moved on. "Nor do I have a mirror on hand."

Thorne snorted in that scoffing way of his that never failed to annoy. "You're closeted up like Christmas linen, only to be let out into the fresh air once yearly."

"I receive fresh air more than once a year, thank you." Holly tapped her pencil upon the draft board. Would the thrust be sufficient for the weight needed to maintain structural stability?

Leather squeaked as he sat forward, setting aside his book and bracing his hands upon his knees. "Responding with obstinate literal-mindedness will not work with me, Miss Evernight."

"No?" She did not take her attention away from her plans. "And here I thought it might silence you."

"Not your first miscalculation of the day." He sounded far too smug.

Holly glanced up to glare at him properly, and he eyed the little flecks of rubber eraser covering her papers like black snow. Bothersome man. His grin grew, stretching past gleaming fangs.

"You do not allow yourself to live," he said, serious once more, his brow furrowing. "Instead you hide away in your laboratory."

"I do not hide, Mr. Thorne. One can locate me quite readily." She teased now, not that he ever caught on.

As she expected, his jaw bunched as if he worked not to curse. Striations of silver flashed in his black eyes. "So help me," he muttered, before going on in measured tones. "Life is out there." He pointed to the windows with his thumb in a sharp, stabbing motion. "Not in here."

A broad sigh left Holly. Carefully, she set down her pencil. "What do you believe the purpose of life is, Mr. Thorne?"

Thorne flinched, his knife-blade features tightening. "What do you mean? Are you asking if I've discovered the secret of life or some other nonsense?"

"It isn't nonsense. One ought to consider how one fits into the grand scheme of things, what his or her role shall be in this play called life." She allowed a small smile as his scowl grew. "Especially an immortal such as yourself, Mr. Thorne. For you'll be a player in it long after most of us are dust."

Oh, but he truly did not like that. His lip curled in a sneer. "State your point, Miss Evernight."

"What is this 'life' you are so keen on me seeing outside of these walls? Is it the sky? The sun? The river? People going about their daily business? What?"

"All if it," he snapped, his fist curling tight against his thigh.

"You still have not answered my original question. What do you think we are here to do?"

"Bloody hell, woman."

"Come now, Mr. Thorne. We are here to create."

He laughed shortly. "You really are a literal creature, aren't you?" His brow was quirked, his expression cool and still vaguely annoyed.

She resisted a smile once more. "To create, in whatever form or manner we choose. To use our minds, bodies, whatever talents we've been given to create something, be it of beauty or practicality. That is the point of life. Anything else is simply a waste of time and opportunity."

She pointed to her drafting table. "Here is where I create. Here is where I am truly alive, using my mind and my body to build things. You have no notion of what life means. You, who find it preferable to sit in idleness, playing cards, drinking, and tupping."

Thorne shot to his feet, his eyes blazing, but he didn't say a word; she didn't let him get that far.

"And what do you create?" she pressed on. "How do you express yourself, your soul, to the world? By killing?" She wasn't being fair; she knew it. But he'd poked and prodded at her feelings, and she'd borne it. Perhaps he'd like to see how it felt.

Needle sharp fangs grew long in his mouth.

"Have you no answer?" she persisted, both hating herself and wanting to know.

"You assume your life has more meaning because you have a talent for creation that I do not?" he ground out.

"Not more meaning, but more satisfaction."

He laughed—a cold, brittle sound. "You are either a pretty little liar or completely deluded. Fear has kept you in this house, going on a year!" In an instant, he was in front of her, his hands on either side of the desk, trapping her against it. His glossy white hair swung forward around his shoulders as he leaned in, going almost nose to nose with her. "That isn't living, darling. That is dying. By degrees."

"Nonsense. I—"

"I was not finished," he bit out, his gaze holding hers, gleaming platinum taking over his irises. "Life is not merely about creating through work. There is joy. Call it the creation of joy, if it pleases you. But joy, love, laughter—they mean something too."

Holly stifled a yelp when he lashed out, grabbing a fistful of her hair. He held on firmly at the base of her neck as his eyes roved over her face. "And you, my perfect Miss Evernight, do not know shit about any of those things."

He released her so abruptly that Holly wobbled on her stool, her sudden freedom dizzying her. Already he was halfway across the room, striding for the door.

"We are going out in one hour." He did not bother to turn around. "I expect you to comply or I will come and collect you. Bodily."

The door slammed behind him. It was then, in the ringing silence, that she collected her wits enough to see that he'd left his book lying open upon her drafting table. Only it wasn't a novel, or a manual, but a sketchbook. There, rendered in pencil and done with unquestionable skill and uncanny accuracy, was her face.

Will fully expected to have to haul Evernight out of the house. Part of him anticipated it. He'd throw her over his shoulder, hold onto her plump arse when she struggled. Then there would be the lash of her sharp tongue he'd pretend to ignore, when inwardly he relished her quick wit. All in all, it would be an enjoyable diversion. Besides, she bloody well needed to get out and about. It well... worried him that she hadn't left the house in these many months. It was unnatural. Especially for a human.

However, the sight that greeted him in the front hall had him coming to a full stop, and his plans dissipated like fog against the harsh burn of sunlight.

Evernight stood in perfectly calm repose, her face a neutral mask as she looked at him. She wore not one of her usual plain house gowns, but a walking dress of dusky purple taffeta. The basque mimicked a man's jacket with black velvet lapels and little black buttons marching down the center. Far from being mannish, it hugged her torso with loving care and made one think of undoing those buttons with one's fangs. The matching skirt was unadorned but swept back into a proper and rather enticing bustle.

Tolerating his appraisal with a mere lift of one graceful black brow, Evernight cocked her head to the side, bringing his attention to the jaunty little purple hat pinned upon her neatly coiled hair.

"Shall I do, Mr. Thorne?" Her tone implied that she did not give a whit what he thought, and just might have been mentally bashing his head in.

"Passably," he retorted with a bored sigh.

Her pink lips curled slightly. "Felix," she called, "my mantle."

Felix drifted out of the shadows, a black velvet mantle in hand, and settled it over her shoulders. Will found himself frowning as old, deeply ingrained lessons learned from childhood rose to the fore. He ought to be helping her, to be the one carefully doing up the onyx toggles to assure she was protected from the cold.

Possessiveness was not a welcome emotion. Damn it all, he'd somehow grown fond of the walled-up little inventor. He was bonding with her. Which made him damned uncomfortable. But he wasn't surprised. Sanguis bonded fairly tightly, and in many forms. Bonds were emotional ties that wrapped about a sanguis's soul tightly and dug in deep. He'd bonded almost immediately with Jack Talent when they were both young lads. His demon side had simply said, *yes, here is one who will be a part of your life, who will be a good friend to you.* And that was that.

But he didn't view Holly Evernight as a friend. Will shook his head and, when Felix moved to hand him his overcoat, he ripped the thing from the man's hands and shoved it on.

Evernight's smile grew amused, yet oddly tighter. In truth, tightness lingered about the corners of her eyes and along the line of her slim shoulders.

"Right, then," Will muttered, putting on his top hat. "Let us proceed."

The crest of her cheeks turned milk white, but she gave him a nod. "By all means." She sounded a little unsteady.

He ignored it and, grabbing her hand, hooked it over his elbow. "There's a cab waiting for us. Nan tells me you don't maintain a carriage." Yet he'd seen the mews. The Evernights certainly could afford to have one, and the staff to care for both it and the horses.

"I sent the carriage and stable staff to Ireland." She shrugged. "I didn't see the need for them here."

Because she never went out. Will liked this less and less. No matter. They were going out *now*. And if she felt the need to dig her fingers into his forearm as revenge, then so be it. He liked the bite of them anyway.

The hack was waiting, the driver hunched against the cold wind that rattled along the pebbled drive. Great, grey clouds billowed in the sky, promising rain. A lovely day.

Will guided Evernight down the front stair then turned to open the hack door for her. Only to find she'd left his side. A snarl of irritation tore from him as he whipped around.

Evernight stood, stiff as marble, at the edge of the portico that hung over the front drive. Her dark eyes were glassy and wide in the pale oval of her face. In truth, she looked moments away from being sick. All over the flagstones.

Something softened within him, and he approached her carefully.

She drew in a sharp breath through her nose, as if she expected him to shout. He kept his voice neutral. "What is it?"

She hovered at the portico, her face utterly white. "I..." Her words broke like glass at his feet. "I cannot." Evernight wrapped her arms about her middle and pressed herself against the stone support pillar. "Thorne..." She swallowed hard, and her eyes filled.

Will's blasted unnatural heart nearly ground to a stop.

His proud, unmovable Evernight, tearing up? Will could not abide such a thing. She had to fight him. It was the one constant he could count on.

He wanted to reach out and draw her into his embrace. But he rather thought she would not appreciate the gesture. Not when she struggled so valiantly to hold back her tears. So he merely stepped close to her, buffering her slight form from the wind, and lowered his voice. "Speak to me, love."

She sucked in a sharp breath that seemed to steel her spine. "You were correct. I hide out of fear."

Tentatively, he pressed a hand to the middle of her slim back. "But why? I promised nothing shall harm you, nor will I let the Nex have you. I swear it. Do you not believe me?"

A breath left her, warming the cold skin on his cheeks. "He might be out there."

"He?"

"Don't make me say his name."

All at once, Will went still. Amaros. She'd been chained. What had she endured? Why hadn't he asked? Shock and guilt shook him. He was a shite for pushing her. And here he was about to take her out of the frypan and into the fire. "He's dead, petal. He cannot harm you anymore."

"I know. I know this!" She glanced about, as if expecting the diseased fallen angel to jump from the hedgerow. "My bloody fool emotions cannot seem to accept that truth, however."

Holly leaned against him, her shoulder just touching his. A gesture of trust. A shock to his system. Slowly, he wound an arm about her cinched waist. He looked up into the grey sky. He did not know how to offer true comfort.

Sexual release? Of course, with pleasure. But to coddle a frightened woman? What could he do?

He could hold her, but it would not take away her fear. Giving her one last squeeze, he drew her back and peered into her eyes. They glimmered like polished lapis. "Here is what we shall do. You put your hand in mine, keep me sane while I keep you safe. And then you shall put one foot in front of the other until you no longer have to count your steps, and I will not let you go."

Her pink lips trembled, so soft and succulent that he wanted to taste them. But he held fast and kept his gaze locked on hers. "One step, petal mine. Surely that you can do."

Dimly, she nodded. "One step. Yes. I can manage that."

Swiftly, he kissed her smooth forehead, just beneath the dark curls of her fringe, then caught her hand in a firm hold. Gods, but she was cold. Her fingers twined with his and squeezed to the point of tender pain. Will did not let go.

"One step," he said, leading the way to the carriage.

She mumbled an agreement, but then looked up at him sharply. "Petal? What sort of nonsensical drivel is that?"

Ah, there was his Evernight. The corners of his mouth twitched. "You are soft and delicate like a petal."

"Bosh." She gave an inelegant snort, her neat, little boot heels clicking against the pavers. "There is nothing soft about me."

This time Will gave her a wicked smile. "Having had my hands on you, I can safely assure the contrary."

She went scarlet. A rare blush. And he reveled in it. "Softer than a petal, really," he pointed out, his chest feeling buoyant now that she'd recovered enough to grouse.

"Especially your arse. Why, just last night, I likened it to a plump pillow—"

"Oh, all right," she snapped. "Enough of that, thank you."

He laughed, happy to note that she climbed the carriage steps without hesitation—afraid maybe, but she was with him, and he would not give her cause to regret it.

Chapter Eleven

~~~~

Being in the carriage was better. Contained. Confined. Holly pressed her spine into the poorly sprung seat and stared straight ahead. She could almost pretend that she was sitting in her study. Only the damned thing rocked and bounced over the road, reminding her at each point that she was not safe at home. All due to the bullying horse's arse sitting next to her.

Had he crowed over her fear or been smug, she would have bitten his head off. No, she would have turned him into a lump of metal and left him on the flagstone drive. But he'd been kind. Comforting. His care had disarmed her enough that she found herself obeying his command, putting herself into his keeping. How horrid. How foolish.

A bitter well of panic rushed up her throat like acid. And though she did not make a sound, somehow he knew. His grip upon her hand—for he never truly let her go—tightened.

"Lovely day, is it not?" he observed lightly.

Rain misted the windows, and the lamps had to be

turned up high to ward off the dark. At her speaking look, he smiled. "Well, for a sanguis, at any rate." He leaned back, crossing one long leg over the other, causing his foot to sneak up under the hem of her skirts. Holly shifted her legs away from him.

"Although," he went on, "I do admit, it would be better if there was a nice, thick fog, and a warm, balmy temperature instead." He winked at her. "I do so love the warmth."

Good lord, had the man turned into her great aunt Patty in the last block? Was he going to wax on about knitting patterns next?

Thorne craned his head to peer out of her window, and his chin nearly touched hers. "Perhaps the rain will soon stop."

She pushed at his shoulder. "Are you attempting to simultaneously bore and annoy the fear out of me, Mr. Thorne?"

He turned, bringing his face, mouth, and eyes far too close to hers. His warm breath touched her cheeks. "Is it working, Miss Evernight?"

"Yes." She gave him another push. "Now give me room to breathe, or your efforts will be for naught."

He hovered there, his eyes lowering to her lips, and his own lips parting. Everything within her went tight and warm, but then he did as bided and sat back. "Interesting to note," he said, his gaze watchful, "that my nearness sets you into a panic."

She smoothed her skirts, thankful that her black leather gloves hid her damp palms. "More like I understand the concept of social distance while you do not."

"Ah, but petal, a demon's sense of social distance is far more intimate than a human's." His sudden, wide grin had her pulse leaping as he added, "I suppose we'll have to meet somewhere in the middle."

Indeed. She needed to be out of this coach. Though Thorne was lean, his shoulders seemed to take up entirely too much space. Properly kitted in a charcoal grey suit and a fine black wool overcoat, he might have appeared the perfect gentleman, were it not for the fall of snow-bright hair over his shoulders. Paired with the top hat tilted down over one eye and his blade-sharp male beauty, William Thorne was something exotic, dangerous, and far too tempting to be allowed to roam through bland and somber London.

"How does a demon end up with such a proper English name?"

"Ah," he propped a polished boot heel upon the base of the opposite bench. "I suppose we ought to thank my proper English mother for that, hadn't we?" His smile was not at all nice. "I come from a long line of William Thornes. However, I have the distinction of being the one inhuman of the lot. Quite the taint to the illustrious line of the Marquis of Renwood. I daresay my ancestors would be rolling in their graves had my family failed to be rid of me."

"You're a Marquis?"

It certainly explained his arrogance and bearing.

"No," he said patiently. "I am a sanguis demon. Left for dead on the streets of the East End while—" another cold, tight smile—"a distant cousin stepped in to take up the title upon my untimely death."

Holly turned to stare out of the window where the grey clouds hung upon a bleak, white sky. "How did you end up in a human household?"

"It is the way of demons, you see." His smooth voice

filled up the space. "We crave luxury, warmth, frivolity. Things that go hand in hand with money and power. Things," he added, "we aren't allowed to obtain in our own right because we must hide our true nature from humans. Thus, when it comes time to procreate, a demon will take on the identity of some titled nob, wealthy merchant, or what have you, and put his seed in the bloke's wife."

Her stomach turned. "And what of the man whose identity was stolen?"

He shrugged, making the gesture appear casual, when the dark look in his eyes was anything but. "A demon needs the person's blood to take on his appearance, and they don't want to be caught. So..."

They used the victim's blood for as long as need be, then killed him. It was the number one crime the SOS fought against.

Seeing her look, he made a noise of dark amusement. "Not the most noble of actions, I grant you. But in the demon's eyes, he is providing his offspring with a step up in life. Alas, many humans never catch on that they've birthed the devil's get. Until it's too late."

A strangled sound escaped her. "It is horrid," she said. "To deceive and toy with the lives of others in such a fashion. To take what you have no right to."

"What is horrid," he answered in clipped tones, "is that we must pretend to be something we are not for fear of your delicate sensibilities. That we must take, like thieves and beggars, when if we were free, we could be something so much more."

Such bitterness there.

"And I didn't say I was planning to do likewise," he said dryly. "Personally, I'd rather make my way in the world upon my own merit. I am merely explaining how I came to be the son of a Marquis. Not—" he lifted a finger as if giving a lecture—"that I can truly claim to be of his blood. Although my mother was an earl's daughter so I suppose there is some true-blue English blood in me after all."

"How glib you're being, Mr. Thorne."

His eyes narrowed, flashing filaments of pure platinum. "How would you prefer me to act, Miss Evernight? Ashamed of something I had no say in? To apologize for my origins? Oh, but I almost forgot. You are SOS." He sneered. "You lot expect us demons to beg and scrape as we crawl back into Hell so that you may pretend we never existed."

Abruptly, he turned away. A muscle ticked in his clenched jaw.

Holly's insides cringed. "You are correct. You had no say in the matter." She frowned down at their clasped hands. How was it that they still held hands and she hadn't noticed? She relaxed her grip. "I apologize for insulting your honor."

His grip eased as well. "No need. It is all rather unsavory. And yet one more reason I loathe the way my kind must hide what they are."

Holly wasn't about to dwell on that discussion to save her life at the moment. "What is your natural form then?"

"What you see is what you get, love." His mouth quirked. "Well, aside from this metal muck."

Holly shook her head. "But you said demons needed blood to take on the appearance of a human..."

He rolled his eyes. "To steal another's identity. Really, you ought to know better. Aside from raptors, and a few unsavory breeds who feed off of evil and are never allowed out of Hell, we are essentially human in appearance." He inclined his head towards her. "We onus are, after all, part human."

Her cheeks heated. "Of course." The onus were the offspring of primus—the original, and rather rare, first demons of creation, and humans.

Despite an inner warning that she'd not tread further upon his feelings, her curiosity was running rampant. "The color of your hair is distinctive. Has no one recognized you?"

"Once I grew out of leading strings and could no longer be mistaken for towheaded, they colored it. Plain brown. Regardless, we see what we want to see. I assure you, my former family turns a blind eye to me. And I them."

"And yet you go by the name they gave you."

When he did not answer, Holly risked a look. His profile was to her, stark and tight with displeasure. "That I do," he finally murmured.

"And you never knew your real father?"

Thorne blinked once, so slowly that it seemed as though he braced himself. "No. But I heard quite a bit about him." He stared out of the window. "He fell in love with my mother, you see. So much so that he revealed himself." He grew silent, and Holly thought he would speak no more. Then his voice drifted out like a ghost in shadows. "She killed him and then waited to see if I'd turn out the same as he. She told me this on the day I began to mature and my demon nature became clear. The day she let me out in the East End and told me never to darken her doorway again."

Idly, he traced a pattern through the condensation upon the window. "I heard she died a few years back," he said, as if remarking upon the weather. Flicking his gaze to her, he leaned forward as the cab came to a stop. "Had enough of chitchat, Miss Evernight?"

"Quite." It was all she could manage to say past the lump in her throat.

Thorne opened the door and hopped down before turning to offer her a hand. "Let us to it, then."

"You won't find a GIM able to bring you to Adam, boyo. That's plain fact. Nothing more. Nothing less."

Sin frowned over his glass of scotch.

Sitting opposite, his companion watched him. "You doubt I speak the truth?"

"I shall ask my sister Daisy." Sin didn't want to involve her; she'd ask too many questions. The woman had the curiosity of ten cats. But he would. She was a GIM and one of Adam's favorites.

His companion laughed. Several rather stuffy gentlemen frowned at them from over the edges of their daily papers.

Sin's brother-in-law Archer had sponsored him for this private club, all in an effort to civilize him. Not that it did much good. And though Sin would rather be in a tavern than this tomb, Mr. Magnus, as his companion wanted to be called today, would only meet in humans' most exclusive haunts.

"Sin, me lad, Daisy Ranulf couldn't help you even if she was willing." Magnus leaned in, and his golden cap of curls gleamed under the gas lamps. "Adam is a being of extraordinary power and foresight. Do you think he doesn't have safeguards in place? No GIM can call him unless it is to his benefit."

"How does he know it is to his benefit without first hearing the request?"

Magnus rolled his eyes. They were so deeply blue that they appeared purple. A little too close to purple. Arrogant arse. Of course, Magnus had picked a handsome form too. It wouldn't do to traipse about in any form that was less than perfect. Sin wondered how many humans had fallen for the glossy façade and never lived to tell the tale.

"Magic." This news was delivered as if the answer were bloody obvious. "A simple spell is all it takes for one such as him."

In short, Sin was bolloxed. Damn, but he hated dealing with ancients. Vain, selfish, and slippery bastards, each and every one of them.

"The answer lies with Holly Evernight." Magnus took a lazy sip of scotch. "Our clever girl has the solution to our problem, to be sure."

Magnus wanted Holly involved. Which made Sin that much more wary to do so. If he'd learned anything, it was to never trust Magnus.

"She has problems enough." His poor cousin was a self-imposed prisoner in her own home. "I'll find another way."

Magnus's mouth turned down at the corners, making him appear like an angel in a pout. "She is an Evernight. She will comply."

For a fleeting moment, a flicker of flame danced within Magnus's purple gaze, a promise of pain and hellfire should he be disobeyed.

"Even if she wanted to help," Sin argued, a little less steady now, "she cannot break the chain that binds Eliza to Adam."

"Right you are," Magnus agreed. "Only one of Adam's kind can do that. For it isn't really a chain made of metal, but of his power."

"Well, there you go," Sin said. "We are at an impasse."

Magnus gave Sin a beatific smile. "You are overlooking the sanguis crawler."

The blood-sucking crawler who was currently camped inside Holly's house. Sin inwardly snarled. Nanny had told him not to worry—that the crawler, Will Thorne, was bound to protect Holly. And wasn't it a cold shock to realize that his cousin had a contract out on her life? *He* ought to be protecting her, not some metallic beast.

Disgust marred the smooth perfection of Magnus's brow. "Unnatural thing, this crawler. Its very existence is an affront to Adam and his creations." He grinned wide and pleased. "He is the next step in their evolution, able to shift his body into spirit form. And stronger for it, if he'd only learn."

Sin hadn't a clue how that would help his cause, nor did he want to ask, not without earning Magnus's painful wrath. He wanted out of this club, and away from Magnus. But it wasn't going to happen until the bastard was good and ready to let Sin go.

Magnus smoothed a hand over the green silk of his waistcoat. "Trust me, laddie, the crawler can be played. I shall insure that."

Sin's gaze drifted over the room and settled upon a group of young men playing whist in the far corner. Laughter and easy insults fell from their lips. They were only a few years older than he was, and yet he felt ancient in comparison. To be like that. Human and carefree. Not bound to serve. Not being taught to deceive and manipulate. The air around him rose several degrees as rage bubbled within his gut.

One of the blokes glanced about in confusion as the drop-crystal chandelier above his head rattled.

Sin drew himself under control with a deep breath. And none of it was lost on Magnus.

"Ah, now, don't fret, my wee pet." Magnus withdrew an ornate silver box set with agate stones from his jacket pocket and selected two fine cheroots. He handed one to Sin and then proceeded to light both of them. To an outsider, it appeared as though he'd used matches. Only Sin saw the flame leap from the tip of his thumb.

When they'd both exhaled and thick, luscious clouds of blue smoke wreathed their heads, Magnus leaned back, settling a languid, pale hand on his flat stomach. "When the time is right, you'll bring the crawler and Holly to heed."

The mask dropped, and Sin stared into a feminine face of such terrifying beauty that his heart froze within his chest and his cods shriveled within his trousers. Rosy red lips curved in a smile that showed just a hint of fang. "I have every faith in your abilities."

Chapter Twelve

꧁꧂

Located on Regent Street, Verrey's was an old and proper French restaurant that had long served royalty and ambassadors.

"Are we truly going to—"

"Have a lovely French meal," Thorne finished for Holly, while taking her hand once again. "Yes."

"But you don't eat," she murmured, as a doorman opened the door for them and the rich scents of roasting meats and butter sauces wafted over her.

"Details." Thorne nodded to the maitre d' as he glided over to them.

"Monsieur Thorne, it is always a pleasure to see you. Welcome."

"A pleasure to be here, Henri." Thorne was smooth and pleasant, as if the upset he'd displayed in the coach was entirely forgotten. She was almost envious of the façade he was able to project to the world. Very useful, that.

"Shall your usual table suffice?" Henri asked, as attendants took their hats and coats.

"If it is available."

Henri's large nose lifted a touch. "For you? Always, Monsieur Thorne."

Thorne a regular? What the bleeding... Thorne put his hand on the small of her back and guided her forward. "Close your mouth, love," he said at her ear. "You resemble a witless fish just now."

Her mouth snapped shut, and she trod upon his foot with enough force to make him grunt as she followed Henri across the restaurant, with Thorne hobbling at her side.

The room was a light-filled space with a wall of windows fronting Regent Street and a lofty ceiling held up by Doric boxed columns. All quite French in design, with its mirrored panels, marble-topped tables, and bentwood cafe chairs.

Henri sat them at a table in the far corner, with a mirror at their back and the view of the entire restaurant at their front. For all of that, they were secluded, set far enough away that their closest neighbor would have to visibly strain to hear them converse. An excellent spot that put her somewhat at ease. It was a spot an SOS regulator would pick.

"Do you remember what sort of work you did for the Nex?" A stirring of guilt awakened in Holly's gut. Nex equaled enemy. Did that make her a traitor?

Keeping his eye on the room, Thorne nodded. "Seeing Aldous Nex brought memories of the Nex flooding in, of how it is structured, who I was friendly with and who I wasn't. But..." The corners of Thorne's eyes tightened, and he touched his temple. It was a fleeting press of his fingertips but enough to expose the sudden tremor in his hand. "Hell, when I try to pull up details of what I did, or of my blasted tattoo, a great black wall looms up in my mind." He scowled down at his gloved hand.

Knowing how quickly the platinum would spread when he grew overwrought, Holly caught his free hand under the table. She'd removed her gloves, thus she could press the tips of her fingers against his wrist and concentrate on stabilizing him. "It will come to you. Just give it time."

He turned to her, his eyes dark and surrounded by the thick fringe of his long lashes. "Ta, love," he whispered, his accent going deep and Northern with emotion.

Flustered, Holly sat straighter. "It is nothing."

"You know that it is everything."

The words punched into her, making her breath hitch. No one had ever talked to her in this manner—as if she, not her inventions, were needed, were as necessary as air or water. She had to remind herself just why he needed her.

Not noticing her discomfort, Thorne's gaze moved over the room, taking everything in at a glance, and so Holly did the same.

They had garnered a fair bit of attention when they'd arrived. Rather, Thorne had. How could one not look at him? His attractiveness was that of a gilded lily. And he played the part up to the nines. Normally, Holly did not make much note of fashion, but where Thorne was concerned, it was almost theatre.

His black, superfine suit was exquisitely tailored, the coat cut in a rather old-fashioned frock style that, paired with his long, outrageous hair, created a picture of continental elegance that Londoners vocally disdained but secretly coveted. Diamonds winked at her from the fold of his cravat and from the edges of his French cuffs when he moved to take a sip of water.

By his careful expression, Holly could guess that he did not find the taste of water appealing.

When the waiter had ambled off with a promise to bring them the specialties of the house, Holly tilted her head towards Thorne. "How shall this go?"

Thorne turned and gave her a small, wicked smile. "You shall eat a delicious meal, and I shall pretend that you are the most fascinating, irresistible companion I've ever had the pleasure of dining with." Without warning, he leaned in, draping one arm along the back of her chair, and nuzzled her temple.

She jerked, wanting to get away, but his sudden hand upon her nape held her fast. "We are here to be seen, love."

Holly kept her attention on the room and off of Thorne. "Why?"

Long fingers found the back of her neck and began to play with loose strands of her hair. "One," he said, as she broke out in goose bumps, "we are waving a red flag in front of a bull. If you are being watched by an assassin, seeing you finally out and about will prove irresistible."

"So you have put me on display as bait?" Holly could see the logic in it. Even if the thought sent a cold wash of fear and dread through her middle.

"Just so." He turned and pretended to nibble her ear. Close enough that she had to quell the impulse to smack him away.

"Two," he went on, "we are waiting."

He paused as waiters marched up, one proudly carrying a silver tureen with long, curving legs that resembled a spider, the other bringing forth dinnerware. Bowls were placed with flourish before them, and a brown broth soup, flecked with colorful bits of vegetables and small cuts of beef, was ladled with care.

"Petite marmite," the waiter explained in an accent that Holly suspected was forced. She waited until they were gone. Staring at her food, a horrid thought occurred to her.

"What if someone poisons me?"

Thorne glanced down at the soup, which suddenly looked to Holly like a vat of devil's brew. He gave her what she assumed was a reassuring smile. "I might not have the sense of smell equal to a lycan, but I can suss out poison in food." He frowned then, his expression drawing inward. "I was trained to notice. However, if you don't believe me . . ." He took a heaping spoonful into his mouth and waited, his expression twisted in exaggerated concentration that made her want to pinch him.

A long moment passed. Then, with a shake of his head, he brightened and nudged her elbow. "It's safe, love. Go ahead and eat."

She'd have to trust him. That both irked and comforted. With a hand that wasn't quite steady, she picked up her spoon. The soup was rather wonderful. Warm and comforting. Strangely, she was famished. As she hadn't been in some time.

"Waiting for whom?" she asked.

He watched her eat, the corners of his eyes crinkling. "I'm not certain. But someone will come. That I know."

"I do not like surprises."

"Now that," he said with a chuckle, "does not surprise me in the least."

Bothersome man. One that kept her entertained, however, with little observations about the restaurant's patrons as the waiters cleared their bowls—his untouched save for a spoon or two of broth—before setting down a silver-topped tray.

"*Oeufs à la Russe*!" With that grand proclamation, the waiter lifted the lid to reveal deviled eggs, dotted with amber pearls of Osetra caviar.

Holly's lips twitched. "It sounds so much more impressive when they say it in French, does it not?"

"I suspect the *hauteur* in their delivery has a bit to do with it as well." Thorne's voice lowered. "I'm going to feed you one now. Appear as if you enjoy the activity."

She had objections. Vehement and persuasive ones. Ones that she would gladly voice. Only, when she turned to do just that, he was there, holding a halved-egg up like an offering. To refuse him would undo the charade he'd concocted.

A playful glint lit Thorne's dark eyes. "Open, love, and let me in."

Heat flushed over her skin, under her too-tight bodice. As if he knew precisely how she was affected, his lids lowered, and his attention fixated on her mouth. Awareness consumed her, of her actions, of the way her lips parted, of the cool slide of the egg against her tongue.

He'd taken off his gloves, and when he slid the tip of the egg into her mouth, his fingers brushed her bottom lip. "Take a bite," he whispered.

She couldn't look away from him. She ought not to be stirred in the slightest. It was merely an egg. Pedestrian fare, to say the least. Yet when her teeth sank into it, she nearly moaned, her lids fluttering with the need to close, to experience the sensation in a dark and quiet world.

A low sound, as if he'd swallowed down a grunt, filled her ears as she chewed. She had to look.

His gaze was rapt and hot. It was indecent, feeding her like this in public. And he knew it. His nostrils flared as he fed her the last bite.

A bit of smoothly whipped yolk, rich and luscious, clung to the corner of her mouth. Holly's tongue swiped out to lick it away, just as Thorne ran his thumb across her lip. She tasted his skin, felt the heat of the rounded tip, and he made a strangled sound. Holly stared. For the life of her, she wanted nothing more than to draw his thumb into her mouth and suck.

"Hell." His chest lifted on an unsteady breath.

His hand, so very warm and strong, cupped her cheek, bringing her closer. Her corset creaked, the cinch of it stealing her air.

Slowly, with languorous intent, he dipped his head. The flick of his tongue at the corner of her mouth sent a tight jolt down her center. His strong, hot fingers caged her cheeks, holding her there as his lips barely brushed hers. "Tell me," he whispered thickly. "Tell me you feel this pull between us."

He was sanguis, ex-Nex, her opposite in every regard. It wasn't real, what she felt, what he felt. It couldn't be. It made no sense. The push-pull of him had her body frozen in place, vibrating like a struck tuning fork.

The tip of his forefinger stoked the crest of her cheek, and she felt it down deep within her as if he'd touched her center. "Holly."

Slowly she drew back, raising her gaze to his pained and pleading one. *William*.

"William Thorne, as I live and breathe."

Flinching apart at the sound of the woman's voice, they turned as one. It took a moment for Holly to arrange the muddled shapes and colors that had become the rest of the world into an understandable picture. A woman stood before them. Tall, thin, with glossy brown hair and a ready smile. Smartly dressed in a wool day gown of cream and emerald green stripes, she made quite the picture. But there was a hardness in her brown eyes and a certain tension along her frame that belied her outward appearance.

Thorne, having recovered as well, rose from his seat and inclined his head in greeting. But he'd yet to answer. Instead, his gaze slid lazily over the woman. Holly was of half a mind to be annoyed, had she not suspected that he was trying to place a name to the face.

As for the woman, her eyes narrowed just a touch. "Have you no kind words for me, Will?"

Will, was it? Holly kept her expression neutral when what she wanted to do was roll her eyes.

Thorne, however, smiled then, a dark and sensual tilt of his lips. "Merely taking in your loveliness, dear Matilda." He swept an open palm towards the unoccupied seat. "Please, join us."

Matilda did so, happily. "Are you going to introduce me to your friend?" She glanced at Holly, disassembling her in one blink.

"Mrs. Matilda Markham." Thorne sat then inclined his head towards Holly. "Miss Holly Evernight."

Rather blunt as introductions went.

A pretty smile lit up the older woman's face, but Holly had doubts as to its veracity.

"I would be careful with how many of those eggs you ingest, Miss Evernight. Such treats run straight to a woman's waistline." The look in her eye said that eventuality was a very real danger for Holly.

"Thank you for the warning," Holly answered in perfect pleasantness, keeping her expression bland as water. "How kind of you to convey your wisdom of experience."

Out of the corner of her eye, she caught Thorne's

quickly repressed grin. Holly ignored it and helped herself to another egg.

Mrs. Markham nearly growled but she regained her composure. "She isn't your usual sort of bird, Will."

One of Thorne's dark brows lifted eloquently. How easily the man could convey a shrug with that simple look. "I should hate to think I've become set on one type of bird. After all, as the poem goes, 'Variety's the very spice of life, that gives it all its flavor.'" His lips curled, not quite a smile, but enough to show a hint of fang. "And I do so enjoy my flavors."

Matilda made a noise of amusement. "So you do." Ignoring Holly, she leaned in, her hip curving prettily as she took her weight upon one elbow. "And what, pray tell, are you here to enjoy?"

Thorne did not answer but stayed as he was, slouched in casual repose, one arm draped along the back of Holly's chair, and somehow managing to look elegant and urbane. Holly might have interrupted, told him to get on with whatever it was he was doing. But, quite frankly, she was enjoying the show. He was a master, hooking Matilda Markham and reeling her in.

The woman's eyes, so deep brown they almost appeared purple, gleamed in the flickering gas lamps as Thorne thoughtfully tapped his bottom lip with one long finger. Matilda's attention lingered upon the action.

Holly resisted the urge to snort into her wineglass.

Then Thorne finally deigned to speak. "Right now, my interest lies not in sweet doves, but in mad dogs."

"Does it now?" Matilda said softly. "Have you a particular sort in mind?"

"Yes. You see, my house has been overrun by rats." Filaments of platinum shot through his black eyes.

"Cook leaves out arsenic-laced biscuits, but the rats prove elusive."

Matilda Markham's answering smile was dark. "Sounds like you need to procure yourself a rat catcher."

"I'd be most obliged if you could recommend one." In a blink so fast that surely most humans wouldn't have seen it, Thorne set the assassin's dagger down upon the table before Mrs. Markham. "I'd prefer the very best."

"Sadly, I am not privy to such information," Mrs. Markham answered smoothly, not even bothering to look at the dagger. "However, I believe I know of where you might find someone who is. Kettil makes a fine stew in his cauldron. Come and have a meal, will you? Tuesday night by way of the Tower Subway." She moved to go, her voluminous bustle a rippling river of green and cream. One kid-gloved hand rested upon the table, close to Thorne's hand. "Tribute is required. On all counts."

Thorne, who had not risen with Matilda, looked up at her. "I wouldn't dare assume otherwise."

They watched her go, then Holly turned to Thorne, a dozen questions on the tip of her tongue. He quelled them with a pointed look. *Not here. Not now.*

She narrowed her eyes. Did he fear being overheard?

Thankfully, he seemed to read her with the same ease as she did him. His nod was brief and tight. "Let us finish our supper, love." His tone was light and normal. One more glance in Mrs. Markham's direction. "Then we can take a stroll along the Pall Mall."

Right then. So Markham might be listening. Holly hadn't touched her skin to see how hot it was, so she could not be sure the woman was a demon, but it appeared to be the best guess.

Patience in short supply, Holly reached into her reticule

and withdrew a silver pocket watch. The piece was rather heavy, but she doubted that would bother Thorne. "I almost forgot, dearest," she said in a stage voice, as she wound the watch. "I've a gift for you."

Thorne's dubious expression was quite amusing. "Do you now, buttercup?" He eyed the piece as though it might blow up in his face. Intelligent man. "How positively delightful of you."

Once the watch was sufficiently wound, she presented it to him. Oh, but he would hate this. Her anticipation in seeing his reaction was a guilty pleasure. "Depress the setting lever to start it, darling."

He stared at her for one long moment, then took the gift. With pursed lips, he did as bided and then promptly hunched over with a hiss. As did two other patrons. And though Holly's human ears could not hear the noise her device emitted, she knew it was unpleasant.

"There." Holly sat back and resumed her meal. "I think that should suffice. Now, start talking."

By all that was dark and unholy, Will was going to paddle the blasted female inventor one day. He fought not to cover his ears as the cursed watch continued to emit a horrid screech. Gods, but he'd have a ringing head when this was over. But the device was bloody clever. No supernatural within hearing range would be able to listen to what he said now. They'd be in too much pain, he thought darkly.

"This thing isn't going to blow up in my face, is it?" he asked, only half-jesting.

"Of course not. It is merely a simple radio frequency, running at a pitch and speed that humans cannot hear but supernaturals cannot tolerate," Evernight explained. "We have precisely ten minutes." She happily took another egg off the silver tray. "Now then, who was she and what did you discover?"

Growling low in his throat, Will surreptitiously pushed his fist against his aching ear. At least the pain distracted him from thoughts of finishing the kiss they'd almost started before Markham had arrived. It had been too strong, the temptation to haul her into his lap and take her, restaurant patrons be damned. "She is an informant, obviously. As to what? There is a moving fight club that goes by the name of Kettil's Cauldron." The moment Markham had uttered Kettil's name, more memories had notched into place for Will. "One needs an invitation to attend. Kettil, the fiend who runs it, knows everything about the underworld. If he can't tell us about the dagger, I fear no one can."

Will did not add that he'd have to fight for the information. Evernight might object to the messiness of the business. Despite being Irish, she acted like a fussy English lady unless thoroughly provoked. As if to highlight that, she used her silver to cut her egg up into neat, precise bites.

Evernight's fork lowered as she gazed up at him. "Us? You want me to go with you?"

"Why, my dear Miss Evernight, were you expecting me to leave you behind?"

"Most men would not want a woman involved in such matters."

"Most human men, you mean." As far as Will was concerned, humans were ridiculous when it came to their rules about what their women could and could not do. It was akin to the way the SOS sought to keep supernaturals in their place. Unconscionable.

Evernight's pretty lips pursed. "Some non-humans as well."

Will refrained from snorting. "Sanguis do not view their females as fragile things." Although Miss Evernight was not sanguis. No matter; he needed her near him. Will gave a negligent shrug. "Besides which, these recent developments have made it clear that I cannot leave you alone in the house."

Her lips now twitched as if she fought a laugh. "You do realize that is a complete contradiction to your earlier statement. Either I am fully able to take care of myself, regardless of my sex. Or I am not, and you need to guard me."

Damn. She was correct. How loathsome to realize that he was acting like an overprotective human. Nor could he really say precisely why the idea of having her out of sight filled him with trepidation. "All right, I'll restate. I find you capable enough to be at my side when I go to Kettil's Cauldron, yet too vulnerable to leave alone. Satisfied?"

"That is hardly a satisfactory answer." Her eyes twinkled, and Will found himself fighting a smile as well. She leaned in, and the lamplight caught the alabaster curves of her cheeks. "I think you'd bend any rule to satisfy your own agenda, Mr. Thorne, but," she continued when he tried to voice his objections, "as your agenda happens to coincide with mine, I'll keep any further comments to myself."

Blasted woman. He ought not to have any sort of fun around her. But he did.

"You bluffed Mrs. Markham," she said after a moment.

"I'd hardly call what I did a bluff. More like a deflection."

Her twilight gaze fixed on him. "I'm speaking of when you first saw her. You had no idea who she was, did you?"

Will flinched, fighting his surprise. "How did you—"

"You are not as opaque as you seem to think, Mr. Thorne. Not," she added, "to me."

Well then. Charmed, Will watched her resume eating. "You think you know me so well already?"

"I know blarney. And you, sir, are full of it."

He could not help it; he tossed his head back and laughed, full out. Patrons turned to glare. He ignored them. "You have me there, Miss Evernight." Still chuckling, he leaned in, drawing in her subtle scent. "I had to play a bit of catch up with my memory."

"Mmm." She took a sip of her wine. "And Mrs. Markham's appearance jogged it?"

The underlying bite of jealousy he heard in Evernight's tone delighted him. "Well," he drawled, "she is quite memorable."

"Oh, quite," Evernight muttered under her breath. "And what payment shall Mrs. Markham expect?"

One thousand pounds, if Will's memory held. He'd tell Evernight as much, only baiting her was far more fun. He gave her a lazy smile. "What sort of payment do you think a woman such as Mrs. Markham would require?"

"Oh, I don't know," Miss Evernight speculated lightly. "One's firstborn? A bag of innocent kittens?"

He wanted to laugh again. "She's a lovely woman, once you get to know her." The scent of wine on Evernight's warm breath filled his senses. "In fact, she holds a wealth of invaluable knowledge within that pretty head of hers. You should meet with her. I'm certain she'd be happy to—"

"If you dare," inserted Evernight sharply, "suggest that I pick up pointers from Mrs. Markham, I shall thrash you where you sit."

Already, she knew him too well. Just as he knew such

a barb would rattle her chain. He grinned. "It's all right to be ignorant in the ways of the flesh. Most unmarried human ladies of your class are."

Then the truth of it hit him; Satan's balls, she was a virgin. Of course she was. Human women—even ones who were elementals—guarded their virginity as though it were the door to their souls. Pass that threshold and be prepared to claim the woman for life. Sentimental nonsense, but perhaps that was why she was skittish.

Evernight's blasted radio contraption wound down, leaving behind a faint ringing in his ears and an awkward silence between them.

"Evernight, you know—"

Evernight rolled her eyes. "I am not ignorant."

"Of course not." Will refrained from giving her arm a patronizing pat, but only just. The temptation to do it was high. Really, the woman's pride rivaled the Queen's. "I'm certain you've read manuals."

Her eyes narrowed, turning to glimmering triangles of deep blue sapphire. "Amongst other things."

He took a sip of his chocolate. "Watching through peepholes, perhaps? Very educational, those."

"I'm certain they are, Mr. Thorne. However, I shall leave the peeping to you. I was referring to practical, applicable experience."

Will paused, the idea of Evernight participating in *applicable experience* filling his head with all sorts of lurid, delicious images. "Do go on."

But a waiter arrived with two steaming plates of what he proclaimed "*Soufflé de filets de sole à la Verrey!*" She paused until he was gone, then her slim shoulder lifted a fraction as she took another sip of her wine. "It is quite simple, really. I hired a man for the night."

Chocolate sprayed over the table as Will choked. And choked. "Pardon?" he managed weakly, his eyes watering.

Oblivious to the turned heads, Evernight coolly looked him over, not a pink cheek or wince of embarrassment to be had. "You heard me perfectly well."

"You *hired* a man?" Hell. Bloody hell. "To...?"

"Demonstrate the process." She took a small bite of the soufflé, and her nose wrinkled, and she added a sprinkle of salt to the dish. "It was very illuminating."

"I am sure," Will muttered, wiping his mouth with his table linen. "Who was this Mary-Ann?"

"Oh, come now. You can hardly call him a Mary-Ann when he provides a service for women."

His hand clenched. "Do not split hairs. You know very well what I meant. Simply answer the question."

"Does it matter?"

He just resisted thrumming his fingers on the table. "I suppose not."

They sat in silence, Evernight taking her little, efficient bites, one after the other. His clockwork heart ticked an efficient, never-ending rhythm. Louder, louder.

Will tossed down his wadded linen. "No, sorry, I cannot let it go. I have to know. You did what, precisely?"

With an exaggerated sigh, she set her fork down and looked him over, her expression implacable. "I visited a man who is paid to entertain ladies. From what I gathered, he is usually employed by wealthy, if somewhat bored, ladies of a certain set who require discretion."

Will grunted. He knew that business, but he couldn't seem to find his voice. Instead, he waved her on with a lazy roll of his hand.

"I asked this fellow," she said, "to...."

"Butter your bun?"

She frowned. "You needn't be nasty. It was a simple experiment. One night, no violence, nothing that gave me discomfort. I would decide when to stop. And he would teach me whatever I wanted to know."

Heat coursed along his thighs and into his cock as Will thought of Evernight being instructed in the art of love. "And did you? Stop, I mean."

"Of course not," she said, with a small, secret smile that made him frown. "He was very..." Her cheeks pinked, and she cleared her throat. "Well, there you have it."

"Paid a male whore," Will muttered under his breath. Would wonders never cease?

"He was not a whore. Well, he was," Evernight corrected. "But not to me."

"Because he was so tender and caring?" He laughed. "Do not fool yourself, darling. He was still a whore."

"I think not. You see, after we were...done, he refused to accept payment. Therefore, we cannot call him a whore in this instance." A small smile played around her lips. "He was quite insistent on that point. Said he found the experience too entertaining to ask me to pay him for it."

Chapter Thirteen

❦

Men were decidedly odd creatures, incapable of acting with cool logic when it came to practical matters. For instance, Holly could not understand why they would tup whomever they pleased with no compunction, but became downright missish when a woman did the same.

Take Thorne, who now wore such a scowl that one would think he'd been forced to drink unsweetened lemonade. He hadn't spoken more than a few gruff words to her since they'd left the restaurant, and she could only conclude that he disapproved of her experience with Mr. Mather.

Honestly, one would think he'd be glad for her. The loss of a woman's virginity had the possibility of being a horrid experience, yet she'd accomplished it with a minimum of pain and a maximum of pleasure.

Nor could Holly believe the man who threw the word "cock" and "tup" around as others did "please" or "thank you" expected her to remain virginal until marriage.

Yes, on the whole, his behavior was illogical and odd. Now she was stuck with a mercurial demon in a temper.

"Are we going home, then?" she asked, after a prolonged period of silence in which they simply walked along Regent Street.

He merely grunted and sidestepped a large puddle of muck, which meant she had to jump over it, for he hadn't let go of her hand. At this point, she'd touched Thorne more than anyone else in her entire life. The constant physical interaction between them ought to be commonplace now. It wasn't. A humming thrill still shot through her every time he took hold of her. And the fluttering in her belly had yet to abate. Especially when he did as now, clasping her in a proprietary manner.

"Ought we hail a hack?" she asked when they reached Piccadilly Circus.

"I like walking."

Three whole words. An improvement.

She glanced down at their linked hands and then up at his stern, sharp profile. "Mr. Thorne, are you perhaps jealous of my encounter with Mr. Mather?"

He twitched before glancing at her sidelong, his eyes now full black. "Mather is his name, is it?"

Oh, but he sounded cold now. Irritated.

"Did I not just say it was?" Holly said.

"You did." He went back to frowning. "And you are also ridiculous. The very idea of my being jealous is laughable. Why on earth would you assume so?"

A twinge of doubt went through her middle. Thorne sounded so sure, so reasonable. But then she steeled her spine. "Given your current petulant manner, it is the most logical conclusion."

Thorne huffed and halted, turning to face her. His expressive mouth thinned. "And it never occurred to you that I might be put out due to the fact that I am virtually shackled to a woman who views one of life's most basic pleasures as a bloody scientific experiment? Everything is an experiment to you." He yanked up their linked hands, holding them high as his lip curled in a sneer. "Even me."

For a moment, she could only blink. Hurt punched into her chest like a spike through a shield. She'd thought, despite their initial strife, that they were becoming friends. She hadn't many, especially of late, but the idea of his friendship had begun to warm her. Now she felt cold. Foolish.

Drawing into herself, Holly shook free of his grip. "You may walk on without me."

Ignoring his stormy expression, she turned and hailed a cab. As the circus was filled with them, a hansom immediately rattled up to the curve. Holly did not look back as she gave her direction and started to climb inside. She didn't see Thorne move, but suddenly she was pushed inside with a brutal shove.

Heart in mouth, Holly fell in an inelegant sprawl upon the dirty coach floor. "What the bleeding—" Her shout of outrage died as she looked over her shoulder.

Thorne moved in a swirl of black, the ends of his coat flaring out, tendrils of shadow licking around him as he fought five hooded figures. Knives flashed as they came at him like a murder of crows, pecking away at all sides.

The coach driver shouted in alarm, and people stopped what they were doing and gaped. But no one came forward to help.

With Holly's blasted corset and the heavy fall of her skirts and bustle, righting herself was a struggle. Her ribs creaked as she heaved upward, trying to reach for the gun strapped to her calf. Next time, she thought bitterly, she'd keep her weapons on her arms and damn what the public thought.

Blood sprayed as a knife caught Thorne along his cheek. He didn't falter, only lashed out with claws that had lengthened to metallic blades. But he couldn't hold back all of them. One figure slipped past, his eyes gleaming onyx and his fangs extended as he rushed the coach.

A scream bubbled up in Holly's throat as she fumbled with her gun. The handle scraped the skin on her leg as she finally ripped the gun free from its holster. Claws ripped into the edge of her skirts just as she fired in rapid succession, massive booms going off, making her ears ring. The bullets, filled with a mix of powdered gold and silver, tore into the sanguis. With a howl, he staggered back, but quickly righted himself. Then he grinned as blood bloomed over his shoulder.

Shite. She'd missed his heart. The gold would weaken him, eventually poison him, but not quickly enough to save Holly.

"For that," he said, "I'll make you hurt."

"Wait!" Holly grabbed Thorne's top hat that had landed upon the coach floor during the scuffle and lobbed it at him. Not expecting it, the demon flinched, giving Holly time to scramble around and escape out of the opposite coach door.

Right into traffic. A horse whinnied and wheels screeched as a driver cursed and tried to swerve away, only to bang into another coach. "What the bloomin' 'ell! Get out of the road!"

Holly darted forward, and the demon assassin jumped out of the coach after her.

"Run, run, as fast as you can," he taunted at her heels.

I can run away from you, I can. Grimly, Holly picked

up her skirts and sprinted, weaving through lumbering coaches and creaking drays that threatened to crush her. Her lungs burned. Blast, but she was reverting to wearing her short stays from here on. The handle of the gun, clutched tight in her sweaty palm, threatened to slip free. She couldn't stop to fire it, not here.

"Evernight!"

Thorne. She couldn't turn to see. The demon's footsteps were nearly on top of hers. Holly's breath came on sharp and raw. An omnibus loomed ahead. Crowded top and bottom with riders, it crawled along like a tortoise in the field of hares.

Cursing, Holly let her gun fall, grabbed hold of the bus's brass stair rail, and hauled herself up. The muscles along her arm and side screamed in pain as the abrupt move swung her in the opposite direction from which she'd been running. The demon, still in a full sprint, skidded past her, swiping at her with his claws and snarling when he failed to catch hold of her.

Distracted as he was, he didn't see the massive coalleaden dray until it was on top of him. The dray driver cried out, but he couldn't stop. And the demon went down in an abrupt thud. Massive wheels rolled over him in a sickening crunch as people screamed. Holly closed her eyes for a mere second before taking a deep breath.

"Evernight!" Thorne's shout cut through the commotion.

He ran towards her, his coattails flapping, his wild hair streaming like a white banner. But it was the four assassins in black cloaks that caught her attention. They'd abandoned Thorne in favor of hunting her down. And they were closer to catching her than Thorne was.

Bloody hell.

Hands shaking, Holly rooted around in her mantle

pocket. Her fingers curled over a round metal object the size of a billiard ball. She didn't want to use it, but she had no choice. Leaping from the bus, Holly pushed through the now-stalled road traffic and headed towards the Shaftesbury side of the circus where pedestrians mulled about, pointing at the downed assassin crushed beneath the dray's wheels.

Too many people. It couldn't be helped.

Her fingernail found the depression in the metal ball and pushed it in. An ominous series of clicks came from her pocket. Holly wrenched the device free and dropped it in the center of the circus.

One. Two. Three steps.

The assassins were almost on top of the device.

A loud hissing sounded, and then, with a burst of green light, the ball shot open, sending a cloud of thick fog whizzing and shooting into the air. Instantly, the circus became a murky bog.

People ran to and fro, crying out and coughing, not able to see or breathe. Holly held a gloved hand to her nose and backed up until her shoulder hit the side of a building. Heart in her throat, she glanced around. Gods, where was she? Disorientation took hold. Her head swam, and her lungs burned. Someone ran past. A man, his hat askew in his panic. Sounds echoed.

Limping from the stitch in her side, she headed away from the smoke and down Shaftesbury. The air cleared as she emerged out of the fog. A hack drove by.

"Hold," Holly shouted. The hack didn't slow. "Ten guineas if you do!"

That got his attention. The driver pulled up short. Breathless, Holly rushed towards the waiting coach. So close. Her hand landed upon the door latch.

Hard fingers bit into her shoulder and spun her about. The back of a hand bashed into her lip, the recoil sending her head into the side of the waiting coach.

"Here, now," shouted the driver.

The assassin grinned down at her, his yellow eyes burning bright. A raptor. "I'll enjoy making you beg for mercy."

He moved to strike again. Instinctively, Holly thrust up the heel of her hand, catching her attacker under his nose. It was like hitting a block of iron, but he staggered just enough for her to get her knee up, skirts and all, and hit him between his legs. Not very effectual, but his next swipe to grab hold of her neck went wide.

She hadn't any opportunity to do more before a snarl like that of an enraged dog tore through the air, and her attacker was plucked away.

Fangs extended like gleaming daggers, rage and murder in his eyes, Thorne held the raptor aloft as though he were a child's toy. He moved to rip the assassin's head from his body when the three other cloaked figures jumped upon him.

They went down in a black heap of swinging arms and razor-sharp claws. Blood sprayed. Then another of Thorne's roars broke out. He disappeared in a maelstrom of ink-black shadow. In a blink, it enveloped the attackers. The black cloud twirled tighter and faster. And then, as quickly as it had formed, it ended.

Thorne reappeared on the ground, one hand resting in a scummy puddle, his legs in an inelegant sprawl, and his white hair covering his face. At his feet, four headless males lay. Someone screamed. People stared, horrified. A shrill whistle pierced the air. The bobbies were headed their way.

Holly slumped against the side of the coach. Even

though she wore a heavy mantle, she shivered as though ice cold. Perhaps it was cowardly of her, but aftershocks of terror quaked through her, and she wanted nothing more than to jump into the coach and hide. She needed heavy walls and a solid door between herself and the world. But she needed Thorne to come with her, and he wasn't moving. Holly stumbled forward and ran to him, ready to assist when he raised his head. Her boot heels skidded against the slate sidewalk.

Not an inch of skin remained upon his face. He was entirely platinum. It shone bright in the weak light of day. Brilliant and beautiful. And causing him extreme pain, by the way he shook and clenched his teeth.

"Mr. Thorne," she whispered. She ought not have spoken. She knew that instinctively. And too late. A sound rumbled low in his throat. A growl. He snapped at her as an animal might. And then whimpered, as he began to pant, his body curling in on itself.

She hesitated no longer. "William."

He flinched as soon as she touched him, rearing back and hissing, his long, wickedly sharp fangs gleaming pure white against his silver-toned lips.

"It's all right." Her hand rested on a shoulder so hard and so cold through his coat that she knew it was completely metal now. "It's all right, big man."

A choked sound left him but he soothed a bit, the violent shaking in his shoulders ebbing, but tension still held him hard.

"Come." She pulled at his arm. "Let's get you home."

Awkwardly, they rose together, him resting upon her. He was ridiculously heavy for such a lean man. Another whimper left him, and she tucked closer into his side. "Easy now, big man. Easy."

Tossing a bag of coin up to the driver and shouting "go!" in a manner that promised pain and suffering if not heeded, Holly helped Thorne into the coach, landing by his side. The coach lurched forward, careening down a side street.

Thorne hauled her close, his hands upon her hips, and rested his forehead against hers. Another shiver lit through him. His neck was torn open. Blood, hot and thick, dripped upon her collarbone. Holly ignored it and carefully cupped his nape. The slashed flesh was already closing, but he didn't seem to ease.

"Where do you hurt?" she whispered.

His eyes were closed, and he swallowed hard. "Everywhere." Convulsively, he clutched her hips tighter. "Are you harmed?"

With clumsy fingers, he touched her lower lip. It throbbed, the curve stinging where it was split. Thorne cursed low and viciously.

"It's all right," Holly assured.

"Do not make light of this," he ground out, his thumb stroking her lip. "You might have been——" His teeth snapped together so hard that she heard them connect.

"But I wasn't." She pulled at the metal that invaded his flesh. As if unable to help himself, Thorne leaned into her touch, his hands moving over her hair, her cheeks, shoulders. He trembled, his movements weak, sluggish. She'd need to do more for him at home. Home. How could it be that she already thought of home as a place they both belonged? It was madness.

When she'd done what she could for the moment, she sank into him. The coach swayed and rattled as they simply held onto each other, holding each other up, their former strife forgotten.

Thorne's fingertips caressed her neck as he spoke. "'Big man'? Is that what you called me?"

"Er..." Holly's cheeks flushed hot. "Yes."

The coach rocked gently.

"You called me that before." Thorne's voice was a mere breath. "In the cellars. I remember your touch upon my face, the sound of your voice."

She had. It was an endearment her grandmother had used on her grandfather. Holly flushed hotter. She had merely wanted to comfort the hurting sanguis. Silence took on a life and weight between them. And then Thorne huffed. "Big man."

He'd said it as though scoffing. But she could hear the question in there, that he wanted to know why she'd called him that. She almost smiled. No, his frame wasn't what anyone would define as "big." He was lean and strong, a sharp blade. And yet what could she say?

"Well, you are compared to me," she settled on. For even though he was not bulky, he towered over her by nearly a foot.

He huffed again, a half-laugh, half-snort, before leaning back a little, weariness lining his face. "Well," he said in a lighter tone, "we have one goal accomplished. We certainly gained attention."

Holly chuffed out a weak laugh. "Oh yes, well done, that." Then she shuddered. "I didn't expect a pack of them to come for me."

With a weary hand, Thorne raked the hair away from his face. "Those were not assassins, love. Those were Nex."

"You gave a rather vivid response to their offer to rejoin them," Holly murmured as though her heart wasn't racing.

His hand found hers and squeezed firmly. "Congratulations, Miss Evernight. You have yourself an army of one." He looked out the window, and his grip went slack. "Pray that it will be enough."

Someone was waiting for them when Holly and Thorne arrived at Evernight House. As soon as Holly descended the carriage step, a figure slipped between the open gates at the end of the drive. Thorne tensed, but Holly held out a staying hand. There was something familiar about the woman coming towards them.

Her black cloak was drawn up high against the cold, but the little hat pinned atop her neat bun left the majority of her hair exposed. It shone copper bright when she passed beneath the massive gas lamp hanging on the portico's ceiling.

Holly's tension eased a touch. They'd not be attacked, but a reckoning was imminent.

Thorne, feeding off of Holly's reaction, pressed himself against her side.

The woman stopped before them. "Mistress Evernight," said Poppy Lane, director of the SOS, and the woman most believed to be Mother, the secret head of the organization.

She was the last person Holly wanted to see now, when blood was drying in Thorne's hair. Keeping her composure, Holly gave her a respectful nod. "Director Lane." It was on the tip of her tongue to say "fancy meeting you here" or something equally banal, but dread kept her quiet. Director Lane never visited Holly at home.

The tension between them pulled tight as Director Lane surveyed Thorne, and a deep frown worked its way across her pale brow. "Mr. Thorne, my sources had marked you as missing and unaccounted for until now."

Thorne said nothing.

"Where have you been?" Lane prompted in the face of his silence.

"Madam," Thorne said, "as I am not SOS, I do believe that is none of your business."

Director Lane's mouth twitched. Holly might be inclined to think the woman was fighting a smile, but it was hard to discern when it came to Lane. "No. But it couldn't hurt to ask." She turned her attention to Holly. "Mistress Evernight, did you allow Mr. Thorne the use of an anti-listening device at Verrey's restaurant little less than an hour ago?"

Despite the frigid air, Holly's cheeks burned. Gods and gadgets but she wanted to kick Thorne's shin for forcing her out of the house to begin with. But she held Director Lane's reproving gaze instead. "Your information is correct."

"I see." Disappointment and censure colored Director Lane's tone.

"You don't see at all," said Thorne. "Only imply with that supercilious look of yours."

Director Lane angled her chin towards Thorne as if only just giving him her attention. "And what am I implying, Mr. Thorne?"

He seemed to invade Holly's space even further, though he'd yet to move. "That Evernight compromised your precious SOS, which is rot."

"Perhaps my concern lies with your loyalties, Mr. Thorne," Director Lane said. "You were Nex, after all."

" 'Were' being the operative word," Thorne retorted. "What occurs between Miss Evernight and myself stays between us."

Thorne's conviction sent something warm fizzing

within Holly. But she didn't revel in it, for Director Lane's gaze pinned Holly down once more. "After leaving Verrey's, you deployed a top secret smoke bomb that has yet to go through proper testing, upon which time Mr. Thorne violently beheaded five supernatural beings in front of several humans." Lane cocked her head. "Or do I have this wrong?"

Well, hell.

Holly fought the urge to cower. "Technically, he beheaded four. I killed one of them."

"Careful, Miss Evernight," Director Lane said evenly. "Your cheek is not appreciated in this instance."

Holly hadn't considered her answer cheeky, but she refrained from clarifying.

"Why were you engaged in a public bloodbath?" Director Lane asked. "In the middle of Piccadilly Circus, no less."

"Because the bloody buggers weren't polite enough to attack us in a back alley," Thorne quipped. "I do so hate an inconsiderate killer."

Bugger all, but Thorne was going to get her sacked. Holly balled her fists to keep from slapping a hand over Thorne's mouth. Lane's gaze narrowed just as the temperature fell. Holly knew it was a sign of Poppy Lane's rising temper. Her particular power was the ability to create frost and ice. Holly was not afraid. Director Lane wouldn't hurt her. That didn't mean that she couldn't and wouldn't make her life miserable.

"Miss Evernight, whether you were at fault or not, the fact remains that you are the head inventor of the SOS and privy to sensitive information. It is the express opinion of both myself and the SOS that you end your association with Mr. Thorne. It is against the rules for an SOS member to fraternize with a Nex agent. Whether retired or not," Lane added with an emphatic look at Thorne.

Never mind that Jack maintained his association with Thorne and was now a director, Holly thought bitterly.

Thorne's fangs flashed on a snarl, and he took a hard step in Director Lane's direction. "You have no right to order Miss Evernight about!"

"Oh, but I do," said Director Lane without flinching. "I am her superior. As SOS, she answers to me."

Holly set a quelling hand upon Thorne's forearm. But she kept her gaze on Director Lane. "I am on hiatus, thus I am not SOS for the moment." A ridiculous distinction, but Holly could think of little else to use as a defense.

The weight of Director Lane's stare was crushing. "Given events of late, that is hardly comforting, Miss Evernight." Lane's pale face twisted with something that appeared to be regret, but she was a hard woman, and not one easily deterred. "Cease interaction now or you'll have to be brought up for review."

Holly's insides heaved. She hated disappointing Director Lane. They were not close, and likely would never be, but it was Poppy who'd given Holly a position on the weapons and gadgetry team. It was Poppy who had promoted her to head of the division. Moreover, Poppy was Sin's sister. Holly did not want to cause a rift between them. Nor did she fancy being reprimanded by the SOS. Her career had always been the bright star in her world. She was so very proud of her work.

Holly squared her shoulders, knowing that she was in danger of losing everything. "I made a promise, Mum. I will not go back on it. You must do what you feel is best, and so must I."

As soon as she finished speaking, she felt ill, ready

to be sick all over the cobbles. What would she do if she could not share her work with the SOS? It was too advanced for normal society. She'd be cut off, silenced in the cruelest fashion. What had she done?

A cold shiver ran through her. And then she felt the soft touch at the tips of her gloved fingers. Thorne, reminding her that he was there for her. Holly didn't want to think on how warm his support made her feel. Or the fact that she wanted to clutch his hand and not let go.

Lane's disappointment was fierce upon her face. And Holly found herself speaking once more.

"However, when I return to work, I will..." Words stuck in her throat. She pushed them out. "I will no longer associate with Mr. Thorne."

At her side, Thorne flinched, though he said nothing. He didn't need to. She knew she'd disappointed him. Did he think her a coward for folding under Lane's censure? Holly rather feared that she was.

Director Lane stared Holly down for an icy moment. "Well then," she said finally, "I see your mind is set." Her gaze went to Thorne, and the temperature dropped so swiftly that their breaths came out in puffs of white. "You harm Miss Evernight or my organization and there won't be a safe place for you in this world, Mr. Thorne."

Holly expected a flip reply, but Thorne simply bowed and touched the brim of his hat. "Duly noted, Mrs. Lane." Then he gave Holly a look of such sheer disgust that she flinched before he turned heel and walked into the house.

Chapter Fourteen

Holly's father had always said that, when cornered, she tended to act rashly. She rather feared she was guilty of this now, that she hadn't disappointed Thorne but rather had injured his feelings after Director Lane had backed her into a proverbial corner.

For tension and some deeper emotion hummed off Thorne's frame as he handed Felix his overcoat and gloves in the hall. Ought she apologize? But what could she say? She had to give up any association with him. He'd been standing at her side; surely he understood why. Was he truly upset over that eventuality? Or was it something else? She did not know. Emotions were ephemeral, fleeting things. She dealt in facts and figures. They were safe, logical. Thorne was anything but.

Not having a solution to the problem, she kept to what she understood: a schedule. When he made to climb the stairs, she stopped him. "Are we not going to do your massage?" Even as she said the words, she knew she'd made an error.

He stopped short, one foot on the first riser. His grip upon the newel-post went knuckle-white. Slowly he turned, and her insides jumped upon seeing his grim expression. In silence, he stared at her as if trying to discover any hidden motive she might have.

She tried to reassure him. "It isn't safe for you to forgo them."

He merely looked at her. As though she were a defective machine. Holly swallowed. "That is, you might slip into madness should you ignore the problem."

Wrong thing to say, apparently, for his eyes narrowed to slits. When he spoke, his voice was a cold whip through the thick silence. "We wouldn't want to put you into any danger, now would we?"

That wasn't precisely what she'd meant, but she didn't want to argue. "I'll wait out here until you are ready."

He'd yet to lower his gaze from hers. "Why wait?" The silky tone slithered over her spine. He took a step forward, watching her like a falcon does a mouse, even as his hand went to his cravat, jerking it free with a tug. "Such common actions as my undressing mean little to you, correct? I am, after all, nothing more than an experiment."

So then, she'd hurt him. Had he no sense of her finer feelings? That he'd stomped all over them more than once? Irked, she lifted her chin. "As I am nothing more than a remedy."

"Just so," he said crisply. Like a perfect gentleman, he made a little bow and held out a hand, indicating that she proceed him into her laboratory. "After you, pet."

Walking with a stiffness she felt down to her bones, Holly did as bided. Thorne followed, closing the door behind them with a decisive click that had her insides clenching.

Instinct screamed for her to beg off, flee. But she wouldn't give Thorne the satisfaction of seeing her unravel. For she knew, with the suddenness of one being caught out unprepared in a rain shower, that he wanted her unhinged. It was in his steady stare and the tight, unpleasant smile tugging at the ends of his lips.

Thorne walked to the center of the room. There, he turned to face her. He watched her as he grabbed hold of the lapels of his ruined jacket and opened it wide like an offering.

A lump filled her throat.

Thorne slipped free of the jacket, and it fell to the floor in a muted thud.

Moving with a languid sort of deliberation, he eased the braces off his shoulders. They slipped along the linen of his shirtsleeves with a soft hiss. Behind her, a log in the fire broke with a sharp crack. Holly clutched the back of a chair and remained caught in the snare of Thorne's attention.

Oh, but he knew what he was about. He wasn't simply undressing. He was putting on a show. For her. As though they would soon tup. His eyes gleamed with rays of silver and black as he unbuttoned his shirt. Slowly. Each button, quietly coming undone and revealing more skin, more of him.

Holly glared. He smiled. And then pulled the shirt overhead.

The silken strands of his hair settled about his shoulders, drawing her attention to the breadth of them, to the way his waist narrowed down to lean hips. His trousers hung low, held up only by the jut of his hipbones and the bulge of his cock.

Gods and gadgets but she didn't want to notice his

cock. Heat swarmed over her skin like a fever. As if he heard her thoughts and sensed her reaction, he paused, and his nostrils flared. Humor lit his gaze as his smile grew crooked, almost smug.

Smarmy bastard. She fought the urge to run from the room. Something told her he'd follow.

Swallowing with difficulty, Holly fussed about with the heavy blanket he would use to cover himself. She didn't want to watch him lower his trousers. She didn't think she could touch him with any sense of propriety if she saw him utterly bared to her.

Obviously not fooled, he made a noise of amusement. She ignored that too and went over to add a few logs to the fire. Something to do, at least. His voice, dark and laced with irony, called out to her. "I'm covered. Your virtue is safe, Miss Evernight."

Holly's back teeth met with a click. Reluctantly, she turned.

The first massages she'd given him had been something of a blur to her. She'd been either exhausted, both mentally and physically, or had managed to remain in a state of detachment, too eager to see if her theory proved correct to truly be affected by Thorne. Now? She was alert. And far too aware.

Saints preserve her, but it was difficult approaching him as he lay spread out like a banquet upon her worktable. He watched, his gaze somnolent yet attentive, like a lazing cat waiting to pounce. And a pulse began to beat low in her neck.

A throw covered his hips and lower limbs. It did not help, for the delineated stretch and dip of his torso muscles were on full display. He'd placed an arm under his head, and his biceps bunched, drawing her attention from there to the little tuft of bronze hair upon his underarm. It was too much intimacy.

Transfixed, Holly walked closer.

When Holly had been a girl of fifteen, her parents had taken her on a trip throughout the continent. They'd visited the Salon in Paris, and there, had seen Auguste Rodin's scandalous *The Age of Bronze*. Holly remembered gaping up at the nude study in darkly gleaming bronze. The metal had sung to her, a low, beautiful hum. But the sinewy grace of the male form was what had held her in thrall.

She tried to think of that now as she looked down at Thorne, whose body, while similarly graceful, was chiseled with greater definition. She tried to view him as little more than another beautiful sculpture. And failed.

He was so very beautiful. So finely made. Wicked, forbidden, wild. William Thorne was all of the things she'd turned away from her entire life. Order, rules, and discipline made up her world, gave her a sense of place and self.

Now everything felt off, as though her center of gravity had pulled away from the earth and affixed itself to him, compelling her inexorably closer. She stared down at his chest, where the ever-present metal expanded outward. His abdomen, arms, and neck were all covered with it.

"You are managing your pain better now," she said, if only to break the oppressive silence.

He simply looked back at her. When he finally spoke, the words came out flippant. "When there is the promise of relief in the form of your touch? How can I not?"

To keep her wits, Holly pursed her lips, looking reproachful, because he expected that. He could not, *would not*, know how he affected her. She refused to let it show. Nor did she want to touch him. Not now, when she feared she'd give herself away, flush with desire, or perhaps linger too long in one place. It took all of her will to lay her hands upon him.

Her palms spread over the cold metal patch that covered his left shoulder. Inside, she began to shake, a slow build of heat growing within. Bugger all, but this would be impossible. Barely daring to breathe, Holly eased her touch along his shoulder, concentrating on her power. *Just a sculpture. Think of him as a sculpture.*

Cool, hard, smooth, hot. The texture of his skin was unlike anything she'd ever felt. The metal made it smooth and cool and hard. Where not altered by metal, his skin was like hot satin, only silkier and tight with strength.

His flesh twitched beneath her palms as she mapped his chest. Every breath he took sounded loud and clear in her ears. And all the while, he watched her.

A quiver rippled along the backs of her thighs, up over her bottom, and crawled along her spine. Damn it, she was better than this. She was not a creature of base desires, but of logic and restraint. Her breath moved in and out, a slow, steady rhythm as she stroked him.

Neither of them spoke. The crackle of the fire in the grate, along with the occasional creak of the house settling, surrounded them. Beneath heavy lids, Thorne tracked her every move. And her touch grew unsteady. A momentary weakness he jumped upon.

"Does it feel good to you?" he drawled, low and easy. "Touching me?"

Instantly, the space between her legs clenched tight. Holly kept her touch impersonal. She could not live with the ignominy of revealing her wants to Thorne, who would treat her weakness as a bloody good joke. "It is a task. Just like any other." A bald-faced lie if ever she told one.

His nostrils flared, the platinum in his eyes shining bright. "Then why do I smell your cunny growing wet with need?"

Holly stopped, her palm flat against his pectoral muscle, as more slick heat flooded her sex. Oh, this was beyond the pale. What on earth had gotten into the blasted demon? "Being crude is not going to get a rise out of me, Mr. Thorne."

A small, cruel smile curled his lips. "Not going to deny it, are you, Miss Evernight?"

"Blather." She took up stroking an area tangled with platinum webbing with more force than necessary. "That is all you're about. Ridiculous blather. And I will not engage in such nonsense."

Holly concentrated on pulling the metal from him. Not on his scent, clean and pleasing in the space between them. Or the way his skin grew increasingly warmer.

When he spoke again, it was soft, teasing. "Do you know that when I said 'cunny' your sweet scent grew stronger?"

Again she stopped. His dense muscles tightened beneath her nails. "Mr. Thorne—"

"Do you wonder," he whispered, holding her gaze with his, "if my cock is affected?" A dark brow lifted, his fangs glinting. "If it is more metal than flesh? Hard for you?"

She would not look down at the appendage in question. It was difficult enough to pretend each time that she wasn't aware of that part of him, or that she hadn't seen it grow and lengthen beneath the covers. Oh, she knew precisely how long and thick he was, and precisely how aroused. Each and every time.

His gaze upon her burned. "Do you want to see my cock, Miss Evernight? Feel it move inside of you?"

Gods, he made her feel empty, made her want to be filled up. Her hands turned to fists. "Stop it. Now, Mr. Thorne."

He rose up on his elbows, his white hair sliding over his broad and dusky shoulders, his defined abdomen tightening. "Or. What?"

Holly sat back on the stool by the table, placing her hands upon her lap so that he wouldn't see them trembling. "Why are you doing this?"

"Why not?"

She could not look away from the black and platinum starburst of his gaze, so very brilliant. So very angry and taunting. Her nails dug into her palms. "Find your amusement elsewhere."

His lean hips canted just a bit, an utterly crude gesture that held her in thrall. "I'd rather find it with you."

"I'm helping you, aren't I?" She hated how the words came out in a near-desperate pitch. But he had to stop. Agitation had her breath coming on hard and fast, pressing her now-heavy breasts against her too-tight bodice.

"Helping me," he scoffed. "Do not skew this into some act of kindness. You do so that I won't kill you."

"Is it kindness that you want?" She laughed without humor. "A funny way you go about getting it." She leaned forward in her anger. "Why are you saying these things? Truly? Why are you acting like such a . . . disgusting arse?"

He shot upright, his chest bumping into hers before she backed away a pace as if seared. "Because you never react during these torture sessions," he ground out. "Because I want that rise out of you. I want you to . . ." He bared his teeth, those evil-looking fangs growing longer. "I want to know if you feel—"

His teeth ground together, his eyes wild and silver-black.

"Feel?" she prompted as if her heart wasn't beating madly.

"Anything!" he roared. "Jesus." He ran a hand through his hair. "You touch me every day. You rub your hands all over me. And nothing! Not a flicker of emotion. As if I didn't exist." The expanse of his chest heaved with exertion, the sinewy muscles along his abdomen clenching. "And all the while I'm lying here aching, fucking dying to... You're driving me to insanity," he finished with a wild shout. "And it means exactly nothing to you—"

She grabbed hold of the back of his neck and kissed him. Just as she'd wanted to, her lips claiming his parted ones, shutting off the stream of words that flowed from him. His lips were soft and warm, and touching them set off a rush of lust that coursed along her limbs. He froze, going so tense that his neck felt like ice. For all of one second. And then he attacked. His hands plunged into her hair and gripped the sides of her head as he fell back, hauling her with him, devouring her with quick, biting kisses, punctuated by helpless groans.

Breathless and dizzy, she answered every kiss, opening her mouth when his mouth demanded it. They both shivered when their tongues slid together.

"Hell," he moaned, licking along her bottom lip. "Hell, I knew you'd taste so bloody good." He angled his head, plunging his tongue in deep as his hands held her captive. The gesture wicked and decadent. Grunting, he spun them, pressing her into the table with the strength of his body. His thigh nudged between hers, and her skirts slid up. Instantly, his hand was there, long fingers trailing along her skin. "I'm not stopping," he growled into her mouth. "So don't ask me to."

Holly tore her lips from his and grabbed a handful of silken hair. She held him fast and hard. "You'll stop if I say so."

Thorne paused, his lips brushing hers as he breathed heavily through his mouth. Hot, black eyes bore into hers. "Are you asking me to stop?" He was so still and careful that she knew he would, despite his claim.

A fire raged through her veins. And the need to suckle his curved lower lip had her voice turning rough. "No."

His nostrils flared. "Then why are we discussing this?"

"I wasn't the one who brought up the subject—"

He kissed her so deep and long that she whimpered. And he ground the length of his hard cock where she ached. Desperately, Holly reached between them and wrapped her fingers around him. No, not metal here, but hard as, with skin softer than silk. And hot. So very hot in her hand. His unhinged groan vibrated through her frame.

"Harder," he rasped, thrusting his cock through her fist. "Make it hurt."

She squeezed tight, tugging as her thumb swept over the smooth, slick tip.

He panted into her mouth, his entire body shaking. "Yes, like that. Bloody hell." He seemed to swell within her grip, go impossibly harder. Holly flickered her tongue against his as she writhed beneath him, impatient, needing him to bruise her too.

With a curse, he canted his hips enough to wrench her skirts up high, bunching them in a mess about her waist. And then the rounded, hot crown of his cock was at her opening. Not pushing in, but slip-sliding over her wetness. A tease. He stared down at her, his lips parted, his brows drawn tight as though he were in pain. Oh, but the look in

his eyes, so filled with need and dark heat that her heart
flipped inside her chest. She was empty. So very empty.

"Will... please..."

With his thighs, he spread hers wide.

"I'm going to fuck you now," he said against her lips,
and she whimpered again. Gods, but she wanted it. More
than she'd ever wanted anything. She hated him for making her want him. But it only fueled her lust. Mad. She'd
finally gone mad.

Her hand ran down the hard curve of his arse and
gripped it tight. "Then shut up and do it."

He thrust. Hard and deep.

On a cry, Holly arched up, and he caught her in his
arms, not giving her a moment to settle before he took
her with rough strokes. With each slap of his hips against
hers, the table groaned and rocked as he fucked her. There
was no polite term for the way he went about it, driving in
and out of her as if he couldn't go far enough.

She grabbed the ends of his hair and kissed him, desperate for more of his taste, for the feel of his tongue sliding over hers. With one hand, he cupped the back of her
head, holding her tenderly. But the other hand gripped the
strings of her corset at her back. The grip turned brutal,
pulling the corset tight, cutting off her air.

She couldn't breathe, couldn't think. Her world spun
in a hot blur of color and feeling. His thick cock invading and retreating, the tender well of her sex, her breasts
aching to break free of their confinement. He pounded
harder, gripped her tight, watching her through heavily
lidded eyes, as though he knew exactly what he was doing
to her, how his hold would affect her.

She became a mindless creature, straining and scram-
bling to get closer to him, her source of pleasure and of

torment. Blackness crept over her vision. And then with a jerk and the slice of his claw along her corset strings, she was free. Her breath drew in on a great gasp, and the orgasm swept her up with such force that she wailed, her body convulsing against his.

Thorne's shout, the sharp buck of his hips into hers, was a distant thing as Holly came down from where he'd taken her.

Spent, he sagged against her, his hold fragile and his skin covered with a sheen of sweat. The weight of him was far too pleasing.

Holly lay limp and panting. Every inch of her thrummed with a sort of boneless, well-satisfied yet aching contentment. But her mind whirled. Intercourse with Thorne was nothing like what she'd experienced before. He'd taken her with coarse, unfettered need. Now she feared she'd give up everything, lose herself body and soul, just to have more. More of him.

A loss of control was unacceptable. The tighter she held onto her emotions, the safer she would be. But the scientist in her needed to understand. How had he done it? Why was the experience better with him? Better. It was transcendent.

"What…" She licked her dry lips. "What did you do to me?"

For a moment, he said nothing. Only the gentle touch of his fingers stroking the side of her neck gave any indication that he was awake. Then he spoke, his voice rough and cracking. "Just the question I was going to ask you, Miss Evernight."

There was pleasure and then there was Pleasure. The latter was to experience the moment with every sense firing and working at top performance. Thoughts fled, joy and sensation roared to the forefront. Will had thought himself an expert in both. Taking Holly Evernight hard and fast on a table top had proven him a dilettante on true Pleasure. She'd decimated him, reducing him to a quivering pile of limbs and aching cock. Was it wrong of him, then, to want to linger over her? To seek a repeat performance?

He'd had the barest of tastes. And he wanted more.

Thus it was to his extreme disappointment when she all but shoved him off of her and pleaded the need for privacy. Had he retained an ounce of his wits, he might have questioned her. Instead, he watched her flee to her rooms with the determined strides of one trying desperately not to run, but wanting just as desperately to give in to the compulsion.

Flattering. Truly. More so when she went to bed, locking her door against him without so much as a good night.

He'd paced his room, wondering whether it would appear too needy should he charge into hers and stake his claim. Eventually, he'd given up the ghost and went to his own, cold bed,

How, he wondered, as he waited for her the next morning, would she receive him?

She solved the quandary by reappearing, all buttoned up in a high-necked gown of deep silver. It called to mind a suit of armor, especially given the way she stood at attention, her little chin up and her shoulders squared.

He couldn't help himself; he smiled. Broadly. "Well, hello again."

A soft, pink blush spread up from her collar. He wanted to nibble his way down her neck to the sweet tips of her breasts. He hadn't even seen her breasts. Why hadn't he completely ripped off her bodice and feasted on them when he'd had the chance? He took a step towards her, and she stiffened as though fearing his touch. Her reaction was so strong that he stopped short.

Before he could say a word, she turned and proceeded to walk away with brisk strides that had her skirts snapping. "I am going to work in the other laboratory today," she said, as Will followed.

"All right." His response came out more a question. Which was apropos, as he didn't quite understand what work had to do with what had happened between them. Was she embarrassed? Shy? Worried how he'd act towards her now? She needn't be. He would adore her if she gave him half the chance.

Her lovely face might have been carved marble. "I don't want to be disturbed."

Something ugly twisted deep in his gut. "By me, you mean."

Her chin lifted a fraction. "As you are the only soul in the house who would think to interrupt me while I work, then yes, I do mean you."

She wouldn't look at him. Will halted. Surprisingly, so did she. When she turned to give him a curious look, he peered down, using his height to loom over her. Hell, he needed every advantage he had with this woman. "Have we a problem?"

"Problem?" she tossed out lightly. "Whatever do you mean?"

A laugh broke from him, although he was tempted to curse. "Do you honestly believe that this Little Miss Insouciant retort will work on me?" He waved a hand in disgust. "You're acting overly formal." And cold.

"Mr. Thorne, as you have been keen to point out on

many an occasion, I *am* overly formal in comparison to you."

A growl rumbled in his throat, and he ground his teeth to keep from shouting. "When a man has spent himself between your thighs, *Miss* Evernight, you may feel free to treat him with familiarity."

A blush tinted her checks as her gaze flicked away. "Charming."

A realization dawned on him, so brutally hard that he felt ill and nearly stumbled.

"You regret it." Will's fists clenched. He was a breath away from grabbing hold of her. "You regret me."

She glared up at him, her blue eyes like midnight beneath her black brows. "Of course I regret it. You disgust me—"

"You did not appear disgusted last night!" He could not believe it. Not how much it chafed or how much he wanted to tup her again, just to hear her moan as she did before. *Disgust, my arse.*

Her fine lips pursed. Damn, but he loved it when she did that with her mouth. It made him want to bite her. "To clarify, it disgusts me that I want you. You are crude. You use every opportunity to rub my base needs and weakness in my face." Her hand cut through the air when his mouth opened again. "I don't want to desire you. Not with this arrangement hanging over us. And continued intercourse without love or, at the very least, affection, is a waste."

"What bloody rot," he snarled past the odd ache in his chest. He didn't expect her to love him. It was a relief, really, that she hadn't become calf-eyed with the emotion. But no affection? Did she dislike him so much? Bloody, irritating woman. "Tupping is tupping. It feels bloody good, *tremendous*, if done right." And they had done it very right. "Fucking is life. The creation of it. Its greatest pleasure. Why shouldn't we partake in it?"

She rolled her eyes and made a move as if to go. Rage, and something uncomfortably near panic, seared his insides, and he grabbed her. "Answer me."

"Because," she said through her teeth, "pleasure or not, when I see that smirk of yours, I feel ashamed." Her eyes grew overly bright as she held his gaze. "I cannot stand the thought of you having a laugh at my expense."

"Having a laugh at you?" His throat constricted. Was she mad?

"I'm sorry," she said, pulling free of his nerveless fingers. "I thought I could silence my mind and give in to simple feeling. I cannot."

She left him standing there, numb all over now, save for that aching place in his chest where the metal heart now lay.

Chapter Fifteen

──────────◆~◆~◆──────────

Will had to leave the house. Or he'd be storming into Little Miss Regretful's sanctuary and bodily showing her just what he thought of her theories. Smarmy, was he? Having a laugh at her? She was utterly without a clue when it came to men. Pride stayed his hand. He would not crawl on his belly for her, or anyone.

For now, he needed to air out his anger. The problem being that he feared that the moment he left, she'd be attacked. Shockingly, it was Felix who solved his problem. The man came across Will pacing a hole in the library rug.

His expression was one of sympathy, which irked too.

"How quickly can you travel by shadow?" Felix asked him after a moment of silence.

Will stopped short. "Why?"

The butler held out a rather large silver pocket watch. Having been subjected to the terrors of another one of Holly Evernight's so-called watches, Will eyed the thing with caution.

Felix gave him a wry look. "This is a communicator.

The model works only in one direction, so you cannot contact the house with it. However, should an emergency arise, I can sound an alarm, which you will receive through this."

Will blinked, then a grin of appreciation crept over his mouth. "That woman is bloody brilliant."

"Yes, she is." Felix sobered. "Go on, sir. We'll look out for her."

Will took the device with gratitude. A strange notion of kinship with the young butler fell over him. "I'd never hurt her," he found himself saying, for he knew without doubt that both Felix and Nan knew what had occurred.

Felix didn't blink. "I know." He hesitated, then added, "Upsetting the order of things is another matter."

It did not sound as though the man disapproved of that, however. And then Will understood. Holly Evernight needed her carefully constructed world shaken up. Unfortunately, Will didn't know if he had the heart to do so. Not when it meant the risk of his being broken.

He laughed without humor as he pocketed the watch. How had it come to this? That he was pining over a woman so unlike anything he'd ever wanted? Will did not stay around to think on it. He fled to the only place he knew he would be welcome. Jack's house.

His friend greeted him with a mixture of surprise and wariness as he opened his own door, still refusing to employ a proper house staff. "You look like hell," Jack said.

"Stating the obvious, mate," Will answered without much heat.

"Come on then. We'll suss it out in the library."

Once in the library, Will sat in one of Talent's ridiculously comfortable chairs and stretched his legs out towards the fire. While he did not have the ability to manipulate fire that many of his brethren possessed, he still craved its roaring heat. Hell was in his blood, he supposed.

Jack handed him a crystal glass filled with crimson liquid. "Madeira," he said, taking the seat next to Will. "One hundred and fifty years old."

Will straightened. "How in the hell did you get your hands on it?"

Jack took a sip of the fortified wine. "Lord Archer. He has an obscenely decadent stock of wines and spirits. This was a birthday gift." A look of bemusement crossed Jack's hard features, and Will knew he was still unaccustomed to such acts of kindness.

"How do you know the fellow?" Will had heard of Archer. At one point in time, all of London had feared him. Well, all the humans had feared him. As for Will and his brethren, they'd admired the way an obviously supernatural creature had flaunted himself in high society. Of course now, Archer appeared as human as the next bloke, which was rather a shame.

"He's Ian's best mate and brother-in-law. So we're family in a roundabout way."

Ian, known to the underworld as The Ranulf, king of the lycans, was Jack's self-appointed father and protector. Will knew Jack had an extended family as a result, but he hadn't paid attention to the particulars. Not when it reminded Will that he essentially had no close family.

"Well, cheers to you, mate," he said, and took a sip. Merciful Devil. Rich, almost buttery sweetness slid along his tongue. "Bloody hell, that's good."

"Thought you might appreciate it." Jack drank as well.

"Where is your woman?" Will felt compelled to ask; the devil help him if he had to face Mary while trying to sort out his feelings for her good friend.

"Meeting with Lucien Stone." Jack's voice, though tight, did not hold the old taint of jealousy it once did when he spoke of Mary's mentor and fellow GIM.

"So then, you're all right with that?"

Jack shrugged. "Still don't care for the prancing peacock, but I can manage a polite word when need be." Which meant that Jack was still a prat to old Lucien. The fact that the GIM was a known seducer and far more attractive than a man ought to be might have something to do with it.

Jack's expression sobered. "It's about GIM business, at any rate. Don't know the particulars, but apparently Adam has abandoned the GIM."

Will frowned into his drink. Adam created all GIM. In a way, Will's predicament was directly related to Adam. Holly had created a replica of Adam's clockwork hearts, and it now resided in Will's chest. Absently he stroked the scar, the raised, thick line obvious even with his waistcoat and jacket buttoned up. "Sounds like a boon to me."

While Adam might be the creator of the GIM, his gift came at a price. Servitude. Each contract varied, but all GIM served him for a time.

Jack made a half shrug before taking another drink of his Madeira. "On the surface, perhaps it is. But when a powerful primus, who has controlled an entire species, suddenly releases his holdings? It's best to sort out why."

"Perhaps he's gone the way of the ancients and lost his marbles."

Jack gave him a look. "I believe we both know what sort of shite that scenario can kick up."

Will cleared his throat and forced himself not to rub his scar again. Yes, he knew too well.

Clearly not wanting to continue down that dark path, Jack sat back comfortably in his chair. "So then, what has you in a mood?"

Will wasn't about to deny his foul mood. Jack knew him too well. What's more, Will never felt the need to hide his feelings. It was the sanguis in him. To deny emotions was a dangerous thing.

Will finished off his glass. Setting down the crystal with a small clink, he ran a finger over the rim before answering. "Holly."

The corner of Jack's mouth curled. "Holly, is it?"

Will sighed and handed Jack his glass. "I'm going to need a top off."

Jack's eyes gleamed as he poured more Madeira. "Got you in a lather, has she?"

"You're enjoying this far too much, you arse." Will took a gulp. His hand was less steady now. How much time did he have? An hour? Less? Christ. He did not want to beg for her touch. Never again would he beg.

"It could be worse," Jack deadpanned. "I could hunt her down and flirt with her just to see you sweat."

Very well, he deserved that, as he'd done the very thing to Jack with Mary Chase. "Oh, please do. I'm certain your wife would find it most amusing too."

"Which is the only reason you're safe." Jack suddenly grinned. "Though, if I gave her my reasons, she just might wish me well."

"She's that certain of your affections?"

"Oh yes."

"You make me ill, you know that?"

Jack wagged his thick brows. "Jealous?"

"Yes."

His oldest friend's mouth fell open. Ordinarily Will

would have relished the fact that he shocked Jack; it was hard to do. But he was too weary to fully appreciate it now.

"I want what you have. I want it with Holly." As soon as the words were out, the truth of his predicament crystallized in his mind. He wanted her. And she'd told him to take a piss. Gads, but he was in the thick now.

Will sat back with a sigh. "But the blasted woman... Hell and damnation, she's a bloody cold fish half of the time." Why couldn't he desire some nice, lusty sanguis female? Never mind that Holly Evernight, in the throes of passion, burned hotter than any bed partner he'd ever had. "And I'm quite certain she'd have nothing to do with me were it not for the initial threat of me killing her."

Jack choked on his Madeira. "Are you still threatening to kill her?"

"Do not be daft." Will waved a heavy hand. "I'm the one bloody keeping her safe, am I not?"

Dark green eyes bore into him. "You used to be better than this. You used to charm women with a look."

Will pressed his fingers over his aching eyes. "I'm out of practice. Besides, it never meant anything before. I cannot function properly around this damn woman."

"Sounds about right," Jack said with a wry salute.

On a growl, Will pounded the armrest with his fist. "Bloody hell, you're supposed to give me advice. Why do you think I'm here?"

Jack snorted. "Me? Advice? Do you not remember the depths to which I bolloxed things up with Mary? You ought to be running from my advice." He tilted his head and peered at Will. "You're hiding out, aren't you?"

Will glanced away and picked at a loose thread on his jacket sleeve. "Hardly."

"You are." Jack sat up straighter, that bloody irritating smile creeping back over his lips. "I bet my best hat that you stormed out in one of your fits of pique."

"I'll have you know, I strolled out, and quite peaceably too. Now then, I'll take the black, flat-topped bowler with the silver band that you fancy so much, thank you."

Jack did not appear convinced, which was bloody insulting.

"I'll wait here," Will said amicably.

When Jack did nothing more than stare a hole through his skull, Will sighed and leaned forward to rest his arms upon his bent knees. "I didn't need to storm out. The blasted woman has locked herself in her laboratory and doesn't want to see me."

"What did you do to earn the cold shoulder?" Jack appeared both amused and empathetic.

"I tupped her." Will winced at the admission.

And so did Jack. "That badly, eh?"

With a snarl, Will launched from his chair and headed for the door. He had more important things to do this night. Jack's laughter followed him.

"Oh, come now," Jack called after him, "you walked right into that!" His tone turned serious. "Will!"

Will halted. "What?"

Jack stood, still grinning but visibly trying to bring his humor to heed. "I'd say you ought to profess your adoration, but in my experience, it won't always work. A woman's mind, once set, is a difficult nut to crack."

Will was rather afraid of that. "I'm buggered." Which meant there was only one course of action to take.

One either fought against nature, or accepted it. For too long, Will had fought against being a crawler, never truly utilizing the power it gave him. Until Evernight's life had been in danger. It had been too close, and he'd waited too long to let his shadow go. Never again would he fail her.

Will decided to embrace what he was. With acceptance, came control. For the first time, his shadow had a mind capable of cold and cunning thought. He called forth skills he'd left unused for long enough. And he hunted.

The Nex thought themselves safe from his wrath. That they could control him, harm what was *his*. They thought wrong. He slid into their den, the safe haven of the elders. They didn't see him coming, didn't have a chance.

Will spread his shadow wide, covering the ceiling of their underground lair. And then he descended.

Blood, screams, terror. Aldous Nex died first. And then the others. They struggled as he engulfed them in a tornado of fangs and claws. Without a purely physical body, he could not be struck down. And he moved with a speed that insured they didn't have the chance to try.

He left them all dead. Shredded beyond recognition. Those who remained in the Nex would see the devastation he'd wrought here. And they'd know: one did not touch Will Thorne's woman and live.

When he was done, he returned to her, flowing into her room and under her covers. And though she slept, she turned to him, her body warm and pliant. He held her until his pain ebbed and the sky turned to pale grey. Only then did he leave her, fearful that she would wake and reject him once more.

Chapter Sixteen

〜✺〜

Tuesday evening found Holly standing in the hall outside of Thorne's door. Dithering. There was no other word for it.

It pained her to think of the callous words she'd tossed at Thorne, fear and the sharp need to put a distance between them making her needlessly cruel. She'd mucked things up between them, and now everything felt off kilter and wrong. With all of her being, she wished she could take back what she'd said to him, or simply take back the moment of weakness when she'd kissed him.

Deep in the secret corners of her heart, she wanted William Thorne. Wanted to again feel his heat, taste his flavor, lose herself in him. But she knew an experiment doomed to failure when she saw one. Holly could not give Thorne her body without eventually giving him her heart as well. He lived for frivolity and pleasure. She lived to work and... Well, she didn't precisely like that vein of thought. It made his life appear more enjoyable. While hers was what? Cold. Lonely.

But work was all she had. Without the SOS, her work would die. There was no place for a lady scientist in the misogynistic world of normal, human society. So she had done what was necessary, and drew a line in the sand between them, assuring that he would neither expect nor want any further intimacies with her again.

Holly's fingers curled into a fist, and she rested it upon the glossy, black wood door. Her reasoning didn't matter. Logic and emotion were two different beasts. Emotions had been engaged between her and Thorne. And she had bruised his. She needed to apologize. She was better than this. But on the next breath, the door swung open, making her stumble forward.

Thorne looked down at her as though she were slightly daft, then glanced about the hall as if checking for possible spies. He was dressed for an outing and far too attractive for her equilibrium. His gaze cut back to her. "Good," he said briskly. "I want to talk to you." Before she could utter a word, he caught hold of her elbow and tugged her into his room.

Once inside, he let her go, and Holly, beset with nerves, drifted over to the settee where the morning post lay upon the seat. A pot of chocolate sat on the table, the sight so homey that she almost smiled. Thorne glanced at her, and his lips compressed in a defiant gesture.

"I killed them."

Holly's head snapped up. "Pardon?"

He gestured with his chin towards the newspaper. There, in bold black, proclaimed *Grisly Slaughter in Wapping! Nine Dead—Possibly More!*

With numb hands, Holly lifted the paper and read about the discovery of several body parts—all that was left—within a wine cellar located at the docks. The bodies had only been found because their blood had seeped under the cellar door to run in a crimson river along the gutters.

Thorne's voice cut through the silence. "I found that my response to the Nex's offer was not forceful enough."

The paper drifted from her hands, scattering upon the floor in ink-smudged sheets. "They were Nex?"

"Elders," he said crisply.

Good God, how had he done it? She realized she didn't want to know.

His expression shifted between wariness and reassurance. "At any rate, the Nex, what is left of them, will no longer come after you." His lashes lowered, hiding his eyes. "I told you I'd see to your safety."

He'd done this mass murder for her. It was staggering, humbling. And it frightened her more than a little. Holly's breath hitched. "Thorne, I don't know what to—"

"Do not say anything," he cut in with a wave of his hand. As if destroying the entire head of an organization that had plagued the SOS for a century was nothing but a slight diversion of his time. "We've far more important things to discuss."

She stared at him for a moment, her limbs refusing to move, and her heart a lead weight within her chest. At her silence, he lifted his head. The look in his onyx eyes pleaded with her to let it go. Being a coward, she took the easy way out.

"Very well," she said, as though her insides weren't shaking. "Tell me your plan for this evening."

Thorne outlined his plan for their trip to Kettil's Cauldron in vague sketches and weighty warnings. Holly needed to do exactly as he said, for they were going into "his world" now, and there was no margin for error.

Master of the obvious, was Thorne. And she was to wear a costume of his choosing.

Holly complied without kicking up a fuss because, in part, she was sensible and knew he was correct. But mostly because that niggle of guilt for rejecting him had wormed through her, burrowing under her skin and making her twitchy. So she held her tongue and complied with Thorne's directives.

That did not mean she had to enjoy the experience. Or that she did not want to knock the supercilious expression off his face while he informed her of his plan. But she kept her dignity and went to her rooms to dress.

The gown Thorne had sent up was, in short, atrocious. One could see that right off. It was hard not to, since the bloody thing was made of a garish red silk that all but shouted "look at me" from its plain brown box. Holly might have borne a rich crimson or a deep scarlet. But no, this was a bright, vivid red, the color of new blood.

It fit her well enough—too well in truth. Which was the second part of the problem. Starting with thin strips that clung precariously to her shoulders, the bodice dipped down low, curving like the top of an insipid Valentine's heart over her bosom. Her breasts had no place to hide, but sat like an offering, two little mounds that jiggled with every step she took.

Her face flamed as she looked down at herself. How very horrid. One deep breath and she would likely pop free and disgrace herself. The skirt was of the same flashy red silk with an intricately folded train and bustle, trimmed in black lace. Holly never truly understood the fad for bustles, but she had once overheard that men viewed them as an enticement, the large swaying fabric drawing their eye and making them think all sorts of lurid thoughts about that part of a woman's anatomy. Men, she thought, could go hang.

One man in particular.

Stomping out with as little grace as she could manage, Holly found Thorne waiting for her in the front hall. With each step she took, his smile grew, until it was wide and boyish with unfettered glee, his dour mood apparently forgotten like last season's gun model.

"There she is," he announced in an almost sing-song manner, "my little devil lass, looking like a vision from Hell."

Coming from a demon, she supposed that was a compliment. It did not quell the urge to hit him square on his elegant nose. Unlike her, he was perfectly kitted out as a gentleman ought to be, with a silver-satin waistcoat and expertly cut black frock coat and trousers.

When she stopped before him, his gaze turned obsidian, and he let it travel over her in perusal. "You are transformed, Evernight." His voice was deeper now, rough and tumble. "A visual feast."

Well then, far better than a literal feast. Holly fought the urge to step back and cross her arms over her breasts. "You are enjoying this, aren't you?"

The smug grin stayed put. "Immensely."

When she scowled, he laughed. "Oh, come now. Surely the gown isn't so horrible?"

"'Horrible' doesn't even begin to describe it." She tugged on her gloves—fingerless, black lace ones that women in mourning favored, but when paired with her red gown they felt like a sin. "I look like a doxy. And not even a well-turned-out courtesan, but a cheap, Covent Garden light skirt."

His glee merely intensified. "You'd rather be mistaken for a courtesan?"

"At least they have some air of mystery and aplomb." Holly waved a hand over her figure. "This all but screams, 'three penny upright for hire!'"

His laugh was booming. "Ah, now, Miss Evernight," he slung an arm over her shoulders as though they were old mates, "I'd say you are vastly underrating your appeal." When she moved to pull away, he merely held her more securely against his side. "Nor are you considering that 'cheap doxy' is precisely how we want you to be perceived."

She succeeded in shrugging him off. "*You*, Mr. Thorne. How *you* want me to be perceived. Do not pull me down to your level."

Unfazed, he led her not to the door but in the direction of the small formal parlor to the right of them. "I rather think spending time down on my level would do you a world of good. Come," he said, "before we go, I need to speak to you in private."

He glanced yet again at her bodice and ran the tip of his tongue over one fang.

Holly gave him a repressive glare. "The sight has not changed in the last few moments, Mr. Thorne."

"Which is why I keep looking," he said lightly. "The fit is perfect."

As if he were merely being helpful by pointing that out. Holly refrained from rolling her eyes. Given the carnage he was capable of wreaking, she ought to be afraid of him. Yet she was not. She felt utterly safe with him. "Yes. As to the fit, how did you manage to ascertain my measurements?"

Fangs flashed in the dim light. "My darling, I've held

you in my arms. How could I not—" He broke off with a laugh as she strode away from him. "I was teasing, love. I simply took one of your gowns with me to the dress-maker's." *Obviously*, his tone implied.

"Very clever of you," Holly finally admitted.

"There," he said, looking pleased. "Was it so very hard to give me a compliment?"

When she was stuck in this costume? Yes. She stopped in the middle of the parlor. This room had been deco-rated by her grandmother, who favored delicate furniture gilded and covered in pale pink satin. Cream damask papered the walls, and china shepherdesses stood guard on the pink marble mantle. Her grandfather often said this room gave him gas, for which he'd earn a light cuff on his arm by her annoyed but smiling grandma. It was a known fact that Eamon and Lucinda Evernight were like oil and water when it came to tastes, yet somehow they still managed to get along famously.

Holly stood in her grandmother's domain, suddenly missing her grandparents tremendously, and crossed her arms over her swelling bodice. "Well," she said to Thorne, who looked as out of place in this room as her grandfather did. "What is it you need to say?"

He did not answer, for he was busy gaping around, his tall, black frame a sharp blade amongst the soft colors. "I picked this room because it was the closest," he muttered, "but hells bells, it's like walking into a pink nightmare." He shuddered and turned to her. "I have the sudden fear that I might be attacked by dozens of French poodles."

Holly's lips twitched. "Focus, Mr. Thorne."

"I'm trying. It's simply unnerving." He glared over his shoulder. "Are those putti carved upon the lintels?" His lip curled at the cherubic winged babies smiling back.

She bit the inside of her mouth. "Yes."

"What man in his right mind would allow a room such as this in his domain?" He'd said it to himself more than anything, but Holly bristled all the same.

"A man who understood that this home isn't solely his domain. A man who loved his wife and knew it would please her." When Thorne made a face, a huff of amusement left her. "You scowl at love as though it were a dirty word, Mr. Thorne."

He laughed at that, the sound dark and weary. "A foreign word, more like. I have never been loved. And the only being I have ever felt that tender emotion for was my mother, who treated me as though I were an asp waiting to strike. So no," he said a little sadly, "I do not understand the finer nuances of love. But I know it exists, that it is something to covet and protect. Even if it eludes me."

Something she could not name punched through her belly. It felt quite a bit like guilt, but worse, like loneliness and empathy.

The fine curve of his lips lifted at the corners as he looked her over. "Now who is frowning? You thought I didn't believe in love or wanted anything to do with it, didn't you?"

Holly balked, feeling her cheeks burn. He was absolutely correct; she had thought that.

Slowly Thorne shook his head, as if amused at her reaction, then he caught sight of the room once more, and the thin blade of his nose wrinkled.

With a mutter about losing one's appetite, he strode forward, stopping just before her. He looked her over, and an emotion that appeared to be apprehension clouded his expression. Her heart started to beat faster. She'd never known Thorne to be hesitant.

Thorne licked his lips—a quick, nervous action. "This

place we are going, Kettil's Cauldron, the dodgy bit is that only supernaturals may enter."

"I am a supernatural."

His lips quirked. "In my world, love, elementals are far too human to be considered true supernaturals. They do not possess the potential for true immortality. Thus, they do not signify."

Lovely. She placed her hands upon her hips. "Well then, what do you suggest?" For she knew Thorne would have a plan.

He licked his lips again, his features drawing taut. "You may, however, enter as my esculent."

"Your *what?*" Outrage had her voice rising.

The curved line of his mouth flattened. "It is merely a term. It means—"

"I know what it means, Mr. Thorne." That she was edible. Food.

His lush mouth flattened. "It isn't simply about providing me with blood. An *esculent* is a treasured companion. Like a courtesan," he added, as though this were somehow helpful.

Now she understood the garish gown.

"Well, I am much relieved to hear it," she said with false levity. "Here I was merely worried about giving you blood." Oh, but she'd given herself to him already, hadn't she? For a heady moment, the memory of him pushing into her assailed her. He'd been so hard. Filled her so perfectly. She glared, forcing the memory away.

Thorne's dark brows snapped together. "All right, we know you aren't pleased . . . loath to touch me again, what have you. But it will be an act." He shifted his weight as he stared down at her, and the muscle along his jaw began to twitch.

"Out with it," she said. "Holding the truth in won't ease the telling."

With a sigh, he ran his fingers through his hair. "The dress is not enough. There needs to be physical proof that I'm feeding from you."

She recoiled, her hand flying to her throat.

Thorne's scowl intensified, but his tone grew softer, apologetic. "It is simply an impossibility for an *esculent* to be free of bite marks, love."

Her cold fingers wrapped about the base of her neck. "Then I won't go."

He held her gaze. "You have to. I cannot risk leaving you alone. Certainly not tonight, when I will be out and distracted for hours." When she didn't answer, his lips curled bitterly. "It isn't as though I want to do this." The sneer grew. "I loathe the thought, in truth."

"How kind of you to say." Holly hated that hurt lodged against her breastbone at the confession. Was she so distasteful? What was she thinking? She didn't want to be considered edible, for pity's sake.

Unfortunately, her tender feeling must have shone, for Thorne leaned close, his white hair swinging over the tops of his shoulders. "You don't understand. I'm afraid of losing control. I don't want to hurt you."

It was then she truly took note of his appearance. Perspiration beaded his brow, and his fists were clenched tight.

"You realize your worry makes this worse, not better?" she said through dry lips.

"I know," he snapped. "Shite." Thorne pinched the bridge of his nose. "May we get this over with?"

The sound of Thorne's clockwork heart whirring and ticking away filled the space between them. Then Holly swallowed. "What if you lose control?"

"You are the one person in the world who can control me. Hit me with everything you've got." He stepped close enough that his legs brushed her skirts, and his warmth washed over her. "It won't hurt when I bite you. That I promise."

The trepidation ebbed from his eyes, replaced by a gleam, hungry and intent. "I will only take enough to make it look convincing." Fangs descended, needle sharp and brilliant white against his lips. Holly's heart skipped a beat. His voice grew darker, altered. "I swear it."

She knew he'd try. Determination tightened his shoulders and creased the corners of his eyes. She knew this, and yet her heart raced, her breath growing short and making her breasts heave against the tight confines of her bodice. As if called, his gaze moved to them, and his eyes went black as pitch.

Heat bolted down her center. Dear God, she was in trouble. Because she was going to let him drink from her.

Perhaps she'd spoken the fact aloud or perhaps he'd seen the capitulation in her eyes, for his warm, strong hands wrapped about her bare shoulders, hard enough to feel his intent but not to bruise, and he was drawing her in. Her palms hissed up his silk lapels, as his head dipped.

Gently, he wrapped an arm about her waist then cupped the top of her neck with his free hand, tilting her head to the side to give him access. Holly's pulse leapt wildly. This was too intimate. She wanted...

Warm breath buffeted her skin, and then the brush of his lips. Her sex clenched, her fingers convulsed on his shoulders. When he spoke, it was low, rough, his mouth tickling her sensitized flesh. "I won't harm you. I won't." Then he struck.

She expected a bite. He kissed her neck instead, a soft,

warm press that made her belly flip. With a little noise that might have been a moan, he angled his head further. The tip of his tongue flickered over her skin just before he suckled her, and she let out a strangled cry, clinging to his lapels for fear of falling.

"Easy." It was a murmur, hot and moist against her neck. "Easy. I'm preparing you."

She tried to ease but he licked her again, and everything within her grew tight and achy. Her head fell back, allowing him more. Thorne took a shuddering breath. And then, without warning, needle-sharp fangs broke through her skin with an audible snap. It ought to have hurt. It didn't. She felt…penetrated.

Holly rose up on her toes, pressing her aching breasts against his chest, and his fangs sunk in deeper. And they both moaned. Gods, but she could hear him swallowing her life's blood, feel the possessive grip of his hands upon the small of her back and the base of her skull. Her fingers tangled in his silky hair, bringing him closer.

Each lap of his tongue, each drawing suck, felt as if it were against the swollen bud of her sex. To her horror, her hips undulated, rocking in time to every pull. Thorne gave a soft grunt, an acknowledgment of her need. The world seemed to dip and sway as he pushed her back against the wall, his thick, hard thigh inserting itself between hers. Relief. And not enough.

Holly trembled. More. She needed more. His fingers dug into her hip, his breath coming faster, sucking harder. She grew dizzy. Her head light. Fear tinged the edges of her perception with hot licks.

"Thorne." She could barely speak, barely think. The little carved putti grinned down at her from their perch in the ceiling. "William…"

In a burst of movement, she was free. Thorne staggered back. His eyes were ice blue and wide, so wide, as if he'd seen a ghost. Or perhaps he was one, with his phantom's hair flowing about his face like a shroud.

Holly sank, her knees too weak to hold her upright. And then he was back, drawing her into his arms. "Easy," he said again. A shiver ran through him and into her, and he tucked her head into the crook of his shoulder. "Easy for a moment. One is often overcome when giving blood." As if her intense reaction was something mundane. "It will pass."

He did not sound so sure. Neither was she.

It took all her strength, but she pushed at his chest. "Please," she said, when he wouldn't budge. "I need air."

Only then did he step away, frowning as he did.

Holly leaned against the wall and took deep, cleansing breaths. Silently, he watched her. Not a drop of blood marred his lips. A fastidious eater? She snorted inwardly at her macabre little joke. "I need water." She couldn't phrase it nicely; she was too weak.

With a curt nod, Thorne burst into action, doing as bided. He left the room, and lovely silence surrounded her. She staggered to the settee and gratefully sank into its silken embrace.

No sooner had she settled than Thorne rushed back into the room, glass in hand, his gaze darting about until he found her. When he did, he headed directly over. His expression was so like Nan's when she was of a mind to mother that Holly bristled.

She'd been in danger of reaching an orgasm, still felt the effects in the form of a delicate throbbing between her legs, and he was fretting about, not stimulated in the least.

"Your water." He placed it in her hand as though she were an invalid. Holly bristled further.

"You took too much blood." Without waiting for his answer, Holly took a long gulp of cold water.

Thorne stood straight. His expression as smooth as fine porcelain. "I took the proper amount. It only feels like too much because it was your first time."

She snorted inelegantly. "Virgin no longer."

To her shock, Thorne blushed at that, a swath of rosy color that ran across his high-cut cheekbones.

She lifted her glass in cheers and finished her drink. The empty glass made a little clink when she set it on the table. "Well. Are we off, then?"

"You're well enough?"

Another heavy, sticky-hot wave of embarrassment washed through her. She'd moaned, writhed in his arms. And he might as well have been having a midnight snack.

"I am fine."

Thorne's lips thinned. "When a woman says she's fine, an intelligent man runs in the opposite direction."

"Too bad for you that we are stuck in this together."

Chapter Seventeen

~~~❦~~~

Walking beside Evernight on the way to the Tower Subway, Will felt anxious. An emotion he loathed. He was bringing Evernight into a world of danger. She was brave; he'd give her that. It was a quiet sort of courage that she possessed. Slow and steady. Methodical. And she'd given him her blood. Her blood to warm his body and give him strength.

From the time Will turned thirteen and his voice began to drop, he had imbibed blood to survive. The first taste of it had made him weak at the knees and shiver with pleasure such as he'd never before known. Here, he'd thought in that moment, was the nectar of life.

The taste of blood varied from species to species. In general, however, the flavor did not vary much more than, say, different types of wine. And every sanguis had a blood preference.

Sanguis blood tasted of watered down wine, and rarely satisfied, which was likely due to some innate repulsion for feeding off one's own kind. Lycan had a rather gamey flavor. Raptor's blood was unpalatable, like bitter coals mixed with mud. Shifter blood was rich and full, like the darkest chocolate and the finest wine. And angel's blood was fruity, delectable, and as addicting as opium.

Human blood, however, was Will's favorite because of the variety offered. He was convinced there were a few set types of human blood, for he'd encountered certain but varied base notes over and over again. However, diet and health could alter the richness and flavor within those set types. Wouldn't it figure that Holly Evernight's blood was utterly divine? A cosmic joke upon him.

Her flavor was subtle, elusive in the beginning, before growing savory and exciting the taste buds at the back of his tongue as he swallowed. Hells bells, nothing since his first taste of blood had given him such pleasure as drinking Holly Evernight.

If it were a matter of simply craving her blood, Will would not be the shaking, distracted mess he currently was. It was the act of taking it that had turned his insides to suet and his cock to granite. It was the scent of her surrounding him, it was holding her slim body against his, the long, white column of her neck so willingly tilted to the side so that he could plunge his fangs in deep.

It had taken far too much control—all of it—not to sink down to his knees and lift her skirts, not to run his tongue along her rosy bud before sucking it to plumpness. And when it had swollen in his mouth, when she was crying out for release, he would have punctured her with his fang and drunk her blood to completion.

Will's step stuttered, his cock thickening all over again. Damn it all.

"What is amiss?" Evernight asked immediately. Damn her observant hide.

He had to say something. She'd not let the thing go.

"I hunger." No need to say for what.

Her pert nose wrinkled. "How can you possibly be hungry? You just . . . ate." She blushed.

Will had the sinking suspicion that he'd always hunger for her.

He gave a negligent shrug that belied his inner turmoil. "I've always had a voracious appetite."

Her blush intensified. Now that he had part of her very essence inside of him, his connection to her was that much greater. Her scent bloomed stronger, and he could identify a buttery rich note of sexual agitation that had his metal heart churning fast.

Patience. He needed it in spades. Either she eventually wanted him for the demon he was, or she would not, and he'd find a way to work through the disappointment. Until then, he'd keep his cock in his damned trousers. And wait. Will took a breath and simply let himself look at her.

Against the bleary backdrop of grey sky and coal black buildings, her profile was a pristine alabaster. Next to them loomed the Tower of London, the great old fortress a dark and hulking shape in the shadows. At his other side, white caps peaked on the greenish waters of the Thames. There, rising up like broken teeth in a dark maw, were the beginnings of two great piers that stretched out to a cluster of barges that held mountains of steel framing. Work had begun on the Tower Bridge. Expected to take years, the project promised a bascule bridge that would give testament to Britain's industrial might and glory. Which, in Will's experience, usually meant it would be big and ugly and gaudy, but he'd wait to bear judgment.

The wind shifted as they rounded a bend, and Evernight's scent surrounded him with fragrant coolness. How was he going to play the part of her master and keep his fangs and hands off of her? His cock wouldn't survive the experience. A growl rumbled in his throat.

Mistaking the sound for hunger, Evernight rolled her eyes. "Here." Briskly, she reached into her inner cloak pocket and then handed him a wide, brass flask. "That should hold you."

He didn't want vodka, or whiskey, or any other alcohol it might contain. However, not wanting to reveal the true source of his agitation, he unscrewed the cap. "It's rather large." Roughly the size of his hand—outstretched fingers and all—the container was bulky and unrefined. "And ugly."

Evernight's mouth pursed, her fine nostrils flaring in that way that told him she was about to blow like a geyser. "There's gratitude for you." Her response was clipped, controlled. Of course. No matter how much she wanted to explode, she wouldn't. What would it take? He fancied she'd be magnificent in a temper.

"I was simply making an observation. It wasn't—" Will stopped short, almost choking as the liquid he'd been tipping into his mouth made contact with his tongue. "It's hot!" Rich, gloriously hot chocolate. He glanced at the flask. The brass surface was cool to his touch.

Evernight's smile was smug. A trifle too smug.

"All right," he said before taking another long pull at the chocolate. *Delicious.* "Tell me how you did it. Have you a secret gift for heat conductivity?"

"Hardly." Then she glanced at him, her twilight eyes sparkling. "It is a simple matter of form and function. There is a smaller inner flask made of glass. A vacuum is created between the sealed space between the brass flask and the glass container, creating a void, which prevents the conductivity of the—"

"Yes, all right," he said hastily. "You are a genius. Understood. Acknowledged." He took another drink. And then smiled at her. "A bloody, brilliant genius. I recant any dark thoughts or murderous impulses I've had about you this day."

Imagine; hot beverages that one could carry about without fear of rapid cooling. He wondered if blood could be conveyed in it with the same results. No matter. Chocolate was better than nothing. He drank deeper, loving the feel of warmth filling his gut.

"I suggest," she said in measured tones, "that you resist glutting yourself on the chocolate. It is meant to be sipped, and your devotion to that flask has become unseemly."

Ignoring her, Will imbibed until only a drop remained, illusively hanging upon the rim on the flask. "I've discovered a design flaw." He tucked the empty flask into his pocket. "It is too small. I suggest a larger size."

Unperturbed, Evernight walked along in her even strides. "I have created a picnic-sized insulated flask. But it would not fit in your pocket."

Laughing, Will just resisted slinging his arm over her shoulder. "My clever Miss Evernight, you let me sort out the inconvenience."

Holly had heard of the Tower Subway. Officially opening in 1874, it had operated as a shuttle service, running beneath the Thames. A long, narrow tube fitted with an omnibus-style car was propelled by cables. Holly had been a young girl at the time, but was desperate to have a ride, wanting to see for herself the mechanics of the process. Her father never got around to taking her, and the business proved a failure in the same year.

Now it operated as a pedestrian tunnel, where persons could pay a halfpenny fare and travel between Tower Hill on the north side to Vine Lane on London's south side. Being close to midnight, the subway was closed. That didn't stop Thorne, who simply shoved the tip of his claw into the locked door at the station entrance. The door popped open, and he slipped inside, fiddling about until a dull, yellow light glowed from the space.

Thorne reappeared and held out a hand. "All set."

It soon became apparent that Holly had not properly thought out this particular task. Inside, the air was dank and cold, smelling of river water and earth. Like a grave. She shivered. A gloomy pit of darkness, visible just over the edge of a rail, seemed to drop to endless depths.

They descended a wooden, spiral staircase so narrow and steep that the ends of her skirts batted the back of Thorne's neck. With each step, the risers creaked and groaned, the whole structure vibrating with the movement.

Perspiration broke out on Holly's brow, and she swallowed down the discomfort that swelled up her throat.

"How far does this go down?" Her voice sounded thin and hollow.

"About eighteen feet, I believe." Unlike her, Thorne appeared unaffected. The rotter.

Down, down, down they went, and the air grew heavier, colder, the stench seeping into her skin. A slow, deep shake built within Holly's lower belly, and the back of her neck tensed to near pain. On all sides, rough-hewn walls oozing with condensation closed in on her.

When she thought she might scream, the staircase ended.

"There now," Thorne said happily. "We are in."

In? Holly licked her upper lip, tasting the sweat pebbling there. Gads but they still had to traverse the actual tunnel. It was a horrid space, a little over six feet in diameter, so low, in fact, that Thorne had to remove his hat and duck his head a bit.

The iron tube stretched out towards the blackness with lines of evenly spaced gaslights fading from sight. Holly let Thorne take her hand, and they walked on. She was going to be ill. The pavers rocked beneath their steps, and every noise was amplified, echoing back at them in this eerie bowel beneath the Thames.

She tried not to think of the many meters of earth and water that lay just above her head. Or the crushing weight of it. She was a scientist, for gods' sake. She understood the principles that kept them safe. It did not matter here. Water dripped somewhere. *Drip, drip, drip.* The floor pitched, and the tunnel stretched on.

Her breathing grew strained. Her corset too tight. Blindly, she put out a hand, but the walls curved in and she fell off balance.

"Hold on there, love." Thorne caught her arm and tugged her to him. "Take a moment."

She couldn't see him. Everything grew fuzzy. A loud ringing filled her ears. Her heart would burst. It raced too fast, too hard.

"Evernight?"

Thorne's voice came as if from a great distance.

Warm hands touched her face. "Breathe, love. Breathe." Another soft touch. "It's all right. You're all right."

"I'm not," she blurted out through lips thick with panic.

"I want to go." She pulled at the hand that held her. "Let me go."

"Shh..." The hand upon her arm slipped to her palm. "I've got you. You are safe with me."

Despite her need to flee, she grasped it tightly, crushing the long fingers. "I can't. I can't."

"Ask me a question."

Holly blinked, trying to concentrate. "A question? Why?"

He laughed, a soft husky sound that drew her attention closer to the surface. "Ask me a better question than 'why,' Evernight."

Holly blinked again, and Thorne came into focus. He nudged her chin with his knuckle, reminding her of how Sin used to tease her. "Ask me anything. Come now, a good question will put you to rights."

She took a shaky breath. Her pulse slowed. Damn it, her mind was a blank. Rubbing a trembling hand over her sweating brow, Holly searched for one. Panic threatened.

"Surely there is something that must rouse your curiosity," Thorne persisted. "About tonight, perhaps? Come along, Evernight. Don't let me down now."

Holly scowled up at him. He grinned in that lewd manner of his. It called to mind the last time he'd been lewd. Just before she'd lost her senses and kissed him.

"Your fangs," she blurted out. "They weren't long." Holly cleared her throat. "That is to say, they weren't there when we were...kissing." There were times when she truly hated her curiosity. Such as now. How was this helping? She'd expire of mortification at this rate.

Thorne's eyes narrowed with a catlike smugness. "My dear Miss Evernight, you haven't been replaying that lovely moment in your head, now have you?"

Her face burned. "Forget it."

"Not on your life." He took a few steps, dragging her through the horrid tunnel. "What is the true question you are bumbling into?"

Holly took a deep, bracing breath. "I don't understand how you can . . . Well, they're quite sharp and . . ."

"They retract."

"Really? I did not realize they could fully retract."

He made a sound of amusement through his nose. "See? Ever the scientist. I knew you had it in you. Well, my dear, I shall explain." He stopped and rounded on her. "My fangs can both retract and extend. It is the equivalent of flexing a muscle. Although," he lifted a finger like a professor at a lectern, "when I am angered or threatened, my fangs will extend on their own."

Thorne paused and gave her a small, patronizing smile. "As for the reason why my fangs were retracted when I kissed you—" his voice was low, intimate, and entirely annoying—"they would have shredded both your mouth and mine." His smile grew into something warmer, disturbing. "And we wouldn't want that."

Holly ignored the flush washing over her skin. "No," she said somewhat thickly, "that would have been painful." She glanced away from his too-steady gaze. "So you don't like to . . ." *Cease! Do not ask it!* "Drink blood when you . . ."

She couldn't finish. Mortification had swollen her tongue.

Thorne grinned wide, appearing almost boyish. "Miss Evernight, if I did not know you were ceaselessly analytical, I'd believe you had a naughty mind."

"Shut up." She tromped along, no longer caring about the dank dark, but he caught her hand and held it fast.

"Oh, no, darling, we cannot leave it at that." He laughed lightly, and she jerked her arm, succeeding only in drawing him closer. He was wholly unrepentant. "You asked the question, now let me answer."

"Fine," she snapped, wanting to kill him.

Chortling, the smarmy bastard wrapped an arm around her shoulders and held her against him. Holly was too annoyed to do anything other than glare up at him.

"Do you usually eat while you tup, Miss Evernight?" he murmured.

"Well no..."

"Neither do I." His hand slid up her back, and it felt so lovely that she shivered. "However, I have been known to eat *what* I tup." He glanced up at the low ceiling overhead, his brow furrowed, and nibbled on his bottom lip in contemplation. "Or is that, I tup what I eat?"

"William Thorne," Holly slapped his chest in irritation, "you are an utter beast!"

When he laughed, it was with his whole body, the gleeful sound of it echoing through the darkness, obliterating the gloomy atmosphere. She gaped at him, drawn to the sight of his taut neck muscles, straining with his laughter. He grinned down at her, appearing more a young, handsome man than an outright fiend.

"I am," he admitted happily. "I can't help it, Holly."

His gaze darted over her face, and the tension in his body shifted to something darker, languid, as both of them realized he held her still. His smile slipped, his lids lowering as he looked at her mouth. "I just can't help myself around you." It was a husky whisper in the silence.

Somehow, she was closer, her lips feeling fuller, parting for him. God help her, but if he kissed her, she'd let him. Here in the dark, it wouldn't really count, would it?

Thorne dipped his head. The scuff of a shoe echoed loudly in the tunnel, and Thorne snapped to attention, rounding and putting himself in front of Holly.

Like an apparition, the little man moved out of the shadows and into the light. They watched him shuffle closer. Dressed in a grimy and billowing sack suit that made it appear as though he'd shrunken within it, he was a boney thing, small and hunched. Tufts of white hair stuck out from beneath a battered bowler of an indeterminate color that sat precariously on top of his large ears.

And though thoughts of trolls who lived under bridges to collect their dues ran riot through Holly's head, Thorne seemed to relax and slapped his hat back on his head as he stood tall. The man came to a stop before them and blinked up at Thorne with wide eyes that glowed milk-white in the weak electric lights.

"Invitation?" came a voice like rust, followed by a long wheeze through his beak of a nose.

"Matilda gives her salutations," Thorne replied amiably.

The little man grunted. Still mumbling, he patted about his suit as though looking for something. He found it in his jacket pocket and pulled out a thick, silver disk. With a flick of his wrist and a little click, the disk unfolded to form a silver cup, composed of three collapsible rings.

The man cocked his head to the side as he held the cup out to Thorne. "Dues."

Far from being lost in this odd interplay, Thorne stretched out his arm, exposing the delicate blue veins of his wrist. As with all demons, his nails could shift into claws with a thought. He grew one on his index finger and promptly speared his extended wrist.

Holly winced, but Thorne did not, as thick, deep crimson blood poured from his vein into the cup. After a moment, Thorne pressed a thumb over the wound and held it, as the little man lifted the cup to his dry lips and drank down Thorne's blood.

Finished with his gruesome drink, the man licked the blood off his lips and grunted again. "Right. House rules apply." He glanced at Holly, and she fought a shiver as that milky gaze travelled over her. It settled on her neck, where the puncture wounds from Thorne's fangs seemed to pulse. "Esculents," the man added with a sneer, "are the responsibility of their master."

Thorne touched the brim of his hat in acknowledgment, earning him yet another grunt. The man said no more but turned. "This way."

"What other way would there be," Holly murmured close to Thorne's clean-shaven cheek. "It only goes but one direction."

Thorne's lips twitched. "Quiet. You'll upset Freddie."

"His name is Freddie?" How positively cheerful.

Though he fought a smile, Thorne shushed her again.

"All right," she murmured. "What was the point of the blood drinking?"

"It's a blood vow of sorts. In giving mine, I am promising not to harm Kettil or attack any of his workers during the duration of the fights." He shrugged. "It's a simple matter of security."

That this Kettil felt the need for safety measures did not ease Holly's anxiety. They followed Freddie further into the bowels of the tunnel. Just when Holly thought she might scream with the need to get out of the subterranean hell, Freddie stopped at a spot and pushed at what seemed to be just another wall panel.

A door slid open, bringing with it the sounds of laughter, shouts, and cursing.

Thorne smiled at her. "Welcome to Kettil's Cauldron, love."

Chapter Eighteen

At first sight, Kettil's Cauldron was nothing more than
yet another dreary tunnel, save for the bright light that
glowed at the end of it. Holly headed towards that light,
holding Thorne's hand as if it were an anchor.

The scent of brimstone and blood thickened the air.
Demons. Holly would soon be surrounded by them.
Exposed. She wanted to turn and run. But she could
not. One did not let oneself be fed from like a liquid
buffet just to flee at the first sign of danger.

It took all of her considerable restraint to refrain from
touching the spots where Thorne's teeth had sunk in deep.
Those two little points throbbed in time with the beat of
her heart. Memories of Thorne's mouth upon her neck,
his tongue sliding over her with little flicks, heightened
her awareness. Her entire body was sensitized, her skin
too thin and her flesh swollen and heavy. Beneath her fine
cashmere cloak, the satin lining slipped and slid over the
exposed tops of her breasts, and she repressed a shudder
of tactile pleasure. As if Thorne felt her response—which

likely he did, the rotter—he tightened his grip on her hand and tugged her closer to his side.

"Touch it," he whispered thickly against her temple. Her nipples peaked at the command. "Caress my mark like you crave another bite." His tongue flickered over her skin, a crude lick that had her step bobbling.

Holly wrenched her head away as much as she could without drawing notice, and his dark chuckle was a warm breath over her now damp skin. "They'll expect these things, love. Expect you to be in my total thrall."

Heat suffused her, and she could not bear to meet his eyes, but she managed a short nod.

"Touch it now," he murmured, impatient, demanding.

Unable to resist, Holly pressed two fingers against that throbbing spot. A bolt of luscious, aching pleasure and heat shot down her center. She nearly moaned.

Thorne's grip became a crushing thing. His breath rough and urgent.

Wild thoughts swam in her head, of Thorne pressing her back against the damp stones with the force of his hard body, and simply *taking*.

Perhaps Thorne felt similarly, for he mumbled something under his breath and doggedly kept them moving forward, their hips touching, their cloaks tangling with each step they took down the miserable corridor.

The path took a sharp turn to the left, and the space grew close, the air hot. Sounds of shouting and laughter echoed. Thorne let her hand go in favor of slipping his beneath her cloak to curve around her waist. The sharp scent of fresh blood mingled with that of stale sweat. Holly's throat closed on a wave of disgust. It was nothing compared to the sight that greeted her.

The space opened up into a massive underground arena

awash with torchlight and writhing with hundreds of demons. Sweat glistened on skin, teeth flashed on a grin or feral grimace. Most maintained their human appearance, but plenty of beings with grey skin and pointed ears were throughout the crowd. Attention centered on a small oval fighting pit at the center of the room. There, what appeared to be a female raptor fought with fang and claw against a tall, pale female sanguis whose black hair fell to her thighs in a tight cue.

"Mistake that," Thorne said in Holly's ear, his voice now smooth and normal. He nodded towards the sanguis female. "Keeping her hair long. Easy target."

No sooner had the words left his mouth than the raptor flipped over the sanguis to land on steady feet just behind her. In a blink, the raptor grabbed that hanging strip of hair and spun the poor sanguis through the air, smashing her down onto the high iron railing that ringed the pit. Impaled, the sanguis screamed.

Holly gagged and did not notice Thorne opening her cloak until the damp air hit her skin. She frowned at him as he folded the edges back over her shoulders, exposing her further. He gave her a slight, reproving look. Right. She was his ornament. Grinding her teeth together, she straightened her spine and thrust her breasts forward. Thorne's hitched breath and flared nostrils were only slightly gratifying. The instant attention she garnered from the males around her, however, had her skin crawling.

Being exposed set her nerves on edge. Noises sounded overloud to her ears, and despite Thorne's earlier cheek, she wanted to cling to his arm like a limpet.

Tucking her hand in the crook of his arm, Thorne headed off, his walk peacock proud, his top hat tilted at a jaunty angle as if to say, "why yes, I am a pretty piece, and top of the mornin' to ya for noticing!"

Though she was loath to admit it, her Irish blood appreciated his showmanship.

The crowd seemed to part for him. Some nodded at Thorne, giving a quick hello or a simple acknowledgment of him; others slid their gazes away as if they were fearful. But all seemed to know him. This was his world, and he belonged. Unequivocally. And because he did, not a soul seemed to question her presence here. They did, however, look her over. Until she felt covered in a sticky film of attention.

Thorne made his way towards a box seat that overlooked the fighting ring at dead center. The box was bigger than those around it and swathed in black silk. Though there were about ten seats within the box, one held an obvious place of honor. Like a king holding court, there a man sat on a gilded, red velvet chair. He was rather large on all counts. And scruffy, for all the airs he put on. A battered stovepipe hat sat on greasy black hair that reached his wide shoulders, and a black-and-white checked waistcoat stretched over his well-fed gut.

Perched as he was, all long-limbed and fat of belly, he reminded her of a great spider, waiting to draw innocent and guilty alike into his great web. He watched them approach, his beady eyes narrowing, and he licked his lips. Holly repressed the urge to draw her cloak back together.

Two overly large bruisers guarded the entrance, but they didn't so much as blink when Thorne moved past them.

"Will Thorne," the man said as they entered his box. "It has been a while, me boy."

"Well you know, Kettil," replied Thorne with his easy smile, "one cannot stay away from your entertainments forever."

Kettil glanced at the two men who were lounging in the seats next to his. That was all it took from them to depart with haste. As soon as they did, Kettil gestured broadly to the vacated chairs. "Join me."

Though Thorne behaved the perfect gentleman, handling her into her seat, he put himself between Holly and Kettil. A move not lost on the man, for he made a small sound of amusement.

"Wouldn't mind a taste o'that. That lass is the jammiest bit of jam I've seen in an age, to be sure." He leaned in, his fat nostrils round and porcine as he inhaled. "She smells off, though. A bit like metal and oil."

Thorne crossed one of his long legs over the other, a seemingly careless shift of position, but one that blocked Holly slightly from view. "She's an acquired taste."

Of all the nerve!

Kettil, however, grinned, exposing the needle sharp fangs of a sanguis. Holly had never seen such a plumped-up demon. The unfortunate image of a tick bloated on blood came to mind, and she fought another urge to gag. Down in the ring, they were hauling off what remained of the female sanguis demon. The crowd, now denied its bout, turned to each other, chatting, shouting, calling in bets. A fug of blue smoke hung in the air, crackling about the hum of electric lights.

"Let me have a taste and find out then," Kettil was saying.

Charming.

Thorne's smile was bland. "Now you know I do not like to share my esculents."

Kettil, not so easily dissuaded, leaned forward, his beady eyes on Holly's breasts. "Always thought that was uncharitable of you, Thorne. Not sharing."

Thorne gave an exaggerated sigh as he pulled a slender cigarillo and a cache of matches from his inner pocket. "Ah, well, you know how it is." With the flick of a wrist, he lit the match, and fire flared right in Kettil's line of sight, depriving him yet again of staring at Holly. "A taste here, a taste there, and suddenly there's nothing left for me."

Thorne dropped the match and drew on his cigarette before blowing a cloud of smoke into the air between him and Kettil.

The smoke did not seem to bother Kettil. No, he simply inhaled, visibly drawing it into his wide nostrils. Still staring at Holly, he licked his thick lips. "Perhaps you ought to rethink that. Especially with a morsel such as this. Put me in a charitable mood like."

As if he anticipated Holly's need to strike out, Thorne set his hand over hers and pressed it into his thigh. "Have I brought the Kellermen twins round before?" he asked Kettil idly.

Twins? Holly refused to react. Thorne eased his thumb under her hand and ran it in a slow circle around her palm.

"You have not," Kettil said, still sounding sullen.

"Ah, gods, but they are a pair. Plump with sweet blood." Thorne sighed expansively. "They have the most exquisitely sensitive breasts and thighs."

Holly twitched. Vile pigs. The both of them. She told Thorne as much by flicking his thumb away from her palm. But his thumb merely returned and pressed hard against the center of her palm. *Hold your fire,* the gesture seemed to say.

For only so long, she squeezed back.

"That so." Interest flickered in Kettil's beady eyes.

"Quite." Thorne flashed his fangs. "They love being suckled."

A snort of irritation left Holly's lips before she could stop herself. The blunt tip of Thorne's thumb tapped her. *Now, now, love. I'm working here.*

Holly dug a nail into the fleshy pad at the base of his thumb. *End this nonsense now, or I will.*

He gave her hand a quick, minute squeeze. *Fine.*

"I'll bring them round next visit," he assured Kettil. "As for now, I have something else that ought to interest you." Thorne pulled a slim box from his outer pocket.

She recognized that box. Why, that ruddy, sticky-fingered bastard. Holly stiffened in outrage; Thorne's warning squeeze a distant thing in the face of it. But she held her tongue as Kettil grabbed the box and opened it with greedy haste.

"Spectacles?" Kettil blinked in confusion. "What need do I have for a bleedin' set o'glass peepers? And right thick ones at that."

As if he deserved to even look upon her exquisitely wrought creation.

"Ah-ah." Thorne lifted a finger. "You have yet to try them on."

Inwardly, Holly howled when Kettil's grubby fingers smudged the finely polished glass as he fumbled to put them on. As soon as they were on, he gave a start of surprise. His mouth hung open as he peered about the room.

"Why, every man is all aflame!"

Holly grumbled. Thorne glared at her while answering in a smooth voice. "It is the spirit glow of demons. The spectacles make it visible. Quite handy for telling friend from foe."

"Quite so, laddie."

As Kettil gaped about like a lack-witted ape, Thorne leaned in close to her until his breath tickled her neck. "Nex stole an earlier model from the SOS last year. I find these a vast improvement, love."

Holly kept her expression serene as she pinched his side hard. Unfortunately, he was too lean to get a good grasp of any flesh. Even so, he gave a little grunt and wisely moved away.

"So, then," Kettil said as he took off the spectrometers, "what will this cost me?"

Thorne pulled a small paper from his pocket of delights and handed it to him.

There, drawn with great skill, was a rendering of the dagger that the assassin had dropped and of the tattoo that graced Thorne's forearm.

Upon seeing the blade, Kettil's expression froze for one icy moment, and it was a look of terror. Then he blinked it away and hastily shoved the paper back at Thorne. "'Twill take more than this for that sort of tell."

Thorne did not appear surprised by the news. "Price?"

Kettil's eyes went to the ring. "A bout. And the spectacles."

Thorne gave a negligent shrug that had his hair sliding like white satin over his shoulders. "Very well."

He moved to rise, when Kettil shook his head. "'Fraid it's ladies night." His oily gaze slithered over to Holly.

Thorne growled—a low sort of rumble a dog would give when guarding his food. "I'll come back another night."

"Don't think so, mate." Kettil crossed his arms over his

ample belly. "You know the rules. Favors only granted at the time of request."

Seemed like a made-up rule to Holly, but Thorne's mouth tightened so perhaps it wasn't.

"Then we leave." Thorne stood, his chair scraping against the slat-board floor.

Leave? He motioned for Holly to rise, but she stayed put. She'd let him drink her blood. She'd trawled down the bloody tunnel to Hell for this. And he was going to leave? When they could have the information they needed tonight?

"Hold on." Kettil raised a placating hand. "You need not be so hasty. Your female can fight."

"Absolutely not," snarled Thorne.

Holly stood then, and Thorne grabbed her elbow, ready to usher her out. She held firm and then threw herself into the thick. "I'll do it."

"You will not," shouted Thorne, just as Kettil slapped a hand on his thigh and cried, "Deal."

He appeared far too pleased. Thorne, on the other hand, bared his full fangs and hissed. "No!"

Holly met his glower without flinching. "You do not get to decide."

"Oh, yes I do." He wrenched her closer. "You are my esculent. *Mine.*"

She leaned around him. "When do I fight?" she asked a beaming Kettil.

Thorne uttered a ribald curse. "No, no, no." With each 'no' Thorne shook her arm. "You are not fighting."

"Do stop," Holly said, pulling free. "You're going to give me a migraine. Besides, I need my strength."

Thorne let go and rammed a hand through his hair instead, knocking his top hat off in the process. He appeared ready to scream.

Kettil rose. "Go to the back. Harlan will get you sorted."

When Thorne rounded on Kettil with a snarl, he tutted. "Now, Thorne, you know the rules. You can't be hurting me here. And the lady has taken up me offer. No backing out of it now without bloodshed." His expression turned ruthless. "And not just yours, either."

Calmly, Holly pulled Thorne to the side of the box. Around wild tangles of his long hair, his expression was mulish, his black eyes turning silver. "You cannot go into that ring and fight, Holly," he said without preamble. "You will *die!*"

"Well, that's a fine thing to say," she snapped back. "How about a little support?"

He leaned closer, until they were nose to nose, and his hair hid them from view. "In case it has slipped your notice, you are human. Who," he added when she meant to speak, "would not leave her house until a few days ago!"

She did not blink. "I am not merely human. I am SOS."

"You are an inventor for the SOS, not a regulator. And your contraptions won't save you in the ring. You won't be allowed any mechanical devices for defense."

"I am trained in combat. Every SOS member is." Before she'd hidden herself away, she'd trained with Mary, the both of them quite enjoying the exercise. True, her skills might be a little rusty. But she was hardly a civilian. "And I won't need any devices."

She could hear Thorne's teeth grinding. "Holly..."

The sound of her given name on his lips, the pleading tone of it, softened her response. "We need this information, do we not?" She did not want to fight. Only a mad woman would. But she was no coward either.

"We'll find it another way."

"How?" She searched his face and saw the frustration there. She empathized. As if it could hide the truth, he avoided her gaze.

"I don't know," he finally ground out.

Holly took a deep breath then nodded. "Then there is nothing for it. I will fight. And we will get the information we need." Because *they* were a *we*. Somehow, they'd become so the very moment Amaros had wheeled Will Thorne into her laboratory and given him her heart.

Helplessness was an emotion Will detested. He'd only felt it a few times, and each had been during the worst moments of his life. Now it gripped him again. His teeth snapped together, his fangs growing so long they pressed over his bottom lip.

Harlan led them into a back room. "Pick two weapons on the table. Two only. You've twenty minutes 'afore the next bout." He stopped as if remembering some pertinent information. "You'll be fighting a raptor."

Will's innards pitched. A sodding raptor? Oh, fuck no.

Evernight, so very small before the hulking guard, nodded briskly, then moved to a quiet corner as if seeking some privacy.

Will followed. "You cannot do this," he growled, his words garbled by fangs and fear. How many times must he repeat this before she heeded, the blasted woman?

Evernight did not look up from her task. "Your lack of confidence in me is certainly not helping with morale." She reached under her voluminous skirts and began to wriggle about, distracting him with the amount of shapely leg she revealed.

His attention stayed on her searching hand. What on this dark, hateful earth? Gritting his teeth, he tried not to shout. "You are human." It was a shout anyway, and it came out far too fearful.

The cage of her bustle rattled to the floor, deflating her skirts. "I am aware."

"And yet you intend to fight a raptor!" Had she lost all sense? A raptor would tear her open in a heartbeat.

Evernight drew a switchblade from her reticule and flicked it open. The blade was shockingly large and lethal. "Must we go over this yet again? It is becoming tedious."

"When you insist on ignoring common sense, then yes," he said, torn between wanting to strangle her and watching as she proceeded to hack away at her skirts, cutting them off at her knees.

Red satin pooled at her feet. Hells bells but her legs were lovely. He wanted to memorize the exact shape of them with his tongue.

"I am not merely a human, Thorne. I am an elemental. Do not underestimate me."

"An elemental who cannot heal as a demon can. Satan's balls, woman, one good slice of a raptor's claws and you'll be dead!" Bile rushed up his throat as he said the words, and he swallowed with difficulty.

Dainty as a society miss, she stepped out of the remnants of her ruined gown. Only then did she deign to look his way. "You know as well as I that we cannot back out now. So cease berating me and give me your waistcoat."

His mouth hung open for a moment. Insufferable woman. He hated that she was in the right. Hated that this might very well be the last moment he saw her whole and unharmed. Since he could not give into that particular fear, he addressed the next most pressing question. "My waistcoat? Why?" He was already shrugging off his jacket and going at his buttons.

Evernight pulled a few hairpins out of her coiffure and re-secured them, tucking in wayward inky strands until every hair was severely secured. At least she'd taken note of what a good target free-hanging hair made.

"I do not want to worry about my bosom popping free on top of everything else."

In the act of handing her his waistcoat, he nearly dropped it. His fist clenched. "Good point," was all he got out, for now he had that image in his head to contend with as well, thank you, Miss Evernight.

She took it from him and finished dressing with brusque efficiency.

Hell, she ought to look ridiculous, with her hacked-off skirts hanging limply around her knees, exposing her black-striped silk stockings and little boots, and wearing a man's waistcoat. The garment did not fit her perfectly. It hung too loose at her waist and strained over her breasts, but it covered the sweet swells of them admirably.

Yes, she ought to look a fright. Instead she stirred his blood. With the determined tilt of her head, her steeled spine, she was a warrior. And she was a human.

"Right, then," she said crisply. "Weapons."

Weary, Will leaned against the wall and simply watched her. His heart was a leaden weight against his ribs as she marched over to the table that held a selection of gruesome weaponry.

Lips pursed as if she were shopping at Harrods, Evernight scanned the selection. She picked up a pair of metal gauntlets first. They were huge, meant for a large man, and crafted of steel. He was about to protest the inane choice when she slipped them on.

As if alive, the metal suddenly undulated, gliding over her hands and forearms, shrinking and stretching, fitting itself to her shape. When the gauntlets had reached her upper arms, they suddenly shimmered and then hardened once more. A perfect fit.

Evernight peered at him from over her slim shoulder, and a quiet smile danced around her lips. Then she made a fist. Instantly four blades shot out from her knuckles. Claws.

Will thought he might be in love.

"And your next choice?" His voice was dry, rough as sand. She only had one more. Two weapons. Two bloody weapons to defend herself against an immortal. The room seemed to sway.

Evernight's thin, pale hand hovered over the rows of battle axes, maces, swords, and blades. She stopped above a Scottish broadsword that had to be over four feet long and weighed at least five pounds. She hefted it high, her slim arms straining against the weight. Then glanced at him.

Will raised one brow. *Truly?*

Her black brow lifted in turn. *Truly.*

And then, still watching him, she took hold of the sword and snapped it in half as if it was nothing more than a dry twig. Like the gauntlets, the halves appeared to come alive. Writhing like snakes, they coiled around her arms and settled in. With that done, she turned and faced the thug looming at the door. "I'm ready."

She was going. Leaving him. Will stirred out of his self-imposed pout and leapt forward, catching her by the shoulders. She gaped up at him as he spun her around.

"What now?" Her tone was short.

He couldn't speak. Emotion, a strange mix of panic and something odd that squeezed his chest with icy hands, rooted him to the spot. He could only grip her fragile shoulders far too tightly and stare. Even in the dank light, her skin was luminous, the bones beneath it delicately wrought and fine. Wide eyes of the deepest blue gazed up at him expectantly. And he could not say a bloody thing.

His chest heaved, his fingers turning cold. Now was not the time to lose his sanity. But he could not stave off the dark tendrils of dread that bled into his sight.

"Thorne." Her voice came at him as though through thick cotton. "I have to go now."

Go. She had to go.

He took a shuddering breath. Calm. Be calm. Don't show fear. Slowly the buzzing in his ears quieted, and his vision cleared. Evernight was still before him. So lovely. Her lips were petal pink. She smelled of mechanical things and fresh blood and the essence of her. A scent that would never be replicated. Were it gone, it would stay gone.

"This fight has to end before it begins," he barked out. "Make every hit count."

"Yes, I know."

"Raptors love blood almost as much as sanguis do. Expect her to make you bleed." Hell. Fucking Hell. "She'll want to draw the fight out. You," he gave her an abortive shake, "don't."

"I know, Thorne." Her exasperation was clear.

His mouth worked; words caught in his throat. She was in danger because of him, and he had to let her go. So he said the only thing he could think of.

"Don't die."

Chapter Nineteen

❧❧❧

Don't die. What sort of help would that drivel be to Evernight, Will thought as he slumped in his seat next to the bastard Kettil. *Jolly good, go and state the bloody obvious, mate.* His guts churned, and he suppressed a growl.

Around him the crowd was chanting, baying for blood. Stomping feet had the floors bouncing.

His fault, all his fault.

"Ah, tops. Just tops!" Grinning around his pipe, Kettil sat back and rubbed his belly in contentment. "Never had an elemental in the ring. Novelty of it should be amusing. Just hope your lass holds out long enough for a good show."

It took all that Will had not to launch himself out of the chair and tear Kettil's head from his neck. His claws bit into his palms. "If she dies," he said to him, "you will be next."

Kettil's beady eyes widened. Will did not blink. He'd make it hurt, and then hunt down everyone who had watched.

The crowd roared. Holly and the female raptor had stepped into the ring. Will sat up straight. Even though his was the finest seat in the room and center stage, he craned forward.

Gods, but she appeared so small. She looked a mere girl with her skirts hanging about her knees and her slim shoulders, squared and tense. The raptor before her was a large bitch, as far as raptors went. Nearly a foot taller than Evernight, the raptor hadn't bothered with a human appearance but kept her dark grey skin and yellow eyes. Thick fangs, designed to tear flesh, peaked out from her black lips as she smiled. She carried no weapons. She didn't need to. Fangs, claws, and superior strength were on her side.

"What sweet treat is this?" the raptor shouted to the crowd, and they cheered with glee.

"That is Calli," Kettil murmured. Beads of sweat now dotted his brow, and he mopped at them with a grimy handkerchief. "She, ah, likes to employ a bit of showmanship."

Calli lifted her arms wide, riling up the crowd. "Shall I gobble her up in one bite?"

Half the crowd swelled with approval.

"Or take small tastes and enjoy her?"

The room vibrated with raucous agreement, and the rank scent of sweat and violence thickened the air.

Fucking hell. Will fairly twitched. He could not stop *this*.

"Look at the little elemental," Calli went on, laughing. "Wearing naught but gauntlets!" She turned her yellow eyes upon Holly. "Shall you slap me with one when I forget my manners, human?"

Holly merely stood watching the bitch. Deep within

himself, Will started to shake, metal working outward from his heart, turning everything ice cold. He sucked down a breath, fighting against the inevitable tide. He had to witness this. He owed her that much.

The chair beside him creaked as Kettil stood and, in a booming voice, spoke. "All right, ladies and gents," he said, though the crowd wasn't anything of the sort, "you know the rules. Fight dirty, double points for first blood, five minutes maximum..."

Five minutes. She merely needed to remain undamaged for five minutes. And it would be over. A bloody eternity.

Kettil's fangs flashed. "But sudden death wins!"

"What!" Will lurched from his seat, his mind screaming *no!* even as the crowd roared in anticipation. He made to swipe at Kettil's fat belly, but the blood voucher kicked in and invisible hands seemed to slam into his chest. He crashed back into his seat, his throat swollen shut, keeping him from shouting his protest.

Kettil glanced his way. "You know very well you can't kill me."

He'd see about that.

In the pit, the raptor crouched, grinning wide and extending her yellowed claws. Holly widened her stance and kept her eyes upon her opponent.

Holly. Terror arced through Will as the bell rang.

Instantly, Calli leapt, her claws swinging down in a vicious strike. Holly lifted her arm at a 45-degree angle, protecting her face, and the claws scraped along her metal gauntlet in a shower of sparks.

Before the raptor could move, Holly kicked out, connecting with a knee. Bone crunched. Calli screeched as her leg bent back at an unnatural angle.

Like the rest of the crowd, Will surged to his feet, his fists clenched at his sides as he shouted an incoherent cry.

Holly's body was a blur of red and black as she spun round and caught Calli's jaw with her booted heel. The raptor slammed to the dusty boards.

"Ho!" Kettil laughed.

"Elemental, Elemental," the crowd chanted.

As for Will, he wanted to sob, shout, laugh, strangle, or kiss Holly senseless. He gripped the rough railing of the box tight enough to splinter the wood.

Holly stepped back, alert and ready as a snarling Calli jumped up, graceless and hobbled in one leg. Black blood trickled from her lips. "Bitch!" Spittle flew. "I'll rip your intestines out and wear them as a necklace!"

Without warning, her tongue lashed out like a long, black whip akin to a frog's. It caught Holly around the ankles and tugged. Holly fell back, bashing into the floor, her palms slapping against the boards.

Will's metal heart lodged in his throat; the railing came off in his hand.

Before Holly could protect herself, Calli yanked her forward, slashing out with her claws. But at the same instant, Holly gave a war cry, sitting upright with the force of it. Silver whips of liquid metal shot out from her gauntlets. With a snap of her wrists, the whips hissed through the air, catching Calli on either side of her neck.

The raptor's eyes went wide, her mouth opening on a cry that never came for, at the last moment, the whips solidified into razor sharp swords that cleaved through her neck as though it were soft pudding.

The room froze, every breath held as the raptor swayed on her feet. And then, without a sound, the body toppled to one side and the head landed with a dull thud on the other. Black blood sprayed the crowd, and the room erupted into pandemonium.

She'd done it. She'd won. Holly's heart pounded so hard and fast that she barely heard the roar of the crowd, the shouts for her. At her feet, the raptor's body began to shrivel, black blood spreading in an ever-widening pool. The raptor's head lay at an angle, mouth agape, eyes wide and blank.

Chest heaving, Holly retracted the metal swords back into the gauntlets and clamored to her feet. The ground seemed to sway. Cold sweat ran down her back, and black raptor blood dripped from the ends of her skirt. From the corner of her eye, a blurred form of a figure hurtled towards her. She tensed, half raising her arms, but stopped when she recognized Thorne's familiar face.

He didn't give her a chance to say a word, but snatched her up and wrapped her so tightly in his arms that her ribs creaked. Holly didn't protest. For the first time in what seemed like hours, she felt safe. Unashamed, she burrowed into him, holding onto his lean waist, her nose lost in the sweat-damp folds of his linen shirt. He smelled wonderful. Dark heat and safe harbors.

She'd never been so afraid in her life as she'd been when facing that raptor. One wrong move and she would have died. It had taken all she had not to break down, but to focus, to formulate a plan: take the raptor out immediately, don't get hit. Now that it was done and over, she found she could barely stand.

That was all right. Thorne would hold her up now.

"My girl," he whispered into her hair. "My girl." Kisses to her head punctuated his words. "So very well done. My girl."

A shudder rent through her at the thought of what she'd just done, and he held her tighter. They stood as one, a quiet cocoon in the midst of a shouting crowd. And for once, Holly soaked up Thorne's power, letting it bolster her.

When she could stand without trembling, she eased back. He protested only for a moment, then loosened his grip. Their gazes clashed, and for one bright instant, they grinned at each other like mad fools. Excitement and victory fizzed through her like champagne.

"I told you I had the situation under control." Her voice was breathless, buoyant.

Thorne barked out a laugh, but his lower lip wobbled before he grinned down at her. "I may have lost a decade of my life watching you, but yes, you managed that quite nicely, love."

Quick as a cat, he slung his arm about her shoulders and hauled her back to his side. His lips pressed hard against her crown, and his warm breath gusted through her hair. "But you are never doing that again."

She wasn't going to argue.

Nor did she get a chance. Kettil waddled up, beaming. "Well now, lass, you certainly took the egg! 'Course, ye lost me my best fighter."

Thorne growled, his fangs elongating with an audible snap. Kettil held up a placating hand and chuckled. "Hold your fire. It was worth it. Best bout we've had in ages." He glanced at Holly. "Would have been better if it had gone on a bit longer, but the upset was unparalleled."

"The contact," Thorne bit out.

Kettil paled. "Alamut."

The name did something to Thorne. He flinched, recoiling as if slapped. Then his expression went blank.

All but his eyes. They darted about as if seeing some other time and place. Silently, his lips formed the word again as if saying a prayer. And then he broke out of the trance.

Thorne lashed out, grabbing Kettil by the neck then wrenching him close. Since Holly was still securely held by Thorne's other hand, she was treated to Kettil's stench as he floundered about, trying to break free. Thorne gave him a rough shake. "Blood vows have passed," Thorne snarled. "You cross me on this and your stones are the first thing I rip off."

"It's square," Kettil insisted on a choked breath. "I swear it."

Thorne let him go so abruptly that Kettil tottered. Thorne wheeled Holly around and marched them out of the arena. The crowd parted for them like the proverbial Red Sea, and quickly, for Thorne's stride was brisk and unwavering.

Though it was a struggle, Holly matched his pace. Her heart was still racing, the knowledge that she'd fought a supernatural and lived coursing through her with increasing strength. For nearly a year, she'd been terrified of every shadow, every sudden noise that occurred outside of her purview. That fear, the helpless feeling, started to dissipate like London fog against a hot sun. Her cheeks grew warm.

"All in all, a productive day's work," Thorne said as they entered the long, narrow corridor that led the way out. As if he'd never been afraid. As if she'd never been in danger. As if he'd bloody planned the entire thing.

Ah, yes, that reminded her. Her spectrometers. The ones currently in that rat Kettil's possession. Holly stopped short, grabbed hold of Thorne's lapels, and hauled him close, setting him off balance. They both stumbled back, her shoulders meeting the cold wall of the tunnel. "Touch another one of my inventions without my express permission again, Mr. Thorne, and I'll cut off your cods and feed them to the dogs."

Heat flared in his eyes as his lips curled into a smile. Irritating man. He leaned into her, caging her smaller frame by bracing his arms against the wall on either side of her head. He watched her, not at all cowed but as if he'd soon gobble her up for his dinner. "We don't own dogs, love."

She gave him a little shake, wanting to push him away, yet somehow bringing those smiling lips closer. "I'll bloody purchase some then." She let him go before she did something irrational, like kiss him.

It was only when they'd climbed into a coach, and the last vestiges of the agitated energy gained from the fight had waned, that she felt the pain and the blood trickling down her side.

Chapter Twenty

Report." Adam cut into the thick slab of steak in front of him. Juice pooled around the tines of his fork.

"Mab is in London," Lucien Stone, his right-hand man and leader of the London GIM answered. Dressed as a man out of the eighteenth century, with a shimmering blue satin frock coat and lime green waistcoat and britches, he appeared more ghost than ghost in the machine.

"Tell me something that I do not know, Lucien," Adam said before taking a bite of beef. Delicious. "I gather she's searching all and sundry for me?"

Lucien's gaze flicked to Eliza May and then away. "Not for you." Predictably, Eliza stirred from her slump against the wall on which she'd been leaning.

Adam and Lucien sat, tucked in a corner of a packed pub, while Eliza stood as far away from them as the chain would permit. Around them, humans supped and caroused with abandon. Which was really quite perfect. Adam remembered being human, and though centuries had passed, he had frequented similar pubs.

"She can try to find her," Adam said, "but she shall fail." Adam had a natural ability to cloak himself from any form of supernatural. He only allowed the humans to see him now. And the GIM who served him.

"*Mon commandant*"—Lucien leaned in, and the rings on his fingers glinted in the gaslight—"will you not tell me why the *fille* is so important as to tangle with Mab?"

Adam paused, his fork halfway to his mouth. Lucien's expression was not only imploring, it was worried. Hell.

"You believe that is what this is about? That Mab simply wants her kin returned?" Adam knew better. Mab could not care less about Eliza May. She was a pawn to Mab, nothing more.

Eliza took a step closer to them. Though she made not a sound, Adam could feel her do it. Damn, she ought not to be listening to this.

"I know fae too well to believe anything they do is altruistic." Lucien's jade green eyes glowed with unearthly GIM light. "However, I cannot know what to believe until you tell me the truth."

Adam set his fork down, his meal now leaden in his stomach. "As much as it pains me, my old friend, there are things in which I cannot confide. To anyone." Bloody, fucking curses.

Lucien stared at him for what felt like an eternity, but was closer to a second. Then he shrugged and took a sip of his wine.

Guilt slid over Adam. Lucien had done much for him and was loyal to his core. Now the man thought Adam did not trust him. It was far from the truth. Bloody rules. Binding him. Adam nearly rubbed his wrist, around which the golden chain attached him to Eliza May. He wanted to howl. If only she'd look at him, let him in, this could all end.

His voice was a ghost between them, so low that Eliza could not hear. "She is the most important thing in my world." She was his existence. Literally. But Adam could not say that.

Even so, Lucien's eyes widened. Slowly he blinked, as if to say, "understood." Then his expression reverted back to its usual insouciance.

"Well then," Lucien drawled as if not having heard Adam's confession, "I would pay particular attention to William Thorne." The one man who could bring about Adam's downfall. And the bloody curse forbade him from causing the bloody sanguis-crawler mutt any harm. Damn it all.

He kept the anger and frustration out of his voice. "I have it under control." Darby would hold Evernight and Thorne, and Adam would discuss the matter with them. Maddening, but it was all he could do.

Lucien did not appear assured.

Adam grunted in annoyance. "You think Mab can force Holly Evernight or William Thorne's hand?"

"She's done so to stronger beings."

"Fae cannot attack humans on this plane of existence. It is forbidden. Nor," Adam added, "would she ever harm one of her own blood." That was the ultimate dishonor.

"You put too much faith in what people *ought* to do, master."

Adam could not help but look over his shoulder at the one soul he needed to put his faith in more than any other. "Yes," he said, turning back to Lucien, "unfortunately I do."

Thorne kept a running commentary on Holly's bout the entire way home, as if she hadn't a firsthand account of

the proceedings. What shocked her the most was how...
proud he appeared. Which annoyed and pleased her in
equal parts. He hadn't been so confident of her prowess
before the fight. Then again, most men underestimated
women. Now he wouldn't. Which was good.

"The use of the claymore to create metal whips was
most inspired, Evernight," he went on, his eyes alight with
demon glee. "I swear, watching that bit got me hard as a
rock."

"Lovely," Holly murmured. She leaned into the side of
the coach, letting the windowpane cool her heated skin as
she surreptitiously pressed the folds of Thorne's overcoat
hard against her wound. She'd left her cloak behind when
they'd abruptly quit the arena. They were nearly home.
There she could tend to her injury. In peace. "Do you not
have an inner censor, Mr. Thorne? Or are you merely
attempting to provoke?"

He grinned, the swaying coach lamp moving his sharp,
handsome features in and out of shadow. "Miss Evernight, you know perfectly well that I live to provoke you.
That it also happens to be the truth merely makes it more
fun for me."

She made an inelegant snort. And he peered at her, a
thoughtful expression gracing his strong face.

"You are still cross about the spectacles."

"How astute you are, Mr. Thorne."

"Ah, now, petal, you know I had to offer a proper
inducement."

"I know nothing of the sort." If she thought too long on
her lost spectrometers, she'd haul off and hit him on his
elegant nose. "And you might have asked."

"And you would have refused."

Precisely.

He must have read her silent retort, for he chuckled. "Would this facilitate a step in renewing our accord?" With a lightning quick move, he flicked his wrist, and the light caught on his hand. And her spectrometers.

Holly's pain ebbed with a surge of joy. She plucked her precious invention from his outstretched hand and held them carefully against her breast. "How?"

Fangs flashing in the lamplight, he chuckled again. "Easy pickings for a former fine wirer." His warm gaze was a caress. "Come now, petal mine. Did you honestly believe I'd let that sluggard have your clever little device?"

Yes. Yes she had. Holly refused to thank him. Not when he'd deliberately teased her, drawing out her suffering over the loss of her invention. She tucked the spectrometers away, then pinned him with a look. "You needled me on purpose."

His inane grin returned. "Of course. I've such fun doing so." He leaned in closer. When he spoke, his voice was low, intimate. "Someday, you'll learn to trust me, Evernight."

"Who is Alamut?"

He winced, looking for all the world like a youth caught out. Then his expression turned inward. "Not 'who' but 'what.' Alamut was a citadel, and the place where the world's first known assassins lived and trained."

In the dim coach light, Thorne's eyes shone like stars of platinum and onyx. "For our purposes, however, the Alamut refers to a band of assassins, named in the citadel's honor. They started out as Nex assassins but the Nex could not control them. Now they are mercenaries and work for the Nex, or those sympathetic to their cause."

Holly glanced at his arm, which rested so benignly against his thigh now. "Your tattoo."

Slowly, he nodded. "I am Alamut."

"You?"

His attention darted to her face. "What? You don't believe I am capable?"

Of murder? Yes. But a cold and calculating assassin? "A hunter needs patience. Something you have yet to display."

An ironic smile flitted over his mouth, but he was pale with sweat blooming at his temple. "I recall having far better patience before I ran afoul of you, love."

She resisted the urge to pinch him. Only just. And because he was an arse, she couldn't help her retort. "You are also rather flamboyant. Both in appearance and in nature. Hardly the sort to blend in with a crowd."

"Oh, I see," he drawled. "You imagine an assassin as some silent, brooding bloke who slips about like shadows in the dark." His upper lip curled, revealing a bit of fang. "Upon entering a public room, who do the wary most focus on first? Who do they instantly fear? It is the dour wallflower hiding back in some corner, not the jolly gent making merry with a flock of doves."

Well, all right, he had a point.

From under slanting brows, his dark gaze bore into her. "A word of advice, Miss Evernight. The devil wears many hats. Believing in appearances, whether pretty ones or ugly ones, could find you skewered."

Chapter Twenty-One

———————————⋙⋘———————————

It was fortunate the coach ride was short, for Holly could no longer pretend that she was well. She did not wait for Thorne or the driver, but opened the door and hopped down. That she managed not to wince was but a small victory.

Unfortunately, she only took a few steps before Thorne's hand wrapped about her upper arm, and he whipped her around. The move was quick, but he handled her as if she were blown glass. Frowning, his gaze darted over her. "I smell blood. Fresh blood."

Without pause, he flipped open the overcoat she wore. A sharp hiss shot through his teeth as he spotted the widening bloodstain upon her side. "Why didn't you tell me?"

Holly winced at the sharp tone. She was not feeling her best and wanted to lie down. "What good would it have done? You couldn't have helped me in the coach—"

"Stubborn, insensible woman." Thorne bent down and swung her into his arms. Holly bit back a whimper. His scowl was ferocious as he marched them up the stairs and through the door held open by Felix.

"She's hurt." Thorne did not pause as he headed for the main stair. "Raptor claw wounds." Thorne's tone stated emphatically that he expected Felix to know what he needed and to provide it immediately. Which, of course, Felix did and would.

Holly, however, held up a hand. "Wait."

"What?" Nostrils flaring, brows drawn together, Thorne appeared capable of mayhem.

She let her head rest upon his shoulder. "Go to the glasshouse laboratory. I have supplies and ointments there."

And it would be warm there, so much warmer than she currently felt. Thorne all but ran them to the glasshouse. Humid heat surrounded her like a soothing fog as they entered. He set her down on the large wrought iron chaise she liked to use for contemplation. Giant palms swayed overhead, and the air smelled of soil and greenery.

Thorne's pinched expression came into view as he hunched over her and began slicing her bodice with his claws. Though quick, his care was evident; he wouldn't cut her. Even so, when he sliced away her corset with a flick of his wrist, Holly swatted out to stop him.

"Get your blasted hand out of the way, Evernight." His brows snapped together, and he grabbed her hand and gently held it down. "Do you want me to accidentally cut you?"

Holly struggled, ignoring the pain shooting up her side. "You are not leaving me unclothed and lying here!"

As if smacked, his head reared back, and he blinked down at her as though she'd gone daft. "I need to see your wound to clean and dress it, you barmy bird."

Holly scowled. "Then cut away the material at my side, you oaf. And keep your hands off my chemise." Bad enough that was all that covered her torso now. She needn't look to know the fine linen was nearly transparent.

Thorne, however, kept his gaze upon her face. Storm clouds gathered on his. "My dear, I can well understand how you might have the impression that I care for nothing more than fucking and feeding, but you must have cracked your nut if you think that I'd take advantage of you now!"

Holly winced and looked away. All right, so she was a bit sensitive. Perhaps she wasn't thinking very clearly at all. She started to tremble, her eyes smarting, when the soft folds of a blanket settled over her shoulders and right side. It felt lovely, and her eyes closed as she heard her chemise rip, and felt small tugs as he pulled the ruined garment free.

"Satan's balls," he ground out, as his fingers lightly touched her battered flesh. "At least she raked you over the ribs." Which was a blessing. Had the demon hit her softer flesh, she might have been eviscerated. And they both knew as much.

Felix bustled in with hot water and clothes. He frowned down at Holly. "Been playing with demons, Miss?"

Holly's snort turned into a groan as Thorne pressed a hot cloth to her side. "I don't believe she appreciated my definition of play, Felix," she said.

At her side, Thorne was bent over, his face close to her skin as he cleaned the wounds. "Sod it all, you are shredded." He pressed a hand on her belly, holding her in place, and such was her awareness that each of his fingertips seemed to burn into her skin. "It will need stitching, which I am abysmal at doing with any neatness."

Holly almost smiled at his put-out tone, save she was feeling rather foul.

Felix went to the long counter running down the center of the room. Several workstations were set up along it, each with a different purpose and experiment. Felix extracted a black, glass bottle with white wings etched upon it. "This will help." Felix tried to hand him the bottle, but Thorne eyed it as if it were poison.

"What is it?" Before receiving an answer, Thorne snatched it up and pulled out the stopper. His nostrils flared as he sniffed. "This is Jack's blood."

She huffed out a small laugh, and immediately regretted it as pain lanced her side. "You can recognize the scent of Jack's blood, but not the fact that I was bleeding all over the coach?"

"I drank from you. The scent of your blood has been haunting me ever since." The set of his mouth turned mulish. "I thought I was imagining things."

"Oh." She would not flush.

"Never mind the fact that you're covered in rotten-smelling raptor blood." He studied the bottle one moment more, then black eyes glared down at her in accusation. "How did you get this?"

"Oh, that's rich, accusations coming from the likes of you." Despite this truth, Thorne did not flinch. And her ire grew. "You needn't look at me as though I'm a thief."

One of Thorne's brows rose eloquently, and she rolled her eyes. "He gave it to me."

The brow did not lower. "Gave it to you."

Jack Talent was notoriously reticent about letting anyone near his blood. For good reason. Demons had captured and tortured him for it, as it had incredible powers. The one that interested her was its ability to heal.

"He felt he owed it to me." For Amaros had been after Jack when he'd taken Holly. "I refused, but Jack wanted me to use some for research as well."

"Why the bloody hell would he desire that?" Thorne appeared incredulous, but he'd reached for a rag and poured a bit of the bottle's contents upon it. The liquid was reddish black and viscous.

"It may not occur to you, Mr. Thorne, but Jack would gladly sacrifice a bit of his blood if the result helps his fellow regulators who have been wounded in the field. He wanted me to see if there isn't a way to replicate the healing properties for use in a healing balm."

Thorne frowned as he dabbed at her wounds. Instantly, her flesh began to heat and tingle. He made a noise of wonder and poured a bit more blood directly onto her skin. "You won't even need bindings in a few moments." Then he glanced at her. "You believe that Nex agents do not look out for each other?"

"Do they?" The Nex had abandoned him to Amaros. And yet Thorne had come after her. As if she were somehow accountable where they were not.

Wiping her as clean as he could, Thorne then dropped the rag and sat back on his haunches. His expression was inscrutable, his eyes dark and striking against the white of his flowing hair. "I betrayed them," he said, answering her unspoken accusation.

"You helped an old friend in need."

Thorne blinked. "Aye," he said slowly. "I did."

"Do you regret helping Jack?"

Thorne's head bent as if he'd lost the strength to hold it up. "No."

Holly rested her hand on top of his. "Tell me more about the Alamut."

"We don't speak of us. Most never hear our name, and if they see us, it is their last sight."

"You never let anyone live," Holly said dully. How could they, when they were the ghosts of the underworld. The SOS hadn't even heard of them.

Thorne nodded, then pinched the thin bridge of his nose. "We certainly don't vow to protect our target, nor take up residence in their houses, unless the ultimate goal is disposal." He laughed darkly. "Though what is one more broken rule?"

Holly blanched, and he caught the sight. His mouth canted on a smile. "Still doubt your safety with me, love?"

"No," she said with feeling. "Only . . . what shall happen to you? Once this," she waved a hand between them, "is over and done with?"

Thorne's expression went cold and tight. "Worried? Over me? I can't quite believe it."

"Stop it." Holly frowned. "Answer the question."

He sighed. "The pertinent point of discussion is that the Alamut has no set number or leader. They rule by consensus vote. To fight them is like slashing at the heads of a hydra. Cut one down, dozens more take its place. Once hired out, the Alamut stop at nothing."

"How heartening." Holly traced the pattern on the throw before meeting his eyes again. "What shall we do?"

"Just as we've always planned. Convince them that you are no longer a desirable target." When she scowled, he gave her a half-hearted smile.

It did not help. The base of Holly's spine went cold. "It does not sound as though they'll agree to your way of thinking."

"Ah, petal, both of us are fighting an uphill battle, are we not?" The hopelessness that deepened his voice was new, frightening, but then he glanced over his shoulder, preventing her from saying anything further. In a fluid move, he rose to his feet just as Nan bustled in tutting and cooing under her breath and holding out a thick flannel nightgown.

"There now, lass," she said, coming close. "You're home, safe and sound."

Holly could have sworn she heard Thorne snort, but did not meet his gaze.

Nan sat on the edge of the settee and touched Holly's rapidly healing skin with careful fingertips. "A bit pink and puffy but you'll do. Here then, let's get you into this and settled down for the night."

Thorne pivoted on his heel and gave them his back, making it equally clear that he would not simply leave.

Nan frowned at him but then quickly eased the soft gown over Holly's head. As Holly slipped her arms through the sleeves, Nan took off her muddy skirt and boots, and put thick, woolen stockings on her feet. "There, now," Nan announced, "a good cup of tea and some hot cross buns, and you'll be right as rain."

At that, Thorne turned back around and, without asking, bent down and scooped Holly up. She hadn't been carried around in such a manner since she'd been in pinafores. The desire to snuggle against Thorne's hard chest was alarming. And unwise.

"I can walk, you realize," she found herself snapping.

He didn't even look at her. "If only you'd lost use of your mouth."

Touché, Mr. Thorne. Holly stayed his movements with the touch of a hand upon his chest. "Don't take me up to bed." An unfortunate choice of words that had her grimacing. "I'm too wound up to sleep."

He frowned. "You need rest."

"Then I will take it here." With her chin, she pointed towards the shadowed end of the glasshouse, where clusters of potted orange trees bore their summer fruit. "There's a little salon arrangement over there." She gave his dubious visage a ghost of a smile. "My parents love the scent of growing things and spend an admittedly inordinate amount of time out here when in residence."

"All right," he answered slowly before his jaw firmed up again. "But if you think I'm leaving you alone, you had better have your head examined."

Holly found the idea of Thorne staying by her side far too comforting.

The far end of the glasshouse boasted a small area set up with two long davenports made of carved teak and padded with linen-covered pillows. Holly's parents had imported the set from the Polynesian Islands, and they weathered the humid environment just fine.

After Thorne deposited her on one couch, he settled down in the couch catty-cornered to hers. A maid brought in tea and sweet buns for Holly and a pot of chocolate for Thorne. And there they stayed, their heads close together due to the placement of the couches, while drinking their tea and chocolate and talking of nothing in particular. At some point, it began to rain, filling the cavernous space with the rhythmic sound of tapping and making the thousands of glass panes fog over.

"You had a happy childhood, didn't you, Evernight?"

Holly stirred from her lethargy and stared up at the painted white iron lattice that divided the windows. "Yes," she said. "Yes I did. Only…" She paused and worried her lip, not wanting to continue.

"Only what?" Thorne prompted quietly.

"Well, it sounds rather petulant when I think to give voice to it now."

"If you believe one thing about me, Evernight," Thorne said with a dry laugh, "it's that I will not judge you for petulance, either real or perceived."

Her lips twitched with a repressed smile. "All right. I was raised with love, surrounded by it, supported and nurtured. And yet, despite the fact that I am not the only inventor in my family, nor the only scientist, I've always felt rather apart from everyone. Which is utterly nonsensical—"

"Evernight," Thorne cut in, "you think too much. That is your problem."

"Whereas you think too little, Mr. Thorne."

"Why yes, actually." Far from sounding put out, it was almost as if he were pleased with her observation. "Not thinking too deeply about anything is precisely what I do. The past, the future—those are dark places full of possible hurts. Stick to the moment is what I say. Concentrate on the here and now, and everything's safe as houses."

Holly did not miss the slight sarcasm in his tone, as if he knew it was an illusion, but one best kept. Surprisingly, she understood the sentiment. Hadn't she done much the same this past year, focusing on the present and literally cosseting herself up behind brick and mortar so that a dangerous world could not get in?

"Thorne?" Holly cleared her throat. "I want to... That is, I apologize. For how I spoke to you. Before. After we..." It was hard, getting the words out, but she'd delayed in saying them for far too long. "I don't find you disgusting. Not remotely. I admire you a great deal."

The silence from Thorne's corner took on a tangible substance. Holly could feel it, feel him listening to her.

"Your joy for life, the way you look at the world, those things *do* have meaning." She cleared her throat again, her skin growing too tight for comfort. "You are brave and loyal—"

He made a low sound, half-pained, half-protesting. Holly spoke over it; if she didn't say this now, she might lose her courage. "You are, William. You risked your life for Jack, and suffered greatly for it. Yet I've never heard you speak ill of him. You risk your life for me now, even though I've done nothing to deserve that loyalty." For she hadn't found him a cure. She was beginning to think that she couldn't, and the very thought terrified her.

Thorne's deep voice seemed to touch at her ear. "You know that is not true. When I am nothing but shadow, you are the light that guides me back." The davenport creaked as Thorne adjusted his position, as though he were as uncomfortable as she was with showing finer feelings. "No one has cared for me, looked out for my well-being and comfort. Until you." He made an abortive attempt at a laugh. "Hell, Evernight, you know quite well that if it weren't for you, I'd be a raving beast right now."

A flush of frustration swelled within her breast. "That is little more than me being self-serving."

"And I could say the same." His usually smooth voice turned rough. "But I think we both know that our motives are no longer what they were."

No, they weren't. She cared about him, to a frightening degree. But she needed him to understand and did not know how to explain herself. "I can take a dirigible apart down to its gears and screws, but when it comes to interacting with others, I . . ."

Face burning, she shut her mouth.

"I know, petal," Thorne said. "And even though you possess...ah...slightly maladroit social skills, that does not negate your kinder actions."

Holly snorted at "maladroit" but then sighed. "Well, I've mucked up this apology, to be sure." She worried the corner of her lip with her teeth before blurting out, "Will you accept it? Believe that I think highly of you?"

Though he made not a sound, she could almost feel his amusement. His tone certainly conveyed it, husky as it was. "Yes, love, I accept." He paused before adding softly, "Thank you."

Holly nodded, feeling a weight lift off her even though she still felt awkward about the entire exchange. Then Thorne, who never could stay put for very long, rolled to his side to spy at her from his spot on the other couch. Though she could only see him in the periphery of her vision, she could feel his study of her like a caress upon her cheek. Finally, when she could take it no longer, she turned to her side as well.

"What is it?" She wondered if he'd been worrying yet again about her wound. She'd insisted several times now that it was completely healed, such was the power of Jack Talent's blood. She'd even revived enough to give Thorne a punch of power to stave off the ever-encroaching platinum upon his flesh, though he'd protested vehemently about saving her strength before she'd simply reached out and grabbed his hand and done the deed.

"How old are you, Evernight?" Thorne's expression was relaxed, almost happy, as though he enjoyed lounging about with her on these old davenports beneath the glass ceiling.

"Three and twenty."

"A babe."

She refrained from rolling her eyes. "And you? Don't tell me your white hair is a sign of advanced age, for I won't believe you."

Amusement lit his eyes. "Seven and twenty."

This time she both rolled her eyes and snorted. "So very ancient. I bow to your advanced age and experience."

"Now, now, Evernight," he flicked the tip of her nose lightly with his finger, "I might not be much older, but my experience is by far superior. In that you can trust."

No, she would not laugh. She pressed her lips together. "Why did you ask about my age?"

He began to grin, a slow, impish smile that broke like the dawn over his features. "Well…" He reached out to her. "It's simply that…" His fingers threaded through her tumbled locks, sending a shiver down her spine. Then he plucked a hair, and she yelped.

"I do believe I've found a grey hair." He looked positively gleeful about it.

"You have not!" she exclaimed. "Give it here and let me see."

She reached for the strand but he held his hand aloft. "I will not. It's mine, I found it."

"How positively infantile. Found it, my Aunt Francis." She attempted to grab it again, only to have him leap from the couch and dance away, keeping it high above his head. Holly got up as well, coming after him. "You plucked it from my head. That is theft at best."

Thorne burst out laughing, tilting his head back with it. "Theft. I like that. Very well, then." He crammed the strand in his trouser pocket, still laughing. "I am a thief. But you aren't getting it back."

"You don't believe I will take it from there?"

In a blink, Thorne's gaze turned molten. "Oh, please do," he said thickly. "I beg of you, go digging around in my trousers."

"Snake." She wanted to hit his head, or dig about in his trousers. Each was equally tempting.

His grin returned. "Trouser snake, you mean."

Holly did not want to know what he meant, but she did, and heat invaded her face. "You really are the most coarse, vile…"

"Handsome?" he supplied with a wag of his brows. "Charming?"

"Annoying," she said with emphasis. "The most annoying man I've ever met."

In a flash, he wrapped an arm about her waist and pulled her against him. "Ah, but you like me all the same."

Pressed as she was to his body, she felt the rising bulge of his cock and the increased rate of his breathing as they stared at each other. Beneath her open palm, his heart whirred and clicked. Yes, she did like him. Heaven help her, she liked him too well.

The air grew too close, too humid, and she found it hard to breathe. This was Thorne, the man who viewed relations as a quick release. Did he really? Did it matter? She'd not test the theory. Not when she had to live with him for the foreseeable future.

With effort, she pulled back, but he tightened his hold with a low, complaining growl rumbling deep within his throat. They paused again, Holly gaping up at him. His dark brows knitted. He seemed almost confused by his reaction, and hers.

"I am tired," she said past her tongue that felt too thick. "I want to turn in." Holly pushed at the solid strength of his chest. "Let me go, Thorne."

For a moment, she wondered if he'd heard her, for his scowl did not alter. Then his arms fell to his sides, and he took a deliberate step back. He said not a word but simply watched her go.

Alone in her dressing room, Holly thought not of Thorne as she peered into the mirror, running a careful hand through her hair. Just behind her left ear, she found another shining strand gleaming against the black locks. Holly's heart pounded as she reached up and plucked it free.

Wincing, she kept hold of the strand and went to her room, where her microscope waited on her desk. But she did not need the scope to know. She could feel the truth clutching her heart with cold hands. Setting the strand of hair beneath the lens, Holly confirmed her suspicions, and a tendril of fear snaked down her spine. It was not a grey hair at all. It was pure platinum.

Chapter Twenty-Two

❧~❧

Will's blood was still up as he went to his rooms. He'd teased Holly too far tonight. And not far enough, for she hadn't cracked the way he yearned for her to do. Perhaps he should have simply kissed her, but he wanted her capitulation. He wanted her to want him. Yet she remained steadfast in her determination to keep him at a distance. But that was not what truly bothered him now. No, it was her "grey" hair. The one resting heavy as a ballast stone in his pocket.

Will caught sight of himself in the mirror above the mantel and winced at the smear of blood on his shirt. It wasn't Holly's but the tainted, foul blood of the raptor that had tried to kill her. It upset him down to his marrow.

Women had flitted through his life, bright and brilliant as butterflies. Here one moment, gone the next. He'd loved them, enjoyed their company, but breathed a sigh of contentment when they'd gone. One could only interact with another for so long before it became tedium. A hard tup, a good laugh, a warm body to hang onto his arm when he went to the theatre—that was what a woman meant to him.

Holly was none of those things. Oh, he wanted to tup her, and she made him laugh, and he'd love to take her to the theatre, if only to hear her opinions. But she did not flit, and he did not want her to go. She was weightier than anyone he'd known before. Her being had a substance that stuck to him.

Which made him all the more irritable. Apparently, he had nothing, not even the novelty of sex, to offer her. Only his protection, and once that ended, they'd part ways. Hells bells, but she'd made that perfectly clear.

Will turned away from his reflection and took the long skein of silvery hair out of his pocket.

Two feet long if an inch, the lone hair danced and glimmered like a gossamer thread. But it was not fragile. He pulled on it just to test. No, it was strong as steel. Or platinum. Will's heart began to churn out a hard pace.

Reaching up, he found a similar shining thread hiding out with his natural white hairs. He plucked the platinum strand free and held the two hairs side by side.

Identical to Holly's. The heaviness in his chest grew as he entwined the threads—his and hers—together.

Will wound the hairs around his ring finger. Over and over, until they made a band. He tied it off in an unbreakable knot and then curled his fingers into a fist. The ring of platinum bit into his skin. Dread filled him. He could not think of a single harmless or natural reason for Holly to be growing platinum hair.

Worse, Will had no clue in hell as to how he could protect her from the Alamut, a group that never went back on a contract. A group whose very honor rode upon finishing the job properly.

* * *

When morning came, Will could barely wait to see Evernight. He found her in her room, perched upon her settee. A tea tray, holding two pots, was on the table before her. Will knew one pot contained his chocolate. The sight of her pouring him a cup as he strode towards her filled him with an almost rabid sense of satisfaction. His chest swelled with it. He wanted to swoop down, claim her mouth, devour it before he drank his cup of chocolate in one gulp, then crawl on top of her and shove himself into her. Like a brute.

So great was his distraction that he almost missed the dagger peeking out from the folds of her gown. She surely hadn't seen it, or she wouldn't have sat almost on top of it. Not wanting to startle her, he came close and touched her shoulder before pointing out the dagger.

"Careful now," he murmured when she stiffened upon seeing it. "Don't jostle it any more than you have. Ease to the side."

Eyeing the thing as if it were a snake, she did as he requested and slid to the very edge of the seat, pressing against the bolsters. The blade, though razor sharp, had no sheen, but was nearly black. Etched in the blade was a tangle of thorns. It was a perfect replica of the dagger Darby had dropped.

There was no message attached to it. Not any that was visible, but with a sudden and cutting tightness in his gut, Will understood what was needed. He picked up the blade. It fit his palm, felt at home there. A shiver of pleasure ran down his spine.

He forced his expression to neutral. "I don't suppose you'd agree to give a length of your petticoats up to the cause, would you?"

She blinked at his odd request, her nose wrinkling in a way that spoke of a forthcoming interrogation. But then she promptly lifted up her skirt, revealing a pristine, white petticoat of fine-spun cotton. That capitulation, the way she'd willingly exposed herself, was like a fist around his cock. He smothered a grunt of surprise and managed to keep his composure as she lifted a brow and looked at him to proceed.

Being as careful as he could, Will cut a square of petticoat free with the knife. The section was as large as a piece of stationery. When he was done, he set it upon his thigh, and she leaned in.

"What now?" she whispered, her ubiquitous curiosity high.

He gave her a small smile. "Now the fun part." Before she could ask more, he sliced through his palm, quick and deep enough that blood welled up and dripped down in crimson splotches on the snowy white.

Evernight made a noise of protest, reaching out to grab his hand, but her gaze strayed to the linen. There, where the blood pooled, a dark, ruby glow began to emanate. Before their eyes, the blood moved, wriggling and shaping itself, much like metal did for Evernight. But here, it formed words.

William Halvor Thorne and Hollis Penelope Evernight, Your presence is required. Abbot Theatre. Box 12. At the dawn of the coming day.

"Hollis?" he asked.

Her smooth brow wrinkled. "After my grandfather Eamon Hollis Evernight."

"I suppose it could be worse," Will offered with a smile. "I could be calling you Eamon."

The corners of her lips twitched. "Do you always deflect with jests?"

"Come now, love. Don't ask questions to which you know the answer."

She made a noise that might have been a snort. "The dawn of the coming day?" she asked him, all business once more.

"Midnight."

When she frowned, clearly dubious, he smiled faintly. "To most of the underworld, the dawn of each day is midnight."

Slowly she nodded, her attention on the words written in blood. "We shall meet the Alamut."

He nodded once. Unease sat heavy in his gut.

"Is it a trap, do you suppose?" Worry creased the corners of her eyes.

"No." In this, Will was certain. "Someone placed this dagger in your room." A cold shiver touched his metal heart. "Had they wanted you dead now, you'd be so." And he'd be seeking vengeance this moment. One thing was for certain: he was never leaving her to sleep alone again.

Evernight balked but swallowed quickly. "Why refrain from killing me now?"

"That," Will said, "is but one of the questions we'll seek an answer to tonight."

Chapter Twenty-Three

———— ❦⟡❧ ————

Holly dressed for the theatre with the slowness of one heading for the gallows. She did not want to face this. Old fear had her wanting to do nothing more than hide away in her laboratory.

With a small curse, Holly tied a black satin ribbon around her neck, a necessary adornment, as the two puncture marks from Thorne's fangs had yet to fade. Then she left the safety of her rooms.

With his hair tied back in a low queue, Thorne looked younger, the handsome lines of his face striking. But he appeared no happier about the outing.

They were silent as they headed to the theatre. At some point, he'd taken her hand in his, holding it with the casualness of long familiarity. Had he not touched her, she'd feel bereft. Twenty-three years, she'd gone through life without the need to hold onto another, and now the touch of this sanguis demon was essential to her.

She was still frowning when they stopped a block away from the Abbot. Long lines of coaches and cabs clogged the street in an effort to pull up before the theatre. Thorne knocked upon the hack's ceiling, and it pulled over.

"We'll walk from here," he said, helping her down from the cab.

Fine by her. Holly breathed in the acrid air of congested London, tasting the rot and coal on her tongue, and tried to relax. Around them, people chatted, their heels clicking on the pavement as they bustled to and fro. Hawkers were calling out their wares, and the warm scent of roasted chestnuts drifted on a crisp breeze.

Holly burrowed further into her thick velvet cloak and glanced up at Thorne, who stood unmoving and stiff. In the grey light of the evening, he appeared paler than usual, a platinum sheen glimmering along the surface of his skin. Metal swarming through his blood.

"You're in pain." She cupped his cheek and found it cold, even through the barrier of her white silk evening gloves. "Why did you not tell me?"

He flinched. "What difference would it make?"

"Because I want to know."

"Leave off with it, will you?" Silence rang out in the aftermath of his harsh reply.

Not meeting her eyes, he looked off in the direction they were headed, where men in top hats and women with intricate coiffures smiled as they walked through the Abbot's enormous front doors. "I apologize, Holly. That was not..." Clasping her elbow with care, he moved them out of the never-ending flood of people flowing past before speaking again. "I'm..."

A silky white strand of his hair escaped its queue and brushed his collar as he shook his head. An aggrieved look tightened his features. "Tonight, I must let you go, keep my distance, for these men cannot see what you mean to me. Any weakness is assessed and preyed upon in an instant."

"I am your weakness." Guilt swamped her anew.

"And my strength." He took a step closer, and his warmth enveloped her in the cold night. "They cannot know that, either."

Heart in her throat, she swallowed hard. "I see."

"Do you?" His thumb slid over her knuckles, and she fought a shiver. "Do you understand how hard it is for me to let you go?" His voice lowered. "To even consider it?"

Thorne's brows knitted as he peered down at her. "I need my wits about me, and though I am growing more adept at controlling myself, I fear that if I become too agitated, I shall fail tonight. Tell me, Miss Evernight, what shall we do?"

"We prepare you properly." She drew him into a shadowed corner, and then opened her arms. "Come here."

He held back for just a breath, then he tugged her close until they were connected from breast to thigh. On a shudder, he rested his forehead against her crown. She cupped the nape of his neck and slid her other hand beneath his overcoat and under his suit jacket. The mad churning of his heart vibrated against her palm. Holly closed her eyes, trying to ignore the soft caress of his fingers along the small of her back, and let all of her power free.

A groan of pleasure rumbled through him as he sagged against her, pressing them into the rough brick wall of the small nook. Warmth, light, calm—she felt it go through her and into him. But it wasn't enough. She knew it instinctively. He needed more than what her power could give him. Her mind flipped through possible solutions until it screeched to a halt on one.

Blood.

Holly eased back to tug down the ribbon upon her neck. When Thorne lifted his head and frowned, she arched her neck. "Drink."

Instantly he stiffened. "No. Not from you."

"Why?" Her breasts lifted and fell against his chest with each agitated breath she took.

He almost snarled, looming over her like a vexed angel. "I don't need it."

Stubborn, petulant… "You are sanguis. Blood is nourishment, and you've been ignoring your basic nature."

His mouth tightened, but his gaze lowered to her neck, and again his grip upon her flexed. "What if I take too much?"

Holly caressed his chest, wanting so badly to soothe him. "Did you not once tell me that to withdraw out of fear is to die by degrees? You are sanguis," she insisted. "Fully grown. You know how to do this without harm. So take it. Take what you need to give yourself strength." She huffed out a breath when he simply stared. "Do so now, or I'll cut myself open and pour the damn blood down your throat."

He chuckled, but when she moved to pull free of the knife tucked into her boot, he growled and grabbed hold of her nape. With blinding speed he struck, sinking his fangs in deep and clean. Sweet, sharp pain lanced down her neck, then turned to base heat as he started to suck. Each pull sent a stroke of sensation over her sex.

Holly pressed her thighs together and tried to breathe through the lust coursing through her veins. She needn't have bothered. On the next breath, he had set her free, backing off with a gasp. His color was high and flush with health. That alone gave her satisfaction.

Weakly, she smiled at him. "Very good. You have a few hours now, at the very least."

The ground beneath her tilted drunkenly, and she leaned into the building. Thorne hadn't taken very much blood. She could tell. No, this weakness, this strange, heavy pain that seemed to push its way through her veins with cold hands was something different. Metal. She could feel it invading her from the inside. Most worrisome. Holly shivered convulsively.

He grabbed her upper arms and drew her closer. "You are too pale. I should not have done this."

Holly managed a deep breath. "It is not the blood. I told you before. Using my power so quickly takes its toll."

His expression turned pained. "Holly—"

"Save your regrets. They won't help us here." She allowed herself a moment to rest against the wall before pushing away and wrenching free of his grip. "Do not make my efforts for naught."

Will used to love the theatre, loved drinking up the laughter, heat, and vibrancy of humans who attended it. The SOS bastards thought that because the Nex wanted to live out in the open, that they hated humans. Maybe some did. But not the sanguis. Other supernaturals never truly understood how much the sanguis loved humans. They were so wonderfully reactionary. Emotions ruled them. Logic only came upon them in hindsight, a convenient little fallback on which they tried to talk their way out of their actions. As emotions were, in essence, energy, a sanguis could walk beside a human and simply soak it up.

And a crowd of humans? Divine. Which was why sanguis tended to haunt public houses, brothels, gaming hells, and the like. Anywhere one could find a guaranteed mass of emotionally charged humans. Theatres were his favorite haunt. The bawdier the better.

Now, however, even the buzz of the humans gathering en masse did little to elevate his mood. Dread held onto Will with icy hands. No matter how he inwardly scolded himself, he could not shake free from the feeling. He hadn't lied when he'd told Holly that tonight's meeting with the Alamut wasn't a trap. He was Alamut, and though he'd forgotten the truth for a time, they certainly hadn't; an invitation to meet with them was expected. He could guess that they'd want to know why one of their own was protecting their mark.

But to invite Holly? That was troubling. The whole situation bothered him. Why couldn't he remember the particulars? He was convinced his memory had been wiped clean. But he was starting to believe that it would be revealed tonight. The thought had his head aching, as though the lost memories were trying desperately to return.

Grimly, he guided Holly to their box. The Abbot, though not as flash as some others, was fine enough, with gilt touches, massive crystal chandeliers that hung from the high-domed ceiling. It rose three stories, with public balconies and private boxes ringing the stage. Their box was a small space with only four chairs available. It was empty when they arrived. And as Holly moved to the rail to peer out at the spectacle of patrons finding their places, Will thrust a chair under the door handle.

It wouldn't hold any real threat out, but it would give him a bit of warning. That done, he moved close to Holly.

Cocooned inside the small box with its red damask walls and heavy velvet drapes framing their view of the stage, he felt a measure of calm. Unable to help himself, he placed his palm against the small of her back where indigo satin lay smooth and tight.

She turned and looked up at him. Still too pale for his liking, she appeared to have calmed as well.

"All will be well." The words tasted like a lie on his tongue. And when the lights dimmed and the curtains lifted, Will sat close to Evernight and tried again to put away his dread.

By his side she sat, enthralled by the bubbly musical that played out on the stage. But Will couldn't watch it. Holly had weakened herself for him, and though he understood her motives, and agreed with them, it sickened him all the same. It was his duty to protect her. From all things. Even from himself.

Will rubbed at the cold spot of platinum that ran down his sternum. It ached, going in deep. He glanced at Holly. He had to leave her. When this was done, he had to get as far away from her as possible. She wouldn't protest, at any rate. The blasted woman couldn't have made that fact more clear.

Anger, futile and pained, rolled within him. Sod all, he was finished with her. He'd had a life before this. One that he'd return to with relish. She'd soon be a faint memory, one he'd look back on with the sort of wry fondness reserved for those awkward moments in one's life that eased with the passage of time. She'd be an anecdote he'd tell on some distant day, and his friends would have a chuckle over it with him.

Will grimaced, pressing a hand to his chest again. Hells bells but he hurt there.

No. He would not fall to melancholy. Holly Evernight had no hold on him. No longer.

Then something extraordinary happened. She laughed. She'd done so before, when he'd first come into her house. A lifetime ago, it seemed. He'd forgotten how utterly beautiful she was when she laughed. How utterly freely she did so. Her cheeks pinked with it, plumping up into soft curves. The corners of her fine, blue eyes crinkled merrily. She was utterly without guile.

It took his breath. His chest hitched—sweet, tight pain holding him captive. On the next breath, warmth invaded his body. And his heart, that cold, metal contraption that he'd hated for so very long, heated. She'd made that heart, with her clever mind and quiet courage. He lived because of her. In that instant, he knew. She was his heart.

When life threatened to sweep him up in a tide of meaningless encounters, she grounded him, made him think about something other than his own selfish needs. What was he to do without her?

Emotion rose up, clogging his throat, stinging the backs of his eyes. It was all he could do not to reach out and grab hold of her. His fists clenched so hard that his palms stung with the prick of his claws.

Awareness stole over her, that he was watching her instead of the show, making her shoulders tense. And she turned, the elegant wings of her black brows lifting in question. She leaned towards him, just a touch, and her intoxicating scent enveloped him. "What is it?"

Searching for his voice, he could only shake his head, and her expression turned to concern. Lightly, she touched the back of his hand. "Thorne?"

Close, she was so very close. Vivid and alive. She was color and life, the glossy ink-black of her hair, the white velvet of her skin so stark against the blue of her gown, her pink lips parted in curious concern. At her throat, the black satin ribbon hid his mark. Will frowned at it, then up at her. When he spoke, his voice came out dry as sand.

"I cannot do this anymore."

Chapter Twenty-Four

~~~

Thorne's confession rang clear as a bell in the small, dark space of their box. Pain lanced Holly through the belly. Did he wish to leave her? Cease his protection of her?

Oddly, it was not the notion of being left unprotected that sent a bolt of ribald fear and sharp pain through her. Death, she could face, could fight with wit and resolve. Being alone? Without him?

Holly knew with the utter surety of finally solving a puzzle that the loss of him would devastate her. He'd become the brightest part of her. In a world of chaos, science gave her life meaning and focus. But William Thorne brought her joy, hope, the promise that each day would show something new and unexpected. How could she have missed it?

Despite the laughter and music all around, silence thickened between them. He peered at her, his expression more intent and serious than she'd ever seen it. And she could only stare back, her eyes surely glazed.

"Do you understand?" he whispered finally. They were sitting close enough that the smooth tenor of his voice rolled over her skin, and she shivered.

"No," she blurted out. "Do you..." Her breath caught and she tried again. "Do you mean to leave me?"

Tears prickled behind her lids, turning her vision watery.

His gaze darted over her face, and then his stern countenance shifted to one of shocking tenderness. "Never." It was a fierce declaration in the darkness.

Slowly, with immeasurable care, he reached out and took hold of the end of the ribbon about her neck, and pulled. The satin slipped free, and a shiver of pleasure licked over her skin as it slid down her breast and onto her lap.

Thorne's dark gaze burned. "I want you, Hollis Penelope Evernight. I can no longer pretend otherwise."

His chair creaked as he leaned forward, closing the distance between them. The gentle press of his lips upon her neck had her eyes fluttering closed. On the very spot he'd taken her blood, he kissed her, as though she were fragile and something to be savored.

"I would show you the world if you let me," he said against her skin. "I would do anything just to see joy and wonder light up your lovely face."

And she nearly sobbed. Again he kissed her, opening his mouth and sliding his tongue, oh so gently, along that tender spot. A strangled sound rose in her throat as heat licked down her body. Eyes watched them, censorious, curious, peering into their box as the show below went on. She ought to pull away, tell him to stop. Instead her fingers threaded through his silken hair, pulling the strands free from their tight queue.

A tremor rent through him, and he sighed, his heated

breath warming her. "If only you'd let me." Soft, seeking kisses made their way up her neck. "Tell me." His lips grazed her jaw. "Tell me you'll let me in."

Her grasp tightened on his hair as she curled into him and rested her heated cheek against the cool crown of his head. "William."

The tips of his fingers cradled her cheek as he lifted his head and turned her face towards his. Beyond them, the crowd roared with laughter. A woman sang shrilly. Will's hand found the curve of her lower back, drawing her into him. His lips moved to the corner of her eye. A bundle of nerves must reside there, for she felt that gentle touch like a stamp pressing into her flesh.

"Happiness." It was a sigh in the dark, his voice softer than she'd ever heard it.

"Happiness?" Holly tilted her head, trying to see him in the dusky light. "What do you mean?"

Only his eyes, silver and gleaming with an internal glow, were visible. His words were a slow moving tide. "You thought I was smirking at you that day we tupped. I was smiling. Because you'd made me happy."

Happiness. The SOS's disapproval, her fears, their troubles, what did any of it matter if she was without joy? Without him? Moving as though through cotton wool, she reached out and tucked a lock of his hair back from his brow. "Make me happy now," she whispered.

His nostrils flared in a sharp, indrawn breath. And then he kissed her, an open, melting glide of his lips against hers. The world around her faded, and Holly shivered, a small whimper of want escaping her as she leaned into him, licked inside his mouth where he was hot and wet. Instantly, he canted his head and explored her with a quiet ferocity.

And it felt so good, so bloody good, that her body went tight with heat. Against the fine linen of her chemise, her nipples grew hard, aching, and she pressed her breasts to his chest to relieve the pressure. He groaned, a low rumble of sound, and slid his tongue in deeper.

Her fingers trailed to his throat where his pulse beat hard and fast. She wanted to sink to the floor, let him press into her, take her. A thunderous applause had her jumping, and Will jerking back.

In a daze, she stared at him. He stared back, his eyes wide and heated. Then he took a breath and laughed softly, as if at his own folly. But his smile slipped as his gaze turned distant. His light grip upon her turned hard. When he looked back to her, his expression was cold, controlled. "They are here."

Will had lost his head, when he needed most to keep his wits. A mistake. And one harder to bear when his cock throbbed and strained against his trousers. Silently he cursed, and when he let Holly go, he tucked himself into what he hoped was a discreet appearance.

Someone was coming for them. He could feel the presence walking up the theatre stairs, heading this way. That the man was being obvious about his arrival was a courtesy. Will took one last look at Holly, touched her cool cheek, the temptation of her kiss-puffed lips calling to him, and then stood and closed the box drapes.

Once done, he pulled Holly up to him. She tucked her hand into his, where it belonged, and he gave her what he hoped was a reassuring squeeze before letting go. It felt like he'd lost his own limb.

A moment later, a dark shadow moved through the door and reformed before them. Golden eyes shone in the near darkness. Will knew this man. They were colleagues after all. Memories of short exchanges, a brusque word or two between them, returned with clarity. The man had been a shifter when last they'd met. And now he was a shadow crawler just as Will was. Only made of gold.

Will wanted to ask him about his alteration. He too had been taken by Amaros, had a clockwork heart forced into him. Did he suffer? Could he control the pain, the madness? It must be so, for the man was completely calm and in control. What had he done differently that Will had failed to understand? Was it the gold heart as opposed to platinum? But gold would have instantly killed Will's demon body.

"Lord Darby." Holly's voice, though low, cut through Will's musings and tugged him back to attention.

Darby's stern gaze moved to her, and Will fought the impulse to pull Holly behind him.

"Miss Evernight," Darby clipped out. "I did not expect you to recognize me." The accusation laden in that statement was not lost on Will.

Nor Holly. Her brow furrowed. "I remember everything."

Darby blinked, his frame going utterly stiff. "Unfortunately, so do I." Only then did he look at Will. "They're waiting."

Darby turned to go, but Will stayed put. When the man noticed, he paused, frowning at him over his shoulder.

"I'll have blood passage for Miss Evernight." It was not a request.

Darby's aristocratic brow lifted. Will had perfected that look when he was in short pants and returned it with measure. Abruptly Darby turned and held out his wrist, while looking at Holly.

"Your hand, Miss Evernight," he said shortly.

Holly glanced at Will, and he gave her a nod of encouragement. "It's all right."

Though, in truth, a part of him hated seeing her extend her vulnerable and fragile arm towards Darby. But it had to be done. When Darby clasped her forearm, placing their wrists side by side, Will stepped forward and, using the tip of his claw, quickly punctured their skin.

Holly flinched, but Darby simply kept his eyes on her. Blood welled and mixed. Will punctured his wrist then and let his blood drip into theirs.

"Miss Evernight," Darby stated, "you are under my protection and that of William Thorne's until our meeting is concluded."

A sizzle rent the air as their combined blood bubbled and dissipated upon the pact. With that, Darby let Holly go as though she were diseased. Will understood his resentment; hell, he had lived with the same. But he did not like it. Not when they were going to the Alamut.

Darby took them to the theatre's basement. There, amongst the sewage pipes and building supports, a door lay hidden in the brick wall. Another memory surged, and Will knew precisely what brick Darby needed to push to open it. Through the door lay a tunnel to one of their meeting rooms.

"More tunnels," Holly murmured under her breath.

Fighting a smile, Will touched the small of her back to urge her forward. The tips of his fingers burned with the need to hold on to her. But he let his hand fall.

Standing in a semicircle within the barren stone chamber deep beneath London, ten men waited for them. Torchlight flickered over their still forms. They wore hooded cloaks to hide their faces, but Will felt their stares. With the inclusion of he and Darby, there were twelve men. Always twelve. Never more when having a formal meeting. Which meant they hadn't yet excommunicated Will.

Though he did not know the outcome of this meeting, and though he'd sacrifice himself to protect Holly, the sight of the men eased something within him. This was his world.

"Thorne." They spoke as one.

Will extended his arm and then brought it up to his face as though he held a sword before him. With practiced ease, he bowed. "Alamut."

At his side, Holly stood rigid and watchful, and Will sensed the attention of the room shifting to her. He brought it back to him. "I request that the contract upon Holly Evernight be voided. I am willing to pay both for it and for reparations."

Darby's stony expression did not alter. "We do not go back on our word."

Yes, Will had rather feared that answer. For their word was their bond.

"However"—a small, evil smile formed on Darby's lips—"there are no rules against the contractor withdrawing his request. With," Darby added, "reparations for our trouble."

Trepidation lay heavy in Will's gut. "Right, then. Give me a name."

A grumble went through the room. Names were never revealed. A member was contacted. And that member would be in charge of disposal or, if it was his wish, assigning another man onto the job. As Darby spoke for the group now, he must be the one responsible for Holly's contract. And yet he'd obviously sent Will to do the deed. After all the others had failed. Will did not feel an ounce of regret for his fallen comrades. Their world held no room for tender emotions.

"What I do not understand," Darby said, "is why you seek to protect Miss Evernight."

"That is my business."

"Is it?" Darby glanced about as if gauging the others' level of disbelief. A futile exercise as the group did not display emotion. Golden eyes met Will's. Darby shrugged. "I suppose it is. Though I cannot say I understand."

"A name."

Darby's gaze bore into his. "William Thorne."

Silence was a slap. Will flinched, not understanding, yet filled with a sick, twisted dread.

"Given that you started this," Darby went on, "wasted our time, men, and resources, reparations will be high."

A high-pitched ringing sounded in Will's ears. He'd requested the contract on Holly? His skin grew too tight. He couldn't turn to the woman at his side. He'd be ill if he looked upon her face just now.

"You are remembering now, aren't you?" Darby said softly. "How you escaped Jack Talent's house to find me. To demand that Holly Evernight be destroyed for what she'd done to you." Darby's gaze flicked up to Holly, who stood just behind Will. "And to me."

He'd killed a woman then as well. A blood whore provided for him. Drank her dry before putting down the blunt to end Evernight. He'd been so angry then. Full of rage and revenge. He'd sought the only recourse he could. To have them kill her. His brothers in death.

"You did not send me to kill Evernight," Will said to Darby, his heart chugging painfully. "Nor alter my memories?"

The man's golden brows wrinkled. "Why would I?

You'd paid your fellow Alamut to do the job." He gave Will a reproachful look. "And what do you do in exchange for our help? Defend the bloody woman." He shook his head as if disgusted. "You must know you are no longer fit to be one of us."

"Yes." Will knew what was coming. He had regrets. Things that he still wished to do. But it did not matter in the greater scheme of things. Holly would be safe. And his pain would end; there was that. "Jack Talent has access to my funds. Tell him I went to visit Nicky, and he'll give you what you need."

Nicky had been Jack and Will's childhood friend, dead eleven years now. Would Jack mourn Will? Will hated that he hoped so. That he wanted someone to remember him.

Though Holly had not moved nor said a word in this time, she sucked in an audible breath then, as if she realized what Will was saying and what would soon occur. As much as Will wanted to turn to her, tell her what she meant to him, he would not endanger her by showing tender sentiment here.

Darby stepped forward, his expression smooth as paper. "You're ready, then?"

Will tugged his collar, exposing his neck. "Aye. Let it be done."

"Stop!" Holly grabbed hold of his elbow, and her dark eyes were wild with panic. "Do you mean to let them kill you? Is that what all this double talk is about?"

"Holly," Will began.

"Your interference is not appreciated, Miss Evernight," Darby cut in.

"Neither is yours," Holly snapped back, before looking up at Will. "Tell me that is not what I am hearing."

Gently, he touched her arm. If he held her closer, he feared he wouldn't be able to let go. "I cannot."

Darby's bored tone cut between them again. "Let us proceed."

"Do not try my patience," Holly growled at him.

Darby laughed. "My dear woman, you'd take on a room full of trained assassins just so that you can uselessly plead for your lover? How very foolish of you."

"I've killed enough of your lot before," Holly said. "I don't see how this would differ."

Will inwardly cursed, and another ripple of discontent went through the men in the room. Darby's eyes were cold when he spoke. "Yes, but you do not have your little gadgets to save you now."

Holly's stubborn chin lifted a touch. "It is a mistake to assume I need them."

Enough. Will pushed past her. "Stop bickering with the woman, Darby, and do your duty."

"Will!" Holly moved to grab him but two men stepped in and held her back. That they were firm but not rough was the only thing stopping Will from attacking. As it was, his heart ached.

"Leave off, Evernight," he forced himself to say before turning his back on her.

"This is utterly ridiculous, bloody stupid male, posturing…"

"Your jacket," Darby said, above Holly's ribald protests.

Will removed it. His knees only shook a little as he knelt before Darby.

"You cannot do this," Holly shouted. "I won't be held responsible—" Her protests cut off as someone put a hand over her mouth.

Will's body shook. He wanted to go to her. Comfort her. But stayed the course.

A member grabbed hold of a torch and brought it over. Darby grabbed hold of Will's arm and wrenched his sleeve back, exposing the tattoo of the Alamut dagger. Stoic and calm, Darby thrust his own hand into the torch fire. It glowed, molten gold. When his nostrils flared and his hand glowed a brilliant yellow, he removed it from the flames and grasped Will's arm.

Agony exploded at the point of contact. Will ground his teeth, his fangs dropping low and drawing blood. The heated gold of Darby's hand, poisonous to Will, ate at his flesh, burning it up in a way simple fire could not. The foul stench of burning demon flesh invaded his nostrils and had him gagging. A sweat broke over him as he panted and hissed through the pain.

And then Darby's hand was gone.

But the pain remained. Trembling, Will swallowed hard and found his voice. "The other one." His Nex tattoo. "Take it as well." He'd go to his creator without the taint of that mark upon him.

Darby did not blink. "Very well." Again he heated his hand in the flame.

The second burn was worse. Will shivered, pain a pickaxe to his skin, a scrape over his bones. He fell forward as Darby released him.

Head bent and neck exposed, Will cradled his ruined arms to his chest and waited for the deathblow. Cool air caressed his skin.

"Get up," Darby said. "And get out."

Chapter Twenty-Five

❦

Agony flared from Will's arms to the point where he actively pleaded with his body to turn them from weak flesh to hard metal. Even so, it was a shock when his body obeyed, and the intense burn altered to the heavy weight of platinum. It took shockingly little effort to change back to flesh, healed now, his skin as smooth as a lad's.

If only all things could be solved so quickly. He cupped Holly's elbow and hurried her along the darkened street, wanting, *needing,* to have her safely indoors. Home. They needed to be home.

"That seemed too easy," Holly murmured, breaking the silence. "Well, aside from what they did to you. That was... I'm not pleased with you, I'll have you know. You scared the devil out of me."

Will ought not be amused. Even so, his brisk stride broke measure, and he fought a small smile. "Noted."

He frowned. "We were let go for a reason, but damned if I know what." Despite the urge to get to relative safety, he stopped and pressed a hand to his aching eyes.

Holly stopped as well. Standing by his side with quiet patience. It lanced his heart anew.

"You haven't said a word about it," he said in a low voice, unable to look at her.

She remained quiet, but her touch upon his arm was gentle, warm. He wanted to shrug her off or pull her closer. Will took a breath, self-disgust making the task difficult.

"Will you not rail at me?" he asked into the silence. "Put me out of my misery, at the very least?"

"William." Her voice, so clean and smooth, soothed his frazzled nerves. No one called him William. Not since his mother. He hated the sound of his full name, snarled at anyone who dared use it. Save her. She made it something special. Something just between them.

He knew she wanted him to acknowledge her. How could he? When he'd done this thing to her?

"Look at me," she commanded softly.

It hurt, lifting his head to face her. He wanted to sink to his knees, wrap his arms about her narrow waist, and beg her to never let him go. Instead, he merely held himself steady, waiting for the lash of her tongue.

By the light of the moon, she was a study of pale cream and blue-grey. Her features were not tight with censure but drawn with concern. "Do you expect me to be cross with you?"

Though he did not deserve to touch her, he couldn't stop himself from clasping her upper arms and drawing her closer. "I am responsible for you being in danger. I asked for them to kill you."

"Yes, and then you came to do the job yourself." She stared up at him, her expression bland as porridge. "Or do you not recall how we reconnected?"

" 'Reconnected?' " he repeated with a weak, humorless

laugh. "Bloody hell, woman, how simple you make it all sound."

"Because it is simple—"

"It is nothing of the sort," he ground out. "It makes me ill, down to my marrow, to think that my selfish ravings could have been responsible for your death."

Her slim hands wrapped about his forearms, warming him even though he naturally burned hotter. "You had a valid reason for desiring it at the time."

"There is no valid reason for ordering the death of another." Only now, after all these years, did he believe it. He was utterly exhausted by death, wanted no part in dealing in it. He simply wanted to *be*. With her.

Her hand came up to cup his jaw, and the tip of her gloved thumb stroked his bottom lip. "Yesterday and tomorrow do not matter. Isn't that what you said?"

Still frozen, he searched her face, wanting to answer but not finding the words. Her smile was wry. "You see? I've been listening to you all along. The rest of the world can go to the devil. I will not regret a thing, because I have you with me here and now—"

He hauled her against him and kissed her. Hard, desperately. With both hands, he gripped her hair and held her in place, his chest heaving as he kissed her again and again. When she simply opened her mouth to his, letting him in, his frantic need tempered. And he slowed, exploring her with greater care.

"Have you any idea—" his mouth brushed over hers, his tongue slipping in between her lips to lick her depths, once, twice—"how much I crave you?"

She stretched up to meet him, wrapping her arms about his neck, her fingers slipping into his hair. "Tell me," she murmured before suckling his upper lip.

Will cursed and held her tighter. Through the layers of fabric and bustle, he found the plump curve of her arse and grasped, lifting her high and pressing her back against the rough brick wall of a nearby building with his hips.

"I go to sleep to thoughts of your cunny. I want to lick those sweet lips, learn the taste of you with my tongue."

She shuddered, delicately, and it inflamed him. He canted his head, opened her mouth wider, thrusting his tongue deeper. In and out, as he ground his cock between her spread legs. He shuddered too, heat and need licking up his back.

"I ache to suckle the tender tips of your breasts," he whispered into her mouth, the heat of her panting breath and the slick warmth of her tongue inflaming him further. "Just the tips. Gently, oh so gently. Tease and lick them until you're out of your head with wanting. Until you're begging for me to fill you up."

"Will…" Holly moaned, her fingers digging into the bunched muscles along his shoulders.

A surge of lust hit him so hard that his knees went weak, and he ground himself against her, his cock throbbing with impatience. "Bloody hell, how I want to come into you."

With trembling fingers, he traced the edges of her mouth even as he kissed her.

"I remember," he said. "With every waking breath, I remember how hot and tight you were around my cock. The way your quim milked me with sweet, firm tugs when you came."

She whimpered, moving her hips as if begging for the same.

"Do you remember, Holly?" He canted his hips, thrusting his cock up along her sex, the layers of clothing between them a maddening barrier. "Does it haunt you the way it haunts me?"

"Yes." She shivered, and her fingers plunged into his hair, as if to keep him from leaving. *Never.* "Yes."

Close. So close. She would come in his arms, and then he'd take her home and start all over again.

He didn't hear the threat, wasn't even aware of it until a hard hand grabbed the back of his neck and flung him into the opposite wall. Will's body slammed into it, sending bits of mortar and old brick flying. His brain sloshed in his skull, his fangs slicing into his bottom lip. Blood filled his mouth as red took over his vision. He struggled to rise but the ground shook as though the very earth were breaking up beneath him.

A shadowed figure loomed.

"You dare touch her," the man said. As if he had the right that Will had not.

In an instant, Will launched himself at the man, his now-metal fist smashing into a flesh-and-bone face. The man grunted, staggering. Not enough.

Will fell upon the man, even as Holly screamed, shouting something. A blow caught him on the head, hard and far too strong. Will lashed out with his claws, only to be engulfed in flames.

Brilliant orange and red, they surrounded him, eating at his clothes with fiery teeth. A violent wind blew over him, giving strength to the flames. He grabbed hold of the man beneath him, hauling him up by his lapels. Pale eyes glared in fury as the flames burned hotter.

"I'm a demon," Will pointed out. "I bloody love the fire." He smashed his forehead into the bastard's nose.

The man didn't flinch, nor lose his grip, but grinned, an evil gesture full of blood and menace. "Thanks for pointing that out."

Before Will could throw another punch, or tear the man's throat out with his fangs, a wall of ice engulfed him. Frozen, he fell to the side, a thousand shards of agony spiking through him as he clattered upon the pavers and lay there, helpless and silent.

"Thorne! Sin!"

Now that flames weren't shooting up in the air, threatening to burn down the entire area, Holly picked her way over the broken pavement to the men upon the ground and promptly smacked the victor in the back of his thick head. "You bloody idiot!"

"Ow!" Sin groused, rubbing the abused spot before he turned and stood. "And you're welcome."

Holly put her hands upon her hips. "For what? Attacking an innocent man? Bloody hell and damnation, unfreeze him." She crouched beside Thorne, who lay encased in a thick layer of ice. His eyes were frozen open, wide and pained and enraged. "Now!"

Sin's eyes narrowed, as he shifted from one foot to the other. Around him an irate wind swirled, picking up the flame red ends of his hair. "He was going to tear my throat out."

"Because you were trying to turn him into kindling. Now hurry up." Her hand settled on Thorne's ice-encrusted shoulder, not letting go even though the contact burned. "You're hurting him."

Muttering, Sin took a breath and let his power surge. The air about Thorne misted as Sin melted the ice. The moment his face was free, Thorne let out a gurgling growl. Chunks of ice fell and splattered to the ground as slush as he tried to rise, staggering and falling back when he could not. Holly wrapped an arm about his shoulder.

"Who is he?"

Thorne and Sin spoke as one, then each glared at the other.

"Will," Holly said, holding onto him harder than necessary, for she could feel his renewed attempts to attack, "this is my cousin, St. John Evernight. Sin, this is Mr. William Thorne, my *friend*."

"Friend," Sin scoffed. "He had his hands all over you."

"Some women," Thorne cut in snidely, "welcome that sort of thing."

Tiny flames flickered in Sin's green eyes. He took a small step forward, his hands clenching. "Fancy another cool down, Thorne?"

Beneath Holly's hand, Thorne's body tensed. His fangs dropped down. "You only get one cheap shot. And yours has passed. Next time, I'll take your head."

"Oh, hush," Holly snapped. "Both of you." She caught Sin's gaze and held it. "Apologize to Mr. Thorne."

Sin's nostrils flared. He appeared both younger than he really was and capable of setting the entire alleyway to blazes. Or destroying it in an earthquake. The ground gave an ominous rumble.

"I realize you were trying to protect me, dearest," she said in a gentle tone. "But the fact remains that you attacked Mr. Thorne in error."

At her side, Thorne began to shiver. He tried quite admirably to hide it, but she was close enough to notice. His clothes were soaking wet and falling off in burnt, black tatters. She moved to pull off her cloak, intent on covering him, when his hand found her hip and gave it a warning squeeze. He would not show a weakness. Even if it made him ill. Bloody stubborn man.

Sin took another sharp breath, reluctance outlining his body and making his jaw clench. "I apologize... No!" He shook his head. "I cannot. You expect me to act politely when I hear my cousin crying out, when I see her being shoved against a wall?" He pointed at her in accusation. "You think I should wait? What if he'd had a knife?"

"A bloody good point," Thorne said mildly. "I would not have hesitated either."

Sin's black brows rose in surprise, but a small smile curled over his lips. "There, you see?" he said to her.

"I see that you're both barbarians."

"Bosh," Sin said. "You'd do the same."

"I'd have the sense," Holly retorted, "to discern between a true attack and a..." She trailed off with a flush.

"A bloody good kiss?" Thorne supplied with cheek.

Shoving away from him, Holly rose and wiped her hands upon her grimy skirts. "I ought to have left you on ice."

Thorne grunted and jumped to his feet. A graceful move, likely designed to convey that he was unaffected. But Holly did not miss the pinched corners of his mouth.

"You her man, then?" Sin asked, his gaze raking over Thorne in assessment.

"Yes," Thorne said.

"No," Holly said.

They eyed each other warily.

"He bloody better well be." Sin's brows rose in outrage. "After the display I just witnessed."

Holly took a step in his direction. "You, sir," she poked his chest, "are not my father. So kindly keep your own council on matters that are not your business."

"Ah," said Thorne with a soft smile, "there's the Evernight I know and love."

Chapter Twenty-Six

St. John Evernight was an odd duck. Will settled back into the warmth of the massive davenport in Evernight House's library and let his arm brush against Holly's. After his having been turned into a demon ice-block, she was far warmer than he, and his body eased in a dozen different ways. But he kept his focus on St. John. Or Sin. With coal black hair—that ended, strangely enough, in red tips—and frost green eyes, he was certainly striking. Almost pretty in his handsomeness. Will recalled that his sisters were all beautiful in their own right, most especially the youngest, Miranda. A celebrated beauty, Lady Archer's portraits hung from shop windows. If one was so inclined, one could buy a postcard of her for a bob.

But St. John hardly appeared capable of any real sin. The boy—and Will hated to acknowledge that he'd been felled by a boy—was no more than nineteen or twenty, tall and lanky, with the tenderness of youth softening his cheeks. Power radiated from him, almost unstable in its vibrations. Will had never encountered an elemental capable of controlling all the elements. More troubling, however, was the darkness that oozed out of the boy. He was no mere elemental. One blow from Will would have killed him otherwise. No, Sin was something heretofore unclassified.

He would, Will concluded, make a most excellent jewel in the Nex's crown. The notion sat heavily within him. Before he'd have found an excuse to leave, go directly to headquarters, and make plans to arrange a meeting between Mr. Evernight and the council.

But Will was free now. Utterly and completely free from any and all obligation. Part of him felt buoyant, ready to laugh and dance about just for the fun of it. But the greater part of him worried. Alamut had let him go for a reason. And he knew very well that it had nothing to do with him. He didn't know for certain but it almost felt as though they'd been paid to retreat. He simply could not come up with another scenario that explained their odd actions. But if that were so, then who'd paid them and why?

Beside him, Holly stirred. Again he fought the urge to gather her close and hide her away from everything.

"Are you here to stay?" she asked.

Will nearly shouted, "Yes, forever, always." But then he realized she was speaking to her cousin.

The lad cleared his throat. "Ah, no. I mean, I'll stay the night. It's late enough." He scratched at a spot just behind his ear. "I came to find you because I have something to discuss with you, Hol." Green eyes turned to Will. "Alone."

Holly suppressed a sigh as the tension in the room expanded. Really, Sin's tact needed smoothing.

"I'm rather weary tonight," Holly said to Sin. "So please dispense of the theatrics and say what you need to say."

Sin shot to his feet and began to pace. "Am I no longer granted a private audience with my own family?" The hurt and irritation in Sin's voice was clear.

"I'll go," Thorne offered. It was kind of him. Right of him.

"No," she said. "I need you here." She was unhinged in ways she couldn't yet analyze, but that much was true. She needed him close to her tonight or she'd go mad.

Thorne's gaze went soft, then hot. "Then you shall have me."

Sin scoffed. "Bloody perfect."

Holly turned her attention back to him. "I'm sorry, darling. If you'd rather speak to me alone tomorrow, we can do that."

Sin paused, his mouth turning down at the corners. "Were you hurt tonight? Are you well?"

"I'm fine. Only tired." And she was. Every day, exhaustion built within her, and that strange, pained weight grew within her flesh.

Thorne squeezed her hand but kept silent.

With an awkward nod, Sin opened his mouth, but then closed it before sitting back upon the chair. "It's about Eliza May."

Holly went very still. She hadn't forgotten her lost cousin, but she had not told Sin about what had happened to her either. "What do you know of Eliza?"

His green eyes narrowed, catlike and glowing celadon green in the firelight. "More than you, to be sure."

"Who," Thorne cut in, "is Eliza May?"

"A distant cousin," Holly answered. "Come over from

America last year. She met a bad end of sorts with a bunch of roughs."

"Aye," added Sin. "And now she's with that sod, Adam."

Holly's brows lifted in surprise. "And just how do you know this?"

Sin grew very interested in the damask pattern covering the chair. "There are things I cannot say. Not," he hurried on, "because I don't want to, but because I literally cannot."

"Sin." Holly grabbed his hand and squeezed it tight. "Are you in trouble? Danger? I cannot think anything less when you say such things. Tell me that, at the very least."

He gave her a squeeze in return. "No, Holly berry. I'm not in danger. But Eliza is. And I need to help her."

Thorne held up a hand as he leaned forward, his gaze cutting between Holly and Sin. "Let me see if I have this straight. Adam, the creator of all the GIM, an immortal of unknown origin and unknown weaknesses, has absconded with your cousin, and you want to hunt him down and take her back?"

"That is the short of it," Sin said tightly.

Thorne snorted, running a hand through his flowing hair. "Oh, well that's bloody good. Good luck to you, lad."

Holly shot him a quelling look before turning to Sin. "How do you intend to help her?"

"We need to . . . no, *you,* with your great big brain box, must figure out a way to contact Adam. To demand to see Eliza."

"Oh, bloody hell," Thorne bit out in exasperation. "You want to draw her into this? Are you bamming me?"

The room heated at an alarming rate.

"Hush," Holly snapped, before sitting back with a huff. "Why haven't you asked Daisy for help? She is your sister and a GIM."

"Even if she wanted to, she'd be unable to call him. The GIM literally cannot call Adam forth unless it is to his benefit. Considering that I intend to take away his new prize, I don't think he'd come." Sin sighed. "You, however, are an elemental. And I'm only asking for your help to call him forth."

"You think I can contact one of the most powerful known demons, who just so happens to live in another plane of bloody existence?" Holly laughed, but there was little humor in it. "I'm inventive, not a miracle worker."

Sin's mouth flattened to a thin line. "But I was told that only you could... You have to, Holly. You simply do."

"Why must I?" She rose to her feet, the fear in Sin's voice making her chest tighten. "What aren't you telling me, St. John?"

He seemed to deflate. "I made a blood vow to see her returned home."

A blood vow. Which meant should he fail, he'd be the property of whoever he'd made the vow to.

Thorne muttered under his breath, and Holly rather wanted to join him.

"Look, all I know is that it has to be you. Don't ask me for details," Sin said, "because I can't tell you."

"No, I don't suppose you can." If the blood vow forbade him, he'd literally be unable to say a word. Who in the bloody hell had he made this vow to? And why? Holly had no way of knowing.

"It's for a good cause, isn't it?" His expression was mulish, defiant. The little idiot.

"At what cost?" Holly snapped, then sighed. "All right, yes. I want to see Eliza home too."

Sin's entire body seemed to sigh with relief. "Thank you, Holly."

Thorne, on the other hand, sat up straight. "You are both barmy. You cannot make an enemy of Adam. He will never let you live." Thorne turned on her, his fangs extended and his eyes burning. "After all we went through to keep you safe, you cannot do this. I won't let you."

Holly had a great deal to say about what William Thorne could do with his grand edicts. He'd soon learn that he would not be ordering her about. But he'd suffered for her this night. He'd suffered due to her sins for a year. So she held her tongue for now and simply rested a hand upon his arm. "I'm not doing anything at the moment. And we'll sort this out in the morning," she added when Sin voiced a protest. "When this is through, St. John, we're going to have words, you and I."

He glared back. "Fine." Sin winced. "There's more."

"Here we go." Thorne tossed up a hand in exasperation. And they both glared at him.

Sin recovered first. "Thorne's involved . . . somehow."

Thorne snapped to attention. "The bloody hell—"

"I don't know how," Sin explained. "But my . . . that is . . ." He grimaced, clearly fighting to find a way around the blasted blood vow. "*They* know about him and seem to find his presence here very . . . shit . . . they approve! They've been pushing you two together."

He'd broken out into a sweat and swayed until he braced himself against the arm of the chair. With a shaking hand, he wiped his brow.

"Oh, Sin." Holly ached that he'd bound himself, for whatever reason, and that he could only feed her crumbs.

"Holly—" his voice sounded weak and rough—"they believe you and Thorne are the key."

Chapter Twenty-Seven

~~~~~~~~~~~~~~~~~~~~

I don't like it." Thorne strode into Holly's bedroom moments after her and slapped a hand upon the bedpost. The steel supports clanged at the hit.

"Nor I." Bone tired, Holly pulled the pins from her hair. Her head ached and sat heavily upon her tender neck.

Undeterred, Thorne raised an imperious brow. Times such as these, she could see the aristocrat he might have been. "It is the height of insanity to antagonize Adam."

More pins slipped from her hair. "I agree."

"Then you'll refuse to help your cousin?"

Her hair ambled free of its bun in a curtain of relief. "I didn't say that."

"Damn it, Holly!" Thorne slapped the bedpost again. "I cannot—"

"Do you wonder," Holly said softly, for her head throbbed, "who talked Sin into a blood vow?"

Deflating a bit, Thorne glanced off towards the fire crackling in the grate. "Yes. And I wonder..." He looked at her with dark eyes. "Nan tells me your family is related to the fae."

"Nan and her tales," Holly muttered, annoyed for she knew the cagey housekeeper would love nothing more than to scare Thorne off. "If the fae had any interaction with my family, it was hundreds of years ago, for I've never seen them."

"Back when the earth was flat, eh?" The corners of Thorne's eyes crinkled.

"Just so," Holly said with a smile of her own. "It isn't easy for the fae to travel into our world. They must pass through as sprit and then create a corporeal body once here. It takes a great deal of power. Not to mention that those crossroads are well protected, as the reality of fae coming *en masse* into our world would be catastrophic."

Fae were powerful and would subjugate all those weaker than they were, which included not only humans but also a great deal of demons and elementals. Old superstitions had Holly wanting to shudder, but she pushed that back by remembering cool logic. "Luckily, only a catastrophic, magical event, far more rare than the fae themselves, can open the crossroads long enough to let them in."

"Amaros came here because of a catastrophic event," Thorne reminded her. "Does it not stand to reason that the fae might have taken similar advantage?"

"Damn. I suppose you have the right of it." Holly sat and removed her shoes. The satin heels landed with a thud on the carpet.

"If you are related to the fae," Thorne continued, "then, by logic, Eliza May is also their kin."

It made sense. And it made Holly's heart grow cold. Fae were mercurial beings. For them, everything had a price, and they often requested favors, usually to the extreme detriment of those with whom they bargained. The sane avoided contact with them at all costs.

"So here we have Nan insisting the fae wanted me to be your champion." The long lines of Thorne's body were taut. "Then someone either paid or bargained with the Alamut to let me go tonight." His eyes met hers. "And now your cousin shows up asking for help to release Eliza May?" The corners of his eyes wrinkled as he gave a small shake of his head. "It is too much of a coincidence for me."

"And me," Holly agreed. Gads, but her body ached. She ran a hand through her hair. "We'll have to talk to Sin—"

Thorne was suddenly at her side, kneeling in front of her and taking her hand. "What is this?" Horror lit his expression.

"What is what?"

"This!" He lifted her arm. "Your bloody arm is platinum!"

Holly's vision wavered as she spied the thick swath of platinum running from her elbow to her underarm. Cold fear and an odd sense of finality pressed upon her insides. She let her arm fall to her lap. "Well."

"'Well?'" Thorne jumped to his feet. "That is all you have to say?"

"What ought I say?" The truth was, she didn't want to talk, or to think.

"I don't know." Thorne raked his hands through his hair. "But something other than 'well.'"

How irritating that Thorne had suddenly become the logical one, wanting to suss out every problem. Holly bit her lip and refused to answer. Which made Thorne growl.

"Do not dare try to sweep this under the rug, Holly. Not when we both know what is happening." Past patience, Thorne lifted his hand, displaying a thin band of shining platinum wrapped around his ring finger.

"Is that—" Holly began.

"Your hair. And mine." Thorne stomped over to the fire, sneered at it, and stomped back towards her. "Like a fool, I held onto some wild hope that this one hair was an anomaly. Yet I am stabilizing, while you're growing worse!"

"I had a suspicion that might be the case." She tried to say this calmly but it didn't ease him.

Thorne reached her in a step and clasped her upper arms in a tight grip. The heat of his hands made her skin prickle. "Why is it happening?"

Holly searched his face, hating the pain and fear she saw in his eyes, hating that she could not fix this. "I do not know."

They stared at each other for a long moment, Thorne's throat worked on a swallow, and then he let her go with a snarl. He paced away, his boot heels clicking on the floorboards. "Bloody fucking hell." He glared down at his hands, spreading his fingers wide as if they held the answers.

Holly sagged against the chair. A thought occurred to her, one she did not favor. "I think…" She took a deep, pained breath. "I think that perhaps we are bonding."

His head jerked up, and he looked at her with sharp eyes of silver and onyx. "Bonding?" It was a quiet query, but there was something almost hopeful in his voice.

With cold fingers, Holly clutched the arm of the chair. "Symbiosis. In biological terms, it means simply the living together of unlike organisms. In this case…" God, she didn't want to say it, but the concept was the most logical conclusion she could formulate.

"In this case..." Thorne prompted, peering at her warily.

A spasm of pain shot through her heart. "In this case," she said, forcing herself to hold his gaze, "it is a parasitic connection."

Thorne reared back as if she'd stuck him. "Parasitic?" His voice was thin, cold. And she recalled how sanguis were often accused of being parasites, feeding off the life force of others to survive. It was one of the greatest insults one could use on them.

"In a fashion," she managed, though her throat constricted. "One organism benefits at the cost of the other. Your mind gains control through the use of my power. Thus it demands it more and more."

He went utterly white, the rivers of platinum upon his neck standing out in sharp, shining contrast. His mouth moved to speak but the words were slow to follow. "I am a parasite to you?"

Oh, William. Her vision wavered before she quickly blinked. "It is merely a term. Not how I think of you. There was no way to foresee this result."

He knelt before her, his thighs moving between her knees as far as her skirts would allow. "But the fact remains, I am draining your power, your strength, to gain mine." Like an asp he struck, grasping a wavering tendril of her unbound hair. His jaw worked as he held it up between them. Pure, gleaming strands of platinum glinted within the dark locks, as if they were winking. "You are turning into me."

Unwilling to see the self-disgust and pain in his eyes, she lowered her lids, her throat sore and her heart unbearably heavy. She wrapped her fingers around his. "All is not lost." It was something her parents often said, taught to them by theirs. Evernights did not give up. Ever. "I will find a solution."

A strangled sound left Thorne's lips, and his arms wrapped around her waist as he burrowed his head into her lap. "Holly," he whispered, his breath warm against the fabric of her skirts.

He gripped her tighter, his touch almost that of a frightened boy, and she instinctively leaned over him, her fingers threading through his silken hair as her free arm wrapped about his shoulders. They sat in silence, holding on to each other, both shivering despite the warmth in the room.

After a long, heavy moment, he stirred, turning his head to rest his cheek upon her thigh. Holly's fingers trembled only a little as she traced the line of his temple, brushing back errant strands of his hair. He merely blinked slowly, as if stuck in a fog, and toyed with the dark fringe on her overskirt with the tip of one finger. She felt the touch, his power, all the way to her bones. When he spoke, his voice swept over her like a caress.

"I am your creature."

"*No.*" She could not bear it if she had to think of him in that manner.

A small smile curled his mouth but he did not move from his place on her lap. "I am. Wholly." The tip of his finger moved to her waist where she was slightly ticklish. Her skin prickled as he traced along her side. "I am yours to command, yours to do with what you will."

"William." She gripped his hair, harder than she meant to, but he wouldn't budge. "You are not. You are not a creature, nor are you my slave."

His strange smile only grew. "But what if I want to be?" He lifted his head, and his eyes were ice blue. "What if I want to be claimed by you?"

Her heart stopped. She still held him, her hand against his throat where his pulse thrummed. Only she could not find the power to speak. Thorne rose to his knees, bringing them eye to eye.

"Do you not understand?" he whispered. "I have never belonged to anyone. Not since I was a child. It is a lonely thing to be unclaimed by another. The idea that I could be yours seduces me more than you can know." His lips tilted in a dry smile. "And if the only way I could belong to you is by this strange bond, then I would gladly accept that." His expression dimmed. "Only now that I know what it does to you, I cannot let it go on. I will not see you hurt."

Her grip on him tightened, and somehow she was pulling him closer, until they shared the same air. "I'd rather you belong to me in another way. It shouldn't be one-sided, this ownership."

Thorne drew in a sharp breath and seemed to hold it as he studied her through narrowed eyes. When he spoke, his voice was rough, cracked. "What do you mean?"

Her mouth went arid. "What if I belonged to you as well?" His arm slid around her waist, hauling her against him as she continued to speak. "What if you had my heart?"

"As you have mine?" His lips brushed her cheek, his breath unsteady. "Do I, Holly? Do I have your heart?"

Her smile was tremulous. "You've had it all along."

Thorne moved to release her, but Holly wrapped her hand around his wrist. "Don't go."

His expression was soft, his voice a warm whisper. "I did not plan to. Let me put you to bed. You are tired."

She was. But she did not want to rest. Holly ran her thumb over the pulse-point at his wrist. "William, kiss me."

Understanding lit his features, and she knew he realized she needed the comfort he and his body could give her. Slowly, he grinned. "Where?"

She found herself slowly grinning too. "Wherever you want."

"This discussion of your health isn't over," Thorne said just before he kissed her mouth. His lids lowered as he gave her another lazy, melting kiss. And then another.

"Noted," Holly murmured against his lips. Languid warmth stole over her.

"Good." Thorne nibbled on her earlobe. Before returning to her mouth. A low, male growl of contentment vibrated in his chest. He learned the contours of her mouth, exploring it from different angles, never rushing. As though they had all the time in the world.

The silk of her skirts rustled in the silence as his free hand eased them up. Cool air hit her shins, then her knees. Holly let him ease his body further between her thighs. His breath brushed over her cheek as his palm ran up her thigh.

Her belly tightened in anticipation, her sex heating as he came closer. At the moment of contact, they both made a strangled, breathless noise. He cupped her, his fingers making a slow circuit through her wetness, and he groaned low and rough.

"Here." The blunt tip of his finger breached her, sliding in deep before pulling out slowly. In. Out. "Here," he said again as he kissed her, "is where my dreams begin."

Holly squirmed, spreading her legs wider as she slumped upon the chair, her aching breasts and heated skin confined by her heavy satin gown.

"Here is where I want to be," he whispered. "Always."

He added another finger, plunging in deep, invading, retreating. And kissing her. Always kissing her. Holly shivered, followed his lips with hers, trying to make the kiss harder, needing some sort of release. He wouldn't give it to her, but continued his steady plunder. The pad of his thumb found the swollen bud of her sex, and he stroked her there. The shivers grew within her, moving outward towards her sensitized skin.

He drank down her little cry of distress. And then he curled his fingers, stroking a spot inside of her. Her orgasm rushed over her with such force that she arched back, her lips slipping from his. A keening wail left her as she gripped the sides of the chair. Still he stroked, his mouth at her ear, whispering dark things, promises of more.

On and on it went, until spent, Holly lurched forward and clutched his shoulders. For a moment, she could only hold onto him and pant. He pressed kisses along her temple as he withdrew his hand from between her legs.

"You, sir," she said between gasps, "are a wicked beast."

He chuckled darkly and then lifted her up, cradling her in his arms. The bed dipped as he set her down. In a daze, she let him undo the buttons of her gown, peeling it from her body. A welcome rush of cool air soothed her damp and heated skin. Off came her petticoats and bustle, her silk stockings and drawers, the crumpled corset cover. But when he moved to free her corset, she swatted him away with weak hands.

"Oh no you don't." She eased herself up on her elbows and scowled at his grinning face. "Not when you are fully dressed. Take off your clothes."

His grin widened. "Demanding miss, aren't you?"

She merely raised a brow. The speed with which he disrobed truly was impressive. As was the sight of him standing before her, utterly unabashed by his nakedness. And why shouldn't he be?

She'd seen him before, revealed in parts. She'd touched nearly every inch of him at some point or other. But Will Thorne, viewed all at once, took her breath away. Long and lean, his was not a body of brute strength but of feral grace. Beneath smooth skin, his muscles were so finely wrought, so perfectly delineated, that it would take hours to fully explore every crest and dip. And she knew she wanted to try.

The proud jut of his cock drew her attention, and her thighs clenched with delicious heat.

"You must know," she murmured, still looking, "the effect you have on the female sex."

He moved then, prowling towards the bed, to crawl over her. Before they even touched, the heat coming off his body enveloped her. She lay back, and he hovered over her, his dark gaze meeting hers. "The only female I want to affect," he nipped her lower lip, "is you."

Holly nipped him back. "Then let me show what you do to me."

"Anything you desire, love."

He let her ease him back onto the bed.

"Rest against the headboard," she told him.

Readily, he complied. There was a glint in his eyes, as though her orders excited him. Or perhaps it was simply that they were both here, at this moment. Together.

"Grab hold of the rails." Her voice was only slightly unsteady. The steel headboard of her bed was composed of several bars, laid out in a grid fashion.

Keeping his eyes upon her, Will spread his arms wide and clasped his hands around the bars. Instantly, the metal grew pliant then wrapped around his wrists before solidifying once more. Bound, Will jerked in surprise. He glanced at his trapped arms then turned back to her.

Holly's heart beat hard within her chest, and tension gathered along her spine. Would he be angry? Demand release? Think her crazed?

A slow, satisfied smile curled his lips, and something within her relaxed.

"I knew it," he said in a low rumble. "Under all that starch, you're as dirty-minded as I am."

It was a lovely compliment. And the pose did lovely things to his chest and arms, stretching those sinewy muscles out and drawing her gaze down to his narrow hips and thick cock, so hard now that it lay flat and pulsed against his tight belly.

Holly undid her corset and let it fall to the floor but kept her chemise on.

"Ah, now love," he complained, as she crawled upon the bed and straddled his thighs, "don't stop there. Take that thing off."

Preoccupied, Holly ran her fingers over his taut chest, pausing to stoke the tiny bud of his nipple. Will shuddered, but his quest did not waver.

"Give me something, darling," he went on thickly. "Show us your tits, there's a good lass."

At his crude words, her nipples tightened. Never one to miss a thing, his eyes focused on the change, and he licked his lips, his voice dipping lower, going rougher.

"Come now, petal. Show them to me." His gaze seemed to burn through the thin material of her chemise. "Those sweet tips are practically begging to be revealed."

Heat pulsed through her sex. Oh, but he was far too adept at destroying her composure. Hands shaking, she watched his face as she pulled the tie that held the front of her chemise closed. His breathing sped up, his attention rapt as the fabric sagged and then parted, exposing her to his gaze.

His chest hitched, the muscles along his torso bunching. "I've wanted to see you for so long," he rasped. "Gorgeous. You're gorgeous."

She thought much the same of him.

He rocked his hips, the movement edging her closer. "Lean in and let me give them a kiss."

A heady sense of power washed over her. Dizzy with it, Holly grabbed hold of the headboard at either side of his head and bent close, bringing her breasts up to his mouth. He wasted no time, but craned his head forward and licked. The flat of his tongue laved her sensitive nipple, and Holly groaned.

Arms shaking, she held on and let him do what he willed. Again and again he came at her, licking and lightly suckling the tip of her breast until she sagged into him, weak with heat and desire.

"The other one," he demanded on a growl, his breath hot on her skin. Without thought, she offered him her other breast, and he gave it the same, thorough attention. When she whimpered and arched her back, he moaned against her and angled his head to draw her in deeper. Each sharp tug of his mouth sent a bolt of heat through her.

Wicked demon that he was, Will bent his knees, bringing his thighs up. The action tipped her further forward, and her sex slid over the hard length of his cock. Instantly, he bucked his hips, grinding himself between her legs.

"Oh no you don't," Holly managed between gasps. "I'm not through with you."

With a punch of power, two of the metal bars upon the footboard snapped out and snagged his ankles. Will yelped in surprise as they drew his legs wide and straight.

"Evil woman." His fangs flashed. "You're going to be the death of me yet."

When Holly settled her weight back onto him, he sucked in a breath between his clenched teeth, and his hips shifted as if he couldn't keep them still. "Ah... gods, put me out of my misery. Put me in you."

She almost relented under the plaintive look in his dark eyes. But she had plans for him. Because while she wanted him more than her next breath, he needed more. He needed to know that he was worth more than idle pleasure. He needed to understand that he was her everything.

"No," she told him, pulling her chemise free from her body. "Not quite yet."

Chapter Twenty-Eight

No demon in his right mind would leave himself so exposed. So helpless. Yet here Will was, stretched out and bound hand and foot as a man upon a cross. And he loved it. Loved that his practical Holly liked to play.

Now fully trapped, with his legs spread wide upon the bed, his cock at full mast and impatient, he waited for her next move. Her pert bottom rested upon his thighs as she contemplated him. And he grinned back, not saying a word. Hells bells, but she had him stirred up. He could hardly wait for her next form of torture.

She cupped his jawline, touching him as though he were something breakable.

Will hadn't expected that. He'd predicted more wet, scorching kisses, frantic touching, pushing up into her slick quim and letting her ride him. But none of those things occurred.

Light as butterfly wings, her lips touched the tip of his nose. Another delicate kiss upon the crest of his cheek. The ridge of his brow, his forehead, temple. A slow shake built up within him as she mapped the lines of his face.

"Holly..."

"Shhh." She kissed his eyelid, then his mouth. Once. Then once more. When he tried to deepen the kiss, she moved off.

"Holly," he said again, more forcefully.

She paid him no heed. Kisses feathered his jaw, moved down his neck. His head tipped back, his gaze alighting on the ceiling. Her fingers threaded through his hair, a light exploration as if she were simply enjoying the texture.

Will's heart churned a hard pace, the need to move, to free himself and end this gentle torture had him clutching the bars on the headboard. Still she kissed him. Breaking defenses he didn't know he'd erected.

Holding his gaze, she leaned forward, her sweetly curved belly pressing into his throbbing cock, the silken tips of her breasts skimming his chest. Will groaned low and pained. Her smooth, cool skin was a balm, yet inflamed him all at once. Her slim arms wrapped about his neck. And she hugged him.

He felt the touch down to his soul. And some dark emotion swelled up within, choking him.

"Holly, love," he croaked out, "sweet petal, let me pleasure you—"

"Shh." She snuggled in closer. "Let yourself feel. It's all right. It is only me. Here with you."

He squeezed his eyes shut and fought against the hot prickles behind his lids that threatened to unman him. His breath came in sharp, agitated bursts. Still she held him.

"I will not let you go, William."

He swallowed convulsively. She held on tighter. "You are mine now."

A choked sound left him—half laugh, half sob. "Evermore."

As if she'd been waiting for his capitulation, she tilted her head and placed a soft kiss upon the vulnerable spot on his neck where his artery lay beneath his skin. Slowly she rose to cup his cheek. Her smile was radiant in the amber light. And when she leaned close and placed a soft, open kiss upon his mouth, his breath hitched, flowing into her.

"I love you," he told her. It needed to be said. She needed to know. So he said it again. "I love you."

His confident Evernight merely gave a Mona Lisa smile. "And I have loved you from the moment you helped me bind your wrist to mine."

Shock, joy, heat slammed through him, flooding his veins. She loved him. She'd loved him all along, just as he'd loved her. His voice barely worked when he found the strength to answer. "Enjoy having me bound, do you?"

He wanted to be set free so that he could capture her, do all the things he'd promised.

"Mmm," she hummed, "I do."

The sound of her contentment seemed to vibrate straight down to his cods. And then she leaned in and kissed his nipple. Forget freedom. Her tongue flickered over the hardening tip, and his hips canted in reaction. Forget anything but letting her do as she pleased.

Her hands trailed down, smoothing over his skin, leaving a wake of warmth and pleasure in their path. He sighed and craned his head down. "Kiss me," he nearly begged. He wanted her mouth. Her taste in his.

Holly placed a series of light, delicious kisses down the center of his abdomen. "I am."

Were she not torturing him, he would have smiled. As

it was, his skin prickled in pleasure, and his abdominal muscles clenched with a sweet ache.

"Do you remember," she murmured almost conversationally, as she nuzzled and kissed around his navel and over to his hip, "when you asked me if I thought of your cock when I massaged you?"

Her hand skimmed over his length, a light tease that had him twitching.

"Yes?" It came out strangled.

Carefully, she cupped his cods, and he whimpered.

"Every bloody time, love," she whispered, stroking him. Bless. Her.

Slim cool fingers wrapped about him, and almost delicately, she lifted his cock up, held it just before her lips. From beneath her long, inky lashes, she peered at him. "Do you want me to kiss you here, William?"

His cock pulsed in immediate approval. "To start," he rasped.

She gave him a sly look then bent over him, her midnight hair pooling about his thighs, and his gut clenched in anticipation. She kissed the very tip. He felt it in his heart.

Merciful hell but she gave his aching cock the same attention as she'd done the rest of him, kissing her way down its length and back up again. The tip of her tongue made a slow, languid circuit around his engorged head, and the bed creaked ominously as he tensed.

Another lazy lick had him groaning. She kissed him again, almost a suckle but not quite.

"Ah now, love, don't tease." It sounded far too much like a plea. The muscles in his arms quivered, his chest aching from the strain, and still he tried to edge lower, tilt his hips up enough to follow the brush of her lips. "Put it in your mouth, love," he whispered, sweating. "Suck me."

She drew him deep into her hot mouth.

"Ah, hell." He strained against the bonds, thrusting helplessly. "Oh, Jesus, yes . . . Evernight, just . . . God! Just like that . . ." He panted as she sucked him harder. The sight of her delicate pink lips around his cock, of her cheeks hollowing as she drew back, had him shaking with restraint. He wouldn't come, he wouldn't.

The tip of her tongue swirled around his head and licked his slit. He bucked, shouting before he ground his teeth and panted.

"Release me." Sweat dripped down his neck, his heart threatening to lock it pumped so hard. "Let me touch you now. I need to touch you."

With a snap, the metal bonds broke, and his limbs, tingling and throbbing from the sudden freedom, surged forward. On a growl, he wrapped his arms about Holly's slim frame and tossed her back onto the bed before following her down. His lips caught hers, devouring her mouth as he thrust hard and deep into her heat, his hands roving, touching skin softer than silk.

"Lovely, perfect, darling." He ploughed into her, all speed and frantic need. He could not get enough.

And she met him stroke for stroke, undulating against him as he cupped her pert breast and held it firm so that he could draw her tight nipple into his mouth. Good glory but she drove him mad with lust. He licked her like cream, following the pale blue vein that ran up her breast to her neck. Up further to her sweet mouth.

Their gazes clashed. Wild tangles of her raven hair spread over the pillow. Her skin was dewy and flushed, and her eyes, dark, pure blue, gleamed up at him. With adoration. For him.

The frantic need that had swept him up eased. He

stopped, holding himself deep within her. Until she wriggled beneath him, her sex clenching in impatience. Will smiled. And so did she.

"Hello," he whispered.

Her smile turned tremulous. "Hello."

Bracing his forearms on either side of her slim shoulders, Will set a new rhythm. Going slow. So that she would feel every inch of him moving through her. It was agony, but he did not abate.

"You're so beautiful." The words burst out of him. "Holly. Petal-mine."

Her eyes glistened. "William." It was a breath of sound. "The way you make me feel…"

She stroked his back, long sweeps that sent ripples of pleasure over his skin. He caught her free hand. Their fingers threaded. "Hold onto me," he whispered.

It shocked him how much it mattered, that she not let go. Her grasp tightened. He swallowed thickly, shivers of heat dancing down his spine. He barely moved, barely breathed, and yet it felt as though he would come at any moment. Heat gathered in a tight fist that held his cods and had his gut tightening with pleasure-pain. His breath came out like a bellows, and he thrust, slow, hard.

Never looking away, Holly wrapped her slim legs about his waist. Her lips parted on an indrawn breath, and the tight clasp of her sex began to milk him as she quietly came. He could hold back no longer. He came so hard that he couldn't breathe, couldn't move. The edges of his sight dimmed as he arched over her, his body locked up and shaking as pleasure rolled through him.

Weak as a babe, he relaxed into her embrace. For the first time in his life, Will knew perfect contentment.

* * *

Not long ago, there was a time when the Cremorne Gardens would have been filled with light, music, and laughter at night. Now it lay forgotten and abandoned. Dry leaves skittered down the wide boulevard that led to the wrought-iron Chinese pagoda.

Adam strolled along, stepping over the cracks in the pavement. Delicate iron archways, once lit up with hundreds of little drop crystal bulbs, now stood dark and creaking against the wind. There was something utterly enchanting about abandoned pleasure parks. If he closed his eyes, Adam could almost hear the ghosts of past laughter, the blaring horns of a trombone played long ago. And though all he could scent now was the moldering of dead leaves and the rot drifting off the nearby Thames, he fancied there was also a bit of roasted chestnuts and the scorch of fireworks lingering like phantoms of yesterday.

Once at the pagoda, whose roof had rusted in spots, he sat comfortably upon the top step that led to the pavilion where brass bands used to play. Selecting the top step had been a calculated move, for Miss Eliza May, whom he'd come to think of as the anchor at the end of his chain, was forced to sit upon the step below.

She did so without grace, plopping down in a puddle of horrid homespun skirts covered with dried and blackened bloodstains. Adam scowled at the sight. He'd gifted her with heaps of gowns, a rainbow of silks and satins, and she had eschewed them all, preferring to wear the gown she'd died in. Like a taunt.

Spine straight, her crown of golden curls facing him, she was silent as usual. And he sighed. A series of wide arches, punctuated by little gas lamps, ringed the pagoda. "They used to dance here." His voice echoed in the silence. "Under the lights. Some nights, there'd be a thousand souls dancing, promenading, laughing in this spot."

Nothing. Not a sound but his own bloody hopeful voice.

"During the days, there'd be equine shows, races. I once lost three thousand quid on a race." He'd been disguised as a bored and spoiled nob at the time. In some ways, losing was more fun for him than winning. He'd paid up, had a laugh with the gents. Just like any other man.

Adam resisted the urge to fidget and stared hard at the back of Eliza May's head. A lone strand of hair, caught by the breeze, danced about on the frayed edge of her bodice. "Over in the gardens," he went on conversationally, "they used to have a maypole. You've heard of maypoles?"

She was an American, after all. God knew the Yanks were sadly lacking in culture.

She didn't move. But that was expected. However, he was becoming more adept in reading her, and by the tightness gathering along her pretty, slender neck, he knew she was listening. Perhaps annoyed with his question.

"Lasses and lads used to dance around it while holding onto long, colorful ribbons," he explained, even though he suspected he needn't. "Up and over, round and round, until they threaded the pole. I fell in love with a lass dancing around the maypole one May Day."

That got her. The length of her back went rigid. He smiled, but it wasn't out of pleasure. The backs of his teeth met as resentment swarmed in. "She was a pretty piece, glossy brown curls and wide, blue eyes. Willing too. But I could not claim her. Because I was searching." He leaned closer, taking in the scent of Eliza May, of wool, woman, and resentment. "For you."

An inward breath, sharp and stiff, sounded. Eliza in shock? Good.

Adam chuckled darkly. "Yes, you. It's always been for you." Cursed to search for the one soul that would complete his. "The irony is that I don't even like you. Seven hundred years I've searched, and what do I find? You. Resentful, hateful, and spoilt."

She nearly turned at that jab. Adam wanted to grin but couldn't. Not when he wanted to shout to the heavens in rage. Why? Why had they given him her? He'd done his penance, hadn't he? He'd followed every edict laid before him when he was cursed. And this was what he received? A woman who wouldn't even look him in the eyes.

"Aye, a spoilt child, you are. You think I'm so bloody awful?" he ground out. "I've fathered countless GIM, given all those souls a new life, new hope. Have you the slightest inkling of how many lives that has affected? You wouldn't even be here were it not for me. No, you'd be rotting in an unmarked grave, forgotten and unavenged. Because the GIM did that for you as well, didn't they? Striking down those who hurt you. And what thanks do I receive? Silence."

More followed. She'd calmed now. Dug in and found whatever it was that gave her the strength to ignore him. Adam growled and yanked the chain that linked them. Hard. On a cry, she fell back, her elbow hitting the top riser, her body twisting to face him. For one instant, their eyes met. He felt the weight of her wide, brown stare down to his marrow. And something inside of him ached. "You agreed to this," he ground out. "You agreed to be mine. Mine!"

His voice echoed over the emptiness. "And now you act as though you've been tricked."

Her gaze narrowed. She glared at him, and though it was progress, for she mostly looked through him, he couldn't stand it. "I gave you life anew. I look after your every comfort, for all that you ignore it. What do you want of me? What?"

He hated the desperation that sharpened his tone. And perhaps so did she.

"Freedom."

Adam flinched, so unaccustomed to hearing her voice that he wondered if he'd dreamed it. But she looked back at him, waiting. Freedom. Oh, how very well did he know what it meant to yearn for it. He'd done so for seven hundred years. And now, at the cusp of his, she wanted the one thing that would snatch it away? She, who'd done nothing for him. She who'd agreed to his terms and then instantly sought to go back on them. Like a coward.

His nostrils flared. Cold night air burned down his throat. He leaned closer, until they were nearly nose to nose.

"No."

Her expression wiped clean. As quickly and thoroughly as if his answer was a door shutting upon her. Then she was looking through him once more, as if he weren't there. And he wanted to roar, pound the rotting floorboards to dust, grab hold of her and make her acknowledge him once more.

He didn't do any of those things. He was a near god among lesser supernaturals. He did not beg or rail. Nor, he reflected bitterly, did he hurt women.

Instead he cut her off for once, turning his attention to the night sky, ignoring her completely. He had business to attend to. A moment later, Darby appeared before them in a swirl of shadows.

"Yes?"

Adam took a deep breath. He had to calm. "How goes it with Evernight and Thorne?"

He had to give Darby some credit; the man did not cower as he faced Adam and answered truthfully. "They are no longer the concern of the Alamut."

Adam clenched his shaking fists. Another deep breath. "You let them go."

"Yes."

"When I specifically ordered you to keep them captive."

Darby's expression might as well have been carved from marble. "While I may have entered a devil's bargain with you, the Alamut are not bound to do your duty. They are now loyal to Mab. I could not persuade them to do your bidding over hers."

Darby had to know that refusal to comply would seal his fate.

"You," Adam ground out, "ought to have asked your brothers-in-arms to kill you."

"Then I would not have had the pleasure of seeing your face when I told you that Thorne and Evernight were free."

The man had a set of brass balls. Adam nearly laughed at the thought. Only Thorne was out in the world, and Mab was likely moving in for the kill. Perhaps she already had. And damn it all, Adam did not know what her next move would be.

"Well then," Adam said with forced levity, "now you've seen it." With that, he lashed out with his power, stopping Darby's heart in an instant. Darby fell to the ground, gasping for air.

"Sad, really," Adam said. "I would have let you go after this." Then he called forth another.

In the next breath, Lucien appeared, scowling and

irritated. "*Putain*, but I hate when you summon me in this manner." With crisp jerks, he pulled at the lace cuffs peeking out from his blue satin frock coat. "Why not send a note like a civilized creature—" He sucked in a sharp breath as he caught sight of Darby writhing upon the ground. Lucien went pale. Which was odd considering Stone had been a cold killer in his youth.

"Concentrate, Stone. He is not your concern."

Lucien jerked at the sound of Adam's voice and glanced at him. "You…" He cleared his throat. "What is it?"

"Find William Thorne and Holly Evernight and bring them to me."

Lucien glanced at the shifter upon the ground, and a spasm lit along his narrow cheek. "And this one? Shall I…" He cleared his throat again. "Shall I dispose of him?"

"If you wish." Adam waved an idle hand. "Hurry along. Time is of the essence."

Chapter Twenty-Nine

In the dark warmth of her bed, William held Holly close. The air was humid, and their bodies slick with sweat. He watched her with a lazy sort of possessiveness that filled her with heat. Gently, Holly ran her fingers through his hair, and in return, he caressed the puncture wounds upon her neck.

"Holly?" His whisper was at once rough yet tentative.

"Mmm?" She leaned in and softly kissed his mouth.

A look of pleasure stole over his face before he grew serious. Against her chest, she felt the pump of his heart. "I want to ask you something," he said so solemnly that she stilled. And so did he.

"What, William?"

His fingertips drifted over the tender spot on her neck. "Would you...?" He cleared his throat, a deep flush washing over his cheek. "Some sanguis take mates. For life." His gaze met hers. "Will you be mine?"

Emotion clogged her throat and stilled her heart. "William." She cupped his cheek. "Yes."

He captured her mouth, kissing her fiercely—once, twice—then he pulled back to study her face. "There is a ceremony of sorts."

"I should hope so."

His lips twitched but he remained serious, almost anxious. "It involves blood. The exchange of yours and mine."

"Show me," she said without hesitation.

The covers rustled as William sat up and pulled her into his lap, so that she straddled him. Firelight gilded his skin pale gold and made his eyes glow. His voice was low and tremulous when he spoke. "If we do this, you will be mine in all ways. And I will be yours."

Holly stroked his hair, wanting to comfort him, for she knew he was nervous. "I am already yours. Make it so, as Sanguis do."

Tension flowed out of him on a nod. "I am going to open the wound in your neck and then make a similar cut on mine."

"All right." Nervousness fluttered through her now too.

With utmost care, he leaned close. His lips brushed her skin. The sweet-sharp pain of his fangs came next. Holly's fingers gripped his shoulders as hot blood rolled down her neck.

He kissed her cheek. "No more pain, lovely petal."

Holding her gaze, he used a claw to slice a small cut at the base of his neck. Crimson blood welled up and began to trickle over his collarbone.

In his deep, Northern voice he spoke. The foreign words dipped and flowed, sounding like a mixture of Gaelic and Norse. Though she knew not what he said, the sincerity in his tone, the way he looked at her, as if she'd lit the night sky for him, had her heart swelling within her breast.

"Now," he rasped, "take my blood as I take yours."

Her lids fluttered closed. The taste of his blood on her tongue sent a throb of feeling into the puncture wounds on her neck. The throb intensified as William's mouth latched onto the spot and softly sucked. Her cheek grazed his as she drew back. His eyes, brightly fierce with possession and love, flickered from iced blue to demon black. And then he smiled.

That smile, so full of joy, took her breath. She couldn't speak, could only return his grin as he eased her back into the softness of the down-filled bed.

"Look." He pointed to his neck. The cut had already closed, leaving behind a small, wine-colored mark in the shape of a star.

"What is it?" Wonder made her voice crack.

His smile grew tender. "The mark of possession. Yours." He touched her neck. "You have one too. In the shape of a thorn."

She wanted to grab a mirror and see, and yet she looked upon the mark on his neck, her mark, and she didn't want to move at all. She threaded her fingers through his hair. "Mine," she said. "You are mine."

A shudder went through him, and his eyes narrowed, intent and heated. "Oh yes, I bloody am."

Will slid over Holly, then slid into her. She was so swollen and sensitive now that she groaned, her body languidly stretching out beneath him. And his pleased chuckle rumbled over her. Slowly he rocked into her, taking his time, and plundering her mouth with soft, deep kisses. "Mine. My lovely Evernight."

"Tell me what the words meant, William."

His long fingers cupped her cheeks as he continued to move within her. But he answered her, his tone warm and seductive. "From flesh to bone to blood of heart, shall we be entwined, never to part."

Holly woke first. Which was rather a shock, considering how little sleep she'd achieved the night before. Her darling demon had demonstrated quite thoroughly how knowledgeable a sanguis could be in the matters of seduction. There had been a point, when he'd made himself at home between her legs and proceeded to lick her sex, that she'd forgotten her name. But never his.

Now she was content to watch the dim room, the light of the sun kept firmly at bay by the heavy, drawn drapes. Warmth surrounded her in the form of Will Thorne. They lay, limbs intertwined, his head currently upon her breast. Absently, she stroked his hair, loving the way those silken strands felt running over her fingers. Every so often, he'd nuzzle against her in his sleep. Holly smiled at that. The smile grew when he uttered a soft snore and burrowed in closer.

And though she wanted nothing more than to laze the day away without moving a muscle, a cramping in her lower belly urged her to gently ease away from Thorne. He made a grunt of discontentment, but promptly flopped the other way, hugging a pillow with one arm. Holly tore her gaze away from the naked splendor of his back and went to the water closet.

As soon as she was out, there was a scratch at the door. Thorne slept on. Holly put on a dressing gown, buttoning it as she walked to the door.

"You've a visitor," Nan said, looking put out. "And he won't take no for an answer."

"Well then, he'll have to see me as such." Holly was in no mood for politeness.

Holly did not know who she expected to be waiting for her, but certainly not the man who stood in her visiting parlor. He turned upon her entrance. Dressed in old-fashioned clothes, straight out of the previous century, with a peacock blue frock coat and pale yellow britches, he seemed a painting come to life.

Surely no one had the right to be so beautiful. With caramel-colored hair that ran to his shoulders, jade green eyes, and a full mouth, he was almost feminine in his beauty. Save there was a hardness in his gaze, and an alert tension about his frame.

"Mademoiselle Evernight." He bowed with flourish.

Recognition hit her. "Lucien Stone." He was the leader of the London GIM and Mary's old friend. Though some said he was a libertine and a fiend, if Mary trusted him with her life, then Holly wouldn't reject anything he said out of hand.

He appeared pleased that she knew him. "The very one."

"To what do I owe the honor, Mr. Stone?"

Weariness seemed to take hold of him. She empathized. It took effort to stand just then. She needed to return to bed. Another painful cramp rolled through her belly, and a sweat broke out on her back.

"I come on behalf of another," he said. "My maker Adam."

Cold swarmed through her limbs. "Oh?"

Did Adam know she meant to help steal his prize? Calm. She'd remain calm. Why hadn't she awakened Thorne? Brought him along with her.

If Lucien noticed her disquiet, he hid the fact well. "He wishes to speak with you and Mr. Thorne. At your earliest convenience." It was clear that was all Lucien was willing to convey.

"And just how are we to contact him?"

Lucien's full lips quirked, and he took a step towards her, going slowly, as though fearful of invading her personal space. "Take this." He offered her a gold sovereign. "When you are ready, toss it in the air and think of him. He'll do the rest."

Bemused, Holly held the weighty coin in her palm. The metal, magically altered, tingled against her flesh. "Ancients. They do so love their tricks."

"As you say," Lucien agreed with a wry smile. "Good day, mademoiselle." He inclined his head. Again, a shadow of pain and misery flitted over his features but then he was gone, exiting as quietly as a ghost.

In the distance, Holly heard Nan let him out, and then the house settled. Her fingers wrapped around the coin. She'd have to talk to Thorne, but perhaps they could settle this feud, or whatever it was, peaceably.

Holly moved to go when another cramp slammed through her, this one so hard that she cried out. It did not end, but grew stronger. She curled into herself, her knees slamming upon the floor. A dry heave wracked her frame as she shook and tried to stand. She was cold. Freezing. From the inside out. And it hurt.

Bracing her hands on the floor, she caught sight of them, and a sob left her. They were platinum. Another wave of pain hit her. She fell forward just as Thorne rushed into the room, shouting out her name.

Hearing a commotion, Sin ran into the parlor. Holly lay in a sprawl of shining platinum limbs. Sick fear punched through him, along with crippling guilt that almost had him doubling over. He ought to have known this was what Mab had planned. He ought to have warned Holly.

Holding Holly in his arms, Thorne glanced up at him, his eyes wild with panic. "What do I do?"

A lump grew within Sin's throat, expanding until it ached. "She's dying."

When Thorne snarled, gathering Holly closer to him, Sin sighed. "I don't like it any better than you, but it's the truth. You know it."

The man seemed to curl into himself, a choked cry leaving him like a sob. "Because of me."

Sin wasn't brave enough to agree. "She tipped the balance, taking so much in. Elementals need that balance, else their power consumes them from the inside out. It's why they hid the truth of her nature from my sister Miranda, for in doing so, she'd strive to contain her fire. It's why my sister Poppy trained for a decade to control her abilities. But Holly here? No one ever thought she'd abuse her powers this way. She was too set in her ways, logical and calm."

"Fucking fae," Thorne ground out. "Manipulating and playing with the lives of others. Why not simply warn them? Why not watch out for the women they claim to be family?" Disdain dripped from his voice.

Sin squatted down next to him, wanting to rest a hand upon Holly, but rather fearing that Thorne would tear it off should he try to touch her. "After all you've seen, do you honestly believe the world to be so black and white? Fae aren't good; they do what they please. It does not mean they don't have some sense of love and loyalty. Only that it is skewed and damaged." At that he almost smiled, but his heart hurt too much. "And they are the only ones who can save her now."

Thorne's head snapped up. His glare was cutting. "How?"

"We go to them, give them what they want. And they will heal her."

"They planned this all along, didn't they? This is why they wanted us together."

Sin sighed. "I fear you might be correct."

Thorne's lip curled, exposing his fangs. "And to save her, we become Adam's greatest enemy in the process."

"What is more important to you? Being a marked man? Or saving Holly?"

"Don't you dare presume to question how far I'd go for this woman," Thorne snapped. "She is my life—" His breath hitched, and he winced, pressing his lips against the dark crown of Holly's head before speaking. "Anything. Do you understand? I will do anything."

Thorne loved Holly. Just as Mab had expected him to. She had played them all.

Chapter Thirty

Holly awoke to find herself in Thorne's arms. The
moment he felt her stir, he gave a strangled sort of yelp
and gathered her closer.

"Satan's balls and hell on earth," he muttered, stroking
her cheek with a hand that shook, "you scared me. I didn't
know if you'd wake."

He appeared as worn out as she felt. "How long? Where
are we going?" For it occurred to her that they were in a
coach. And then she saw Sin. His expression was sorrowful and grim.

"We're on our way to Mab," he said.

"The fae queen?" Holly struggled to sit up, partly ham-
pered by the fact that Thorne wouldn't let her go. She gave
up the fight and relaxed against his chest. Her very bones
hurt. "She is here?"

"Aye," Sin said slowly. He and Thorne exchanged a look.

"What is it?" Holly's insides dipped.

Delivered in sharp agitated sentences, Thorne and Sin
told her why they were going to Mab. Denial warred with

panic, and Holly found herself snappish. "You've no proof of this. I might simply be ill."

"Holly, you were entirely metal not twenty minutes prior." Sin gave her a pointed look. "You're not entirely flesh now."

She kept her attention on the coach window, refusing to look down at her arms, which shone with a platinum luster. But she could not ignore the invasive pain along her left side and down her back. How bad did she look? How long did she have before it washed over her again?

Thorne's tender touch upon her cheek had her stiffening. "Petal, let us see what she has to say."

The coach stopped before the Tower of London, of all places. For a moment, Holly simply stared up at the great old fortress, the four finials atop the copper domes of the White Tower glinting in the rays of sunlight that managed to break through the cloud cover. Thorne seemed just as shocked.

"Come on," Sin muttered.

Though the Tower operated as a garrison, with guards living and working there to protect the Crown Jewels and other national treasures, no one came forth to stop them. All was quiet. Too quiet, as though the place had been abandoned. Odd indeed since the Tower was also a grand tourist attraction, usually filled with gawkers who loved to soak up the lurid tales of torture and treachery in England's bloody past.

Then Holly spied the slumped form of a yeoman, gently resting against Byward Tower, the brim of his iconic, low-crowned hat shielding his face from view.

"Sleep spell," Sin whispered. "And likely enchantments set around the grounds to dissuade others from visiting now."

Walking along past more sleeping guards, their footsteps echoed in the eerie silence, bouncing off ancient stone walls. Holly suppressed a shiver and was almost glad when they finally made it to The Green. The emerald green lawn seemed a peaceful place, surrounded by The White Tower, the chapel, and an expanse of pretty Tudor-styled buildings.

A raven hopped about, pecking the ground in search of a meal. And, in the center of it all, smartly dressed in a waterfall of purple and green silk, Matilda Markham reclined with a regal air in a carved wood chair. But it was the woman standing next to her who truly shocked Holly.

"Nan?" Holly couldn't believe it.

Nan raised her chin, her pale eyes flashing. "I'm here to bear witness. For you, love."

Matilda gave them a nod of acknowledgment. "Lovely place, isn't it? This fortress that has seen so much of death and torture." She smiled. "It quite reminds me of my home."

"Dear Matilda," Thorne sneered. "You might have saved us a world of trouble had you simply stated that you were working with the fae."

"Working with? My dear boy, I *am* the fae." Her brown eyes bled to pure purple, and her hair shimmered to dark red. "You may call me Mab."

"Fae give themselves away, you know," Sin murmured to Holly. "If you look for it. Names that start with the letter M in honor of Mab, wearing green and white, flashes of purple in their eyes." They'd been there all along. Fae, playing Holly and Thorne, guiding them along the path the fae wanted them on.

"Mab." Thorne gave an exaggerated bow. "Would you mind explaining why you simply didn't tell me about the Alamut?"

"Now how would that have fostered togetherness between you and my kinswoman Holly Evernight?"

She smiled at Holly then, but there was evil in it. "Young kin, I am so glad St. John persuaded you to call upon me."

Sin had the grace to duck his head, avoiding Holly's gaze.

"I see you are unwell." Mab stood and reached out to touch Holly's cheek. Holly flinched away, and the fae queen laughed. "Angry with me, are you? When I am here to help."

"Let us not be coy," Holly said. "You orchestrated this. Tell me your terms."

With a sigh, Mab leaned her hip against the arm of her chair. "Very well. I want Eliza May returned to me."

"What is your interest in this woman?" Thorne asked her.

Mab's eyes flared purple fire before quelling. "She is kin. Close kin." A fond, faraway look settled over her pert features. "Long ago, when your grandda was a young lad," she said to Holly, "I took in his brother Aidan. Not wanting to marry his intended, he needed advice and called upon me."

Mab closed her eyes, a smile on her face. "Oh, but he was a beautiful lad, golden curled and bright eyed. For the first time in centuries, I wanted. I wanted him." The smile slipped, and she opened her eyes. "But he proved... elusive."

"Because the boy fancied men," Nan snapped. "And you wouldn't take no for an answer."

That earned her a vicious snarl from Mab, before the fae queen went on as if Nan hadn't spoken. "In return for my help, Aidan agreed to be mine for a night."

A cold wash of pity went through Holly at the thought of Aidan sacrificing himself when he'd had no desire for Mab's attention.

"There was a child. I didn't expect that." Mab frowned before shaking it off. "Being part human, the babe couldn't live in my land, so I brought her to Aidan. He raised her, and that child gave birth to Eliza May."

Mab looked around at them. "So you see, I am the girl's grandmam."

"I can understand why you want her back," Holly said. "But why involve us?"

"Not you, actually," Mab said. "Despite what your cousin St. John might have thought, my interest was never in you, but in William Thorne here."

"Me?" Thorne croaked.

"The simple fact is that you are the one, the *only* one I figure, who can free Eliza. Thus, I need you to cooperate."

"Why Thorne?" Holly did not like this one bit.

"Eliza is chained to Adam's side. The chain cannot be broken by magic other than his. Only he and his kind can remove it. And you'll not find a GIM willing or able to release Eliza. But you, Mr. Thorne," Mab gave him an approving look, "though not GIM, are of his ilk. Adam's magic will recognize you. The chain will break for you."

"'Ilk,'" Thorne repeated with sarcasm. "I am an experiment gone wrong. Nothing like the GIM."

Holly touched his hand, and he caught it up.

Undaunted, Mab shook her head. "Adam's first creations were shadow crawlers. The magic will respond to you."

"Darby is the same as Thorne," Holly said. "And he is Alamut. Why not order him to do it?"

"Darby." Mab all but spit out his name. "He saved his hide by entering into a soul bargain with Adam. Thus he could not break the chain. No, there is only Thorne to help me."

Thorne looked at Mab sharply. "It was you who freed me. You sent me to Holly."

Mab pouted in a pretense of innocence. "I did it to help you."

"Help yourself, you mean," he snapped back. "I might have killed her."

Mab laughed. "Holly Evernight is a metal elemental. I knew she could handle you. And I knew you'd be beholden to her." She smiled in a flash of small, sharp teeth. "You were an utter mess. I could not have your help until Holly healed you. Then it was simply a matter of forcing you two to work together and fall in love."

Thorne looked appalled.

"All in all a good plan," Mab said. "And then there is the simple fact that you, Will Thorne, were not meant to have a heart of metal. My kin Holly cannot save you or alter nature's course. Her science has no solution, and I suspect she knows this already."

Holly stared fixedly at a point beyond the green. She hadn't been able to figure out a way to fix William. She simply did not know how. He was not a machine. He was a living being. That she had failed the one person she loved above all others made her want to rage, and made her want to sob in despair.

Thorne did not appear half as distressed. "Your point?"

Mab ignored him and looked at Holly. "Worse, in your efforts to heal Will Thorne, you've killed yourself as well. The scales of nature have tipped within you and you are as infected as he. You cannot control this."

Thorne's teeth snapped and his fangs dropped. "Then. Fix. Her."

"I will. If," Mab added, "we have a bargain."

"Fine then," Thorne said. "I'll go."

"No." Holly held him fast. "You had the right of it last night. Adam will not let you get away with this. He'll hurt you."

"If you are healed of this malady, I don't care." His fierce expression eased to sorrow. "If I am done for anyway, love, then let me do this for you."

"No, Will." She held him fast, feeling close to panic. "Do not say that."

"Oh, come now," Mab said with a sigh. "You needn't fall upon your sword, Thorne. There is a solution to both problems. And we have not yet discussed the terms of our bargain."

Thorne glared at the fae. "Explain."

"I really do not find your tone pleasant, Will Thorne. However, as we are bargaining, if you do this for me, I shall heal my kin Holly and you as well."

Thorne's gaze narrowed. "But?"

For there was always some hitch to a fae's bargain.

"You will be human."

Thorne's head snapped back, color leaching from his pale face. "Human?"

"Yes. I cannot alter magic that has already set in. But I can shift the course. You will once again be the Marquis of Renwood. Leave the details of your return to me," she added when Thorne tried to speak. "And my dear Holly shall go back to her normal self."

"That cannot be all of it," Holly said, cautious hope trying to rise within her. She pushed it down.

"Alas it is not. You will end this union. And I will have

assurances. When Thorne changes, he will forget your existence. Should you reveal who you were to him, he will return as he was, and you will go back to dying."

"Why would you demand this," Thorne bit out, "when I have already agreed to bring back Eliza?"

Mab's pleasant countenance twisted into one of ugly contempt. "It disgusts me to the core that one of my kin would take up with a sanguis. That she should sully herself with a dirty blood drinker is a sin against our noble nature. I'd rather see her dead than suffer such an indignity."

"He is a better man than you could ever hope to know," Holly snapped. Thorne's hold on her arm held her back from charging the fae. But Holly was not finished. "And I have no interest in your foul and twisted bargain."

Mab merely looked at her as if she were a recalcitrant child. "You want my help? You will comply. Am I clear?"

"As glass," Holly snapped. She turned to Thorne. "Let us go. We are finished here."

"You will die," Mab shouted. "Have you no care for your own mortality?"

"No." Holly tugged on Thorne's arm, for he'd yet to move. "We are going. Now."

"Holly..."

"No!" she said to him. "Don't you start."

Mab's gaze darted between them. "Do nothing and your fates are sealed. Help me, and you both live."

"We don't even have a way to find Adam," she ground out, hating the lie but desperate to keep control of the situation.

"You do," Nan cut in. "Lucien Stone visited you just before you collapsed. I heard what he said."

"Nan," Holly hissed, utterly betrayed.

The witch lifted her chin a fraction. "He gave you a coin to call Adam forth. Toss it in the air and think of him, he said." Her expression went soft and regretful. "I have the coin here." She held the gold sovereign aloft, and Thorne snatched it.

Then he took Holly by the arm. "Come with me."

"Do we have a bargain?" Mab called as they walked off.

"Give us a moment," Thorne said over his shoulder.

"Go to hell," Holly snarled over hers.

When they were at the edge of The Green, Thorne stopped in the shadows made by the Bloody Tower looming over them.

"Holly—"

"No." She bit her lip, hard enough to draw blood. "Do not make me do this. I cannot lose you. I've only just found you."

He grabbed her forearms and held tight. "You think this isn't tearing my insides out?"

"Then refuse. We'll think of another way."

"What way? It cannot be solved by science. Can it, love?" He gave her shoulders a little shake. "Look me in the eye and tell me there is a way to solve this problem with science."

"Testing has not yet proven..."

"I'm not referring to me," he cut in softly. "But to you. Do you know of a way to cure yourself?"

She looked away, a thick lump choking her throat.

Gently, he touched her cheek, his fingertips so hot that she knew her flesh was cold metal there. It hurt, but not as much as her heart.

"There is no one with the power to restore you, save Mab," he said.

Helpless, Holly ground her teeth and refused to meet his eyes. "William…" Her breath hitched. "I cannot." The space between them grew so silent that the click of his heart could be heard. Then he touched her jaw, forcing her to look at him. The love and desperation in his gaze speared her fleshy heart.

"See now," he whispered, "while I can manage giving up my own life, I cannot give up yours. Not if it is in my power to save you."

"I am not worth this."

His thumb caressed her cheek. "To me you are."

She shook her head, because he did not know her darkest truth. "I can recall the sound of your screams. The exact pitch and tenor of them—"

Distress darkened William's eyes. "Holly—" He made a furtive attempt to touch her, and she held up a hand to ward him off.

"No. Let me finish this. I need to." She took a deep breath. "I remember each and every face, every cry. For nearly a year, I relived those dark moments down in the cellar. What happened to you…" Tears pooled in her eyes. "I know, William. I *know*," she ground out between clenched teeth, "that what I experienced was nothing compared to the agony you felt."

Through a veil of tears, she saw his expression crumple, as if her crying was too much for him. She let him gather her close, but she did not relent.

"But seeing that being done to you." Holly shook her head and pressed her palms against his solid chest, where his metal heart churned. "It broke something inside of me. To watch that *thing* rip into you."

Against her, William shuddered, and she snuggled closer. His arms tightened around her.

"It's over, love."

"No," she said. "You do not understand." Holly leaned back and looked him in the eyes. "Being forced to watch Amaros rip you apart, when I could do nothing to stop it—I just wanted it to end. I couldn't...to see you in agony. Will," she touched his scar, "I wished..." A sob burst free. "I wished that you would die."

He went stiff against her.

"I begged to heaven, hell, and anything in between that you would die. That it would all end. The pain. The screams."

And then he was clasping her head to his heart, his hold enveloping her as she cried, guilt and the horrible memory of that day swamping her anew.

"Hush, petal." His deep voice was a vibration in his chest. "Hush now."

But she couldn't. She couldn't bear it. "I'm so sorry."

"I wanted it too." He grasped the back of her head and forced her to look at him. His expression was taut, pained. "I too begged for death. And if I'd had to watch that monster do that to you?" He blanched. "I would have lost my bloody mind. Do you understand? I would have wished for your death too, if I couldn't help you."

"William." She had so many regrets.

He read her well, for his gaze turned fierce. "Don't you dare take this upon yourself." He leaned in and pressed his lips to her forehead, breathing her in. "I wouldn't change a thing. Because it brought me to you."

Holly sucked in a sharp breath, and he blinked down, his dark eyes filling. "Everything, all that I endured, was worth it because I found you."

She wrapped her arms about his neck, drawing him down so that he hunched over her, and squeezed him tight. His grip was crushing, and he breathed hard into the crook of her neck before pressing his lips to the spot that held his mark.

When she found the strength to speak, the words were muffled and hot against his chest. "How am I to go on without you, when you give my life color and joy?" A choked sound left him, and his body quaked. She held on tighter, until her arms ached. "I'd rather die."

A great shudder went through him. "I'm killing you now." His voice broke on a sob, as if it had only just truly hit him. "Oh gods, I've done this to you."

"No, love, no."

But he was past hearing. Blood rimmed his eyes and stained the tops of his cheeks, but his expression was set. "You are in this danger because of my misguided need for vengeance. Do not make me live with the knowledge that I ultimately succeeded in killing you. Please, Holly. I could not bear it."

All at once she crumpled, because she could not do that to him. Nor could she condemn him to a life as a shadow crawler, stuck in pain and madness. She had to be as brave as he was. And it broke her heart. William held onto her, stroking her hair and shaking with her.

Too soon, she released him, her arms heavy as lead.

He took a deep breath. "I was not yet ready to let you go either, you know." He looked away, quickly, as if the sight of her pained him, but he held her hand in a bruising grip as he turned them back to the green. His stride was brisk, nearly a run. And she jogged to keep up. But she wouldn't slow him. To delay would destroy what little resolve they had.

Mab waited for them, her countenance bland as they stopped before her.

"You have a bargain, fae witch," William snapped out. His hand in Holly's trembled.

Mab smiled brightly. "Excellent. A wise choice."

Holly longed to tear the bitch's eyes out. But William jerked her round to face him, his treatment rough, though she knew it was done out of pain. Stark lines of hurt and regret sharpened his features. And the platinum filaments in his black irises began to thicken.

"I would have stayed with you forever," he said. "Until you were bloody-well sick of my face."

"Never." Her entire body hurt at the very thought of being without him. She wanted to cling to him, soak in his scent and the warm texture of his skin.

"It doesn't matter if she takes my memories of you," he said in a thick rush. "My soul knows yours. And that part of me will always love you. It will always be yours." His fingertips hovered above his mark upon her, but he did not touch her, as if it would be too painful for him.

Holly's lips trembled. She was breaking. And she would not recover this time. But she couldn't let him see it now. "I love you, William Thorne." And though it hurt to do so, she reached up and pulled down his cravat, exposing the small star-shaped mark that said he was hers. Gently she kissed him there. "With all that I am."

William whispered her name and then cupped her cheeks. His kiss was tender and fierce and not enough. His gaze burned into hers, and then, in a swirl of shadows, he was gone.

Chapter Thirty-One

~~~❦~~~

Will moved as though through a cold fog. At his side, Holly's cousin Sin followed. He didn't want him here, didn't want any reminders of what he was about to lose, but he could not do this alone. He needed someone to take Eliza May back to Mab.

In all likelihood, Adam would tear Will apart after this deception. And Will would not play fast and loose with Holly's life. Thus Sin was his partner. Damn it all.

"I did not know it would play out like that," the lad said in a small voice. "I did not know Mab would make you choose. I did not know Holly's life was in danger because of…" Sin ducked his head, wincing.

Will's chest tightened. "Do not speak of it. Ever again."

He did not check to see if the boy understood or not. If he mentioned Holly again, Will would split his lip to shut him up.

When they reached the privacy of Will's old home—for he could not return to Evernight Hall without losing his sanity—he headed towards the empty ballroom. If

Adam came here, he'd need room to maneuver. If they were transported to Adam, well then he'd figure it out there.

"Do we hold hands, you think?" Sin asked, as Will pulled out the enchanted sovereign. "In case the coin takes us to him?"

Will sneered, annoyance rivaling his broken heart, then grabbed hold of the lad's arm. "Let us see."

He tossed the coin high and thought of Adam. Bloody, fucking Adam.

Cold air rushed by, and blackness descended. In a blink, they stood beneath a domed pavilion in the middle of an abandoned pleasure park. "Cremorne Gardens," Will murmured, despite his rancor. He'd played here as a child.

"Pretty, isn't it?" a deep voice remarked.

As one, Will and Sin turned. He wasn't prepared for the sight of Adam. Hells bells. Will could not see anything particularly special about him. True, he was handsome. Will could admit that much about another man. But there was a scent, a power, coming off the fiend in waves so strong, so blatantly sensual, that an unwelcome heat stirred within Will's belly.

Sweet Satan, but that brassed him off. At his side, Sin scowled and shifted his weight from one foot to the other, as if he too felt it.

Adam's mouth quirked with knowing amusement. "Sorry. I don't intend to attract men. It happens to everyone. Well," he paused, "almost everyone."

It was then that Will noticed the woman standing ten paces behind Adam. She was a pretty lass, with the clean yet lush features of an Evernight. Defiance lined her every curve and set her face with stony resolve. She stared through them as though they were not there. All this, Will thought bitterly, because of this one girl. And then he felt shame. She was just as much a pawn as the rest of them.

He turned his bitterness to where it would be more effective. Towards Adam.

"You wanted to see me?"

"I'd hoped to see you and Miss Evernight together." Adam cocked a black brow. "Yet I find a boy in her place."

Sin snorted.

"This is St. John Evernight," Will said. "He comes in Holly's stead because I am unwilling to risk her safety."

"And why would you assume I'd hurt her?" Adam frowned, and a pulse of power emanated off of him. Hard enough to make the pavilion's iron struts creak. "I do not harm those I invite to meet me. Nor can I harm humans."

"With the old ones," Will explained, "you can never be too careful."

Adam gave a dry laugh. "Touché, Mr. Thorne."

"What is it that you wanted?" Will asked, though he could guess.

"You will be approached by Mab the fae queen," Adam said. "She will want you to return something to her." The hard line of his jaw twitched. "Something that is not hers to take."

Behind him, Eliza's eyes flared with resentment.

"I gather that 'something' is the young lass there?" Will inclined his head towards her.

Adam's eyes glowed, flashing brilliant gold. Will knew that look. It was a male in danger of falling into a territorial rage. This woman, Eliza, meant far more to the demon than he let on. Likely she was his mate. Which narrowed Will's chance of survival significantly.

Easily, Will held up his hands. "You've a gold chain about her wrists. It stands to reason."

Adam grunted. "You shall tell Mab no."

"And in return?"

"I was the one who told Darby not to kill your Miss Evernight." Adam gave him a tight smile. "So as I see it, you owe me a boon."

Will wondered if Adam had a clue how far ahead Mab had played her hand.

"I'll need some reassurances," Will said instead. When Adam quirked a brow, Will went on. "Despite what you might have heard of me, I don't harm women. I cannot in good conscience leave behind a woman if she's being ill treated."

It was a risk, calling Adam's honor into question, but it was the only way. And for a moment, Will wondered if he'd failed, for rage licked over the demon's face. But on the next breath, he calmed.

"I admire that, actually," Adam said lightly. "As you can see, however, she is fine." Not once did he look at Eliza.

"I'm afraid I'd rather speak to her myself. Give her a quick look-over. I won't," he assured, "touch her."

Because that would certainly set the primus off.

"I'm afraid that I do not trust you that close to what is mine, sanguis."

So Will's reputation with females had preceded him. Undaunted, Will shrugged. "Let the boy here do it." Sin had remained quiet, as he'd been told to do, but at that, he managed somehow to look both innocent and earnest.

Adam studied him for a moment. And then, with clear reluctance, nodded. "Be quick about it."

At those words, Will's heart began to churn. Sin had a fae key within his pocket. One of transport. He merely needed to touch it, and they'd be gone. Back to Mab. But Will needed to break the chain first.

Forcing a look of bland calm, he watched Sin walk steadily over to Eliza May. Far from snarling at him, Eliza gazed steadily at the boy. Had she any idea what they were about to do?

When Sin drew near, he spoke to her in a clear voice. "Are you well, Miss?"

"I am unharmed, if that's what you mean." She'd a flat accent, betraying her American origins. But at the sound of her voice, Adam went rigid, his entire body leaning towards her as if he craved hearing it. Will felt a twinge of sympathetic pity for him.

Sin, the brilliant lad, seemed to pick up on this as well, for he kept her talking. "I'm St. John. Though most call me Sin."

"Pleased to make your acquaintance," she replied. "I am Eliza. Eliza May."

"You're a Yank," Sin remarked with good nature.

"And you're a Limey."

He laughed at that, and so did she.

At the sound of her laughter, Adam's eyes fluttered closed. And that was when Will struck. Drawing on every ounce of power he possessed, Will flashed to shadow. He had to trust that Sin would grab hold of Eliza and do his job properly.

Will reformed a second later, right behind Adam. He grabbed hold of the golden chain and yanked it apart. The metal snapped just as Adam roared, the sound so loud and encompassing that Will's ears rang.

"No!"

Will didn't have to look to know Eliza and Sin were gone. Nor did he have the strength. He fell to his knees as a wave of nausea hit him. The only thought on his mind was of her. "Holly."

* * *

Will Thorne rose up. He was utterly human now, a weak and defenseless thing. Yet he stood before Adam's rage without any visible fear.

"You dare remain behind?" Adam snarled. His chest was so tight that the words came out garbled, spittle flying from his lips. Only a mere thread of control kept him from tearing Thorne's head off. But he couldn't touch him. Perhaps Thorne knew as much because he simply regarded him with something close to compassion.

"I gave you the chance I never received," Thorne said in his softer human voice.

"What chance?" Rage had Adam panting. It broke on a roar. "I want my property back!"

Thorne didn't flinch. "That's just it, mate. She's not a piece of property. And if you want any chance of having her with you, she had to be free."

Adam did not want to listen; he'd been searching for so long. And now she was gone. It hurt. It burned. He could barely see through his frustration. On a curse, he lashed out, smashing his fist into the stone. "You had no right."

Thorne's expression hardened. "Just as you and your ilk had no right to play about with my life. With Holly's." Something sharp and pained passed over his face, but he hardened his features. "I've done you a favor. A great one. If there is any logical means of thought left within you, you'll realize this."

Adam spun on his heel and paced. Bloody hell, but the bastard was correct. He'd achieved precisely nothing with Eliza while holding her to him.

"She can't disappear on you," Thorne said in a low voice. "You know who she is now."

Aye, that he did. But that wasn't the point. He ached

when she was gone. It was a wound that bled into his damned soul. Unable to bring himself to look at Thorne, he stared unseeing into the abandoned pleasure gardens.

"What do you want," he said, "in return for this *favor*?"

"Kill me or leave me alone."

Despair hung on the man so thick that it clogged the air. Adam knew that depth of hopelessness. He felt it now. Gnashing his teeth, he bit out his reply. "Get. Out."

Thorne turned and left without a backward glance. A man walking as if headed for the gallows.

Chapter Thirty-Two

William Halvor Thorne, seventh Marquis of Renwood, Earl of Carlay, Viscount Durham, stared into the dressing mirror and tried to find himself. But a stranger stared back at him in the reflection. For seven months he'd studied this face, and though the sharp blade of his nose, the basic shape and form of his features felt right enough, the light brown hair and pale blue eyes that made up his coloring were utterly foreign to him.

Frowning, he made a face in the mirror, peeling back his lips and baring his teeth in a primitive snarl. Even, white teeth shone in the mellow glow of the gas lamp. Wrong. Everything felt wrong. His body was sluggish, his senses dulled. He knew this to his marrow. But how could he be sure, when he could not remember his life?

A tragedy, they said. A horrible accident. Will had awakened one day to find himself in a strange bed with a ring of servants peering over him. They'd told him he was William Thorne, that he was Marquis of Renwood, and he'd hit his head while riding in the country. He couldn't remember ever riding a horse. Everything felt off-kilter, a lie. And yet not. His name he recognized. And his house, once he'd walked through it, letting his fingers skim over oddly familiar surfaces. But those memories were filtered through a haze, as though he'd been absent for a decade rather than unconscious for months.

As for his staff, they too walked about as if in a half-dream. Oftentimes, he felt the weight of their gaze upon him, and when he turned quickly enough, he'd see their frowns, the confusion resting in their eyes. It matched his own.

Why, he'd asked Mr. Mason, his man of business, had he no friends, nor associates? Had he been an evil man? An outcast? That felt…right. Which bothered him in equal measure.

Mason's answer only made things worse. Will had been abroad these many years, feared dead for a time. A distant cousin had taken the title, only to haul off when Will had been found. Now society wanted to meet the newly restored Marquis.

Lies.

Will knew it. But he could not prove it. He was stuck in a nightmare with no way out.

With reluctance, Will straightened the white tie at his throat and adjusted the cuffs of his evening suit. His valet could do such things for him, but Will would be damned if that man was getting near him again. Not after he'd shorn Will's hair in a close, "proper" cut when Will had still been unconscious.

That had been the first thing he'd noticed that was off about himself. He couldn't even explain why, but he'd *known*, without a shadow of a doubt, that his hair ought to be long. Finding it cut short had filled him with rage.

A rage that had yet to abate. For he was missing something else. Something essential to him. And he could not remember what it was. His hands shook with it. And when they did, he caught sight of the gleaming strip of platinum that he wore about his finger.

The ring was fairly thin and of a strange woven design, as if the jeweler had twined two thin platinum threads together and wrapped them round and round. Will could almost see its creation, as if he'd been there to witness the unknown jeweler making it. The ring disturbed him most of all. His soul seemed to scream at the unfairness of life when he looked at it, yet he could not, no matter how hard he tried, compel himself to take it off.

A scratch at the door had him turning.

Mr. Mason's round face appeared at the edge of the doorway. He caught sight of Will and smiled, disingenuous and broad. "Ah, you're ready. Excellent. Shall we go and meet your public then, my lord?"

Absently, Will rubbed the cold spot that never warmed on his chest. His heart ached. Constantly. "Very well."

And though he was about to greet a room of hundreds of people, he felt utterly alone.

Sin caught sight of Holly before she noticed him. In all likelihood, he might have fired a round of bullets into the air before she gave him the time of day. Though it was late, and all the other inventors had long ago left the SOS laboratory, she sat hunched over her worktable. As she had day in and day out for the past seven months.

His heart ached for her. She was too thin, her collarbones visible beneath her drab, grey gown. And she was too pale, dark circles ringing her once-bright eyes. They were dull now, seeing yet never engaged. At least she was here, at headquarters, instead of wasting away in Evernight House.

She'd gone kicking and screaming, in her own stubborn way, back to work. Forced there by the combined efforts of Mary, Poppy, and himself. In the end, Jack Talent had stepped in, thrown her over his massive shoulder, and physically removed her from her house.

Perhaps it was the ignominy of being hauled about like a side of beef, or perhaps she realized the futility of further struggle, but she'd calmed then and accepted that she needed to get back to the familiar, to life.

But she wasn't living. Sin knew. His cousin was dying. Of sorrow and of loneliness. And though her body would go on, indefinitely it seemed, she'd slowly fade into a ghost of herself.

Anger licked through him at the thought, and the room heated about him.

On a curse, he strode forward, making certain that his boot heels struck the floor with definitive thuds. Holly stiffened as he approached. Only when he was right before her did she put down her pencil and acknowledge him. Fine lines pulled at the corners of her lips.

He stared at her for a full minute, until she scowled and broke their silence. "What is it then?"

"You are coming out with me tonight." He'd take no argument. And he'd haul her arse with him if he had to.

Holly's nostrils flared as though she were preparing to lash out. He beat her to it. "I need you, Hollis." Oh, but he was playing dirty. He didn't care. "I need your help. Please."

She sagged, her eyes reddening. "You are a right pest, Sin."

A lump gathered in his throat. He wanted to hold his cousin and tell her all would be well. But he couldn't promise that.

Chapter Thirty-Three

✦✦✦

Holly was in hell. Consigned there by her formerly favorite cousin Sin. Hell came wrapped in a pretty package, a lovely ballroom in an equally lovely house. Crystal chandeliers dripped light upon hundreds of elegantly dressed ladies and gentlemen. Fragrant white flowers, caught up in massive bouquets that flanked each of the large French doors, thickened the air with their perfume. A light waltz played.

All was hazy and gilded. A swirl of colorful silk skirts and smiling faces. And Holly wanted out of it. Immediately. While she could manage to push through life, putting one foot in front of the other, wearing out each day in an endless cycle, she could not tolerate happiness. She could not hear laughter without wanting to tear her heart out. Without thinking of *him*.

And she tried very hard not to think of him.

Heat prickled behind her eyes, the smoke coming off the candles making it worse. She turned to Sin, who stood dressed in immaculate white and black. "I cannot stay here."

He peered down at her, his handsome face drawn in a frown. "We've just arrived." His expression softened as he touched her arm. "Give it a little longer, Hol, and then we can go, I swear."

Gripping the folds of her skirts, she nodded once and then tried to smooth the damage she'd wreaked upon the crimson satin—if only for something to do. Oh, but why had she worn this color? Why had she let Sin talk her into this dress?

Her hands shook. And so she clasped them together. She might have protested again, but Sin uttered a choked sound and turned pale. Holly followed his gaze but could see no threat, only a young woman in butter yellow taffeta. She was a pretty thing, not in a showy sort of way, but in a clean, elegant manner. Mahogany hair swept up in intricate braids gleamed in the candlelight.

She was too far off to see the color of her eyes, but they appeared lively and tilted up at the corners.

"You know her?" Holly asked a gaping Sin.

At the sound of Holly's voice, Sin flinched, and with a tiny shake of his head, looked away from the girl. "It's Layla."

"Layla Starling?" A vague recollection came to Holly. Of a young girl, perhaps six or seven, living on the property abutting Evernight Hall in Ireland. "The American heiress who moved away years ago?"

Dully Sin nodded. He looked as though he'd seen a ghost. For the first time in months, Holly found herself wanting to smile. Sin had always been shy around others. But she remembered him being thick as thieves with little Layla at one point. "Go say hello to her. I am certain she—"

Whatever Holly might have said fled in a hot rush as two men entered the room, their arrival causing a stir through the crowd. The younger of the two men was clearly the cause of all the attention. Tall and proud, his strong features striking against the crisp white of his collar, he stood out amongst lesser men.

Dimly, Holly felt her flesh prickling. A loud buzzing filled her ears. Her vision narrowed down to him. She ought not to have recognized him. His hair was short, combed in a proper English fashion, and plain brown. His skin had an almost ruddy cast, blooming with basic human vigor. Nothing that resembled the man he once was. Oh, but his face, that blade thin nose, the sharp angle of his jaw, the narrowed gaze, and the firm lips that had touched every inch of her body long ago. Those things remained.

William. Her mouth moved over the name, but she hadn't the heart to utter it.

A lady whispered something in his ear, and he canted his head, giving the woman a tight smile.

Thorne. Her wicked Thorne.

Holly's breath caught with such force that it shredded her throat. The floor beneath her swayed. Blindly, she turned on Sin. "You bastard." She could barely speak through her rage. "You bloody, sick bastard—"

He caught hold of her arm—the one she'd raised to strike him with, though she hadn't recalled lifting it—and tugged her close as those around her started to stare. "I know," he said under his breath. "I am, and you can hate me all you like." His head dipped closer. "But I could not watch you waste away any longer. Not when it could end here."

"I cannot..." She struggled not to cry. She would never cry again. That much she had promised herself. "Do you mean to torture me? Do you have any notion how much it hurts, Sin?" So bloody much that she felt as though a barely scabbed-over wound had ripped open upon her chest.

"I mean to set you free," he shot back. "Go to him."

Holly wrenched her wrist from his grip. "He cannot see me," she hissed. "You know this. If I let him see me, it will undo everything we sacrificed!"

Damn Sin to hell, but he knew better.

Her stubborn cousin simply shook his head. "No. I've been thinking on this. You aren't remembering Mab's words properly. She said that you couldn't remind him of who you are. It cannot be your doing. But he"—Sin inclined his head towards the other end of the room where William roamed—"he is not bound by those rules. He can remember on his own without breaking the bargain."

Holly flinched, Sin's words a hard punch to her belly. "He won't remember. Those memories are gone." Just as Will was from her life.

"Fae tricks," Sin said. "The memories are there. Only obscured." His mouth tightened. "Believe me, I know this well." And Holly remembered that Sin's real father had been a master of altering memories and of playing with fates.

"Go to him, Holly." Sin stared at her. "There is nothing in your agreement that says you and Thorne cannot be together. Is it not worth the risk? Is he not worth it?"

She was afraid. Afraid of coming face to face with him and seeing nothing more than bland politeness. Of missing the way he used to look at her, as though she was the world to him. As he was hers.

As if pulled by a cord, Holly's gaze went to William, tracking him as he slowly made his way through the crowd with the reluctance of a man merely doing his duty.

Dear God, but he was beautiful to her. So very foreign now, with his short brown hair and darker human skin, but so very familiar in the way he moved, in the stark planes of his face. Her breath hitched.

Though it was impossible, it was as if he'd heard her, for he suddenly stilled and turned his head. His gaze collided with hers with the force of a bullet. And held. She could not breathe. Could not think past wanting him. Yet somehow, she found the strength to put one foot in front of the other. To go to him.

Being the center of attention, Will decided, was hell. A very pretty version of it, but hell all the same. People pressed in on him, their sour scents and heavy perfumes clogging his nostrils and making it hard to breathe. His insides heaved, though he was starving. He never ate well. Aside from soups and soft, whipped vegetables, he could not tolerate many solid foods.

His sole delight, he eventually discovered, had been hot chocolate. Until the day he'd taken a sip and a spring breeze had drifted in through an open window, carrying with it the sweet fragrance of lilacs. He'd dropped his cup then, unable to stand the rich, warm taste of chocolate a moment longer. His heart had hurt so badly, a deep, unending ache that had him wanting to cry like a lad. So then, no more chocolate for him.

Yes, Will thought, as he bowed over yet another gloved hand in greeting, he was in hell.

At his side, Mason leaned close, his breath stale with the stink of old cigars. "At least try to smile, my lord."

Smile? He didn't know how. He'd never felt the urge. But he tried.

And then he felt the weight of a stare. It tickled the back

of his neck, a hot finger of awareness stroking his skin. He hadn't felt heat, not in all his living memory. Shock had him tensing. He turned, seeking the source of this heavy gaze. And caught sight of the woman.

Everything within him tensed, prickling in an alarm that was close to panic. His breath stilled. Deep inside of him, a voice seemed to scream, *yes, her, that one*. Will blinked, trying to focus on the woman who stood at the opposite side of the ballroom.

Surrounded by ink-black hair, her face was a pale oval, solemn and sorrowful. And beautiful. She was heartbreakingly beautiful to him. Delicately wrought features and a direct gaze that bore into him and set his flesh aflame.

The deep crimson color of her gown stood out amongst duller colors. *She* stood out. Apart from everything, as though she was the only one in the room with him. And then she was moving, her stride slow but as confident as a man's. Something shifted in his mind, like a breeze blowing through, trying to stir the cobwebs. But then it was gone.

It did not matter. She was walking towards him. *To* him.

Will broke out of his stupor, and without a backward glance, went to meet her.

Anticipation clenched low in his gut. He wanted to break into a run, so great was his desire to get to her. He forced himself to remain calm, lest she find him as mad as he suspected himself to be.

Closer. Closer.

They met in the middle of the room, stopping when there was little more than a foot between them.

Hells bells, but she was even lovelier up close. Her eyes

were blue. A dark blue that called to mind cool lakes and twilight skies. A man could lose himself in such eyes. And not even mind if he were drowning.

"Hello." He found himself smiling. Like an idiot.

She blanched, her gaze going to his inane grin then back to meet his eyes. Ruddy, bloody hell, he'd bolloxed this up before it had truly begun. But then she cleared her throat and spoke. "Hello."

Her voice sent a shiver through him. It was calm and smooth, just as it ought to be.

Will fought not to lean forward and crowd her. Awkward silence fell over them. He ought to ask a mutual acquaintance for a proper introduction, but she was alone, and he was impatient. From the sweet swells of her bosom, gloriously displayed by her evening bodice, came the scent of lilacs and something sharp that he couldn't quite recognize but somehow gave him comfort enough to blurt out the first words that came to mind. "I feel like a fool."

She blinked up at him, the black wings of her brows knitting in confusion.

Will's face heated. "What I meant is that I feel as though I know you. I have so much that I want to tell—" He broke off, mortified at his inane babbling. "Bloody hell," he muttered, pinching the bridge of his nose.

Her lips twitched again. Likely she thought he'd escaped Bedlam.

Will pulled himself straight. "Let's try this again. I am William Thorne." He extended his hand, propriety not allowing him to take hers, but hoping she'd offer it all the same.

She hesitated, the tendons on her neck moving as she swallowed, but then she relented. Her slim, gloved hand rested lightly on his fingers. Just that small touch sent a shock of feeling through him.

"The Marquis of Renwood," she acknowledged faintly.

William. Call me William. Having acted the idiot more than enough this night, he kept his council. "I've been... out of the country." The words were a bitter lie on his tongue.

But she accepted them with a short nod. "And are you..." Her voice grew fainter. "Have you been well?"

It was too intimate a question for polite society. But he wanted to answer. He wanted to confide in her. *No, I've been in hell. Until you came.* It hit him then. She made his backward world feel righted. It made no sense.

Will did not know if he'd ever believed in love at first sight, but he knew with utter conviction that he wanted this woman in his life. "Dance with me." It was blunt, not at all a request.

And she blanched. Her twilight eyes going wide. "I... I don't dance."

"You don't? Or won't?" The words were out before he could stop them, and Will silently cursed. Satan's balls, but that was rude.

Shockingly, she did not frown at him or turn away. The corners of her pink mouth twitched, as though she fought a smile. In turn, it made him smile. "Then take a turn about the room with me," he pressed. "Tell me about yourself." It occurred to him that she hadn't even given him her name. "Come now, love. Surely one turn cannot be so great a task."

As if slapped, she closed her eyes, and a look of such utter pain twisted her features that he feared she was ailing. Horrified at the thought, he took a step towards her, his hand moving to clasp her arm, when she opened her eyes and quickly stepped back.

"I'm sorry," she whispered. "I have to go."

No, no, no!

She was drifting away, being swallowed up by the crowd.

"Good-bye, William."

Chapter Thirty-Four

———❦~❦———

Will stared at the spot where the woman in red had been. Every instinct he possessed howled at the wrongness of her absence. From the center of his heart, pain spread. It filled him up then spilled outward.

He fancied he might find his blood pooling on the waxed parquet floor beneath his feet. But there was none. No, he simply stood alone. Without her.

Absently, he stroked his thumb over his platinum ring as their strange conversation played within his head, flickering over and over like a child's zoetrope. Her eyes meeting his gaze without flinching. Her scent, motor oil and metal and lilacs. Her smile reluctant and hard won. Her blood, rich, savory. Blood. Delicious and flowing down his throat.

Will's canines throbbed.

Her voice saying his name. As no other had done save his mum. She'd called him William. She always called him that. Or Thorne.

"William Thorne, you are an utter beast."

Will gave a violent start. Why was he still here?

His legs propelled him forward before he even had the thought to move. And then he was striding, weaving through the crush of people, heedless of anything but getting to her. She was gone. His gait quickened.

Out of the house, down the front drive. The scent of lilacs and metal hung in the air like a tracer. He drew it in, his pace turning into a jog. Then a run. Faster. Faster. He needed to find her. His life depended on it.

Out on the street, people danced, laughing and singing, enjoying the fair weather. May Day. Or the drunken end of it. Brilliant. Will shoved past a Jack in the Green, the brittle foliage on the man's costume scraping Will's cheek. Still Will rushed onward, leaving behind a band of dancing chimney sweeps and three foxed May Queens.

But no sign of a red dress. Frantic, he sped on, following her scent. Not knowing how he could, but smelling it as clear as a bell. His body ached, his lungs burned with effort. Useless, tiresome human body. He hated it. Hated its weakness, when he needed to be fleet of foot and strong.

He turned a corner, and the edifice of Victoria Station loomed in the distance. And he *knew* she'd gone inside. Bugger. Her scent took him to an outbound train platform. There, against the soaring arches of steel and glass, was a flash of red skirts. She was headed for a train. She would be lost to him. Again.

He could not move fast enough, could not get to her in time. Desperation, want, need, rushed up from his chest.

"Holly!" he shouted without thought, his feet flying over the hard ground. The crimson bustle of her skirts swayed with her quick steps. And his soul cried out in wrongness that she should be apart from him. "Evernight!"

＊　　＊　　＊

Holly couldn't stay. She couldn't look at William and not have him. So she ran.

Her corset pinched her side, her legs ached. She ran through Victoria Station, down to the ticket booth. She would go home to Ireland. To her parents. She missed her family. She needed arms to hold her.

Ticket purchased and in hand, Holly wove through the slower moving passengers, heading out to the platforms. She could not stand still; it gave her too much time to think. Ahead of her, the train waited to take her away, a dark, snaking beast, hissing white steam from its valve.

"Holly!"

She nearly stumbled at the sound of his voice, the desperate pitch of it. So quickly had she been moving that she took three more steps before she could slow.

"Evernight!"

Sweet pain lanced through her heart. Panting, she stopped, her skirts swaying, even as footsteps pounded up behind her.

He'd been running like a fiend, for he skidded to a halt as she turned around. Not three feet away, William Thorne stood before her, sweat darkening his temples, his chest heaving as he fought for breath. She struggled to calm her own.

They stood facing each other, he with a pained expression as he panted, and she likely looking the same. His rapid breath slowly eased, and he straightened, his gaze never leaving hers. "Sodding useless human body," he said in his dark Northern voice. "I don't know how you stand it."

A half-sob, half-choked laugh broke from her. And his mouth trembled, caught, it seemed, between a smile and a frown. He stared at her for a beat of silence, and then an anguished sound left him.

"Holly." His voice broke, and his body moved.

Two strides and he had her. His warm palms cupped her cheeks, and then his lips covered hers. He wasn't polite about it, or careful. He devoured her mouth, plundering deep. And it felt so bloody good, like sweet relief and home, that Holly sobbed. He swallowed the sound down, licking it up with the lap of his tongue.

She wound her arms about his neck, pressing closer to the familiar heat of his body. Time and a sea of people passed them by as they kissed. Until she was dizzy with need and happiness.

Slowly, taking little nips as he went, Will pulled back. With a broad sigh, he rested his forehead upon hers, his hands still cupping her face as though he'd never let go.

"Holly," he whispered. "Petal mine."

"You remember." Her voice cracked.

"Everything." Soft kisses peppered her face, the scent and texture of him surrounding her.

"William." Clutching his shoulders, she kissed him back. On his jaw, the warm crook of his neck, the tip of his sharp nose. "Man of my heart."

Impatient fingers plucked at the satin ribbon around her neck. "Let me see my mark, love." The ribbon slithered away, and he let out a satisfied sigh before tenderly pressing his lips to the thorn-shaped mark that had never faded. "I was lost. So lost without you."

Exhaustion washed through her. She rested her head upon his shoulder and let him hold her. "You are my joy," she told him.

"And you are my lodestone," he said. "I will always come back to you."

He smiled. And she smiled.

Until the scent of earth and moss invaded her happy sanctuary. He too caught the scent, for he stiffened and his nostrils flared. Around them, silence fell, the once-crowded train platform now deserted.

As if struck, Will lurched, doubling up on a sharp hiss before falling to his knees. Holly cried out, sinking to his side as he convulsed.

"Will?"

The scent of earth grew thicker, and a fog rolled in, filling up the cavernous iron canopy that made up the depot. Will remained hunched over, his body trembling.

"Talk to me," she insisted, trying to ignore the tendrils of fog that tickled her neck.

"Oh my," said a feminine voice. "It appears Will Thorne has regained his memory."

Mab sauntered out from the billowing fog, a vision in green satin and white bows. Her rosebud lips pursed. "Looking a bit worse for wear, isn't he?"

"Shut up," Holly snapped, her hand still upon Will's shoulder.

Mab stared at Will. "You are not supposed to be here."

"You have no control over where I go," Will said between gasps.

"What are you doing to him?" Holly snarled.

Mab ignored her. "We had a bargain, Mr. Thorne."

"And we kept it. There was nothing in it about me remembering Holly on my own."

Mab sneered. "How I hate when you demons wiggle by on a technicality."

Again Will writhed, doubling up as though trying to hold his guts in.

"Stop!" Holly's cry was sharp and strong enough that

Mab paused. "I want another bargain," she told Mab, knowing a fae could not resist the temptation.

"Oh?" Mab said. "Request?"

"Leave William alone." Holly lifted her chin. "Name your terms."

Will made a gurgle of protest. Gently, Holly touched his cold cheek, and Will's gaze held hers. "Stay down," she said in a low voice. "This is my fight."

His nostrils flared, the expression on his face shifting towards stubborn refusal. But then he gave an almost imperceptible nod. Love, gratitude, and protectiveness flooded her and gave her strength. This man. He knew her. He was her partner in all things. And she would not lose him again.

In a single move, Holly rose and spun to face Mab.

"Now dear girl," Mab said with a patronizing smile, "no male is worth such upset. Do the sensible thing and never become attached to one."

"As you did not become attached to Aidan? So desperate for his affections that you forced a man who did not desire you into your bed."

Mab's eyes flared dark purple fire as she sneered. "He was being unreasonable. As are you."

The fae stiffened as Holly's fists clenched. "Do not," Mab suggested, "make threatening gestures towards me, young one. You shall not like the consequences."

Holly smiled then. This fae believed her to be a rational creature, ruled by logic. Perhaps once. But not today. "As you dared to threaten William?" Holly stalked forward. "You dared lay a finger on him, after we played your game?"

"His very presence here insults me. I am Mab. I shall not be made to look a fool by a lowly sanguis turned even lower human." Her expression turned mulish. "And I cannot say I am pleased by your lack of gratitude for the gift I bestowed to you."

Ah, yes, her "gift." As soon as William had left her, Mab had informed Holly that, because of her kinship and the trials she had to face by being stuck with the sanguis, Holly could have the *gift* of immortality. It had been the height of cruelty, to make Will a human while forcing Holly to live an eternity without him.

Holly had said as much, and Mab, in a fit of pique, had made the gift irreversible. The bitch.

Holly's anger burned hotter now. "If it's gratitude you're wanting, pray look elsewhere. Only a fool would desire a 'gift' from you."

Mab's nostrils flared. She cuffed Holly on the face, sending her to her knees.

A roar rang out, and Will staggered to his feet and grabbed the fae about the throat. Though human, Will was not weak. He shook her like a rag before tossing her far. But Mab landed upon light feet.

And she laughed. "I see lessons are in order."

She snapped her fingers, and Holly heard the sickening crack of Will's arm bone. Instantly, Will's body went rigid, a scream pushing through his clenched teeth. Mab snapped again, and Will toppled, his legs bent at unnatural angles.

Chapter Thirty-Five

～～～

"No more!" Holly shouted, stalking towards Mab.

With a bored expression, the fae lifted a hand and sent a wave of power through the air. Holly tumbled back, skidding until she stopped at the edge of the train platform. And Will, human and vulnerable, flopped about on the ground as Mab continued to break his bones one by one.

Rage, blind and all-encompassing, lit through Holly. She welcomed it, letting it fuel her. Looming behind her was a great, black steam engine. The massive iron locomotive began to shake upon the track, the sound of metal groaning then tearing with a series of sharp screeches. Holly narrowed her focus, and the iron panels along the engine ripped free. They flew through the air and landed before Will, clanging as they formed a wall around him. Higher and higher, blocking him from Mab and her power.

Struggling to her feet, Holly pulled more iron. A violent rattle sounded around the platform, ominous and strained.

Mab glanced about, taking in the wrought-iron fence dividing the wide platform that lay between two tracks. The iron posts began to quiver. And her gaze narrowed. Iron was quite deadly to the fae, and they both knew it. "You would not dare."

Holly flicked her wrists. The iron spears on the fence flew through the air in a blur. Mab screamed as they slammed into her, throwing her back and impaling her upon the stone wall of the station's entrance.

Breathing through her teeth, Mab hissed at Holly. "Insolent little—"

Another sliver of iron caught the fae in the neck, going in deep enough to cut off her words but not yet her head.

Holly stopped before the woman. Mab snarled, unable to move against the iron spears. The metal was doing its work, leaching into her body, poisoning her blood and weakening her.

"You ought to have chosen a safer place to launch your attack," Holly advised. "Or did you assume that I would not fight back? That I would cower and fear you?"

Mab's expression promised retribution and pain.

"Now you listen to me," Holly said with quiet conviction. "You will never touch William Thorne, nor any of his kith and kin, again. You will never contact me or interfere with my life, either directly or indirectly, again."

The fae uttered a noise that might have been a snort before glaring back at Holly.

Holly stared into those ancient eyes without fear. "You may have more power, and perhaps one day, you'll have the luck to catch me unaware. But you do not have my resolve. You come between me and mine again, and I will slice you into ribbons so slowly, it will take agonizing hours for this mortal shell you now wear to die. And when I am done, I'll send you back without another thought for you. I'll do it over and over. I will not stop defending what is mine."

Mab bared her teeth. She could not respond, however, not with the iron bar lodged in her throat.

Holly didn't flinch or blink. "Am I clear?"

Resentful capitulation filled Mab's eyes. Holly waved her hand, and the iron shards sliced through the fae's flesh like it was suet. On a garbled cry, the fae's head fell off, her body breaking apart in a mess of limbs and gore before it sizzled and bubbled an instant later. Before the iron finished falling to the ground, her remains were nothing more than a pile of ash.

Holly turned heel and ran back to Will, flinging the iron panels aside with a flick of her wrist. Will lay on his side, shaking.

"William." Her knees hit the pavement, and she reached for him, half frightened to touch him and cause more pain. White streaks shot down from the crown of his head, growing thicker and thicker, until the brown was gone.

"William?" she whispered.

Snarling, he reared back, and the light of the moon shone down through the glass ceiling and upon his face. Platinum. Razor sharp fangs extended from his open mouth. And then he simply sagged in on himself. The platinum faded away as if on a breath. For a moment, neither of them spoke, until he lifted his head and looked at her with demon black eyes.

A sob of relief broke from her. "Are you well?"

"I've had better nights." He glanced over at Mab's mortal remains and then back to Holly. His firm lips twitched, but his eyes remained tired and wary. "Destroying the fae queen will likely bring wrath upon your head."

"I did not destroy her. I sent her back to her world. She'll have to find another way to return here, and make another body." The thought of Mab returning made Holly shudder. But Will was safe and whole. And so was she.

Slowly he stood, extending a hand to help her up. Around them, the station filled up with people once more, all of them bustling about as if they'd always been there. Shocked voices broke out as people took in the skinned steam engine.

Ignoring them all, Will only had eyes for her, his expression almost stern. "My brave, clever love." He tugged her into his arms and held her tight. For a moment they simply breathed, his lips against her hair, her nose burrowed in the warm crook of his neck. Her palm flattened against his chest where his mechanical heart once again pumped away.

A wave of despair hit her. "What shall we do about you?" Though she was once again in balance, he was not.

"Petal, my capitulation to Mab was never about saving myself. It was about saving you." Will's hand came to rest over hers. "Watch."

Before her eyes, his hand went pure platinum and then back again to pale flesh.

Holly raised her head. "What does it mean?"

Though fatigue lined his face, his smile was cheeky. "Do you know, I've been sitting around that drafty old house pretending to be a marquis and having nothing to do."

"William," she threatened.

He laughed, a light, happy sound. "I'm getting there, love. I must have been thinking of you in some capacity, for I found myself reading scientific tomes. And there was this volume by that chap Darwin."

"You read Darwin?" Really, the thought of Will Thorne sitting quietly reading like a studious scholar was shock enough.

"Mmm." Wrapping an arm about her shoulders, he tucked her close and walked them away from Mab's ashes. "And he had this interesting theory on evolution."

"I've read it."

"Always interrupting." Will shook his head, grinning wide. "It occurs to me just now that perhaps I haven't been dying but evolving. A true marriage of science and nature. Why fight this new step? When fighting it has only brought me pain."

Holly stopped short. "That is your great epiphany? William Thorne, you have no proof—"

He kissed her, slow and leisurely. When she melted into him, he pulled back. "I've gone entirely metal many times now and still have my sanity. In truth, I've had control over myself since I destroyed the Nex elders. And the change to metal stopped hurting just after the Alamut let me go." He shrugged. "That's good enough for now."

Though she could voice various counter-theories and objections, Holly found herself smiling. "I missed you."

"Well I didn't, *couldn't*, you see," he teased, laughing when she poked his ribs. Then he sobered. "And I was in hell."

He kissed her once more. Softly. "I love you, Holly."

"I love you, William." Gently, she unwound his cravat and found her star-shaped mark upon his neck. She kissed the spot with possessive pride and utter contentment. And he returned the favor, nuzzling the little thorn upon her neck before tucking her once more against his side and guiding her down the platform.

"Where are we going?" Holly asked as they walked out of the station and into the clear night.

His grip on her tightened. "Home, petal mine. We're going home."

Epilogue

❧

Seven months earlier, London

Once upon a time, superstitious humans would bury those who died by their own hand at the crossroads. Six feet under with a spike through their hearts so that the dead would not rise. The dead, humans realized on some level, did not always stay dead. Sometimes, they changed into immortals. And while humans thought of a crossroad as a simple intersection, it was something far more powerful. A real crossroad was, in actuality, a gateway to other worlds.

Victoria Station, London's massive homage to locomotive transport, was once such a crossroad. And while the old crossroad was buried under brick and mortar, glass and steel, it still operated as a gateway.

As Adam strolled down a train platform, hands tucked into the pockets of his fine wool trousers that went with his fine English suit, he could not ignore that his freedom had come to an end. He had tried to break his curse, and he had failed. Time to pay the piper, as it were.

Around him travelers went about their business, thinking Adam nothing more than an ordinary gentleman waiting for the train. He waited for something far worse. And far too soon a sickly, yellow-green fog began to roll in, snaking along the track gullies and up onto the platform. No one took notice. London was often plagued by "pea soup" fog. Little did the humans know that this certain color fog heralded evil.

Inside his pockets, Adam's fists tightened against the urge to smash something. He focused on a distant spot, where a woman was gliding along, her green skirts swishing through the fog. The closer she came, the harder his heart beat. There would be pain, humiliation. An eternity of it. He did not want to be afraid; he loathed the idea. But he was.

The woman came into focus, her smile glinting with a sly bit of fang, her eyes a dark, smoky purple. He wanted to retch.

"I thought you might run," she said as she stopped before him. The scent of earth and green things surrounded him. Since it was her scent, it turned his stomach.

"I never run." He'd fight, but that was different.

She smiled, and the sweet visage she wore dropped for a mere instant, showing him her true form, the green tint of her skin, the black lips, and pointed teeth. Fae. Not beautiful and gentle, but ugly and cruel. "I've waited a long time for this, *Cù-Sìth.*"

It had been a long time since anyone had called him *Cù-Sìth*, the dark hound, harbinger of death. Knowing she'd revel in it, Adam refrained from flinching at the moniker.

"I'm certain you have, Queen Mab," Adam said as though he were without care.

Her simper fell. "Aodh MacNiall of Moray, ye have failed to bond with your soul's true mate."

"True." Quite the burn to discover that his other half found him repugnant. And now he'd never know how it felt to be complete. He'd never know peace.

Mab licked her lips, a greedy flick of her tongue. "Thus your soul is in forfeit. To me."

Did you miss

Shadowdance?

Discover the great love that Jack
Talent has for Mary Chase.

Once a heart is lost in shadow,
only someone who lives in
darkness can find it...

Please see the next page
for an excerpt.

Chapter Two

It was inevitable that Jack be called into headquarters. The Bishop of Charing Cross had struck the night before. Murder was nothing new in London. Strange ones of a public nature, however, were another matter. Jack had been the regulator in charge of this particular case for a year now, a blight on his otherwise stellar record. This time a shifter had been murdered. As one of five—make that four now—known shifters living in London, he took it personally. Having intimate knowledge of certain facts, Jack was also unnerved by this new murder. Deeply. And he wanted answers.

Cool shadows slid over him as he strode down the long, echoing corridor that led from the SOS common rooms to the main meeting area. Headquarters was full of regulators updating their intelligence before going out. He did not like being around them, or anyone. Not that he had to worry on that account. The others steered clear of him, their eyes averted and their bodies tense. Fear he could handle, hell welcome, but pity?

One younger agent lowered her lashes when he passed, and a growl rumbled in his throat. She started and hurried off. Rightly so. No telling what sort of beast would break free should he lose his temper. Not even he knew. That was the way of a shifter, not owned by a single monster but possessed by all. He was everything, and he was nothing in particular. In truth, being a regulator was the only certain and good thing in Jack's life.

At the end of the black marble hall, a guard stood beside a massive steel door. He saw Jack coming and swiftly opened it.

"Master Talent," said the guard, "they are waiting for you."

He was precisely on time and the director was already waiting? And what did the guard mean by "they"? His meeting was to be with the director. Who the bloody devil would be here—

Her scent slammed into him like a punch. And what little equanimity he'd maintained flew out the door. Oh, no, no, no... they wouldn't dare. He eyed the inner wood door that blocked him from the meeting room. She was in there.

His muscles clenched tight as he forced himself to enter.

"Ah, Master Talent," said Director Wilde from the head of the table. "Right on time. Excellent. Let us proceed." His clipped voice was unusually animated, as if he knew Jack's displeasure at the unexpected third person in the room and reveled in it. Which wouldn't be surprising. Wilde loved to keep regulators on their toes.

Jack heard every word, but his gaze moved past the director and locked on her. Mary Chase sat at Wilde's right, serene and ethereal as ever. Her face was a perfect replica of Botticelli's Venus, and her body... no, he wouldn't think about that. It was one rule he refused to break. He never, ever, thought too long on Mary Chase.

Mary Chase would have liked to think that, after years of being on the receiving end of Jack Talent's hateful glare, she'd be immune to it by now. Unfortunately it still worked through her flesh like a lure, hooking in tight and tugging at something deep within her. One look and she wanted to jump from her chair and hit him. However, knowing that he found her presence bothersome gave her some small satisfaction.

He stood in the doorway, filling it up, poised for a fight like an avenging angel of Old Testament wrath. Over the last year Talent had reached his physical prime, shooting up well past an already impressive six feet, and adding what looked like twenty pounds of hard-packed muscle to his frame. It was as if nature had given him the outer shell he needed to protect himself from all comers. The change was unnerving, as the man had been intimidating enough before, mainly due to the sheer strength of his stubborn will.

With a sullen pout, Talent dropped his large body into the chair opposite her. She suspected that he sought to convey his displeasure, but the blasted man was too naturally coordinated, and the move ended up appearing effortless. "Director Wilde."

Talent turned back to Mary again. His rough-hewn features might have been carved from stone. "Mistress Chase."

Oh, but the way he said her name, all oil and flame, as if it burned him to utter it.

Mary dug a fingernail into her palm and modulated her voice. "Mr. Talent."

He paused for a moment, his brows raising a touch in reproach. She'd been childish in not giving him the proper form of address, but some things burned for her too.

His quick, irrepressible smirk said he knew as much. "Master," he reminded her.

He loved that she had to call him master. In their first year in training, he'd taken every opportunity to make her use the official title for all male regulators. Their gazes held, and heat rose to her cheeks. Thank God she hadn't the complexion to blush or he'd be all over her. "Master Talent," she ground out.

His annoying smirk deepened, and her nails dug deeper into the flesh of her palms. One day...

"Now that we have our forms of address clear," cut in Wilde, "might we proceed with the actual investigation? Or shall we continue with this little pissing contest?"

"Pray continue. If Chase can manage to refrain from straying off track, that is." Talent adjusted his broad shoulders in the chair and crossed one leg over the other.

Never react. She turned her gaze upon the director. "I was ready to hear the facts of the case twenty minutes ago, Director."

Talent bristled, and she let a small smile escape. He bristled further, but Director Wilde ploughed ahead.

"Good." Setting his hands upon the polished mahogany table, Director Wilde proceeded to give them the facts. Mary had already memorized them, and so she let the director's words drift over her as she studied Talent. The man was good, his strong, blunt features not revealing any hint that he might have personal knowledge of the Bishop of Charing Cross's most recent kill.

One powerful arm rested upon the table, and the fabric of his plain black suit coat bunched along the large swell of his bicep. Talent did not so much as twitch when the director set down a photograph of the last victim.

"Mr. Keating of Park Place," said Director Wilde. "As with the other murders, he has been branded with the Bishop's cross. The sole difference in this victim is that, while the others were demons, this man was a shifter, and by all accounts a law-abiding citizen of London."

Mary glanced at the photo, featuring a young man stripped naked. The cross branding his chest was a raw, ugly wound, but it was his eyes, wide and staring, that made her clockwork heart hurt. It was the expression of an innocent man pleading for mercy.

Talent looked as well. And when he did, she watched him. The ends of his brows lifted a fraction, and she was inclined to believe that he was surprised. Then again, he had always been a fine actor. In the beginning of his association with the SOS, Talent had made a name for himself by successfully tricking a powerful primus demon into believing he was Poppy Lane. Of course being able to shift to look exactly like Poppy had been part of it, but it was his mimicking of her character to the letter that had made the difference between success and catastrophe.

How could a man who had nearly died defending others be a murderer? But Mary feared she understood all too well. Although he was arrogant, obnoxious, and a general ass, he'd survived an ordeal that would break most men. Was he irrevocably broken?

"Do you recognize the victim, Master Talent?"

Wilde's query had Mary focusing once more.

Talent's heavily lidded eyes lifted from the photograph. "Shifters by nature are a solitary lot. No, I did not know Mr. Keating." His long fingers curled into a fist upon the table. "I was under the impression that the SOS kept the identity of shifters secret."

The director's mouth tightened. "We do. There is no indication that the files have been breached."

Talent made a noise that might have been construed as a snort, but it was just soft enough to get by Wilde without earning any reproach. For once, however, Mary agreed with Talent's sentiment.

After researching long into the night, Mary had learned that, in the last hundred years, the SOS had made a concerted effort to locate and document the existence of all shifters living in Europe. A daunting task. However, when the Nex began hunting shifters for their blood— whose properties gave demons the ability to shift into anything—the SOS, realizing its mistake in outing shifters, provided as much protection as it could by offering them new identities and keeping their whereabouts hidden. But it was a constant battle, for the Nex, an organization dedicated to seeing supernaturals rule the world over humans, was resourceful and ruthless.

Talent leaned forward a fraction. "Who was Keating? Before?"

"Johannes Maxum." Wilde pulled a paper from his file and handed it to Talent. "He's an older shifter. Date of birth unknown, but he once worked as an alchemist for Augustus the Strong in the quest to discover the Chinese's secret to making porcelain."

Talent scanned the page, then set it down. Protocol dictated that he hand the paper to Mary, and she might have been insulted at his obvious slight, had she not been expecting it. No matter, she'd read about Maxum as well. Besides, Talent's juvenile tactics would not cow her.

In any event, Director Wilde was now looking at both of them. "Research has been instructed to provide any and all assistance you might require."

"Thank you, Director," Mary said. "We shall keep you informed as the case proceeds."

Talent's jaw snapped up as if he'd been punched. "We?"

The force of his inner agitation was a maelstrom creaking against the walls. Any moment now it would break. Mary remained calm. "We are to be partners now, Master Talent. Or haven't you been paying attention?" *And I will stick to you like a barnacle until I find out the truth.*

The small vein at his temple pulsed. "I work alone. Always have."

Wilde laid a hand over the file. "There is a time to every purpose under the heaven, Master Talent. Which includes knowing when to receive help." The steely look in the director's eyes made it clear that Talent would find no leeway should he protest.

The sound of Talent's teeth grinding filled the room. "I was under the impression Mistress Chase was here in a clerical capacity."

"You hoped," Mary corrected. "Otherwise, I have grave concerns regarding your propensity for jumping to conclusions."

Talent leaned his weight on the table as his gaze bore into her. "Keep baiting me, Chase, and you'll find out what else I have a propensity for."

She leaned in as well, until they faced each other like dogs in a pit ring. "I am quaking in my knickers."

"There you go, mentioning your knickers." His mouth slanted, and his eyes gleamed dark green. "What I cannot discern is if you only do so to me, or if you want the whole of the SOS to be thinking about them."

"Why, Master Talent, are you trying to tell me that you think about my knickers?"

His lips pinched so tight that she had to bite back a grin. A low growl rumbled from the vicinity of his chest.

"Children." Director Wilde's expression was stern, but his eyes held a glint of amusement. "The discussion is over. You will work together on this." His good humor fled. "And you will not fail the SOS. Now"—he motioned to the door with his chin—"take your squabble out of here. Perhaps you can pull Mistress Chase's braids in the common room, Master Talent."

On the outside Mary knew she appeared serene as she left the meeting room. On the inside, however, she quivered in anticipation. For years she and Talent had detested each other. He treated her as if she were some low, conniving wretch. Solely because she was a GIM. *Lousy, arrogant bounder.*

The outer hall was cool and quiet. A calm before the inevitable storm. And that storm was right on her heels. Although, in truth, Jack Talent reminded her more of a panther, all dark and brooding, his powerful body so still when at rest, yet capable of instant, violent action.

Mary headed down the corridor, knowing that, while he made no sound, Talent stalked her. The skin at the back of her neck prickled, and her heart whirred away within her breast. With his shifter's senses, he'd hear her spinning heart, she was sure. *Oh, yes, come and get me, and we shall see how well you dance around the truth now, Jack Talent.* It was torture not to quicken her step or turn around.

By the time she reached the shadowed corner that led to another section of headquarters, her breast was rising and falling in agitation. Damn him.

And damn her too, for some small, traitorous part of her liked the chase, reveled in it. Gripping her weapon, she waited until his heavy hand fell upon her shoulder, and then she spun.

He grunted as they both hit the wall. The hard expanse of his chest barely gave under her weight as she pressed against him. For a moment they both panted, then his gaze lowered to the knife she had at his throat.

She had expected his rage, but not his grin, that wide, brilliant grin that lit up his dour features and did strange things to her equilibrium. His cheeky smile grew as he spoke. "Pulling iron on me, Chase? How bloodthirsty." His hot breath fanned her cheeks. "I knew you had it in you."

She did not ease her grip. Training with Mrs. Lane had honed her skills. The slightest move from him and he would be tasting that iron. "Trying to intimidate me, Talent?"

His body tightened, but he kept his hands at his sides. "What the devil are you playing at? You aren't a field agent. You've been hanging on to Mrs. Lane like a limpet, and now you want to partner." He leaned in, not flinching when the tip of her iron blade cut into his skin. "With me."

A rivulet of crimson blood trickled down his throat. She tore her gaze away from it. "This is the most important case the SOS has seen all year. Any regulator would be mad to pass up the opportunity to take it." When he snorted, she gave him a pretty smile. "Who my partner is makes little difference."

His lips pressed into a flat line. "This is my investigation. It always has been."

From the moment she'd asked Poppy to be assigned to the case, she'd known she'd face his rage. But she'd told

Talent the truth: Having the opportunity to move away from her assistant's role into fieldwork was not to be missed. And if he was guilty of murder, she would be the one to take him down. Keeping that little personal victory in mind, it was easy to give him a bland look. "Oh yes, and you've done a bang-up job with the case so far."

His growl seemed to vibrate through her, but Mary ignored it and the way the hairs lifted along the back of her neck. "What gave you reason to believe that it would remain yours alone after all this time, when you have nothing to show for your efforts?"

With an unfortunately easy move, he shrugged free. She let him; bodily contact was not a situation she wanted to prolong, as it was far too unsettling. He loomed over her. "Toss out what insults you will, Mistress Merrily." He poked her shoulder with a hard finger. "But do not for a moment try to undermine me. You think I'm a bastard now, try handling me in a temper."

He turned to storm off when she grabbed his lapel and hauled him back. Taking pleasure in the shock that parted his lips, she smiled. "I've seen your temper, Master Talent. You haven't been privy to mine." With lazy perusal, her gaze took in his heightened color and narrowed eyes. "While you'll be shouting about like a tot who's lost his lolly, I'll be the lash you never saw coming."

It was quite satisfactory to leave him open-mouthed and silent—for once.

Read on for a sneak peek into Kristen Callihan's other dark, sensual tales of Victorian London – where magic and passion lurk in every shadowy corner . . .

FIRELIGHT

London, 1881

Once the flames are ignited . . .

Miranda Ellis is a woman tormented. Plagued since birth by a strange and powerful gift, she has spent her entire life struggling to control her exceptional abilities. Yet one innocent but irreversible mistake has left her family's fortune decimated and forced her to wed London's most nefarious nobleman.

They will burn for eternity . . .

Lord Benjamin Archer is no ordinary man. Doomed to hide his disfigured face behind masks, Archer knows it's selfish to take Miranda as his bride. Yet he can't help being drawn to the flame-haired beauty whose touch sparks a passion he hasn't felt in a lifetime. When Archer is accused of a series of gruesome murders, he gives in to the beastly nature he has fought so hard to hide from the world. But the curse that haunts him cannot be denied. Now, to save his soul, Miranda will enter a world of dark magic and darker intrigue. For only she can see the man hiding behind the mask.

'Debut author Callihan pens a compelling Victorian paranormal with heart and soul'
Publishers Weekly

MOONGLOW

Once the seeds of desire are sown . . .

Finally free of her suffocating marriage, widow Daisy Ellis
Craigmore is ready to embrace the pleasures of life that
have long been denied her. Yet her newfound freedom is
short lived. A string of unexplained murders has brought
danger to Daisy's door, forcing her to turn to the most
unlikely of saviours . . .

Their growing passion knows no bounds . . .

Ian Ranulf, the Marquis of Northrup, has spent lifetimes
hiding his primal nature from London society. But now a
vicious killer threatens to expose his secrets. Ian must step
out of the shadows and protect the beautiful, fearless Daisy,
who awakens in him desires he thought long dead. As their
quest to unmask the villain draws them closer together,
Daisy has no choice but to reveal her own startling secret,
and Ian must face the undeniable truth: Losing his heart to
Daisy may be the only way to save his soul.

'A sizzling paranormal with dark history and explosive
magic! Callihan is an impressive new talent'
Larissa Ione

SHADOWDANCE

Jack Talent is tormented by the demons of his past. Though Jack loves his position in the SOS, he cannot forget what was done to him. And so he hunts down the remaining demons that tortured him and metes out his own brand of justice as the Bishop of Charing Cross. The only thing that soothes him is his secret visits to fellow agent Mary Chase. But while something about Mary calms him, she is also his greatest torment, for she is a reminder of his worst crime – the night he lost his soul by taking her human life.

Mary Chase is now free. After years of service to the Ghosts in the Machine, she now assists the head of the SOS and is finally enjoying life – except for the one thorn in her side: Jack Talent. The temperamental shifter unsettles her and awakens a need she's never felt before. But when a copycat killer begins to mimic the Bishop's signature and Jack is assigned to the case, Mary volunteers to join him, eager to unravel Jack's mysterious façade. Can Jack protect his secret – and his heart – from the one woman who could be his ultimate ruin?

Do you love fiction with a supernatural twist?

Want the chance to hear news about your favourite authors (and the chance to win free books)?

Keri Arthur
S. G. Browne
P.C. Cast
Christine Feehan
Jacquelyn Frank
Larissa Ione
Darynda Jones
Sherrilyn Kenyon
Jackie Kessler
Jayne Ann Krentz and Jayne Castle
Martin Millar
Kat Richardson
J.R. Ward
David Wellington
Laura Wright

Then visit the Piatkus website and blog
www.piatkus.co.uk | www.piatkusbooks.net

And follow us on Facebook and Twitter
www.facebook.com/piatkusfiction | www.twitter.com/piatkusbooks

piatkus